AF427387

Trail of Sunflowers

Book Three of A Texas Bloom Series

Tanya Fischer

Trail of Sunflowers

Copyright © 2024 by Tanya Fischer

All rights reserved.

No part of this publication may be reproduced, distributed, or transmitted in any form or by any means, including photocopying, recording, or other electronic or mechanical methods, without the prior written permission of the publisher, except as permitted by U.S. copyright law. For permission requests, contact Tanya Fischer at her email authortanyafischer@gmail.com

The story, all names, characters, and incidents portrayed in this production are fictitious. No identification with actual persons (living or deceased), places, buildings, and products is intended or should be inferred.

Print ISBN: 979-8-9864085-2-1

Edited by Britney Waldrop @britneywaldropedits

Cover Art by Eudorna

Contents

Content Warning

This story contains content that might be troubling to some readers, including, but not limited to, depictions of and references to death, discussions of a past suicide attempt, gun violence, dubious consent, one on-page spanking scene, death by hanging, signs of depression, discussions of suicidal ideation, and mention of off-page rape of secondary character(s).

To Rasa for believing in me. To Dagmar for encouraging me. And to my Book Fairy, Susan, whose honesty, love, and support helped pave the way for my books.

Prologue

1891

Texas near the Mexican border

The sun rose indolently above the horizon, spreading crimson light across the charred remains of a farm. A figure sat cross-legged beneath a mesquite tree, sunlight glinting off the revolver in his lap. The heavy weight of a hanging man brought creaks from above. A dull-gray star winked reflectively on the dead man's left breast, a symbol of protection and allegiance to the great state of Texas. If Junior could have destroyed that as well, he would have.

Instead, he inspected the heavy Colt in his lap. It was a Single Action Army revolver bestowed upon him after having completed his training—another symbol of protection. All the chambers were empty but one, and the single lead bullet remaining whispered suggestively, promising ease.

A bullet? Or prison?

Twice, he brought the muzzle of the gun up tight against the bristly underside of his bruised jaw. And twice, the faces of his family forced his hand back down to rest impotently in his lap.

His brother wouldn't just mourn; Ben would grieve and blame himself for the rest of his life.

Junior's best friend wouldn't understand, but Sol would forgive in time.

And Sol's little sister—the tagalong in braids who had been the bane of Junior's existence for years—would spit on his grave. Isa would understand exactly why he did it, and she would curse him to an eternity in a hell she didn't believe in. It was her response to his potential death that stalled him.

Ignoring the dried blood staining his hands, he pulled his wallet from his jacket pocket. A worn, faded letter in Isa's sprawling handwriting lay tucked in the leather lining. Gingerly, he tugged it out and read it for the thousandth time. Its contents recounted exhaustive details of college life for a woman. Isa had written of the adventures she experienced, what her classes were like, and how she was adjusting to life in a new city. When she wrote this letter, she'd been seventeen years old with her whole life ahead of her. She had a knack for making a person's problems feel small. That was what he loved the most about her. God, what would she think of him now?

The letter trembled in his fingertips.

The shock was wearing off.

He wiped the sweat from his eyes with his sleeve, mindful of the eye that was nearly swollen shut, and returned the three-year-old letter to its rightful place.

I'm not a coward, he thought and struggled to his feet. Junior welcomed death, but not if it would mean Isa thought him a coward. He staggered to the horse grazing near the smoking ruins of the farmhouse, carefully avoiding the covered bodies of the family who had resided there, and mounted his dapple-gray gelding. As he turned in the direction of town, he muttered, "Whoa."

Five more bodies were lined up between the smoldering farmhouse and the mesquite tree, a star on each breast. Their dull shine held him immobile, mocking him. Each body had succumbed to a gunshot wound. Junior stroked the handle of his six-shooter, eyes glued to the men on the ground. Unlike the family, they were uncovered. Vulnerable. He didn't spit on or curse them; it no longer mattered if they deserved it. He had done enough.

Something caught his eye, and he dismounted and approached the body at the end. Junior tugged the stolen ivory-engraved Colt from the waistband it was tucked in. A gift from Captain Havelard when Junior had been made lieutenant, the .45 was worth a pretty penny. The captain would want it back. Resuming his seat in the saddle, Junior spared the dead men one last look. Once their cold, frozen faces were carved into his brain forever, he nudged his horse forward again.

Towards town.

Towards prison.

Chapter One

October 1893

Austin, Texas

"What in God's name is that stench?" David Corner fluttered an embroidered handkerchief in the vicinity of his face, peering through the darkness around them. "And where, exactly, have you brought us?"

Isadora Williams pointed her gloved finger at a bulky black square in the distance. "That building is a slaughterhouse, and the culprit of the stench is its rendering factory approximately a quarter of a mile behind it. That's the stockyard." She pointed again, but David was busily goggling at her.

"I thought," he said slowly, "you were purchasing a horse?"

"I am." She studiously ignored the indignant noise that was erupting from him and flicked the buggy reins.

"At a godforsaken slaughterhouse? Have you taken leave of your senses?"

"There is no need to scream, David."

His voice lowered several decibels. "And enlighten me, please, as to why we are journeying under the cover of night? I assume

4

you need me for more than just a buggy mate or my titillating conversation."

A grin flashed across Isa's face in the glow of the buggy's two lanterns. She led the buggy horse around the immense brick building to the yawning darkness of the stockyards beyond. A southerly wind blew the rendering factory's evil vapors directly into their nostrils, and David shoved his handkerchief, lovingly initialed by his young wife, hard against his nose. The smell of animal fat seeped into their pores and lingered in their clothes.

Isa's nose wrinkled.

It smelled precisely how a slaughterhouse and rendering factory should: simmering fat and sinew gone slightly off, singed hair, and the sweet, rancid scent of old blood. The stockyard contained intricate mazes of corrals, stables, and bisecting cattle panels. A semicircular holding pen was visible near the back entrance of the sprawling building, funneling to a gate used to transfer cattle into a chute. Compared to the ranches she'd grown up around, it felt industrial. Cold.

This place was a way station for the "knackered." Old cattle, sheep, pigs—any four-legged hoofed creature deemed no longer useful for anything other than meat or glue.

"Isa?" David hissed. "Why did you feel the need to travel here at midnight?"

He had never liked being ignored.

A shadow creeping across the yard captured Isa's attention, and she whispered from the corner of her mouth, "The man I'm purchasing the mare from demanded a nighttime transaction, and I brought you so he wouldn't get any romantic notions about a woman meeting him alone."

David snorted into his cotton hanky. "Please. You could cut him down to size in a trice. Did you remember to bring your firearm?"

"Don't be stupid." She patted the unyielding lump in the reticule at her hip.

"As I suspected. You need me not at all. The only thing I've ever saved you from is boredom." The words were tinged with bitterness.

"A more horrible way to perish, I cannot imagine. You are a saint."

David reached to squeeze her knee familiarly, good humor restored. She retaliated by slapping his knuckles soundly with the ribbons of her reins. His laugh was muffled.

City boy, she thought wryly.

Their conversation halted as an obscure figure led an inky-black horse forward. She felt David stiffen beside her. It had been nearly effortless on her part to convince the slaughterhouse manager to sell the Arabian mare for a sack full of twenty-dollar gold pieces instead of leaving it to its fate. Isa suspected if she hadn't ridden directly there the day before, the man would have taken the horse home for himself. The mare was worth a fortune.

"Mr. Northam, is that you?" Isa knew it was him, but the rounded shoulders relaxed an inch at her crisp tone.

"Who's that with you, miss?" he asked suspiciously.

"Why, my husband," Isa lied, sounding taken aback. "You cannot expect me to travel alone at night, good sir."

He muttered something and brought the mare closer.

Oh, but she was a beauty.

Dim lantern light gleamed off the dramatic arch of the horse's neck and shimmered against the white blaze on her dished profile.

Perfect.

Even David was speechless beside her, a rare event.

Isa took advantage of his shock, relinquished the reins to him and alighted from the buggy without assistance. She and the man, who was reluctant to vacate the shadows, were eye to eye. Her ability to look a man in the eye from her considerable height could be either a blessing or a curse. Tonight, it was an advantage. She reached into her reticule, fingers brushing the gun, and pulled out a leather sack bulging with gold pieces. The whites of Mr. Northam's eyes reflected greedily at the jingling sound.

"The other half, as agreed," she said lightly, holding the heavy bag out. "And I truly appreciate your discretion."

Glancing from her eyes to her proffered hand, he accepted the money and replaced it with the lead rope.

Smile tightening, Isa reminded him, "And the title?"

He hesitated. "It's to the slaughterhouse, miss. If I sign it, it's my job."

"I understand," she said, reaching into her reticule again. His eyes followed, his bearing taut. She presented a fountain pen. "But where I'm going, no one will even know your name."

Mr. Northam accepted the pen as though it were a snake. Reluctantly, he dug in one pocket, then the other, and retrieved a folded paper. He unfolded it, awkwardly signed it on his knee with a surprisingly flourishing script, and transferred the title to her waiting palm. She tilted it to the lantern light, read it, then folded and stowed it in her reticule with an air of satisfaction.

"Good doin' business with ya." Mr. Northam tipped his hat, pocketed his money with a wary glance at David, and backed into the shadows. Moments later, they heard hoofbeats pounding in the opposite direction.

"You'd think we came here to rob him," David mused from his perch. The white square of cloth had wrinkled in his clenched hand.

"Some likely would have," Isa pointed out, running her fingertips along the bony line of the mare's blaze. Its equine eyes were liquid black moons. Sable ears flicked forward and backward skittishly, and delicate nostrils flared.

"If you're quite finished gloating over your prize, may we depart from this level of hell you've dragged us to?"

Grinning at her unbelievable fortune, Isa pulled the mare's lead rope and giddily led her toward the rear of the buggy. On passing the brown buggy horse, the ebony mare pinned her ears. She squealed, high and sharp, kicking out with her front hoof, nearly making contact with the brown gelding's leg. In response, he lurched away, jostling the buggy despite its set brake. David cursed, straining against the reins to keep the horse and carriage immobile.

"What the devil was that?" David's shout echoed in the empty yard.

"*That* is the reason she's at the slaughterhouse in the first place," Isa said matter-of-factly. She pulled the mare behind her, circling wide around the other horse. "She has appalling manners for a circus horse."

"A *what?*"

"Didn't I tell you?"

"I loathe these games. Every time you shock me, you turn as smug as my father when he liquidates another business."

"Don't be dramatic. Mirage is a circus horse that was sold to my friend's father. Jacquelin's father has a notoriously foul temper and more money than sense. Apparently, he was riding Mirage through the street and lost control of her. He fell off and broke his leg. Jacquelin said he was so embarrassed and enraged that he sent the horse straight to the slaughterhouse to be turned to glue. Can you imagine?" She smiled broadly up at the mare. "His trash, my treasure."

Isa securely fastened the lead rope behind the buggy.

Through the carriage's leather back cover, David's voice was faint. "Can't be much of a show horse if she tries to kill all the other horses."

Isa didn't want to think of that, so she rounded the carriage wheel and said optimistically, "At least she's friendly with people."

"Much good that will be riding her in a street full of *horses*." David clambered down to her.

Ignoring his hand, she pulled herself up and sat on the bench, straightening her gloves. "She just needs a bit of training."

"Spare me," he sighed, then gagged at the lungful of polluted air he'd inhaled. In an exhibition of athleticism, David hopped back into the buggy on Isa's side, shaking it and causing unnecessary commotion. "I can scarcely believe you're leaving."

Isa held onto her hat, glaring. "Believe it. I'm leaving this week."

"You don't have to sound so damned pleased with yourself. My guts are torn out, and you laugh all la-di-da." He snapped the reins with needless force, and Isa had to grab hold of her hat again when they turned sharply around.

Isa stifled the urge to laugh. "Your guts are perfectly well. You're a physician; you would know."

"Maybe if I toted guns and roped cattle like your childhood sweetheart, you'd stay." David's mutter was low and dark, raising Isa's hackles.

Slanting a look at him, she snatched the reins from his hands and steered the carriage horse around the slaughterhouse toward the long, narrow drive.

David ignored the warning signs. "What was his name? Something ridiculous, not even a real name. A *suffix*. Senior?"

"Junior." Isa pretended the name didn't send sparks of animosity through her. "As you well know. And he is *not* my childhood sweetheart. He's a family friend."

"Junior," David scoffed. Arms crossed, he pouted at the swinging lantern. "That's a child's name."

"I'd love to see the day you tell a Texas Ranger he has a child's name." She'd had the same unkind thought countless times over the years, usually amidst imaginary debates where she argued with that self-same man. Naturally, she won every argument. And yet, hearing the callous opinion from another person's lips compelled in her an age-old response to defend. No matter how much Junior had neglected her in recent years, her loyalty persisted.

Grumbling, David asked, "Who says I'll be around to tell it to him face-to-face? I'll insult the fellow in the comfort of others' company like a gentleman."

"He doesn't like his first name."

"Is it odd, like yours?"

"'Isadora' is not odd, you dolt." When her insult made him grin, she elbowed him in the ribs. "His first name is John."

David affected a shudder. "Ghastly common name."

"Nearly as common as David."

"Touché."

Isa dug into her reticule and pulled out a package wrapped in crinkly brown paper. One-handed, she opened the paper and extracted a thin sliver of beef jerky. When she offered a piece to David, he declined. While she tore a strip off and chewed, Isa thought of her brother's best friend.

The truth was, Junior was a bit of a sore spot. Nearly seven years her senior, John "Junior" Stone was one of her brother Sol's best friends. Growing up, Junior had been a constant presence who tweaked her braids, teased her, and pranked her until she flew into a tantrum. He was the one who'd taught her how to spit, race horses, and throw a punch. More handsome than Adonis and as charming as Byron, Junior had broken more hearts than stars in the sky.

Such a number was empirically impossible, but it was appropriate in theory.

Isa chewed furiously on the desiccated beef. She wanted to pretend that Junior had been a childhood friend to her and nothing more. But a friend wouldn't write to her every month for three years and then suddenly stop. A friend wouldn't avoid her when she happened to be visiting home at the same time as him. A friend wouldn't be the only person who could make her laugh until she cried and then, one day, take it all away. An old frustration buried like a mussel in sand began to emerge.

As though disdaining the telling silence from his buggy partner, David was far from finished with the subject of Junior. "This fellow is supposed to ride the train with you to your parents' house?"

"Yes."

"That means he's in Austin now?"

Silence.

"Has he"—David cleared his throat—"come to visit you? Have you seen him?"

"No." Said through gritted teeth.

"Why hasn't he come to pay a call on you? If he's such a close family friend, it's a little odd to meet you at the train station with not a word before then, isn't it?"

"David?"

"Yes?"

"Shut up."

He mimed affront, buttoned his lips, and crossed his legs and arms.

Amused despite herself, Isa said, "You should have been a famous actor in a play, not a physician." She pulled the buggy to the left fork, listening intently to ensure her new purchase trotted along behind.

"Bodies are much more fascinating than a script."

That's how Isa felt about numbers. She didn't say that aloud; David would gag. He was famously bad at mathematics and said formulae looked like scribbles on the page, but he could look at an uncaptioned diagram of an autopsied cadaver and name every bone, every organ. Latin words on labeled diagrams fascinated Isa, if not the bodies themselves. David had even taught her a few choice Latin words for body parts in the two years she'd known him, which she'd stowed away for a later date.

Pressing matters shifted her thoughts. She needed a favor from David.

"I'm going on Tuesday's train, not Thursday's," she blurted, her fists tight around the reins.

"Tuesday's—" David began, but she cut him off.

"Pride dictates that I not wait for Junior. I can travel to Dogwood without him." Oh, to be a fly on the depot wall when he discovered she had already departed earlier in the week. "Will you accompany me to see us off?"

"Well, of course—"

She reached over and patted his leg. "Thank you, David. I knew I could depend upon you."

His thigh tensed beneath her gloved hand, and he was effectively silenced.

TUESDAY'S TRAIN CAME and went, and Isa was still stuck cooling her heels in Austin. Her devil-horse had made certain of that.

At Mirage's first sight of the train, her head had wrenched up; nostrils flared, ears perked, and neck sharply arced. When the whites of the circus horse's eyes had shown and her feet had danced, Isa had braced herself against the lead rope, and David had rushed to her aid and grabbed the halter.

"Easy," Isa had murmured. "Easy."

It hadn't made a bit of difference. As soon as the train had appeared amidst the yard of green and red box cars, whistling and billowing streams of gray and white smoke, the Arabian had attempted to bolt. It had taken both Isa and David to stop her from charging through the depot. Porters had rushed to help and shoved a hood on the mare, escalating Mirage's panic. In the end, itchy with sweat, Isa had been forced to exit the depot with her tail tucked between her legs. Her useless animal and a shaken David had followed behind to the ticket booth where she'd been able to wheedle a refund from the depot clerk.

It was presently the blush of dawn on Thursday morning, and Isa was trying not to panic.

Much to Miss Pickney's consternation, David had arrived when it was still dark. He sat on an uncomfortable, straight-backed walnut armchair in the parlor with a decorative pillow embroidered with a Bible quote in his lap, watching with some interest while Isa laid out all her supplies on the coffee table.

"My father wants you to come by his office to pick up last month's wages," he said, absently fondling the stiff corner of the pillow with his thumb. "I believe he was hoping to say goodbye."

"If I have time," Isa said distractedly, moving back and forth between the saddlebags on the tasseled mustard couch and the table cluttered with travel gear. She wanted to be miles away from Austin before Junior discovered she'd never intended on boarding that train with him to Dogwood.

As if reading her mind, David asked, "When is your...'family friend' expecting you at the depot?"

"The train leaves at four. He probably won't get suspicious until a half hour before then." She tucked a trailing, honey-blonde lock behind her ear, thinking. "If I tell Miss Pickney I'm leaving early to say my goodbyes to your father at the bank, she'll be far less suspicious."

"Glad to be of service." David didn't sound glad at all; he positively moped. It grated on her nerves. "You don't think he will be angry that you've deceived him?"

"I don't give a fig how Junior feels. He would have called upon me and come here to collect me if he cared. Even Miss Pickney says so." Isa rifled through each item in her leather saddlebags. "Slicker, knife, currycomb, matches, picket pen, *soap*, mustn't forget soap…"

Junior not only avoided her when she visited Dogwood, but to add offense, he had written to Sol that he could accompany Isa to Dogwood as he was already in Austin. When her brother had written to her of these plans, it had flummoxed her. Why hadn't Junior just told her in person? He was in Austin; why not pay a call and plan it out together? They had been friends once. To be in town and to not see her…The two of them on a train together to Dogwood would be their first opportunity for conversation in years, and Junior hadn't had the gumption to tell her himself; Sol had needed to write it in a letter.

She preferred being angry to being hurt; Isa had crumpled Sol's missive fiercely in her fist and begun to plot.

"He killed for you, didn't he?" David asked conversationally. "*Mr. Suffix.* That night, you spoke at length about him."

Isa closed her eyes for several seconds to gather whatever scraps of patience remained.

"That night" was the night David had proposed, the one she dearly wished he had a duller memory of. She was beginning to think that he hadn't been quite as drunk as she had been, and her mouth flattened. After an evening of rabble-rousing at a gaming hall some months before, their eyeballs had been floating in beer (the second-foulest beverage she'd had the misfortune of imbibing). The man's shirtwaist she'd been wearing had been stained, reeking of beer. That night had begun with a flurry of cards, spirits, and an armload of banknotes. Later, she and David had gone back to his bachelor's apartment to divvy it up, and she'd drunkenly ripped the bowler hat from her head, let down her dirty-blonde hair, untucked her shirt, and unbound her breasts. Having thought of David as a brother, she'd paid no mind to his gaping mouth and sat on the floor with their loot, drawing it closer to her spread legs which were encased in men's trousers.

She frowned at the memories. Had she spoken of Junior that night? Isa recollected dividing the money, David joking about playing doctor, and later, the physical exploration that had been fun on her end and a bit more serious on his.

"I don't recall speaking of him."

"I do." David's voice lowered unhappily, and he glanced at the open parlor door for Miss Pickney. "You called him beautiful. I also know he killed a man for you."

Another memory materialized. An old one.

One.

Two.

Three.

Shoving the cold bite of metal away, ducking, just avoiding her head getting blown off. Junior's bullet meeting its mark. Junior killing in defense of her and the awful, sobering feelings later. Her puppy love converting from liquid to solid; some element forever changed in its chemical components that therefore could never be *un*changed.

Loving Junior, a normal—albeit beautiful—cowboy from the smallest corner of the world, was like discovering the formula that made sense of the universe.

Wonderful. Awesome.

Wholly unsettling.

But Isa had been sixteen. Six years had passed since then. A degree in mathematics, five years in a new city, and a small fortune from gambling with impunity, disguised as a man, drove a wedge between past and present. Isa could no longer relate to that part of herself. She hadn't just turned a new leaf; she was a new species of plant entirely. Her dreams had changed. No longer did she envisage yellow hair and deep-blue eyes. She imagined new places, new people, wonderful new worlds nothing like the sharecropper farm and impecunious folk who had raised her.

"You don't have to talk about him," David said softly.

Reverie broken, Isa saluted him. "My thanks."

David threw the pillow aside and said mercurially, "Perhaps I'll just come with you."

Snorting through her nose, Isa shoved cartridges into the gun belt she'd hidden in her bags. "And what would your wife think of that?"

"That doesn't matter a whit." His hand sliced through the air.

"It should. If I were your wife, I'd snatch you bald."

"Jealous, are you?" He sounded delighted at the prospect.

She shot him a nasty look over her shoulder, and he laughed so hard his feet left the floor. Smoothing her features, she said coolly, "If you're quite finished distracting me."

He buttoned his lips, and she returned to her meticulous packing. Suddenly, his voice was at her shoulder. "Dora. I *am* going to miss you."

From the mawkish intensity behind his words, she could tell he wasn't referencing her trip to Dogwood. Isa closed her eyes briefly, then turned and accepted the embrace from the closest friend she'd made since relocating to Austin. "I'll miss you as well. You must visit me in Dogwood before I leave."

"When will that be?"

"Just after the new year."

"So soon?" His sigh was deep and warm on her neck, and his arms tightened around her when she made to slither away. "I could accompany you."

Face set, Isa peeled his arms from around her and gave him a very stern look from beneath her brows. "You'll do no such thing."

"Traveling abroad alone isn't safe."

She pecked his smooth cheek, effectively erasing the mulish line from his normally smirking mouth. "I can take care of myself." And she looked forward to it. She couldn't wait to ride through the verdant hills of Italy, see the Colosseum in Rome, Notre Dame, the Louvre, and every place Robert Tomes so richly discussed in the *Harper's New Monthly Magazine*. Her family wouldn't be happy about it, but that was why she'd keep it to herself. The last time she'd mentioned traveling alone was to Sol, who had then insisted on sending Junior to chaperone her.

As if I need a chaperone.

"But what about me? Who will take care of me?"

She laughed. "Your wife, of course."

He was unamused. "Not that tired argument. All I'm saying—egad, is that him?"

The alarm in David's tone caused Isa's head to swivel to track his stare out the parlor window.

Striding up the stoop on long, muscular legs...was Junior.

Chapter Two

H e'd always hated his name.

Junior.

John Robert Stone, Jr.

The senior John Stone owned Circle S Ranch, or the "Big Stone Ranch" to the locals. People seven counties over tipped their hats to the cattle baron, neither knowing nor caring that he was the meanest son of a bitch in southeast Texas. His missus, Loretta Stone, liked to call their towheaded little boy, the only fruit of their loins, Junior. Thus, it had followed him into adulthood, clinging like a bad joke.

A dog's name.

A child's.

The minute he'd sworn an oath to the Texas Rangers, he'd abandoned the nickname for Private Stone. His last name was a good one; he shared it with his half-brother Ben. And when "Private" became "Lieutenant," Stone was a name he could be proud of because of himself. Marshals transcribed it on foolscap and stamped it with their insignias. Men shouted it across campfires with grins and raised fists.

Until two years ago, when everything went to hell.

Smiles withered. Faces hardened. Only eyes, dark and distrustful, would lift from campfires when he walked by.

He hadn't worn a Texas Ranger badge in two years. Not even his brother knew.

Now...now he was plain Junior again.

Incompetent.

Pretty-faced, spoon-fed, useless mama's boy.

And the girl who always saw through all of it was right in front of him, clinging to some other man through the college's staff apartment window.

He took a drag of his hand-rolled cigarette, fragrant White Burley tobacco smoke streaming from his nostrils. He wanted to be strangers with Isa. Needed it. Isa was closer to him than a sister; she was a brother wearing the skin of a young woman. Seeing a young woman instead of a girl in braids and bare feet always unsettled him. Sometimes, it knocked the breath clean out of him. The first time it had happened was when she was sixteen. She'd been stolen away by bandits who'd been set on trading her at the border with a dozen other girls, and an oozing, cloying fear he hadn't felt since he'd thought he'd killed his brother had seized him.

A group of men passed him on the street, blocking the shapes of Isa and her gentleman in the window. The men's raucous laughter brought Junior back to dusty, stinking earth. Exhaling the last remnants of smoke hard out of his nose, he shoved his buckskin Stetson low on his forehead, shading his face from the cool October sun. Across the street, Isa pulled away from the man standing two inches shorter than her. Junior crushed his hand-rolled cigarette beneath the heel of his worn boot.

His boot stopped grinding when Isa kissed her gentleman caller on the cheek.

Ben's wife, Lucy, had fondly communicated that Isa had received more proposals from beaus than she and Poppy combined. Junior had only been able to roll his eyes and crack jokes because what the hell else had he been supposed to do? Two giggling college-aged women walking past glanced from Junior's face to the engraved .45 low on his hip and hurried along.

Calm down, Stone. It's not like they're swappin' spit.

Nevertheless, it wasn't proper for Isa to kiss men for the whole world to see. What would her brother say? Stretching the tense lines from his shoulders, relaxing his face, Junior strode across the street and the brick building's front yard to the maroon door labeled with a bold number six on a brass plate. Tied to a post beside the stoop was a beautiful black mare with a hood on, her inky tail swishing temperamentally. The saddle's leather was etched with strange numbers and symbols.

Mathematical equations?

He rapped his knuckles beneath the brass number plate with enough force to start a couple of small dogs barking in the next apartment.

Someone unbolted the door to the modest dwelling, and surprise lit the features of an aging woman. *Miss Persimmony.* It was what he and Sol had dubbed Miss Pickney, an elderly spinster who hated misshelved books and voices louder than a whisper. Break any of her rules and she looked as though she'd sucked on an unripe persimmon. Over the years, the librarian's salt-and-pepper hair had turned silver and the lines in her face had multiplied, fracturing across her skin like worn vellum.

"Mr. Stone. What a pleasant surprise." The terse tone belied the pleasantry.

He tipped his hat to her. "Miss Pickney. It's good to see you looking so well." The charm came out rusty and dull. It had been years since he'd practiced sweet-talking anyone, much less spinsters with no use for it.

Indeed, her sparse eyebrows rose. "You're early. Are you here to meet Isadora?" Only she could get away with the use of Isa's full name.

"Yes, ma'am." He withdrew an envelope with Sol's latest letter from his jacket pocket and handed it over. "I'm to escort Isa to Dogwood on the train today. Has she packed?"

Miss Pickney pulled a pair of spectacles from her apron pocket, settled them atop the bony knob on the ridge of her nose, and scanned Sol's letter. Her lips pursed impossibly tighter. "She has been up since before daybreak packing. But here it says she's not to depart until four o'clock...oh, Isadora." The last was said with a dissatisfied sigh.

He shifted his feet in the doorway, and she jolted.

"Do come in. I'll inform her that you're here."

"I know he's here," said a familiar voice.

He shut the door behind him and looked for the voice's owner, but it had come from beyond the parlor threshold, out of sight. Standing just within view, however, was Isa's beau. Junior noted the young man's eyes were as wide as silver dollars, an expensive suit, and shiny shoes. A tapering mustache, glossy dark hair, and neat sideburns may not have added years to the fellow, but it did add dollar signs. Junior quashed the impulse to smooth his unkempt beard. He hadn't shaved in months, and the hair he'd scraped back beneath his Stetson touched his collar. Isa's gentleman caller, however, was a city dude, Junior's opposite in every way.

"Mr. Corner, may I introduce Mr. Stone? He's to escort our young charge to the train station. It appears you won't be needed after all."

There was a moment where the two men stared blankly at each other before Mr. Corner jumped forward, hand outstretched. "What a relief! I thought I'd never be rid of her. David Corner, a pleasure to meet you." The young man sounded friendly, cheerful even, but when they shook hands, David Corner gave the taller man a decidedly frosty look from beneath his brows.

"John Stone. Likewise," Junior said softly, his eyes like spear points stabbing into the other man. Their handshake was a hard, finger-cracking pump.

"So. Shall I call you John?" David flexed his hand and slid it into his trouser pocket.

"No," Junior and Isa said in unison, and that was when he finally caught his first glimpse of her in close quarters.

In the light from the parlor window, Isa's wide-set eyes were glittering topaz with flecks of peridot green. Cat's eyes. She looked good. Different. The fringe she'd cut when she'd been seventeen had grown out and was swept into a sizable knot at her nape. As she'd matured, her blonde hair had darkened to the color of pale honey. It made him conscious of the years between them. She felt like a stranger: elegant, confident, and cold. Her face had grown into her long nose and wide mouth, and her expressive brows were darker. His eyes carefully avoided her generous bosom and settled on the gargantuan poofs of her sleeves.

He felt a ridiculous urge to poke one.

Before the sudden hush could become awkward, Isa abandoned the saddlebags on the settee, wiped her hands, and approached him. "Hello, Junior."

"Izzy." Junior nodded at her, arms dangling uselessly at his sides. Once upon a time, he would have tweaked a braid. Bopped a nose. Maybe blocked a punch. Instead, he folded his arms, hands curling into fists. *This is a normal day*, he reminded himself. *A normal encounter.*

Isa blinked. "No one's called me that since you swore into the Texas Rangers."

Resentful at being forgotten, her friend piped up. "I call her Dora."

Junior raised a brow. "In front of her?"

Her stony exterior cracked. He saw a flash of big white teeth with a narrow gap in the center. It used to make a perfect funnel to squirt water through when they'd swum in the creek and was the only thing unchanged about her. He wondered vaguely if she was too ladylike to do such a thing anymore.

"Coffee or tea?" Miss Pickney asked suddenly, her shrewd gaze on Junior from above wire-rimmed spectacles.

"Coffee, ma'am. Much obliged."

Her eyes flicked to the hat he'd neglected to doff. With a disapproving little sniff, the starched, prim woman turned on her heel toward the fussily decorated house's kitchen. While a kettle clanged on the stove in the other room, uneasiness trembled between the three people in the tiny foyer.

"Why are you here, Junior?" Isa asked, breaking the silence.

"I'm getting on the train to Dogwood with you."

Hostility pulsed beneath her careful reserve. "I'm not taking the train."

What the hell was she talking about? "What, you gonna ride home on horseback?"

"Yes."

"No, the hell you're not."

After craning her neck around to guarantee Miss Pickney wasn't around, Isa hissed, "Yes, the hell I am!"

Suddenly, she was a snot-nosed brat again. Something inside Junior stood at attention. "Such language," he tutted. "You don't have a choice, half-pint. Your brother gave the orders."

"And you follow them like a good little soldier," she taunted. "If you must know, I tried to get on Tuesday's train, but it proved impossible."

The small hurt gave him pause. "Why would you get on Tuesday's train alone?"

She smiled. "So you wouldn't have to trouble yourself with escorting me today, of course."

"I don't mind." He unwound his crossed arms and braced himself on the doorframe above her head. "I'll just ride with you back to Dogwood. It'll be three days on the open road, and rain is coming, but you'll survive it. You're not sugar; you won't melt."

Isa's chin lifted. She was a tall woman, and it gave him satisfaction that she still had to look up at him. "That won't be necessary."

Junior shrugged like it didn't matter to him. "Just pretend I'm not there."

She folded her arms beneath her bosom (which he'd accused her of stuffing when they were younger) and said cooly, "That will be effortless, considering the practice I've had the last couple of years."

"I don't know what you're talking about." The muscles in his jaw tensed. When had he last written back to her? Had it been years? He still had all her letters in his nightstand, bound in order by date. He was annoyingly aware of David Corner's eyes darting back and forth between them.

"Of *course* you don't," she said slowly, patronizingly. Ever since she'd been a gap-toothed little spitfire half his height, she'd endlessly trailed his heels, always needing to be right, always needing the last word. It made him want to swat her behind. It wouldn't be the first time. But that was when she'd been in braids and overalls. Now, any touching of her person was out of the question. It didn't matter if she was getting under his skin, pulling at every hair trigger he had.

Miss Pickney chose that moment to back out of the kitchen door with a tray. David pulled his attention from the two locked in a battle of wills and hastily offered assistance. Junior released his steely grip on the doorframe and dropped his arms.

"Well," Isa said unnecessarily loudly. "I'd better pack my bag." And with a last parting glare, she strode past Junior down a hallway.

Miss Pickney wiped her hands on her apron. "You two keep each other company," she ordered. "It's best that I help her pack her bag. She's bound to put something absurd in it." Then she shuffled off after her young charge.

Junior turned his eyes slowly to David, who swallowed. "Tell me why she couldn't get on Tuesday's train."

"Er—"

Using all the authority he'd assumed during his Ranger days, Junior shifted his stance until he loomed imposingly in the doorway. "Tell me everything."

"EXPLAIN TO ME why you're riding to Dogwood on horseback," Miss Pickney snapped, her hands fluttering over Isa's open gunnysack on the bed.

"It's poor manners to eavesdrop at doors," Isa said lightly to cover up her sudden guilt.

Miss Pickney ignored this. "You elucidated you'd be taking the train in some detail. Not only have you lied, but your brother will consider me most unfit to act as your guardian!"

"I no longer require a guardian," Isa defended, pulling several articles of clothing from the back of the little armoire in her room. The small bedroom was as full and cluttered as the recesses of her mind. "I would like to train Mirage while I spend time with my family, but the dadblamed animal—"

"Language!"

"—won't get near a train. I was afraid if I told you the truth, you'd have found some way to stop me."

"You're quite right about that." Miss Pickney's voice was shrill. "Gallivanting across Texas with a bachelor—your poor mother shall expire from shock!"

"He's not a bachelor, he's *Junior*. Family. He doesn't count." The latter was said with too much vehemence.

"Family or not, it is unseemly, Isadora." Miss Pickney's rheumy brown eyes sharpened behind her spectacles. "What are you doing with those?"

Blast.

Feigning ignorance, Isa shoved the pair of jeans she wore when in disguise into the nearest corner of her bag. "Just some travel clothes—Miss Pickney!"

The little librarian plucked the balled-up jeans from the corner of Isa's gunnysack and held them behind her. "I insist you practice a little decorum, dear," Miss Pickney whispered savagely. "You cannot travel in trousers across seven counties. Think of what your brother would say."

"He wouldn't say anything because he wouldn't know!"

An arthritic finger pointed so close to Isa's face that the girl's eyes crossed. "You keep that sharp tongue where it belongs. I shan't have you sassing me. As soon as you depart, I shall telegraph your brother of your exploits and to expect you to be...delayed. Now, I know very well that you have riding skirts, so I suggest you gather and fold them properly. No, don't wad them up and crease them. Have I taught you nothing?"

Despite the old woman's stern diatribes, she loaded Isa's already-full war bag to bursting with staples for the road, packing tea, sugar, and a sturdy tin cup with tender care. When Isa said her goodbyes for the second time that week, Miss Pickney grasped the youth by her cheeks and kissed her forehead with dry lips. "You had better take care."

"I will." Isa patted the frail hands. "I'll send a letter as soon as I arrive in Dogwood."

In the parlor, both men stood holding delicate blue-and-white printed teacups of half-empty coffee. They set the cups down at the women's entrance like two strangers inhabiting a funeral parlor, stiff and uncomfortable. The relief and guilt on David's face at her approach made her wary. What had they been talking about?

"Getting along?" she asked, looking narrowly between the two men.

Junior's eyes were obscured by his hat, even in the bright room. Through the thicket of his golden beard, his sensual red lips were unsmiling. His blond hair, streaked with natural highlights from sun exposure, touched his collar. A cowboy Adonis. In Miss Pickney's grandmotherly little parlor, he looked immense. His shoulders, encased in a cream shirt and brown vest, were broad and square. He had always been fond of Levi Strauss denim pants, and he wore a faded pair beneath leather chaps. Teeth clenching, she forced her eyes from his person.

"I get along with everyone," David quipped in the little silence following Isa's query. Again, his eyes flickered between her and the other man.

"I am sure the two of you are anxious to get started." Miss Pickney folded her hands together, caught Junior's eye, and asked pertly, "Are you still misshelving books, young man?"

Junior's unyielding façade softened minutely. "No, ma'am. You taught me the error of my ways."

Miss Pickney nodded once. "I had to run you out of my library enough times before the notion stuck, I daresay."

"Yes, ma'am."

"He only did it to inconvenience me, I assure you." Isa hefted her bag higher. "I'll bet a twenty-dollar gold piece he hasn't stepped foot in a library since I left Dogwood."

"There will be no betting in this house, thank you." Miss Pickney's lips cinched tighter.

Isa shared a secretive smile with David, who turned a laugh into a cough behind his fist. Still smiling, she tossed her substantial bag at him. "Will you be a dear and take this outside for me?"

"Certainly." David trotted out of the tiny parlor, huffing at the bag's weight, and sunlight streamed into the open front doorway. Miss Pickney followed behind, doubtless to chat with the neighboring professor.

Isa turned a sly smile on Junior, whose hidden gaze was sharp upon her. "My saddlebags—"

In a voice torn between exasperation and anger, Junior pointed a finger at her and snapped, "Try that on me, and you can carry your own bags."

Chin squaring, Isa let her smile wither. "A smile would be wasted on you in any case."

"You're damned right," he muttered, grabbing the bulging saddlebags from the ugly-as-sin couch. When he halted in the foyer, Isa perceived how he favored his side. "Lead the way."

Isa placed her palm flat against the front door, eyeing him. "What's wrong with your side?"

Ignoring her inspection, Junior made to shoulder past her. "Got shot."

"What?" Isa leaned harder against the wood panels, unbudging.

"Happened a month ago. Went straight through. I'm fine."

"You're *fine*?" Her face scrunched as if she smelled something rancid. Even to her ears, she sounded incredulous. "It could have hit a vital organ. Or festered."

"It didn't."

"But what if it had?" She'd seen the effects of bullets traveling at high speeds through the human body; men rarely survived. The thought of one going through Junior made everything in her protest. She wanted to know who had shot him and whether he had gotten his revenge. She wanted to know whether it had hurt very much and whether he'd become feverish.

"What are you, my ma?" he jibed. "And you look just like Miss Persimmony when you make that face."

Isa's unwilling concern deflated. "You're impossible." Turning her nose up, she opened the front door and strode out. David was struggling with Isa's bag behind her saddle's pommel, and she stifled a sigh. She walked to Mirage and pulled the gunnysack from David's hands.

"You have to wait until the saddlebags are attached before you can tie this on," she instructed, tugging her saddlebags from Junior and slinging them over Mirage's twitching rump. "Why don't you take her hood off instead?"

David raised his hands, backing away. "I'll not be getting near either end of her. She's a demon in disguise."

"I'll do it." Junior's voice was disconcertingly deep, and Isa tried to ignore the shiver it sent up her shoulder blades. From the corner of her eye, she watched him walk to her horse with the confidence of someone raised on a ranch who lived and breathed horses. "Why does she have a hood on?"

Isa turned away and fiddled with the saddlebag's buckles. "Because she acted a fool at the train station when the porters put one on her, so I'm training her to become accustomed to it."

Junior grunted, and Isa couldn't resist another peek at him. He didn't act surprised about the train station. David must have told him in the parlor. *Traitor.*

Junior deftly pulled the hood from Mirage's elegant head and whistled low. "Where'd you find her?"

"I'll tell you where she found her," David said with relish from behind them.

"*Et tu, Brute*?" Isa asked, slanting a warning look at her friend.

A corner of Junior's mouth turned up as he stroked the white blaze on the Arabian's dished forehead. The October sunrise cast his features in warm tones, glinting off eyes that were like indigo coals beneath the brim of his buckskin hat. "You got your Black Beauty."

She suppressed a shock at this. Ever since her childish eyes had combed the pages of *Black Beauty*, she'd dreamed of purchasing an embodiment of her favorite fictional horse. She'd begged her pa for a true black horse with a white star.

"You remember."

"How could I forget? You never shut up about it." Something brilliant flashed in his eyes, hinting at that same wicked humor his younger self had possessed. It made her want to tease him. To poke and prod and enrage him the way she used to. As if he sensed her thoughts, his face shuttered. He settled his hat more securely on his head, tugging an old, tarnished timepiece from his vest pocket, one his brother had gifted him on his eighteenth birthday. She remembered thinking he had been mad to forgo the more accurate, ornate Elgin he used to own in favor of something more sentimental.

Mirage, having curiously scented the human male with some interest for the last several minutes, lifted her head high and nimbly plucked Junior's hat from his head. Feathery yellow locks fell forward into his eyes.

"What the hell?" He was so flabbergasted that Isa burst into laughter. Junior raked his hair from his forehead and yanked his hat back from her horse, scowling. "Your damned horse just took my hat. What kind of animal is this?"

Isa temporarily forgot that she was supposed to be angry with him. "She's a circus horse. The ringmaster trains them to do little tricks for the audience's enjoyment." Then, because she was a mischievous child again, unbothered by the strictures of past hurts or time apart, she teased, "Perhaps she took you for a clown?"

"Isadora!" Miss Pickney called from the neighboring stoop. Beside her, a middle-aged man smoked a pipe and leaned against his door. "Where is your hat?"

Growling softly, Isa secured the last strap and trudged back inside.

Chapter Three

Forcing himself not to follow Isa's trek to the apartment with his eyes, Junior trailed his fingers along Mirage's glossy coat. When he patted the mare's rump, shining in the morning sun, her long black tail swished in his face. He almost smiled.

"Looks like Dora found a horse that matches her temperament, eh?" David asked conspiratorially from a safe distance. "Tries to kick and bite a chunk out of every horse within reach."

Junior pulled his brown kerchief higher up his neck. "Too old to be acting that way. Probably isn't worth a damn to ride."

"Oh, Dora's certain she can train it right." David pulled a snuffbox from his jacket lining, took out a pinch, and snorted some before returning the modishly decorated box into the recesses of his fine jacket. "We picked the thing up under the cover of night like a Grimm fairy tale. I thought she'd shown me everything, then she takes me to a godforsaken slaughterhouse to pick up a five-hundred-dollar horse." He laughed wryly, wiping his nose with a starched handkerchief from his back pocket.

Dislike curled its way along Junior's arm to his trigger finger, making it twitch. In the parlor, the young Mr. Corner had admitted he'd accompanied Isa to the train station Tuesday. Now, he told Junior that she went off in the night to make expensive purchases. What if it had gone wrong and they'd been robbed or killed for their efforts? And where the hell had Isa gotten five hundred dollars?

"The two of you spend a lot of nights alone?" Junior asked.

David's next laugh was forced. "I'm not answering that."

"Miss Pickney know about this? She's supposed to be watchin' out for Isa, making sure she's not being…taken advantage of." The threat in his soft words was clear.

A hint of challenge flared in the other man's eyes. He was a city boy through and through, pretty enough to make plenty of ladies flutter their lashes, and Junior resented his begrudging respect that Isa's beau wasn't backing down.

"I would never take advantage of her. I have looked after Isa for the last two years. Where have *you* been?" When Junior only glared, David's lips twisted up. "Besides. Have you ever tangled with her? A greasy eel is less slippery. I doubt many men could take advantage of that woman."

Now Junior really hated him. Only his training kept him from wrapping his fingers around the smug bastard's neck. This dandy had wrestled her? Put his hands all over Isa, tried to overpower her? It didn't matter if it had been in play. An outpouring of protectiveness stiffened every one of Junior's muscles.

You don't have a right to feel this way, a voice sneered.

No. He didn't.

Forcing his stony expression not to crack, Junior approached the other man, who was smiling unpleasantly. "You're right. Her brother and I taught her how to fight; I doubt anyone could pin that one down for long." David's smile melted away as the blond cowboy clapped a hard hand on his shoulder. Junior positioned himself imposingly close. "As for keeping an eye on her for the last couple years, I reckon her family and I owe you our thanks. Why don't you make yourself scarce? I can take it from here." Junior squeezed David's shoulder.

"I—" David swallowed and glanced at the front door. "I should say goodbye."

"No need. I'll tell her for you." He released the man's shoulder with a little shove. "Get goin'."

"Well...tell her I'll be waiting at my father's bank—"

"Sure, I'll tell her." Like hell he would. He grazed the pin-striped suit jacket with his plain work shirt as he passed and sauntered across the road to where his dapple-gray gelding and pack mule were tethered. He didn't spare Isa's beau another look, and when he returned with Champion and Red, David Corner was gone.

Isa stepped out the front door as Junior was checking his timepiece for the third time, and he nearly choked on a laugh. She wore something that couldn't decide if it was a hat or a bouquet of flowers. She was fashionable, yes, but at what cost? Reflexively, he thought of things he could say to her.

Did your head turn into a vase when you went inside?

Here's some water. You're wilting.

She was muttering and adjusting the wide brim of her gargantuan hat when she noticed his expression.

"Not a word," she growled, tying a ridiculously wide blue satin ribbon beneath her chin. "Miss Pickney bestowed this on me when I earned my degree."

Not a word would pass his lips...for now. He was in too big of a hurry to worry about starting a long-winded argument.

She made a face at him, then paused. Looked around. "Where did David go?"

"I told him to leave."

Isa's brows knitted. "Why did you do a thing like that? I didn't get to tell him goodbye."

"I'm sure he'll cry into his pillow tonight over it."

Shooting darts at him, Isa untethered Mirage's reins from the post.

"So. She's a circus horse." Junior eyed the intractable way the mare nodded her head, ears back.

"She was before the owner sold her, perhaps because circus animals are conditioned to travel by train and this one breaks the mold. Not only does she spook at trains, but she's also hostile toward other horses. I assume she had an act alone. She's young, has never been bred, and is intelligent. Her manners, however..." Isa trailed off as Mirage pinned her ears at Champion, squealed, and stamped her foot.

He'd been right. The horse wasn't worth a damn. Champion, a veteran cow pony that was used to untrained quarter horses at the ranch, remained good-natured and unbothered. "Circus trainers couldn't tame her, but you think you can?" What an arrogant, foolish notion.

"I know I can train her." Her smile was a sickly sweet grimace.

"It'll be a long ride home—"

But she'd had enough naysaying. "Oh, why don't you put a stocking in it and ruin someone else's dreams." She mounted Mirage, who had stretched her velvety nose toward the gelding to scent him. Her ears lay flat against her handsome head, and her foreleg lashed out. Prepared for this, Isa pulled the reins and brought the horse's sleek black head up. "No! Don't even think about kicking!"

Miss Pickney and the professor looked up.

An untrained, kicking mare was dangerous, striking at another horse without thinking of a person standing between them. Many a kneecap had been shattered by an intemperate horse aiming a kick at someone's mount. The last thing Isa and Junior needed was an easily avoided injury before their journey.

"Yep, I'd say she needs some lessons in manners," Junior drawled, mounting his unperturbed gelding.

Isa, who had been tucking her skirts modestly around her legs, turned to look at him. Her hat was so large it created its own breeze. "I forgot how much you love stating the obvious."

"You'd better get a crop if you're going to ride her around people."

"But what would stop me from using it on you?"

"Stubborn brat," he muttered.

"What?"

He didn't repeat himself. If they continued to rib each other all day, they'd never get out of Austin. He rode Champion over to Miss Pickney with Red behind on the lead rope and Isa's devil-horse prancing sideways in their wake. Junior had planned to tip his hat at Miss Pickney, but she stalled him with a liver-spotted hand on his boot.

"Promise me you will keep a keen eye on Isadora. Let no harm befall her, Mr. Stone."

Before he could get a word in edgewise, Isa said, "It's quite alright, Miss Pickney. Junior is a Texas Ranger. I'll be on the right side of the law with him by my side."

"Then, I am grateful to you, sir, for doing your part in service of our great state's police force. She will be in capable hands."

Junior's upper lip prickled with sweat, and his underarms grew damp and humid. He tipped his hat to her, waited for the fragile hand to release his boot, and nudged Champion forward. Behind him, Isa said something low to Miss Pickney, then called out to Junior that she needed to pick up her last month's wages from the bank.

But all he heard was dry, burning wood.

"PLEASE. WILL YOU reconsider?"

It was the only time the eldest Mr. Corner had ever said please.

Typically, his demands were offered on a serving platter of suggestion. He was perfectly polite, certainly within his realms as the direct manager of the small bank he supervised. Sometimes, he'd share a humorous anecdote with her, typically watered down, with no interesting bite of wit for the only woman who worked for him.

"I'm sorry, Mr. Corner." Isa had already cleared off the desk tucked neatly in the corridor outside his office. To everyone in the building, she had been his secretary. But, under the guise of bringing in his coffee and sweets from the shop next door, she'd ignore the review of that week's secretarial duties and would instead advise him on the more fraught natures of his personal investments. By the end of this, her first year with him, she had earned Mr. Corner nearly a quarter of a million dollars. She could not have conceived of such a fortune as a child raised barefoot and thin on her family's sharecropper farm. Now, real money was just as tangible as the poker chips she and David raked in on weekends at the gambling casino.

"Is it a promotion you want?" Mr. Corner's hands fondled the 14-karat gold chain drooping from his vest pocket. "You know I cannot—"

"Eleanor Brackenridge is a bank director in San Antonio and has been since '87." She couldn't resist goading him and was pleased when his cheeks went florid beneath his frothy white mutton chops.

"Now, I can't give you my job, Miss Williams. We've been over this."

Isa tucked her face away so he wouldn't see her smile. Did the old man genuinely think she wanted his job? What a farce. She had more than enough money holed away for a year's travel abroad, plus up to three years of living comfortably without working. In no way was she interested in delegating work to resentful men, or managing a bank during this depression, one newspapers dubbed "The Panic of 1893." She'd warned him to get out while he could, but the man had dollar signs in his eyes and greed in his heart.

Still...to not work at all? She shuddered at the thought. Even now, her mind raced and her fingers twitched to do something, anything. A fountain pen forlornly lay on the bare desk, and she picked it up, touching its silver filigree.

"My son is in love with you, Miss Williams."

Isa's fingers halted in their investigation.

"If you leave, and if I know my child—which I do—he may come after you."

Setting the pen down, Isa faced Mr. Corner. He looked a little at a loss, tugging at the bush of his facial hair, fingers plumper now than the year before.

Carefully, Isa reminded him, "David is married."

Mr. Corner waved that away. "He did propose to you first if you'll recall."

Isa winced. "I recall."

"Against my good judgment, I might add."

"I recall that as well."

"Don't take it personally—"

"I don't."

"—but you hadn't worked for me yet. I didn't know..." He trailed off, and the awkward stillness made room for past discomforts.

Befriending David in her fourth year at school.

Tutoring him in mathematics so he could pass his rigorous exams—and in return, him helping her financial situation.

The drunken night months before when they'd won thousands at gambling and celebrated by pushing the boundaries of their friendship. The subsequent proposal and her gentle refusal, the only time she'd ever been gentle with him. And David's dignity-preserving mistake that had landed him in a spot of trouble with a lawyer's daughter. He'd married the girl the following month, strangers. Isa had not been invited to the wedding. No, that was untrue. David had insisted she attend, but with his young fiancée's missive, pleading that Isa not cause a scandal by showing her face at the wedding, burning like a hot coal in her pocket, Isa had stubbornly refused to go.

David didn't act unduly miserable with married life, but he also didn't spend a day away from Isa either. The elder Mr. Corner and Isa had both been bullied and beleaguered by David until she'd had a position at the bank. In a fit of temper, David had shouted, "I may not have you as my wife, but I will by God see you supported."

Guilt and exasperation had encompassed Isa's first day on the job. Mr. Corner, who had very exacting opinions of women in a man's environment, had been disgruntled until he'd seen with his own two eyes what she could do with numbers. The minute she'd interpreted the cash flows, balance sheets, and income statements that had piled and creaked precariously on his desk, he'd blinked owlishly at her. And when she'd gone head-to-head with his top investment banker, arguing vehemently over the stodgy fool's investment decisions of the last two quarters, Mr. Corner had actually chortled.

She'd been relegated to his personal secretary that same hour. A year later, he was her sincerest advocate.

Pitying David's father, the sufferer of a man incapable of changing his child's strange ways, Isa strode forward and gave the proud manager a swift hug. "It will all work out for the best, me leaving," she soothed.

From the narrow stairwell, David's voice called, "Dora! Has he convinced you to stay?"

Sharing one final look with Mr. Corner, she called back, "No, but it was a valiant effort." The oath that floated up the stairs made her laugh. "Goodbye, Mr. Corner. It was mostly a pleasure to work with you. I'll be sure to stop for a cup of coffee on my next visit."

She hid a smile at his mutters of "mostly a pleasure" and left him.

Downstairs, David stood with his arms folded and mouth petulant. The floor-to-ceiling window revealed Junior in the street on Champion, holding tight to Mirage's reins, a cigarette between his lips.

"I don't like him," David said soberly.

"I don't like him particularly well, either," she agreed, pecking her pouting friend on the cheek. "Goodbye."

He didn't say anything, just squeezed her hand between their outstretched arms until she walked away and he was forced to let go.

Chapter Four

Something was amiss with Junior. Isa couldn't put her finger on it, so she studied him from the corner of her eye as their horses clopped through the streets of downtown Austin.

His shoulders had certainly broadened in their years apart. At twenty-eight, Junior was built like a mountain man during a lean season. Isa peeled her eyes from his narrow hips and contemplated the other changes in him.

"You have a new scar," she said. It was above his left eye, just below the tail end of his eyebrow.

"It's not new." He seemed uninterested in discussing it. "What did you and your boss man talk about?"

"He gave me my wages and asked that I not leave." Isa fiddled with the ribbons of her hat. They were so wide they acted like blinders, which was precisely why she'd tried to leave the apartment without the hat in the first place. One couldn't safely travel if one's peripheral vision was hindered, but Miss Pickney had insisted respectability was more integral than practicality.

"Sounds like he respects you and your work," Junior offered, glancing at her surreptitiously.

"Mr. Corner respects money. He does not respect women."

"You one of those suffragists?"

"Yes, I'm 'one of those suffragists.'" She glared at him. "I'm a part of NAWSA."

"What-uh?"

"The National American Woman Suffrage Association. You don't pay it any mind because you can have a bank account, and decent pay, and you have the right to vote. Among a thousand other things I won't bore you with details of."

"Thank God."

Isa's head snapped his way so sharply that her hat went askew. "I ought to wallop you."

"I'm only teasin'." He sighed. "Hell, Izzy, if anyone has taught me that women are just as capable as men, it's you. You're the cleverest person I know. And not just out of the women I know, out of *everyone*. I'd put you in Congress if I could. You'd have the world set to rights after a day. No more panic, no more depression. Though I can't say you would be levelheaded if another country wanted a piece of us; you need to work on that temper."

If words could club one over the head, his could. Her jaw was suddenly without working hinges.

"Still want to wallop me?"

No. "Yes."

The noise he made wasn't quite a laugh, and he grew quiet again as the smell of the Colorado River strengthened. A waterfowl cried out as it flew overhead, feathers gleaming white beneath its tapered wings. Junior paid it no mind and continued to scout the way ahead, every face receiving a once-over as they rode sedately by. She had seen him in many moods over the years: angry, petulant, jolly, drunk. She'd never seen him vigilant. On high alert. A fury lay just beneath the surface, boiling beneath an icy layer. He was changed. More unsettling. In the apartment, his long-lashed indigo eyes had been eerily steady. On David. On Miss Pickney.

On her.

The consistent stillness was so unlike the Junior of old that it unnerved her. And Isa did not like to feel unnerved.

He's just disappointed to be babysitting you across half a dozen counties.

She frowned down at her gloved hands.

As a child, she'd pestered and needled him relentlessly, but he'd returned the favor in kind. He would best her at her own games until it was *she* who exploded into frustrated emotional uproars, not him. There hadn't been a time in her life when her brother's friend wasn't there, scuffling and wrestling with her in the dirt, shouting from her pinches while she screeched at holds from which she couldn't escape.

She could not imagine trying such tricks with him now. Had he finally grown out of it...out of her? Had her presence ultimately become a terrible trial for him?

An unexpected ache stirred behind the bone of her sternum, and she rubbed it resentfully with two fingers. By her seventeenth birthday, she'd come to terms with the fact that Junior would never see her as more than just a sister and that any love he held for her in his heart would always be platonic. She'd inured herself to that truth, and her love for him had morphed into something deeper. Softer. All its sharp edges had smoothed so that it no longer cut nor wounded nor incited her to wound back. She had loved him for who he was, whether he returned her feelings or not.

Of late, she felt prickly and hurt all over again. Once more, she felt ignored. Discarded. She was unsure if she could soften toward him again.

Not this time.

Their grim little procession rounded street corners and parked wagons. Once, they had needed to wait for a harassed-looking older gentleman to push a stalled automobile out of the way. The automobile looked like a horseless carriage with its cover down.

"Have you ever driven an automobile?" she asked.

"No."

"Oh. I have. It's wondrous fun. It goes as fast as a galloping horse if you can find a road not riddled with potholes."

She sensed his face turn her way. "When did you get your hands on an automobile?" A pause, then, "Did you steal it?"

Isa couldn't help it—she laughed. "Egad, no! Calvin Cheswick's father purchased one and took David and me out last year. I drove it perfectly well. It has countless gauges you must manipulate to control the steering. David was hopeless when it was his turn; he drove us straight into a ditch. Do you know how heavy steam engine automobiles are?"

"As I've never had much use for 'em, no."

She ignored this lackluster response and continued excitedly, "Calvin had to arrange for a group of men and horses to pull it out. Then the blasted thing wouldn't start for a half hour. Steam engines are very temperamental and would do far better with flash boilers. I advised Calvin's father to sell it and buy one of those automobiles with an internal combustion engine."

"Are you going to be like this the whole trip?" Junior asked politely.

Isa didn't hesitate. "Yes. Do feel free to ride ahead if you get tired of it."

Junior groaned quietly but made no other objection.

"Have you seen the new dam yet?"

"Why would I want to see that?" His peeved tone made her bristle.

"Because it's one of the tallest dams in the country?" Her voice rose. "Because it will power street cars, and people won't have to walk or ride horses everywhere? Because electricity in the city will industrialize Austin by leaps and bounds?" She continued to spew facts like weapons at him all the way down the street, and several men gave Junior pitying glances from their buggies or the sidewalk. His response to her scolding was to look blankly at her. She shook her head incredulously at his lack of enthusiasm. "Are you such a Luddite that you don't wish to see new things? Wonderful things?"

For the first time since their uncomfortable reacquaintance in Miss Pickney's parlor, Junior peered at her as though he truly saw her. The steady onslaught of his gaze made her uncomfortably aware of how her body moved on Mirage, how awkward her arms felt in her puffed sleeves. Gradually, the harsh planes and lines of his face eased until he was the old Junior again. The young man who had witnessed Isa's awkward transition through puberty as a tomboy reluctant to appear girlish during her shift to tentative womanhood.

This Junior gestured a hand outward, encouraging her to lead the way. "Alright, then. Show me this dam."

"IT'S INCREDIBLE, ISN'T it?" Isa shouted over the surging water of the Austin Dam. "This is what will power the city with electricity. Did you see all the new street lights on the way here?"

Junior had to stand close to hear her, even with the shouting. He'd known about the dam; hell, that's all that was in the newspaper these days. Hearing it from Isa, with her icterine green eyes sparkling excitedly, piqued his interest in ways the written word couldn't. He studied the flow of water rushing over the dam with astonishing force. Behind them, their horses were tied in some shrubs. Mirage's lower lip drooped sullenly, ears at half-mast. He'd made damned sure to tie up Champion and Red far away from that heathen.

Isa went on about the man-made waterfall in front of them.

"Did you know this is one of the tallest dams in the country?" she was shouting at him. "It's sixty feet high! See that power-house? It looks like an English lord's manor, doesn't it? Mayor McDonald spared no expense on this project."

He nodded, pretending to be interested. "Must be why Austin is in debt up to its ears."

"What?"

"Nothing."

They stood beside the crashing water until Isa eventually sat, tossing small rocks into the water. With nothing better to do, he sat beside her, plucked a piece of brush from the rocky soil beneath them, and pulled its leaves off, one by one. Over-head, the clouds rolled across the horizon, a dark, ominous shelf promising miserable traveling weather. He swore aloud, but the roaring waters swallowed it up. Twice, he glanced behind him and pulled his watch out.

"Ants in your pants?" Isa called out, her eyes following his movements. Her hat was so expansive it looked like a gi-ant baby's bonnet. The way she watched him irritated him. Made him feel like a bug scurrying at the feet of a magnify-ing-glass-wielding being.

"I'd like to get home at some point this week. Look at that storm rolling in."

Astonishingly, she didn't argue or complain; she hopped up, dusted off her skirts, and held her hand out to him. A brow raised, he smacked her hand indignantly away, rising of his own accord. Her quick, wicked grin gleamed before she turned her back on him and glided to their horses.

Chapter Five

They crossed the Colorado River by flatboat, ate the lunch of cold cuts packed by Miss Pickney, and sipped from their canteens while people teemed by. A farmer with a buckboard loaded with hay rattled past and tipped his hat. Two colorfully dressed women giggled on their phaeton, finger-waving at Junior, their ribbons fluttering in the wind. Junior tipped his hat and pulled his brown kerchief over his nose, going from respectable to bank robber. Isa noticed but said nothing. Later, when a group of boisterous young men rode by on flashy thoroughbreds, whistling appreciatively at Isa in her fashionable poof sleeves and broad-brimmed hat, Junior's loose fingers slowly grazed his Colt, his eyes steady on them.

The men laughed and made a quick escape.

"We need to get off the main road," he said, glancing behind them at the group's retreating backs.

Isa followed him off the main road onto a narrow, rocky trail snaking sharply along rugged terrain. She muttered complaints under her breath, thinking how it would add hours to their trip and for what? It didn't escape her notice that the brown kerchief made its home back on Junior's neck the longer they rode without encountering anyone else on the rough trail.

Junior broke the silence an hour into their journey east to Dogwood. "Is that city dude your beau?"

Isa reined Mirage closer to Champion. "What?"

He curtly repeated his question without looking at her, and she resented how distractingly handsome his profile was. There was not much he would approve of regarding her friendship with David.

"Is *David* my beau?" Isa laughed. "No, we're friends. We attended college together. Well, he only attended it with me during his last year. I tutored him through his final exams."

"Men and women can't be 'just friends,'" he elucidated as though imparting some elementary knowledge on her such as *the sky is blue* or *rain falls from storm clouds.*

"Yes, they can," Isa argued, feeling the warmth of a promising debate bloom in her face and extremities. "Look at you and me. Or you and Lucy."

"Lucy's married. It's not the same." He ducked beneath a low-hanging limb, unconcerned by the disgusted face she made at him.

"David is also married, so it *is* the same," she countered.

Animation livened the stubborn set of his jaw. "What? You let a married man see you off, hold you, and look at you all moon-eyed? I saw you kiss him, Isa!"

That little peck on the cheek? That had been a friendly kiss! But a worrisome, slinking sensation crawled up from someplace within her, one she had long repressed and locked away. Isa disliked feeling shame and typically never acknowledged it if she did. Experiencing it now was like finding slime growing in the corner of a carefully manicured room. Junior had drawn attention to it like a Roman soldier blowing a horn during battle.

"I am not answerable to you," she said stiffly, chin in the air.

He nudged Champion ahead of Mirage, who reared her head unhappily at being cut off. "Let me guess, he's one of the half a dozen proposals you got?"

"One of three, there were no *half a dozen*—"

Junior laughed rudely. "Tell me about them, then. What was so wrong with them that you denied their hand?"

"It wasn't that anything was wrong with them; it was just that we didn't suit each other." Her brows were severe, low and dark over her eyes like the storm clouds overhead.

"How so?" He was staring at her, a mythological god in cowboy gear waiting to dole out judgment.

"You truly wish to know? Fine." She shrugged like it didn't matter a whit. Inside, however, she squirmed at the prospect of telling him about such intimate affairs. "Walter was my first proposal. He approached me one day as a dare by his friends and tried to humiliate me for being the only woman in Trigonometry class."

"Did you set him straight?" Junior asked.

"I bet him twenty dollars that I could get a higher grade in class by semester's end. He took the bet and made the rest of the semester most uncomfortable for me. I had no choice but to reply in kind. Remember the time you gave me chocolate sawdust?"

Junior refused admission, but his mouth curled up at the ends like a cat.

"Well, I suggested a truce and gave him chocolate sawdust decorated with a pretty ribbon. He was so receptive to the truce that I almost felt guilty when he spat it out during a lesson." Isa grinned, remembering the handsome Walter's watering eyes and red face. "Of course *his* tricks tended to ruin my clothes; he spilled ink on my skirts while I was working and hid buckets of molasses over doorways."

"Are we still discussing someone who asked for your hand in marriage?" Junior asked disbelievingly.

"Hush, I'm getting there. I eventually grew angry enough with Walter to pay one of my friends to approach him and flirt a little. He was a fool for a pretty face and was completely enamored. Just as he was touching her cheek, a great giant of a man ran out and threatened to do Walter bodily harm for touching his intended. I'd never seen him so afraid; it looked like he was facing a firing squad."

Junior rubbed his face. "God, Isa, what if he'd gotten afraid enough to shoot someone?"

"Firearms are not allowed on campus. But not to worry, Walter discovered me. He heard me laughing by a potted shrub, and my friend fessed up that it was only a trick. If he'd had the brass to shoot anyone, it would have been me that day. The week the professor posted our marks, I was top of the class, and he was forced to give me twenty dollars."

"What, did he drop down to one knee and give you a ring along with twenty dollars?" Junior sounded doubtful.

"Heavens, no. He hated me for months. He didn't like me until he mustered the courage to ask for help with exams."

"Like David?"

"Yes, like David. They had mutual friends. That's how I earned money; I'd tutor some of the men in secret. In any case, once he got over his initial dislike of me, he would call upon me. One day, he asked for my hand in Miss Pickney's parlor. I told him no, and he hasn't spoken to me since."

Junior scratched the back of his head and glanced behind him; no one was there. "It can't be an easy thing, asking someone like you to marry them. I guess he had the brass, after all."

It was said as a compliment. Isa's chest heated as though a falling star lit her up from the inside out.

"Who was the second man?"

"Hm?" Isa blinked. "Oh. The second one was a professor."

"*What*?" A flock of blackbirds took flight from a nearby tree, their angry cries fading as they flew to quieter woods.

"Yes, he was very enthralled with my brain, but he reminded me of a kindly grandfather. I was much kinder to him than Walter in my refusal. I made excellent marks in his class and didn't want that to change." Junior was shaking his head, so she wisely changed the subject. "You would know all this if you hadn't stopped writing me."

Narrowed blue eyes slid to her. "Were you always this whiny?"

"I don't know. Were you always this ugly?"

"Good grief," he groaned. "And I've got three more days of this?"

"As I've said before, you're welcome to go ahead by yourself. Don't stick around on my account."

He grunted something and jammed his hat down so far that the tips of his ears bent. Unmoved by his sudden crossness, Isa stopped fighting Mirage and gave the mare her head. It was far easier to enjoy the scenic trail when Junior wasn't in front of her to spoil it. The forest around them focused into an Albert Bierstadt painting: splashes of oranges, crimsons, and sunflower yellows amidst a backdrop of twisted, craggy trees bracketing a rock-laden trail. It took her breath away.

Hours went by, and the storm-dark skies became blacker until the landscape of vivid colors turned duller than dishwater. Isa eventually grew bored. And hungry. She was always hungry. She rummaged in her saddlebag and pulled out a sack of roasted, salted sunflower seeds. She popped a few in her mouth, and Mirage's ears swiveled back while Isa's teeth broke open the striped seeds. Isa gently pulled back on the reins until Junior sidled up on Champion.

"Are you involved in clandestine undertakings for the Texas Rangers?"

Junior's hips stopped moving so easily in the saddle. "What do you mean?"

Isa spat a sunflower seed out, joyfully watching it tumble pell-mell to the ground. Miss Pickney never let her eat them because it wasn't *ladylike*. "You disguise your face, you haven't stopped looking behind us since we left, and you're as jumpy as a puppet."

His answer was a grunt.

Undeterred, she tossed more seeds into her mouth and talked rudely around them. "Well, what sort of work do the Texas Rangers have you doing these days?"

"Nothing much." There was no inflection in his voice.

"The last you wrote about your work was when they made you lieutenant and sent you down to the border. Which assignment was that one?"

Junior was quiet for so long that she opened her mouth to repeat the question when he gritted out, "Rogue Rangers."

"Texas Rangers go rogue?" She gasped at this exciting bit of news and turned in her saddle.

There was only stiff, foreboding silence from her companion.

"Oh, come on, Stone, I want details. It cannot be so serious and secretive as all—"

"You don't know a damned thing about it, Isa, and it's gonna stay that way. You understand?" His voice cracked like thunder.

Isa's titillated expression soured. "Well, pardon the hell out of me!" The retort was muffled behind a cheek full of sunflower seeds, dulling its edge.

A flash of lightning in the distance brought the animals to a halt, and the resounding crash of thunder spooked Mirage. The mare bolted. For an eternity, Isa did corrective maneuvers, keeping the half-trained mare's head up high and turning her in circles. Meanwhile, the storm rolled closer. Dense, steely storm clouds settled heavily above them, darkening the woods and dropping the temperature. Treetops went from gently swaying to lashing back and forth. Red and orange leaves rained down upon them, violently torn from limbs by the force of the wind.

They needed shelter, fast.

"Where are we?" she shouted over rushing leaves and creaking limbs.

"Just outside Brenham," Junior answered, his deep voice carrying. His face had paled beneath his tan, and he kept his rope in hand to lasso Mirage if Isa failed to control her. "We should be close to the fork that'll take us to the main road."

For twenty minutes, they traveled, their animals' manes and tails tangling in the wind. Isa's skirts flew up twice, and her hat was in constant threat of taking flight. Cursing, wishing she was wearing the trousers Miss Pickney had so heartlessly confiscated, Isa tucked her skirts beneath her legs. Reminded of her guardian's mercilessness, Isa doffed and stuffed her bothersome hat in the space between her saddlebags and gunnysack. They arrived at the main road just as the bottom dropped out of the sky. Isa stubbornly looked away when Junior furtively tucked his kerchief back over his nose. Let him act like a member of the James-Younger Gang.

She was far too involved in her own dilemma.

There was nothing Isa hated more than to ride while wet. Raindrops on her bare head made her scalp itch like it was crawling with bugs. Moisture trickled down her neckline, soaking her collar. She gritted her teeth and followed Junior along the main road—her horse was finally, mercifully, serene—to a nondescript building with a tiny sign with "Hostel" painted in yellow and outlined in black. They tied their horses to the hitching post and shuffled inside, boots squishing with every step. It smelled heavily of cabbage and the mustiness of improper airflow, and Isa's eyes followed the plain paneled walls to the single tiny window that was painted shut. In a little back room, a strapping man was hunched over a desk. His complexion was ruddy, and his thinning hair lay like corn silk along his scalp.

The door, too tight in its frame, squeaked shut behind Junior, alerting the proprietor.

The man made a little exclamation of pleasure. "Oh! Hello. You need a room?" His accent was strong with softened h's and gargled r's. Brenham was known for its vast population of German immigrants, who had arrived in droves the decade before. Fluent in the language, Isa perked up.

"*Ja, zwei.*" She could only hope the man had two rooms.

"Oh!" This time, the man's robin's-egg blue eyes widened. "*Sind Sie Deutscher?*"

Smiling, she mopped her wet hair out of her eyes; it had fallen around her shoulders in the downpour. "No, I'm not German. But I speak it."

"Leon Meyer." He bowed a little, chortling.

Junior cleared his throat and pulled his damp, flat case wallet from his vest pocket. "You got two rooms?" He was unnecessarily stern.

The hostel owner rushed to obtain what looked like a ledger from the desk in the back room, glanced through the last page's contents, and scratched his scalp with a pinky nail. "Ah, no, we have but one room, *Herr*. Many have looked for shelter this day."

Junior's red lips turned down at the ends. Beneath his bearded chin, his kerchief hung limp, revealing the shining white scar stretching across his neck beneath the jawbone. "You sure there's only one?"

Leon Meyer's eyes drifted low to the dull glint of metal at the younger man's hip, and his friendly smile slackened.

Oh, for heaven's sake. "One room will be perfect, thank you, *Herr* Meyer." Isa scowled up at Junior, the only man she'd ever had to look up at besides her brothers and father.

Perhaps noting his guests' impressive heights and similar coloring, Meyer cautiously asked, "*Sind sie Schwester und Bruder?*"

"*Ja,*" Isa lied. "We're sister and brother."

"Izzy—" Junior growled under his breath.

Isa cut him off without fluttering an eyelash. "Do you have a bundling board?"

Comprehending, Mr. Meyer nodded and bent beneath the counter, his fine hair swaying around his face. He pulled out a large plank used to separate two unmarried people in a bed. He accepted Junior's coin, wrote a receipt for one room, and chatted animatedly with Isa in his native tongue. Isa enjoyed this exchange until she caught a glimpse of the names Junior was writing in the hostel ledger.

Robert and Silvia Winslow.

Junior stepped forward, blocking Isa's view, and she saw a glint of a ten-dollar gold piece. "This is to keep our presence here to yourself. Do you understand? Don't answer any questions about us."

When Mr. Meyer wiped his palms on his sturdy brown trousers, Isa crossed her arms. There was no need to frighten the man! The hostel owner soberly pocketed the coin, leading them up a rickety staircase and down an unlevel hallway. They passed a couple of ripe-smelling railroad men leaving their rooms and reached the last door on the right. Mr. Meyer unlocked the door to a small, quaint room. There was pink everywhere. The curtains, the ruffled bed, and even the doilies on the washstand were embroidered with tiny pink rosebuds.

It was the beige, paneled divider in the corner, however, that excited Isa. She could change out of these wet clothes! Through a tiny square window, the world outside was gray and damp.

"Is there anywhere to bed our horses down for the night?" Junior asked, pocketing the key and lifting the wooden plank from the other man's arms.

"Er, *ja*, a stable in the back."

"Got any feed?"

"Hay is a dollar."

"That'll do." Another transaction was made, and Junior turned to Isa when the proprietor finally quit the room. "What were you saying to him downstairs?"

Disliking his tone, Isa seized the bundling board from his hands. "I told him all of our plans in detail for the next few days, including the fact that you're a Texas Ranger hiding out from someone." His jaw turned to stone, and she shook her head in amazement. "How stupid do you think I am? I didn't say anything of importance!"

Junior wrapped his fingers around her arm, pulling her closer. "You didn't say anything about where we were going?"

Isa looked down at the offending appendage that was wrapped around her biceps, pulled it off with two delicate fingers, and said slowly, "No, I did not tell him where 'Robert and Silvia Winslow' were traveling. Get that bee out of your bonnet."

"And you didn't tell him our real names?" he continued in an angry whisper, cracking the door to look down the hallway for anyone within earshot.

"No!"

"Because if I *was* on a mission for the Texas Rangers, it wouldn't be real smart to bust my cover."

"For Pete's sake, Junior, all I did was ask the man where he hailed from."

"Oh."

"So you can stop shouting at me."

"How could I be shouting when I'm whispering?" he hissed, pulling their room key out and ensuring their lock engaged properly. It did. He then prowled to the window and tested if it was tight within its sill. "I'll bring the saddlebags in and put the horses in the stable. You can ask about supper. I can't argue with you on an empty stomach."

Isa scoffed. "You're just as useless arguing on a full stomach. I don't see how eating helps slow wit."

Junior glared at her and pointed to the side of the bed closest to the door. "That's my side."

She tore her narrowed eyes from him and hauled the heavy bundling board to the bed, settling it in the center. It wouldn't stay upright. "I didn't want that side, anyway."

"Good." He strode to the door and unlocked it.

Before he walked out, she blurted, "*Is* someone following you?" She couldn't conceal her suspicion any longer.

Only his profile was visible, but she could see his left nostril flare. "No."

Liar.

"Well, you're acting like—"

The door shut in her face.

Chapter Six

I sa pressed as close to the window as she could, sporadic lightning in a pitch-black sky illuminating her face's reflection into a pale death mask. She loved lightning storms as much as she feared them. Every explosion of thunder made her start, compelling her to go outside and flee into an open field. She wanted to feel the ground quake beneath her feet and see the lightning grant sight to a darkened world.

Fingers trailing through condensation on the chilly glass pane, Isa breathed in the scent of cold glass, rain, and mildew. It couldn't be much later than seven at night, and already, the yard beyond the little inn was only visible with each fork of lightning.

Booted feet walked up the hallway, and she cocked her head, listening.

It was Junior; she recognized the smooth, purposeful gait.

The door clicked as it unlocked and opened, and a hulking Junior entered, weighed down with two sets of saddlebags and her bulging gunnysack. Rainwater dripped steadily from his buckskin hat and their bags, soaking the pink rag rug at the door with water and mud. She winced, feeling sharp guilt that the proprietor's wife would see the state of the floor on the morrow. Kind Mrs. Meyer had been thrilled to speak in her native tongue when Isa had gone begging for a meal and a pitcher of hot water.

"You know, you're supposed to leave the mud outside, not bring it in," Isa said casually, pushing off the windowsill.

"Damned fool has his stables in the lowest part of the yard," Junior groused, dropping the bags without ceremony to the floor. He pulled his hat off, set it on the hook beside the door, and shook out the damp ends of his hair. When wet, the straw-colored strands changed to dishwater blond.

The room felt too small with him in it.

Manners Miss Pickney had hammered into Isa stood sullenly at attention. "Thank you for getting our bags. Hot water is on the washstand, and Mrs. Meyer said she'd bring our supper to our room shortly."

"Oh." Junior looked at a loss at how diminutive the room seemed when occupied by the both of them. He didn't move from the pink rug. "You're welcome."

Amused, Isa ventured to her bags on the floor and, with much digging, retrieved her night wrapper. "You can come in. I won't bite."

His snort broke the awkward tension, and he stopped play-acting a statue long enough to sit on his side of the bed and toe his boots off. "That's not true in my experience."

"Well, I don't bite *now*. It's against the Women's Athletic Club's rules."

"Since when do you follow any rules?" he asked skeptically, tucking his boots beneath the bed frame. "Wait, you're tellin' me you found a circle of women wrestlers? They all odd like you?"

"Yes, and any of them could give you a run for your money. They're catch-as-catch-can wrestlers, boxers, and more. You should try boxing with me. I excel at it; I have the height and reach that most women don't."

"Guess they couldn't teach you a little humility in that school, huh? Next, you'll tell me none of them could beat you."

Instead of rising to the bait, Isa laughed. She got to her feet and gesticulated with a bar of soap. "Fiona got awfully close."

"I'm sure you have some excuse as to why she almost had you."

"I was running a fever that day."

"You're full of horseshit."

Isa grinned at him, crossed the room, and stepped over his stockinged feet. She poured hot water into the chipped enamel basin, dropped her rag in it, and took her toiletries to the divider in the corner. "If you want to clean up while I'm behind here, I promise not to peek."

"Better not," he grunted, the bed squeaking.

"I'd probably go blind if I did," Isa remarked, spreading the divider's panels to her satisfaction. On a milking stool was a clean bedpan, and she slid the latter out. "Here's this if you need it."

"I'll go outside before I use that in a room with you."

Snickering, Isa peeled off her wet things and draped them one by one over the divider. Stockings, tapes, petticoats, underskirt, overskirt, bodice, and finally, her bright white lacy combinations. As a child, she'd had nothing but her mother's tattered old unmentionables to wear. Never again would she wear dingy, yellowed undergarments. Everything she owned was new and in fashion, the whites bright, no frayed hems, everything fitted—her ensemble was a far cry from the secondhand clothing she'd owned as a child. Her brother's wife, a seamstress, had taught Isa all she knew about patterns and fashion. Normally, Isa couldn't give a hoot and a holler about fashion, but it didn't escape her notice that if you acted the part of a successful, modern woman, people tended to treat you like one.

"How are the horses?" she asked distractedly, scrubbing her face and neck with the soapy washcloth.

"Behaving." It was muffled, and Isa fought the urge to peek behind the panel. Something soft fell to the floor. A shirt? "Your devil-horse stopped acting so spooked in the stable."

"Good. Thank you." She analyzed why it was so difficult to thank him. Why was it so challenging to break childhood habits? Perhaps she was experiencing growing pains, not of her bones, but of the character.

"I wiped her down and curried her. Damned thing stole my hat again."

"It's how she shows her gratitude." Isa smiled, scrubbing beneath her arms and then her intimate areas.

His unintelligible answer was followed by splashing, and Isa slowly slipped on her sturdy cotton wrapper, listening. Imagining. She reached up to braid her hair, but it was curling wildly around her temples and ears. The tresses wouldn't be tamed into a night braid and needed to be brushed. Her fingers froze. Had she brought her hairbrush? *No.* She'd forgotten it. Miss Pickney would fuss if she knew.

A knock on the door jolted her from her fretting. Junior cursed.

"Do you need me to answer it?" Isa asked from behind the divider, assuming the noises she heard were him struggling to get his trousers on. She realized almost too late what she'd see if she did.

"No!" he snapped. "I'll get it."

Isa bridled. "It's probably just Mrs. Meyer with our supper." Giving in to temptation, she peeked around the screen's edge. A shirtless Junior stood to the side of the door, gun in hand, his back to Isa. Just below his ribs on the left-hand side was a knotted purple scar, recently healed.

"Who is it?" he barked at the intruder.

A woman's timid voice spoke German through the door, and Isa gave up pretending to care about propriety.

"Put that down and let her in!"

Glancing around, he glared at her floating head beside the divider and pulled their key from his pocket. But when the door finally swung open, the hall was empty except for a tray on the floor. Two plates of sausage, potatoes, dark-brown rolls, and a jar of sauerkraut beckoned. Isa's stomach growled ferociously.

Sliding the food tray in with a bare foot, he relocked the door and set down his pistol. Isa came flurrying around the divider.

"Get our food off the floor. What sort of animal are you?" She bent to pick up the tray, pausing at the eyeful of bare feet, unbuttoned jeans, and long, tanned torso. The entry wound of the gunshot injury was smaller and less ragged than its exit wound. Faint greenish-yellow bruising orbited the month-old wound, a colored portrait of the bullet's impact on the smooth skin around it. It was a miracle he'd survived. A nick to the bowels and he would have died a slow, painful death by sepsis. David had said even with a doctor, getting gutshot was certain death. Even if the intestine was repaired, the contents of the bowel would corrupt the stomach cavity. Feeling suddenly chilled, Isa glanced away. "You can finish washing up behind the screen. I'm done."

Blue eyes followed her to her bedside table, where she gently settled the tray of hot food. "Why?" Junior asked. "You gonna look if I don't?"

Isa's heart stuttered, but she refused to be cowed. "While I'm trying to eat? I think not."

His chuckle was dark behind her, and her pulse responded, racing—racing as if trying to reach some obscure finish line. *Impudent heart.* It sprinted to see how foolish she could be when tempted. Was she tempted by him? Afraid of the answer, she cruelly ignored her body's rising excitement. This was one game she refused to play, beating heart be damned. She frowned at her plate of food, curiously not hungry despite her stomach's protestations minutes before. She ate supper facing the window and watched the storm's frenzy while Junior finished his nightly ablutions. The sausage and bread were good; she studiously ignored the sauerkraut.

Finally, Junior padded from behind the divider, smelling of Ivory soap and leather. He wore clean, faded jeans and no shirt, and Isa felt heat creep past her collarbones and up her neck. Did he not own a union suit? It was cold enough at night for a pair of the red underwear. He had no right to parade half-naked right in front of her. She stiffened when he strode to the tray, the dry material of his trousers brushing against her knee, and she tried not to think about him taking the wet pair off behind the screen.

"You save me any?" he asked, pulling the tray to him one-handed.

"Yes. I'm stuffed." Isa sighed, twisting her knees away from his legs and falling back on her side of the bed, arms behind her damp head. She checked the ceiling for stains, hoping it didn't leak. Beside her, Junior had stopped moving. He stood in the same spot, staring down at her prone form on the bed.

Curious, she glanced up at him. His eyes were twin sapphires in the ill-lit room. Something in them held her like a hare in a live trap.

"What?" Her voice sounded loud despite the rain lashing against the window.

Junior blinked. "Nothing." He turned, tray in hand, and walked to his side of the bed, his perfect profile sharp against the plain wall plaster. The bed dipped when he sat on it, and soon, the sounds of a fork scraping against ceramic added to the ambiance of the storm outside. Since his back was to her, Isa studied her body on the bed unabashedly.

What had he seen?

Her night wrapper was a garish green print with long sleeves and an altered neckline grazing her collarbones. No lace adorned it except an ostentatious ruffle above the swell of her breasts. Miss Pickney had gifted it to her years ago to walk around the house in, as Isa had scandalized the old maid by wandering from her bedroom in nothing but a white lawn nightgown, translucent and suggestive. What she wore now was an old lady's gown. Had Junior looked down at her, wearing something a maiden aunt would wear, and stifled the urge to make fun?

Trying to see herself from his point of view, she looked again. *Oh.*

The skirt of her gown had tucked between her legs, outlining their shape clearly. The area at the junction of her thighs was defined, a risqué triangle drawing the eye. Her breasts, partially flattened from her supine position, sported pointed tips because of the room's chill. Feeling her cheeks warm, Isa wiped her palms over her breasts, trying to smooth her nipples into submission.

They stayed impudently erect.

Frazzled, Isa sat up and hopped off the bed. She needed to check her saddlebags for her hairbrush and ascertain how her books had fared in the rain.

"What are you doing?" Junior judiciously closed his eyes.

"Checking my books. I want to give them to Poppy and Lucy for Christmas." Both of her friends loved books. She crouched at the foot of the bed where their bags lay in a soggy pile and played tug-of-war to get hers out.

"What are they, *Black Beauty*?" Metal slid on wood as he placed the tray on the washstand against the wall.

"No, they already have that one. Lucy's is a cookbook, and Poppy's is *The Adventures of Sherlock Holmes*. Have you heard of it?"

"Nope." He sighed behind her, and the bed creaked. "What's it about?"

"It's about the exploits of a detective who is very, very smart."

"So, he's like you?"

Isa almost strained her neck to look back at him. "Was that a compliment?"

One of Junior's eyes opened, saw her looking, and closed again. "No."

Smiling now, Isa went back to her task. "Blast."

"What is it?"

"I can't find my hairbrush."

"You can use my currycomb."

"Ha ha." She looked for several minutes, making a mess of her saddlebags, especially her gunnysack, but found nothing to tame the drying waves of hair that promised to be a gnarled mess tomorrow. Eventually, she ended the search and inspected the two books in her saddlebags. Both were thankfully dry, so she retrieved the smaller one and got to her feet. Junior pretended to be asleep, and Isa's lips curled up again. On her side of the bed, she adjusted the bundling board until it was vertical between them, and asked, "Shall I read some to you?"

One of Junior's eyes slid open again. "If you want."

Wriggling her way up to the headboard, Isa opened the first page. She cleared her throat and began, "'To Sherlock Holmes she is always *the* woman...'"

For an hour, she read animatedly. By the third page, Junior's eyes remained open, staring at nothing while he listened. Occasionally, he smiled, scoffed, or laughed. They lived in another world together as the oil in the lamp ran out, making the shadows stretch and darken until the light petered out completely, turning everything into shadow.

In the sudden absence of light, Isa closed the book and set it gently on her bedside table. "Time for bed, then."

He didn't laugh at her dry tone. It didn't even sound like he was breathing. Isa flipped her bedclothes up and maneuvered herself between the sheets.

"We forgot to check for bedbugs," he mumbled, half-asleep.

Snuggling deeper, Isa said, "We'll discover in the morning whether the bed is infested or not."

Junior's laugh was stifled. "You're a strange one."

"You're one to talk." Isa curled on her side and faced the long plank of wood. She touched a finger to it and slid the digit down, imagining the body of the man on the other side, warm and sleepy. Lightning flashed, bringing the rough board into stark relief, unpainted and hastily sanded. "When was the last time you saw everyone at home?" Her voice was magnified against the wood.

The mattress undulated as he shifted around. It felt strange and exciting to be sharing a bed with a man. She'd never even slept beside David—not that he hadn't tried.

"I saw everyone this summer, just before I got shot. I stopped and spent some time with Ben. Helped him deliver some horses. And Mother, of course." The latter was admitted with the utmost reluctance. Isa was renowned amongst the cowhands for calling Junior a "mama's boy," an unforgivable slur amongst men.

"Will you tell me what happened with the man who shot you?"

"No." It was a growl.

"Very well. Is there any news from the Circle S Ranch?"

His hesitation was curiously long. "Nope. No news from home. Everything's the same as it's always been. Mother and Father are getting old, but that's about it. He's still a bastard, and she's still hosting dinner parties every Saturday."

"That's good, then. My parents are getting older, too. It's odd. Every time I visit them during holidays, it's a shock. They'll have more gray hairs, more wrinkles. They stoop more like Granny did when she was alive. It's probably a sad fact of having so many children—three sets of twins on top of that—and I was so late in life…While they decline, I'm in my prime." Her feet rippled beneath the blanket like fish. The pillowcase beneath her cheek smelled of cheap soap, and the sound of rain against the wooden planks of the inn's siding sang a lullaby. "Poppy wrote that she's expecting her baby any day now."

He cleared his throat awkwardly. "Yep, this'll be her third."

Tickled by his distress, she corrected, "Fourth."

"Well, the first one was your sister's baby."

Isa frowned at the wooden plank in the darkness. "Not to them, he's not." Then, "Have you heard anything of Kat?" Her oldest sister was a prostitute at The Hound Dog Saloon in Lufkin, but the last her family had spoken to Katherine was when she'd given up her latest son, Timothy, for Poppy and Sol to adopt.

"Not that I recall."

"Oh." Isa's frown deepened, and she plumped her pillow beneath her head, flipping it over to the cool side. "I haven't seen her since I was little. I used to imagine her brushing my hair and giving me fashion advice, but she left when I was still little. Lucy and Poppy…they're the closest things to older sisters I have."

Junior grunted sympathetically. "Well, you're the closest thing to a sister *I* have." Isa had just begun to smile when he added, "Pesky and bothersome."

Reaching a long arm over the bundling board, she swatted without aiming and made contact with a flat stomach.

Chuckling, he shoved her hand away. "Stay on your side, missy."

They joked and talked back and forth until Isa's eyes burned, her heavy lids closing, but his voice, rough yet soft from drowsiness, made them pop back open.

"I had a friend, a Ranger, who would've liked you."

"You think so?"

"Yeah. Randal liked to tease the girls. He got shot in the leg, and on his sickbed, he'd while away the time by sparking the nurses. Some of 'em were old enough to be his ma." Junior chuckled again, and Isa's fists clenched the blanket from the vibration against the board.

Sensing a pall over his reminiscence, she asked softly, "Do you still talk to him?"

Silence. Then, "Naw. We went our separate ways. He was honorably discharged after he lost his leg."

"I see."

"I haven't talked to him in two years."

Isa thought quickly. "Two years ago was when you went to the border?"

This time, when the silence stretched longer than the board between them, he didn't break it.

A SHARP PAIN in his arm roused Junior from a restless slumber.

Half-asleep, he grabbed the hard, splintery thing on which he'd walloped his elbow and tossed it from the bed. Compared to the din of the raging storm outside, its crash against the hardwood was insignificant.

He rolled over and promptly fell back to sleep.

JUNIOR WOKE UP a second time to a cold back and a warm front.

Junior's limbs had wrapped as tightly as climbing ivy around something soft and warm, and he was breathing in an irresistible scent. Something floral. Sweet. His hand, full of something round and pliant beneath the covers, squeezed. His morning erection throbbed. Half-asleep, he nuzzled the tantalizing fuzz his nose had burrowed into, tugging the warm, soft thing tighter to him.

That "something" moved.

Eyes popping open, Junior released the feminine body he was clutching, horror replacing cozy amorousness. His movements woke Isa, who blinked blearily across the pillow at him. Following the storm, a cold front had settled over the land, and the room felt like an ice house. The little iron grate in the corner was black and cold. He and Isa must have snuggled together for warmth.

They stared stupidly at one another for several disturbing seconds before they scrambled from their sides of the bed to the floor. Isa, tangled in the top sheet, fell, arms akimbo. Junior tripped over the bundling board and sat hard on the floor, knocking his back and crown against the washstand. Searing pain arced through the healing wound on his side. There was no storm outside to stifle the ruckus, and they both froze, afraid of a stampede of running feet. Fortunately, no one came to investigate.

Across the rumpled bed, they watched each other, wild-eyed and feral.

"Where did the bundling board go?" Isa whispered forcefully. Accusingly.

Until then, Junior hadn't noticed the throb of his sore elbow; he absentmindedly rubbed it. "I must have whacked my arm on it and thrown it off the bed."

Her eyes narrowed suspiciously. "A likely story."

Glowering, he stood from his undignified sprawl on the floor, stifling the urge to wince at the pain in his side. "You think I want to curl up with a prickly cactus like you? You were on *my* side of the bed."

"We were in the middle," she whisper-shouted, standing as well. "You had your arms and legs all over me!"

"So did you!"

They glared at each other for another beat until, inevitably, both pairs of eyes drifted down. And down. In the cold, Isa's nipples had pebbled, and not even the hideous print of her wrapper could hide it. The sight of her loose breasts made Junior swallow. He could feel her eyes on his bare chest, its mat of flaxen hair tapering to a thin line down his stomach. The clean pair of work jeans he'd donned the night before were sturdy but not enough to disguise the contours of his morning erection; he cupped his privates.

Cheeks suffused with a rosy glow, Isa dragged her eyes back to his face. "Never speak of this," she commanded, a captain of her army of one.

When he didn't argue, couldn't argue, she whirled on her bare heel and disappeared behind the divider.

Chapter Seven

Breakfast was a quiet affair in the little hostel's nondescript dining room. Isa self-consciously ate the poached eggs and leftover sausage Mrs. Meyer had served them while thinking of Junior's bare, golden skin. She could still smell the Ivory soap on him. The fresh scar marring his side had stood out in the morning light, and she'd itched to touch it. She wanted to ask a thousand questions about the injury but rejected the idea like a column of incorrect sums. Junior would tell her to mind her own business and stop being a Peeping Tom. Battling between her curious nature and newfound embarrassment, she didn't look above his hands while they ate; the callused skin was dry and cracked.

Isa's confidence returned on the road east. Dressed in a slicker protecting her split skirt, sage-green blouse, and gun belt, Isa turned her face toward the sun breaking gradually through patchy cloud cover. She'd shoved the ridiculous hat Miss Pickney had insisted she wear into her gunnysack, and her long, honey-gold hair lay in a thick braid behind her back.

She needed a hat. A *real* hat, not one made of flowers and bird nests.

"Are we going through Brenham?" Isa's voice disrupted the hour-long silence. "Or are we going to take another cut road?"

"Why?" Through his bandana, Junior sounded put off. He hadn't looked at her since their bedroom stalemate.

"Because I need a hat," she said, irritated by his prickly mood.

Long-lashed eyes shifted to her, running over the flyaway hairs that had broken free of her braid. His gaze traveled to the enormous yellow oilcloth slicker she wore in case it rained; its corduroy collar was unbuttoned as she couldn't bear for things to touch her throat. Despite the sun's weak yellow rays highlighting the vividly colored trees that bracketed the narrow lane, a miserable drizzle quenched thirsty mud in grooved ruts and deep puddles along the road. Sunshine and rain. *The devil's beatin' his wife,* Sol would say.

Finally, Junior shrugged a reluctant acquiescence. Isa brightened.

Brenham was a growing town with factories puffing smoke in the distance, grand Victorian houses within white picket fences, and an ornate city hall. Isa peered around with interest as they crossed a little wooden bridge on Pecan Street. Above a storefront hung a distinguished bottle-green sign with "W.T. Carrington, Groceries" written in yellow paint. Isa reined Mirage toward its hitching post.

"I'm going to get a few things here."

"Alright. Meet me at the barber. I need a shave." Junior scratched beneath his bandana with a forefinger.

"Tired of the fleas?" she asked innocently, dismounting.

"Yeah, probably caught them from you," he said over his shoulder, heading toward a barber shop's red, white, and blue pole down the street.

The bell above the door tinkled when she entered the store, much like Hobb's General in Dogwood, and the familiarity soothed the disquiet of traveling. The interior of the brick building was spacious, its shelves laden with goods in eye-catching colors and shapes. Fiddling with her reticule, Isa wandered around until she found a little section of hats: bowlers, felt with creased crowns, and bonnets with happy ribbons.

A thin man with a gleaming bald head watched her, his impressive mustache not quite hiding the slack, open mouth beneath. "Can I help you, miss?" he asked, peering up at her.

At ease with being observed like a sideshow, Isa gestured to the hats. "Are any of those Stetsons?" They clearly weren't, but she prayed he had some stocked in the back room.

"Uh, no, ma'am. But they're good quality."

While he combed through the wide-brimmed hats for an appropriate size, Isa glanced through the rack of medicinals on the counter. A tin of cream advertised that it soothed rough, cracked hands. She snatched it up, reading the label.

The kindly man moved behind the counter, a hat in hand. "That stuff is real good in the winter. Better than that horse liniment people use."

Isa paid the fee, shoved her new coffee-brown hat on her head, and slipped the hand cream into her reticule.

Mirage stood rigidly at the hitching post, her eyes rolling. Eyeing the mare suspiciously, Isa stowed her reticule in a saddlebag and untied the reins.

"What's gotten into you?" Isa muttered when Mirage jerked her head away from a pat. "Burr under your saddle?" Erring on the side of caution, Isa walked the mare across the street to the barber shop instead of mounting her right away. The circus horse wasn't used to this much travel, and in bad weather, to boot.

"If you'd gotten on the train, we wouldn't be in this mess," Isa informed her flighty companion as they sidled beside Junior's big dapple-gray gelding.

"Talking to yourself?" asked a deep voice. Junior walked around the pack mule.

Isa glanced up, chagrined at being caught talking to her horse. Her mouth went dry. Junior's hair was trimmed and cut square at the nape. Thick golden layers brushed back from his forehead in waves. His tawny beard was gone, revealing devilish dimples and a cleft chin. Isa had teased him for it once, saying God gave him two rear ends instead of one. Unfortunately, her ma had overheard, and she was still haunted by memories of scrubbing Granny's bedpan that month.

With his strong jaw and chiseled features, Junior Stone was handsome as sin.

"I forgot how ugly you are," she lied to cover up her staring.

Junior startled her again by throwing his head back and laughing. A group of women across the street stopped as one to look. Isa impatiently shook her head at the downfall of womankind's pride around men like Junior. She shoved her muddy boot in the stirrup and mounted Mirage; right away, the horse sidestepped, tail swishing.

"Someone's full of vinegar," Junior mused, mounting his docile gelding.

"She's spoiled and intractable," Isa grunted once seated, and was turning Mirage in a tight circle when the mare attempted a school jump on two feet. "Oh, no, you don't, you little hoyden."

Casually, Junior said, "I had a helluva time saddling her this morning. Kept stealing my gloves out of my pocket."

Isa wasn't listening. The group of women ogling Junior had stopped again to stare openly at the young rider on the recalcitrant horse. Fisting the reins, Isa settled more firmly in her saddle with boot heels securely wedged in the stirrups and steered the black mare toward the center of Pecan Street. Mirage sidestepped again and reared. Molars grinding, Isa leaned over and whispered in the horse's pinned ears, "You're acting plumb embarrassing."

It was true. Not much embarrassed Isa, but appearing as if she couldn't control her mount in a busy street full of people? It was about the worst thing she could think of, even more so than facing Junior across the bed that morning. Speaking of Junior, he probably wouldn't let her live this little street debacle down.

The drizzle remained steady as they trotted out of town. Isa knew all her corrective maneuvering must look preposterous. She was a giant eyesore in her bright yellow slicker, sitting atop a black Arabian who insisted on charging forward, rearing, and running ahead of Champion. After each appalling misconduct, Isa would mercilessly turn the mare in fast circles, whispering profanities. They weren't a mile out of town before Mirage was winded, head low and blowing, her ears close to her head. Isa was no longer cool and collected. Her hair fell down in long, limp strands, her teeth were bared, and her cheeks were full of angry blood.

Junior watched cautiously from his side of the road, stoic but poised and ready to lunge forward on Champion to help. After observing her from his saddle for the dozenth time while Mirage was put through her paces, he called out, "At this rate, we'll get home by Christmas."

"Feel free to offer assistance," Isa barked after spitting another round of invectives at her misbehaving horse. "She's just being diffi—whoa!"

Mirage, seeing a window of opportunity, bolted.

Behind Isa, Junior cursed, and Champion's hoofbeats pounded in tandem with Mirage's. Although an excellent rider, Isa struggled to keep her mare on the path. They were slowly veering toward a stand of trees on the right side of the road.

"Whoa, whoa!" Isa screeched, pulling on the reins with all her strength. Head high and at an awkward angle, Mirage gracelessly jumped over the narrow ditch on the side of the path, and Isa's stomach floated into the recesses of her ribcage for a breathless moment before jolting harshly down again.

"Isa!" Junior roared behind her. She hardly heard it.

A thick, low oak branch, mossy and black from constant rain, loomed chest-high before them. Junior shouted another warning, but Isa disregarded it. What did he think she was going to do? Get herself killed? Grunting, Isa jumped from Mirage and rolled into the high, wet grass to offset the impact. Her expensive Arabian mare was an onyx blur under the low branch, barely clearing the space beneath it. Full of adrenaline and violence, Isa scrambled from her improper sprawl in the grass, a shock of bright yellow against lush green.

"Izzy!" Junior shouted, halting his gelding and pulling a boot from the stirrup as though to dismount.

"I'm fine, go get her!"

Junior whistled to Champion, dug his heels into the big gelding's sides, and sprinted after the rogue mare, the pack mule hot on his trail.

"Blasted she-devil," Isa spat, prodding a stinging spot at her hip. She'd landed on a spindly branch hidden in the high grass, and it had punctured her oilskin, scratching her in the fall. *I'm going to kill that horse for trying to kill me,* she thought maliciously as she examined the sore spot through the hole in her clothing. Her fingertips came up red when she checked them, and her blood boiled further. Her new hat lay several yards back on the road, and she limped out of the ditch and back into the mud. Her new purchase had landed on its crown, and she brushed it off as well as she could while Junior spent the next couple of minutes roping the runaway horse.

Once caught in the little field beyond the treeline, Mirage trotted sedately behind Junior, her dark, watchful eyes on Isa.

This biddable pretense was the final straw.

"You miserable little bangtail," Isa growled, stomping toward the accursed animal. "That's the last time I will ever throw myself off you. The next time you act up, I'll ride you off a cliff, just see if I don't!"

Above her, Junior flattened his lips tight against his teeth.

"And this." She grunted, tugging at the cinch of the saddle that had listed to the side. "I'll be damned if I plant my rear on you for the rest of the day..." Her voice trailed off while she struggled, fumbling with the cinch strap. She finally freed it and moved to the other strap. Then she disentangled her saddlebags from it all, letting them drop to the road. Isa pulled the saddle off like a sack of potatoes and marched toward the pack mule.

"What are you doin'?" There was a suspicious tremble in Junior's voice.

"I'm riding Red. What does it look like?" she asked savagely. "Help me get all these supplies off."

Junior transferred the supplies to a curious Mirage for the next quarter hour while Isa saddled the brawny red pack mule.

"I cannot believe I had to fling myself from you like a damsel in distress," Isa told Mirage, pulling the bit from the mare's mouth.

Junior, securing the last of the bags on Mirage, began to laugh, rich and from the belly.

"Shush up!" Isa snapped. "You can lead that fiend from Hell. I'll ride the pack mule all the way home, by God." With that announcement, she slid the bit into Red's mouth, adjusted the harness, and mounted him. Her split skirts were soaked through at the hem, her yellow slicker coated in mud on the left side, and her hair—unbraided and loose—straggled to her waist.

Still laughing like a braying jackass, Junior mounted Champ and rode beside her. Behind him, Mirage trotted unhappily.

"A five-hundred-dollar packhorse," Isa said conversationally. "Isn't that something?"

"Maybe you can trade her for a couple good mules." Junior chuckled at the look she gave him.

"I wouldn't wish that horse on my worst enemy."

Sparkling blue eyes roved the top of her damp head to the ends of her trailing hair. "You look like you escaped Bedlam. You'd better hope no one sees you like this, or they'll admit you."

They argued good-naturedly for a couple of miles until Mirage, bored and resentful of her demotion, trotted closer behind Champion and the mule. Her wet forelock over her white blaze and ears forward, the black mare wedged her way between them. Isa stared straight ahead, jaw tight. Junior pulled a cigarette out and observed interestedly. Extending her neck out, Mirage reached until her trembling lips nibbled at Isa's loose hair; Isa swatted her away, expression thunderous. Mirage tried again, this time tugging at Isa's hat brim until the frustrated woman was forced to nudge her heels into the mule's sides.

The horse would not be ignored. When one thing didn't work, Mirage would try another tactic, bumping, teasing, playing. Red shook his head in irritation, his long ears flapping. Junior smoked his hand-rolled cigarette, lips curved softly.

"I think she's apologizing." He nudged Isa's boot with his stirrup.

She glared at him. "I don't care if she learns to write 'sorry' on a piece of paper and mails it by pony express, I'm not forgiving this—ow!" Mirage had pulled a hank of Isa's hair, her head bobbing up and down excitedly. Isa rubbed her tender scalp, denying mercy all the way to the Brazos River.

WASHINGTON-ON-THE-Brazos had one street—a path, really. The town was so small that its church also acted as a schoolhouse. A single mercantile stood across from a nondescript building. Isa peered closer at the latter and suspected it to be a saloon. Half a dozen people stopped what they were doing to watch the two blond strangers ride through their little hamlet. They nodded when Junior tipped his hat, but they whispered and pointed at the handsome black horse trudging dourly behind them.

Isa checked the sun's position in the overcast sky. It was high noon. They reached the ferry street not much later, where an off-kilter sign read "La Bahia Road."

The river was high through the trees, its muddy brown waters full of swirling currents and bits of foam. An ancient rope lay between the two banks, its dark, drooping center grazing the Brazos River. Attached to the rope was a rickety flatboat with two men pulling a family and wagon across. The algae-slick rope slapped the water with every heave. Off to the side was a dilapidated shack; its only decoration was a sign with a faded list of services, load allowances, and prices. Its door opened, and a stout woman with graying hair, a toothless scowl, and bowed legs strode out. Isa and Junior dismounted, paid the sour-faced woman, and led their mounts closer to the bank.

Beneath a shade tree, a group of men loitered on their horses. They watched attentively as Isa pulled her slicker off.

"Hold my hat," she commanded Junior, her voice muffled against the dense fabric.

"What are you doing?"

"I'm sweating through my blouse." Miss Pickney would have been horrified at such a statement. Isa's puffed sleeves had wilted forlornly, and she smoothed back tresses, knotted from her tumble in the ditch. Junior's long quiet spell made her look up in suspicion, expecting censure. But he wasn't looking at her with condemnation. His heavy-lidded gaze was dragging slowly down the contours of her body, pausing at the tuck of her blouse in her waistband. She quickly checked her person, but there was nothing untoward about the fitted sage-green fabric. No mud, no stains, no bugs. When she met Junior's gaze, her cheeks were hot. *Confound it.* She never blushed, and here it was the second day on the trail, and she'd done more blushing around him than she had all year.

Isa held her hand out. "May I have my hat, please?"

"Yeah." His voice was gruff, and he handed her hat over, eyes skittering away. "Stay with the horses. It looks like they might need help." The two men pulling the family on the ferry had reached the bank, but one was elderly, mopping his brow with a black-stained handkerchief. The two oxen stumbled in front of the wagon, making the whole flatboat sway. Junior draped his jacket and vest over Champion's saddle, turned to leave, then stopped and eyed the group of dawdling men. They had sidled closer to the bank. He leaned in and said softly, "Don't look at those men."

Isa looked at them anyway. Scoffed. "Why would I want to?"

The four men were unkempt, clustered together on hungry, travel-worn horses.

"Just stay out of trouble. I'll be back."

She mock-saluted him, and her lips curved up as he shook his golden head the whole way to the water's edge. Junior's shoulders were broad beneath his cream shirt and black suspenders, and the fringe of his leather chaps swayed with his slow stride. Pulling her gaze from the oscillating leather, she settled her hat on her head. Isa bundled up her oilskin, got it as small and tight as possible, and packed it into her saddlebags. From the smallest compartment, she withdrew her sack of sunflower seeds. Red, pleased to have been such an essential part of the journey, perked his long, fuzzy ears, his enormous brown eyes on the sack in her hand.

"Would you like some?" she asked, running her thumb along the length of the mule's ear. Red stretched his neck out, lips quivering in bliss. She laughed softly.

"Think she'd do that to me?" asked a voice just loud enough to be heard to her left.

The group of men, who had wandered closer once Junior left, laughed. A second one replied, "Reckon the mule's ear is cleaner than your'n, Jonesie."

"Wasn't my ear I was talkin' bout," growled Jonesie, and the men laughed again.

Don't look at them, Isa sternly told herself, good humor shriveling. *Don't you open your big mouth.*

Determined to ignore the men who were acting no better than schoolyard boys, Isa cracked a few sunflower seeds open between her teeth and fed them to Red. An ebony muzzle crept closer, its whiskers twitching. When the velvet-soft lips tugged at her cuff, Isa sighed and gave the ungrateful mare a seed. Before long, all three animals pressed close, wanting more hard-earned treats, and Isa pulled away from their hovering heads.

"You're going to smother me for treats," she muttered. Gathering their leads, she led them further from the whispering, laughing men and tied the animals to a hitching post. Leaning against the post, Isa doffed her hat and watched Junior help the youngest man lead the frightened oxen from the swaying flatboat. She hung her hat on Junior's saddle horn, chewing on seeds and working them open with teeth and tongue. Sick to death of her hair tickling her ears and neck, she finger-combed her unruly locks, sectioned out her hair, and began to braid it.

In the distance, the oxen lowed directly into Junior's ear—just as the men began to whistle and jeer.

The bold one, Jonesie, had pale-gray eyes and an old scar running down the right side of his face. He called, "Why don't you ditch your brother and ride with us?"

Don't say anything. Isa kept her eyes straight ahead.

He drew close enough that he no longer had to shout for her to hear him. "Want to know what it's like to be with a real man?"

Isa bristled. All her silent vows not to speak fizzled away like water in a hot skillet. "I'll ask one when I see one."

Slightly vacant gray eyes blinked at her. Grime gathered in black lines along the creases of his neck.

Impatiently, she spat a couple of empty shells out. "Paint a picture, it'll last longer."

His expression curdled. "You're an uppity bitch, ain't you?"

She was spitting shells out like an old farmer, but she was uppity? What a hoot. "I sure am. Now go toddle back over to your friends. You're not wanted here." Isa faced forward, popping more seeds into her mouth, a picture of indifference. She tied off the end of her braid, and it slithered, snakelike, down her back. Disregarding the man, who still hadn't moved, Isa plucked her hat off the saddle horn and set it atop her head.

Drat. Junior was walking up the trail toward them, his expression thunderous.

"Jonesie," hissed one of his friends.

"You'd better go before he gets here," Isa warned, refusing to look at the foul man to her left. Her heart began to pound. Adrenaline sounded warning bells in her ears.

"I ain't scared of him."

She imagined an ape beating his chest.

"You should be afraid of that .45 at his hip. He can hit a snake between the eyes at fifty paces." When Isa looked at him this time, she was openly hostile. The last thing she needed was for some backwoods ignoramus to start trouble. Junior was still healing from a gunshot wound and didn't need another because this fool got fresh with her. "Go back to your friends. Go!"

Too late.

"Hey." The word cracked like a whip, and Jonesie stumbled back as Junior aggressively positioned himself between the other man and Isa. "There a problem here?"

"There's no problem," Isa said quickly.

"What are you sayin' to her?" Junior crowded the other man. From her vantage point, Isa could only distinguish Junior's dark-red neck beneath his fresh haircut and a sliver of Jonesie's blanched face.

"I wasn't sayin' nothing," the other man assured, hands up.

"Not how I saw it from down there. You have something to say, you better say it to me."

"I don't want no trouble."

Junior shoved the man once, hard. "You heard her, then. Go. Get outta here!"

Staggering, Jonesie turned and made a quick getaway to his friends. The other men looked like they wanted to intervene, but Junior didn't move. His hand hovered over his gun, steady as a sharpshooter. Jonesie mounted his thin brown horse, sent Junior and Isa a withering look, and rode off. Reluctantly, his friends followed, and they vanished into the shadows. Prickles rose along Isa's arms at the man's parting glare, one of the most malevolent she'd ever received.

Junior and Isa unhitched their animals when the men didn't return and led them to the waiting flatboat. From the corner of his mouth, Junior asked, "What the hell was he saying to you?"

"Nothing worth repeating." Her lack of defensiveness seemed to put Junior more on edge. It didn't help when the ferry man spoke up.

"You two better watch your back." He spat in the water and took Champion's reins. "That outfit is bad news, yes sirree."

"They outlaws?" Junior asked, inspecting the wood line where the four men had disappeared.

"Don't know. Bunch o' local thieves and murderers. They take this ferry all the time to Navasota."

"Navasota." Junior's face was impassive the whole ride across the river, except the deep line furrowed between his brows.

Chapter Eight

"'One day on the prairie while riding along, my seat in the saddle, the reins on my dong—'"

"Junior. Stop."

"'Who should I meet but the girl I adore, the pride of the prairie, the cowpuncher's whore—'"

Isa wanted to rip her ears off. She hated this song, and he knew it. "Stop singing, or I will shoot you off your horse."

As if unbothered by this threat of violence, Junior rode easy in his saddle and quietly hummed the next verse. They had wisely circled the dangerous town of Navasota, regularly checking behind them for unwanted shadows. Now, halfway to Anderson, Isa was a hair's breadth away from murder. They were suffering from entirely too much togetherness, compounded by his idea of prime entertainment—infuriating her.

"Don't hum it, either," she bit out. He was nearing her least favorite chorus.

Instead of listening, he sang, "'I got off my pony, I reached for her crack—'"

"Junior!"

"'The damn thing was rattling and bitin' me back.'" He didn't sing so much as shout as Isa began to furiously chase him on

Mirage. "I took out my pistol, I aimed for its head, I missed the damn rattler and shot her instead!'"

They found a place to camp at a pond's edge, hidden from the main road by a thicket of trees. The horses and mule were watered, curried, and hobbled near a little clearing by their camp. Red brayed long and loud when his feed was brought out, a habit Junior said the mule exercised at breakfast and suppertime. It made Isa laugh.

Temperatures dropped, and the chill was brisk from the lingering dampness around them. Finding dry firewood was a chore, but Junior worked his cowboy magic and had a crackling fire sending red, glowing embers into the swaying treetops. The sky above changed from indigo to midnight blue, and stars appeared by the hundreds of thousands. Isa breathed in the air, her eyes closed. This was the best part of traveling: little quiet moments between tasks.

"'Nature is the source of all true knowledge,'" she sighed, kneeling by the mound of their belongings at the foot of an oak. "City living is nice, but this is what poets speak of when they write about peace."

Junior crouched next to her and detached a skillet from the supply bags. "Cold, wet, and smelly?" He nodded at Mirage a few yards away; the animal's tail was high as she evacuated her bowels.

Nose wrinkling at his coarse lack of romanticism, Isa grabbed a horse blanket and her bedroll and laid them out by the fire. "No. Existing in nature is beautiful. Listening to every animal within a mile of you go about their business? Seeing so many stars that you could count them until your dying breath and you'd still never have tallied them all? That's beautiful."

There was no response from the figure by the oak tree, but his head was cocked her way, his movements slow. He was listening.

Bolstered, she asked, "What do you think the stars look like in Rome?"

"In Rome?" He filled the skillet a quarter full of a dry flour mixture, brought it to the fire, and poured water from his canteen into it.

"What are you making?" Curiously, she watched him mix up a batter in the skillet and pull coals to the side of the fire.

"Camp bread. Figured it's better than just dried beef and fruit. Want to make us some coffee?"

Together, they worked in silence for a time, and Isa forgot about being irritated with him. She put a handful of coffee grounds in an old metal percolator, filled it the rest of the way with water, and joined Junior by the fire. Soon, the aroma of coffee and cooking biscuits softened the air's cold bite. Isa settled on her bedroll to glimpse the stars through gaps in the darkening treetops.

"What were you saying about Rome?" Junior's deep voice cut through the stillness.

"I'd like to see it one day." She turned to look at him across the popping fire. His hair was leonine in the lambent light, the angle of his jaw sharp as a boomerang. She let her eyes drift along the edge that squared off to form his strong chin where a cleft lay, a tiny shadow in its center. "When…if I travel abroad, I want to sleep out in the open just like this. I want to see if it feels the same."

"I always figured you'd go off somewhere. See the world." The central tilt of his straight brows gave him an aspect of earnestness.

"You did?" This was news to her.

"Hell, look at you. You're not a woman who'd be happy staying in some little town with us common folk. You should've been a politician's daughter or some lady in a manor somewhere. Not a cowgirl." He said it as a revelation, some fact so long disputed that, once it could no longer be denied as false, it astonished the doubter.

It was the first time he'd called her a woman.

Isa lay speechless on her bedroll. As children, he'd told her more than once that she'd never grow up; she'd simply evolve into a taller version of a snot-nosed kid. When Isa said nothing, only stared, he shifted to his feet and muttered something about plates and cups.

They ate slightly scorched camp bread in silence. Afterward, they drank coffee while the horses and mule stood beneath the oak, heads drooping and eyelids closed in slumber. Junior sat, relaxed, on his bedroll, his saddle acting as a pillow at one end. His boots and stockings were off, his toes buried in the leafy grass.

Isa was far less relaxed.

Her stays dug into her armpits and stabbed at her hips. She had raw spots from riding in her corset for hours. Not caring that it was dreadful comportment, Isa began to unbutton the front of her blouse. Attuned as they were to each other's movements, Junior's relaxed slouch stiffened.

"What're you doin'?" The piece of grass he'd been stroking along his lips stopped moving.

"Readying for bed." She was down to the fourth button, and her breasts bulged against the constraints of her corset through the top of her open blouse.

"In front of me?"

Isa looked around. "I don't see a screen anywhere, do you?"

"Why don't you just sleep in your clothes?" He grabbed another blade of grass, his eyes looking anywhere but at her.

She scowled at him. "Have you ever slept in a corset? No? Then hush up."

"All I'm sayin'—"

"When did you become such a prude? Have you been attending church with my ma while I was away?"

That sealed the bigmouth's lips shut.

The sage-green blouse had a preposterous number of tiny buttons, so Isa untucked it and pulled it roughly over her head. Next came the stays. The corset arced high in the air, landing on their pile of bags at the base of the tree. Firelight cast a weak glow on the pile, turning the shadows and hills into something mythical, like a gnome colony or a fairy hideout. Sighing audibly, Isa stretched her back and sat cross-legged on her pallet.

"That's better." She settled her gun belt beside her pallet, close enough to grab in the night. Around them, the woods were black and eerie, and she kept her gaze firmly on the fire.

Junior's eyes were downcast. Once, then twice, his blue irises flitted to the hint of cleavage above the bodice of her combination underwear. An owl hooted above them, pulling his attention up, and his fingers unconsciously tugged his bandana high over the silvery pink scar beneath his jaw.

Without considering the wisdom of it, she said, "You don't have to hide it. Not with me."

Junior's head lowered until his gaze was level with hers. Slowly, he dropped his hand, letting the kerchief fall. He reached into his saddlebag, felt around, and drew out his tin of tobacco papers, and leather bag of tobacco. Isa's eyes lingered on the lean line of his side, noticing the wince when he sat up.

"Still bothering you?" She tried to forget that icy image of him dead somewhere had the bullet gone an inch or two to the left.

He didn't pretend ignorance.

"It's not so bad." Pausing from his task, he loosened the knot behind his neck and slung his bandana towards their bags in the same dramatic way she'd done with her stays.

She laughed.

Returning her smile with a devastating one of his own, he began to roll a cigarette. "Want to know what happened?"

Isa sat straighter. "Naturally. You've been very close-lipped about it."

"I was trailing after a pair of outlaw brothers about a month back—"

"By yourself?" Isa frowned. "Didn't you have a company of Rangers with you?"

"Do you want the story or not?"

Isa squeezed her lips shut between two fingers and held up a hand, a solemn oath of quiet.

Eyeing her dubiously, he continued, "As I was saying, I was following the Grenert Brothers..."

According to Junior, he had trailed the brothers in rain or shine. They had a bounty of a hundred dollars each, dead or alive. Isa squirmed on her bedroll. She wanted to ask if it was a normal occurrence for Texas Rangers to take mercenary jobs but held her tongue. The Grenert Brothers were wily and talented at covering their trail, leading Junior on a wild goose chase for two weeks before he stopped following them and took a risk.

"They knew I was gaining on them, and after weeks of running in circles, I knew they'd need supplies soon. I took a chance, left the area where they were campin' out, and made my way to Fredericksburg. It was the closest town big enough that they'd feel comfortable getting supplies and a drink without detection, so I put my horse up and waited them out. After about the third day, I thought I'd made a mistake. Then, halfway down the street on Champ, I saw their horses hitched in front of a cathouse. I took their horses, hid them, went inside, and gave the mistress a ten-dollar gold piece to get her girls out and not make a fuss."

The first brother was the youngest and dumbest. It hadn't taken much to sneak into his room, knock him over the back of his head, and tie him up.

"His, uh, lady friend made a ruckus, though." Junior carefully avoided her eye. "When I went next door, I'd lost the element of surprise, and his older brother was waitin' for me, gun cocked. He got me in the side, but I got him in the chest." He looked down at his rolled cigarette dispassionately. Isa's excitement at the story faded.

"Killing people never sat easy with you," Isa murmured.

"No." He pulled a match out and ran it along his boot sole. It flared to life. "No, it never does."

"What had they done?"

"Robbed a stage and made sure no witnesses were left alive. A young family was on it."

A sick feeling soured her comfortably full stomach. "The lengths people will go for money."

"Yep. It's usually money. Takes what little soul some people have left and obliterates it." The flame on the match had reached his fingertips, blackening them, before he lit his cigarette and shook it out. "Money. Power. Women. The people who want them but gotta run over folks in the process are weak. Work a little harder. Get it honest."

Isa listened raptly, having been unaware of this philosophical side of Junior. "And you help bring them to justice."

Two thick fingers pulled the slender, tightly rolled paper from his mouth. "Sometimes I feel just as bad as them."

"'*Exigo a me non ut optimis par sim sed ut mailis melior.*'" It was one of her favorite quotes by Seneca.

"You gonna tell me what that means?" he asked sardonically.

"'I require myself not to be equal to the best but to be better than the bad.' And I believe you to be far better than the bad." Isa plucked a burning twig from the fire and studied it while he sat, oh so still, across from her. "Human beings are flawed creatures as a rule. Most are the result of careful rearing, indoctrination, and learned behaviors. Two siblings can be born to the same family and treated similarly, yet their realities will be far different from one another. At the end of the day, whether you are a good person or not is a choice."

He absorbed this, smoking, watching her with glittering eyes. "A choice?"

"Yes. For example"—Isa poked glowing coals with the end of her crooked stick—"you chose to stop drinking, say, a decade ago?"

He nodded, lids narrowing. Junior hadn't touched a drop of alcohol since he was eighteen, astonishing everyone who knew him. Since his first wispy facial hair had come in, he had caroused in saloons every weekend on his father's dime.

"And every choice you have made from then on has been affected by that decision. Lord knows, you could have continued. Who knows where you'd be?"

"I'd be dead." The utter surety in his voice scared her. He looked over her shoulder and into the velvety black night beyond the brush. "You know why I stopped drinking?"

Isa ceased poking the fire. The question could be a trick. Instead of answering honestly, he could say something smart-aleck and laugh at her disgruntlement. When he didn't tease her, her curiosity grew. Worried he'd change his mind, she said nothing.

Finally, his glazed eyes focused. "Remember when Ben, Sol, and I were on that cattle drive years ago? Everyone thought my brother drowned in the Red River?"

"Yes, I remember." She quivered with curiosity. Ten years ago, Junior's older brother's death by drowning had been announced. For almost a week, the townspeople had reeled before word had gotten out that Ben Stone had managed to swim downstream from where he'd been separated from his horse in the floodwaters. Having aspirated river water, he'd become ill and delirious and had holed up at an elderly couple's shack until he was well enough to travel. Before this good news was released, however, rumors that Junior blamed himself for Ben's death had spread. Lucy was oddly reserved about discussing this period in their lives, and Isa never pressed.

"I acted like a jackass the whole trail drive," Junior began. He threw the butt of his cigarette into the fire and began rolling another one. "Ben had his hands full with the herd—it was a good two thousand head—and I made it worse. Drank every day. Bellyached. Didn't work for shit. Stopped in a town and whored instead of helped." The spikes of his lashes were long against his cheekbones as he concentrated on rolling tobacco into another paper, one knee high, the other lolling wide.

"I even stampeded the herd one night because I hollered at Ben. God almighty, just remembering it—" He broke off, grimacing while he rolled each tip tightly.

Cautious of his mood, she offered, "You were just a dumb kid, Junior."

"Yeah." When he closed the lid to his tobacco tin, something was wrong with how he smiled. She didn't like that look on him, like he'd been possessed by something dark. Some specter trying to appear as him, a beautiful façade hiding ugly insides. He stretched to the side to tuck his paper tin and tobacco back into his saddlebags, a move that had to put a strain on his healing wound. When he straightened, the ugly look was gone. Behind the golden halo of his hair, the woods were sinister; his shadow stretched eerily into the void. "Yeah. Just a dumb kid who almost killed his brother. My cousin Leonard was on the trail drive, too, and he was even stupider than me. We'd finally made it to the Red River. It had been raining for weeks; I'd never seen a river so flooded. Whole trees were doing flips in it."

He stopped to scrub his forehead. The bleak expression was back, and Isa wanted to smack it off him.

"Anyway, Ben saw I was drunk again. He grabbed my booze and threw it in the river. Leonard—he was even drunker than me—rode his horse right in like he was gonna get it. Well, that was the last of him. I tried to stop him." He paused.

When the pause stretched forever, she supplied, "And Ben tried to stop you." Her eyes were riveted on him.

Instead of answering, Junior put the tip of his cigarette between his lips and leaned forward. Taking the hint, Isa lifted the flaming point of her stick from the fire, lighting the end of his cigarette. Smoke streamed from his nostrils. It should have revolted her the same way Mr. Corner's pipe-smoking did. But it didn't repel her. Not one bit. Junior's gaze caught hers, and they sat, marionettes with their strings caught. She'd known him for most of her life, but it felt like this was their first meeting. Two strangers alone. Acquainted, yet unfamiliar.

Her lips were moving, an industrious mind speaking aloud. "You stopped drinking around the time you got that scar on your neck."

Firelight glinted off the sheen of the scar in question. He spat a leaf of tobacco away, lips flat. He neither denied nor confirmed her statement, but he didn't look away from her, either.

"May I look at it?" she asked, holding her breath, waiting for Junior to quip sarcastically that she *was* looking at it.

Instead of a jibe, he lifted his chin a fraction. She stood and walked around to his side of the fire, unhurried in case sudden movements changed his mind. Lowering herself to his bedroll, she felt her body react in response to his proximity. Her mind, however, was firmly on the puzzle of his scar. She'd seen it before, of course, but only in glimpses, as it had been hidden beneath the bandanas he never went without. Without looking at her, he took another drag of his cigarette. The fragrant smoke made her head dizzy, and she reached up to touch his neck as if she were underwater. As soon as she touched him, he went completely still. Not even smoke left his nostrils. The mark was similar to the scars Sol had on his wrists from when he'd been tied and dragged behind a horse. *Rope burn*. The ligature mark was in the shape of an inverted V, and several smaller scars riddled his neck. Scratches?

Mouth twisting, she studied them. The more she investigated, the more she disliked what she saw.

His Adam's apple bobbed. "What do you think?"

"You'd like me to...theorize?"

Junior's shoulder brushed against her wrists when he shrugged.

"Very well. I shall play Sherlock Holmes." Clearing her throat, she shuffled closer on her knees. "It's clear that you were either hanged or pulled by the neck, according to the direction of the rope burn. It is a rope burn, correct?"

"Mm."

She took this as an affirmation. Grasping his jaw, she turned his head and looked at the other side. Leather, tobacco, and horse sweat clouded her senses, drugging her. Besides their accidental entanglement in bed that morning, she hadn't been this close to him in years. "And these are scratch marks. Deep ones." Her heart began to race for a different reason. An ominous dread extracted all the fun from the game, and she sat back on her heels. "It appears that you were hanged by the neck. You struggled."

Cricket song and the pop of an occasional ember were the only sounds in response to this declaration. It was as good as an affirmation.

"Junior." She'd never felt so angry on someone else's behalf. So heartbroken. "Who was it? Who did it?"

She saw the answer before he opened his mouth. He looked at her, his lashes long, his lush lips turned down. "*I* did it, Izzy. I did it."

Chapter Nine

One of Junior's least favorite tasks on a ranch was punching a trocar and cannula through the sides of cattle suffering from gassy bloat. The animal would bellow in pain as the deadly gasses were released from its distended abdomen. This was usually done as a last resort but was in the animal's best interest; such a diagnosis could be fatal within fifteen minutes of its first symptoms.

Junior felt akin to a bovine with gassy bloat, uncomfortably obstructed by his many secrets. His shame. Confiding in Isa provided Junior an unexpected relief, a sharp stick to the side with a blade, releasing mortal pressure. The weight of it—the *burden*—peeled away from his body, molting a heavy skin he'd suffered beneath for ten long years.

Beside him on his worn bedroll, Isa was silent. Usually, her response to anything was as fast as a rattler strike—sometimes in warning, sometimes a fatal hit. Strangely, she didn't seem to be pondering the best way to strike him. She sat, hugging her legs tightly, as though he was the one who had doled out the blow. Flames licked along the logs he'd found, red light giving Isa's dark-blonde hair an auburn sheen.

"I never knew," she said finally.

"I regretted it the second I did it." He touched the smaller scars peppering the column of his neck. "Thank God Lucy followed me to see what I was up to. She got one of the ranch hands to cut me down." He remembered every detail. Lucy's fragile strength beneath him, holding his legs and pushing him high enough to put slack in the rope. Her screams for help. Hay, stacked high in the loft, floating everywhere—in his hair, in his clothes. The ranch hand, Crew, sawing at the rope when the noose wouldn't loosen from Junior's neck. Junior still couldn't believe he'd done it. If Lucy hadn't followed him to the loft...

"Have you told Ben?" Isa had inched closer to him, so close he could see the tips of her brown lashes framing translucent hazel eyes.

"I told him when he asked. He made me promise not to do such a thing again. To tell him if I ever felt like repeating history." A burning farmhouse, an old haunt, flickered in his mind's eye.

"Good. Add me to the list of people you're forced to talk to if you get those feelings again." Isa said it sternly.

He wanted to scoff at her. To smile. But he couldn't. Discomfort quickly replaced relief, and he wanted to change the subject to something else—*anything* else. His attention drifted over to her, falling to the inch of cleavage above her white undergarment.

Guiltily, he looked away, clearing his throat. "You wanna borrow one of my shirts or something?"

Her mouth, soft and dewy from chewing her lips, parted in affront. The gentle concern hardened. "No, I do not wish to borrow one of your shirts."

"I was just asking—"

But she was a coiled rattler again, striking for the jugular. "Did you stop drinking around the time you stopped whoring?"

"Christ, what kind of question is that?" He reeled back from her, singeing his blanket with his cigarette. Quickly, he dabbed the last of it out and stowed it away for later.

"I heard a man can catch more than just a good time from a painted lady," Isa added, heedless of his mortified groan. "Did you know that coital-related maladies men catch from scarlet women can make their peckers swell up like a—"

Junior clapped a hand over her mouth, unable to believe his ears. "What in God's name are they teachin' you at that school?" he bellowed.

She ripped his hand off. "College didn't teach me that; David told me about it. He said they studied such things on both living people and cadavers in medical school. Consider yourself lucky you never caught anything. Or did you?" Her scrutiny drifted lower, searching for a tell-tale sign that he had a few important parts missing or maimed.

He was sick to death of hearing about David. His ears turned hot enough to steam. "No, I haven't caught anything from whores, not that it's your business. And if you won't put a shirt on, go back to your side!"

Sparks flew from her eyes, and she defiantly thrust out her chest, putting her breasts further into relief against her neckline. "They're just bosoms! Every woman has them."

"I don't care if your precious David has them; they need to be covered up." He rubbed the back of his neck, feeling panicked.

More ruffled than ever, Isa snapped, "It's not my fault you can't keep your eyes to yourself. I bet you like looking at them, and that's why you want them covered up."

"You're bein' a brat." She was too close, within arm's length. It would be too easy to wring that long, skinny neck. "You can't just say everything you think to men, damn it!"

Her nose went in the air. "I can say whatever I want. It's reasonable that your proclivity for big bosoms is because you grew up a mama's boy—everyone knows mama's boys take forever to get off the tit."

It was the wrong thing to say. Junior had been ribbed for being a mama's boy his whole life, and it was the surefire way to prick his temper. Through a haze of irritated fury, he gripped her body with strong hands and pulled her over his thighs.

"Junior!" she shrieked. "Don't you dare!"

"It's about time someone gave you the licks you deserve," he growled through her struggles. *Swat! Swat, swat!* Each strike of his palm on her upraised derrière incensed her more. His arm was an iron bar over her back, and her maddened shrieks cut through his ire like hot iron dipped in water. She had morphed into the aggravating brat she used to be, pulling pranks on him and her brother and then caterwauling when she got her just deserts. Mirth replaced righteous anger until he shook with it.

Suddenly, strong teeth bit the muscle of his outer thigh.

Hard.

Shouting in pain, his grip slackened, but she'd no sooner scrambled to her knees than he was flipping her to her back on his bedroll. They scrapped in his blankets for what felt like hours, and it was worse than trying to catch a greased pig. Straining and grunting with the effort of overpowering without harming, he asked, "Where did all that catch-as-catch-can practice get you, huh?" The words hadn't left his grinning lips before she rolled him. She had the upper hand for two seconds before she was flat on her back again. Half on his bedroll, half on the grass, Isa was neatly pinned, his body heavy upon hers. Her thighs were indecently spread, feet trying to find purchase, until her long legs eventually wrapped tightly around his hips to offset his center of gravity.

Junior was as unbudging as a thousand-year-old boulder in a field.

"Cry Uncle," he said in her ear.

"Never," she gritted, red-faced and straining, her hair coming loose. She tried to shove him off with her forearms. But no matter how she pushed on his shoulders, chest, or neck, she couldn't move him.

It almost made him feel guilty. Almost. "Yield, half-pint. I figured you'd get better at wrestling as you got older, not worse."

"Oh yeah?"

Her face was close, so close. Her mouth reached up, and Junior's smile froze. Was she about to...

Isa licked his face from jaw to temple.

Of the hat of tricks she had, licking was the dirtiest. She well knew that other people's spit filled him with disgust. Dog drool was a close second. The wet warmth of her tongue along his cheek, the incredible closeness of her face pressed against his, made his body immediately respond. He was already painfully aware of all her soft places pressing against him, but now his nerve endings flared to life. The wriggling body beneath his had stilled, and he sensed her smiling from ear to ear even before she lay back in the grass. She was waiting for revulsion followed by surrender. But he wasn't repulsed. His blood was simmering in his veins. He felt primitive. Furious. Isa's smile faded, and her crinkled eyes widened until the golden depths became something turbulent. Wild. Breathing hard, she struggled against his weight—she felt as weak as a kitten beneath him—and only managed to squirm towards the top of his bedroll.

With this action, her undergarments slid down, revealing more of her breasts. Junior looked down at them helplessly; her nipples were hard and dusky just beneath the neckline. Tension thickened between them, and only the rough sounds of their panting broke the lull. His eyes dragged from her breasts to her mouth, the crisply defined upper lip, the lusciously pink lower that curved sweetly, begging to be bitten. Black pupils spread, catlike, inside her citrine irises. He was very aware of her thighs around him, cradling his hips. His belt buckle was flush against her most private parts.

When her back arched sharply beneath him, he was unsure if it was to get away or get nearer. He lowered his mouth, no longer in control of his faculties. Isa strained against him—and accidentally bumped his mouth with hers. Had it been an accident?

The barest hint of softness took possession of his intoxicated mind.

Junior lowered his lips, molding them tightly to hers until their mouths were one. Slanting his head, he pressed her head deeper into the grass and bedroll, plundering her lips until they opened. The smooth slide of her tongue made a silken entrance into his mouth. He met it with his own, feeling the kiss not just inside his mouth, but lower, where he was hard and thick beneath his denim trousers. Their tongues mated in a sensual glide, and their hands gripped each other closer, fingers rigidly curled into suddenly constrictive clothing. She tasted sweet, and he drank her in like he was both starving and fatally thirsty, knowing he could survive on this kiss alone.

It went on forever. Junior barely came up for air, his eyes closed, their mouths finding a rhythm that started at a leisurely pace and then increased in both pressure and speed. The interior of her mouth was hot, her tongue tangling boldly with his. Even with kissing, she imbued confidence. Challenge. The rougher she became—fingers threading hard in his hair, lips and tongue demanding—the deeper inside her he wanted to go.

He wanted to go so deep she'd finally be still. She'd stop challenging him and would lay there, overwhelmed. Limp with surfeit.

Fantasies of overcoming Isa, of her giving in to him, dissolved whatever reason had remained in a mind already mindless with lust. His body was damp with sweat. Tense. The pulse in his cock was more insistent than his own heartbeat. It throbbed, uncomfortably hard, too full for the delicate skin encasing it, and he slid up a little to press the straining clasp of his jeans against the notch between her legs. It was relief and torture in equal measures.

Isa made a soft, fierce noise in the back of her throat.

Clothes off, he thought savagely, his dominant hand reaching purposefully toward the breasts that had plagued him since Austin.

A log rolled off the fire, throwing a shower of sparks into the air. Flames soared, startling them so that their flushed faces turned as one toward the fire, eyes blinking at the sudden blinding light.

What the hell are you doing, Stone?

Junior was moving before Isa had caught her breath. Before she could decide to be disgusted. He sat up, eyes fixed and forehead creased. His trembling fingers scraped through his hair, his palm rubbing his forehead, but the lines remained. While he tried to calm his racing heart, she sat up, observing him. Guilt swiftly cooled his ardor, but even with the shame of what he'd been doing to his best friend's little sister, a part of him was tempted to turn back to her. To finish what they'd started.

Isa began to unbraid and re-braid her tangled hair. The normal activity she did several times throughout the day focused him. Made breathing easier.

"You should see your face," Isa commented, her voice husky in the silent woods around them. She appeared coolly rational as she slipped her leather band between her teeth.

"What?" Junior risked fully looking at her, but it was like seeing a priceless piece of art he'd defaced. He'd ruined something precious. Broken it because she was wild and alluring, and he was a fool with no resistance against her.

"That was not my first kiss. And it certainly wasn't yours." She tied the leather around the curling tip of her braid. "You don't have to look so upset. You'd think your favorite aunt had died."

It *felt* as though his favorite aunt had died. He smoothed the lines of his face. Shuttered his eyes. "We can't do that again," he said hoarsely, thinking what it would do to his friend if he'd seen them a minute ago.

Isa shrugged, picking bits of grass and leaves from her skirt. Faint red marks marred her arms and neck from their scuffle. "We won't."

"If Sol found out—"

Her sudden laughter startled him. "Oh, please, as though I'd say anything. The world won't fall out from under us because of one insignificant kiss."

Junior mouthed the word. *Insignificant.*

She stood and dusted her backside off. Despite her bravado, he could see the pulse flickering in her neck. It was racing. "It wasn't even that good. I suppose this is why friends don't kiss."

Another line formed on his face, between his brows. "'It wasn't even that good,'" he echoed, trying the words. Testing them. He heard them as clearly in his mind as though they'd been announced through a megaphone.

No one had ever told him his kiss "wasn't that good" before.

"No," she said above him, looking down at the top of his head. "Was it good for you?"

"Hell no!" he said vehemently, staring determinedly at the fire.

Liar. They were both rotten liars. He could still feel her. Still taste her. He licked his lips.

"Excellent," she said brightly, practically skipping to their supply pile. He wished for a limb to wedge between her ankles, tripping her. "Would you like it if I read some more Sherlock Holmes?"

Junior made a noise that could have been assent or denial.

"Good. We'll probably discover who the killer is."

BEFORE THE SUN made its sleepy appearance over the horizon, Isa woke to the sound of scuffling. Straining to see in the dark, Isa felt around for her gun belt.

"Lie down," Junior hissed across the banked coals.

Half-asleep, she whispered, "Is it coyotes?

"Sh," was his reply, and the cock of his pistol cracked loudly in the tense quiet.

Mirage whinnied in the distance, and Isa came to full attention. Her horse sounded very far away. Too far.

"Damn it," Junior cursed, and she heard him get to his feet. "Stay down. I don't want to shoot you."

She followed orders but twisted her head, listening. It was dark as pitch.

Cursing louder, Junior uncocked his pistol. The sound of their mule's and horses' hoofbeats disappeared in the distance, headed east on the main road. At least two riders yipped and shouted, urging them on.

Someone had just stolen their horses.

Chapter Ten

"It was that bounder Jonesie from the river, I just know it," Isa said hotly, sweating despite the bite in the air that reddened their noses and the tips of their ears beneath their hats. They walked along Navasota's outer street, having hitched a ride from a couple of barefoot boys on a buckboard.

Junior, carrying their bags, shook his head.

Seeing this, Isa snapped, "What?"

"I told you not to talk to those men." His voice was an accusing growl, his profile hard, set, and stubborn. Eyes firmly on the road, he looked like a pack mule, overloaded with saddlebags and supplies. Fastenings trailed behind him, slapping his back with every step he took. Isa carried their saddles, and her arms screamed at the persistent weight.

"How is this my fault? It isn't as if I expressed to him that I wanted our horses to be stolen, Junior." His name was bitten out like a bad taste in her mouth. She hoisted his saddle higher on her back, a deformed turtle with their two saddles making for an awkward shell. Junior paused with her, only walking when she continued on. "And considering how forward that juggins was being, I was immoderately kind to him."

He grunted as though doubtful at her ever having been kind to anyone.

"We should split up. I'll go to the livery while you visit the sheriff," she suggested, needing a modicum of distance between them. The urge to club him over the head was increasing.

"We'll split up when pigs fly. Navasota is dangerous."

Downtown Navasota was so wild that women and children were discouraged from visiting it in broad daylight. During their trek along back roads and trails to avoid it, Junior had explained that only the lawless frequented the downtown buildings. Lawmen were known to hide and watch while criminals overran the area that was full of gaming halls and saloons. On Sunday morning, an undertaker hitched up his buggy to collect the bodies after every wild Saturday night. Not only was the town notorious for its shootouts on Main Street but some claimed outlaw John Wesley Hardin used to frequent its gaming halls.

Junior had tracked the horse thieves right into its streets.

Although they were on the outskirts of the town, Isa felt the sizzle of excitement. She'd finally get to see downtown Navasota, a place filled with gamblers, prostitutes, and drunks.

"There's the livery," Junior gritted out next to her.

Her excitement fizzled away. Sulkily chewing her lip, she watched him. He regretted escorting her to Dogwood; she could see it in every taut line of his body. He'd been a reluctant companion before their kiss. Now that their horses were stolen, he probably couldn't wait to be rid of her. She worried about their animals. Isa hoped Mirage sank her teeth into the men's sorry backsides.

As soon as they entered the livery's threshold, Isa and Junior dropped their burdens, groaning and stretching.

A man walked out of the shadows, his small brown eyes curious. "Help you?" he asked, wiping his hands on a greasy rag. A revolver handle peeked out of his overall pocket.

"Sure can. A couple of men come by here in the early hours with a couple of horses and a mule?" Junior gave descriptions of the animals and the possible culprits who had stolen them.

The beady eyes narrowed slyly. "Now, I'm not real sure."

Jaw bulging, Junior reached for his wallet.

Isa peered into the shadows of the livery, eyes adjusting. On a whim, she called, "Red! Red, you want some breakfast?" The loud braying of a mule echoed from the depths, and a satisfied smile crawled across her face. "Found one, Junior."

The livery owner's mouth widened in a disingenuous smile. "I was sold a mule just this morning, but only a mule. You can see why I'd misunderstand."

Junior didn't smile. His eyes were coldly fixed on the other man. "You go get our mule, and then you show us every stall in this place, mister."

The man swallowed hard, tucked his rag in one overall pocket—carefully avoiding the revolver in the other—and led Junior through the livery. Isa stood guard over their belongings, gun drawn and eyes watchful. When Junior returned a few minutes later, he was alone except for a swaybacked nag and a happy Red, whose long mule ears perked at seeing Isa.

"Got this beauty for fifty dollars." Junior patted the deep dip in the old mare's back. "The men rode at dawn. Overalls in there says he overheard a scarred man talk about selling a horse in Bryan."

Isa's stomach fell. "That's north."

Junior nodded. "Couple days' hard ride. I'll leave you in a hotel a town over—"

"The hell you will." She holstered her revolver and tugged a saddle blanket out of their pile of things. "I'm going with you."

Temple flickering, Junior wordlessly saddled the nag while she saddled Red. Without another word to each other, they overloaded their animals with their bags and headed to the sheriff's office.

Half an hour later, they exited the sheriff's office in disgust.

"Those are the most worthless law dogs I've ever met," Junior sneered, angrily untying his livery mare from the hitch. "They wouldn't even take out their goddamned wanted posters."

Isa agreed. "We'll just have to track them ourselves. They went north—"

"*We* aren't doin' anything. *You* will stay behind somewhere safe while I catch these horse thieves myself. Bryan's law enforcement is better than here. Hell, anywhere is better than here."

Grabbing his arm before he could mount, she said, "You're not leaving me anywhere, John Junior. You're taking me with you."

"The hell I am. You'll just slow me down."

"I will not!"

"The answer is no, Isa." His jaw ticked, and his eyes glittered beneath his buckskin hat.

Isa didn't care if steam came out of his ears.

Swallowing her anger, she released his arm and said smoothly, "Of course. Go ahead. Catch them by yourself."

He lifted a boot in his stirrup. Paused. "You'd better not be planning anything stupid."

"Nothing I do is stupid." She pretended not to hear his snort of disbelief. "I'll warn you just this once—if you leave me with a stranger somewhere, I will follow you."

Junior pulled his boot free and turned on her. "You'll do no such thing, or that paddlin' I gave you last night will feel like child's play."

"That *was* child's play, and if you touch me like that again, I'll break your trigger finger. Don't think I won't!" A group of cowboys with droopy mustaches walking toward the mercantile glanced their way. "I will follow you. You know I will. Sol taught me to track, and just who was it who found the bandits when Poppy was taken? *Me*. I'm coming with you!"

He cursed and turned his rigid back on her, mounting with enough force to make his horse stumble. Once mounted, Isa had to kick Red to a trot to catch up. They left the muddy streets of Navasota without hassle, and she felt a twinge of disappointment that there had been no shootouts or street brawls. Perhaps it was because it wasn't even noon; all the troublemakers were asleep. Junior didn't seem to think that mattered—he stayed annoyingly close, his bandana up and his hand relaxed over the engraved ivory grip of his .45 Colt. He was a lookout in a crow's nest, his hawk eyes everywhere at once, focusing on every walking or riding body for a hint of danger. By the time they reached a point in the road where four sets of hooves, two carrying men, veered off to a cut road, Isa was as jumpy as him.

"That's Mirage, alright," Isa murmured when Junior dismounted to study the ground. She pointed at markings in the dirt. "She drags her right hoof when she trots."

"I don't know if my nag will keep up with this pace." They were the first words Junior had spoken in an hour.

"Their mounts won't be able to, either." Isa tossed a few sunflower seeds from her bag into her mouth. "Remember how skinny and poorly they were? Here. Let me get on the mare. Red will take your weight better."

He acquiesced, and they set off at a brisk pace. The swaybacked mare looked eager for a run, and Isa's heart softened for the poor creature. Over the horses' hoofbeats, Junior asked, "What are all these symbols all over your saddle?"

"My favorite mathematical equations," she said around her shells. "Calculus, the standard model, Euler's equation, a few more. A series of numbers and symbols as answers to the workings of our world is beautiful, don't you think?"

Junior said nothing. He watched her, his face carefully blank. It was a far cry from the man who had pinned and kissed her last night. There wasn't a moment where The Kiss didn't loiter in the corner of her mind like some predator in wait. Or a poisonous gas. The memory of his hungry mouth on hers made her self-conscious, so she jerked her head forward like the chicken she was, unable to face him.

JUNIOR'S BLACK MOOD followed them from Navasota to the rocky creek they spied through the trees and brush. Their lathered animals raised their heads excitedly when they smelled water. After they dismounted and watered their thirsty mounts, Isa grew conscious of Junior quietly stewing on something next to her. She nodded at a low, mossy shelf where water ran off into a miniature waterfall.

"Care to take a dip?"

"It's too cold," he grunted, checking his timepiece. According to him, their steady pace had shrunk a couple of hours between them and the thieves. Evidently, Jonesie and his cohort made constant stops.

"It's not that bad. It'll wake us up. The animals need to rest anyway."

"No." There was enough bark to the word to make Isa bristle.

"What happened to you?" She turned her back to him and made her way to the little waterfall.

Junior stopped brooding long enough to glare at her. "Nothing happened to me. I grew up. Maybe you should try it out."

Isa sat next to the bank and began to unlace her boots. "Growing up isn't the same as being a stodgy wet blanket. And that's what you are. When's the last time you let yourself have fun?"

"The last time I wasn't around you."

It took everything she had not to throw her boot at him. "Go ahead and pout, then. But I'm at least going to dip my feet in before we get back on the trail." Boots and stockings off, she set them to the side and scooted closer to the sandy, rocky edge. The water shimmered, reflecting the cloudless evening sky. When her toes touched the surface, she jumped, bunched up her split skirt, and resolutely shoved them the rest of the way in. "This water is freezing!"

"Told you," Junior said behind her, and she could hear him tying the animals up, followed by the crunch of horsey teeth eating grain. When his footsteps came closer, she twisted around. Wouldn't it be just like him to push her in? At the warning flash in her eyes, his lips twitched. "Don't you trust me?"

"Hell no."

He tutted. "Didn't Miss Pickney teach you not to cuss?"

"I've never been so idiotic as to curse in front of her."

Wonder of wonders, Junior plopped down on the bank beside her to tug off his own boots and stockings. She hid a surge of approval. The Junior Isa had known was adventurous and unable to resist a dare; the old Junior would never back away from a taunt. From the corner of her eye, she watched him hold his breath and slowly ease his long, pale feet into the water. She quashed the urge to splash him in case he retaliated with something worse.

Sensing her thoughts, he glanced warily at her. "If you push me in, I'm taking you with me."

"I wouldn't do any such thing," she defended hotly.

"Like hell. You were thinking about it."

"Thinking isn't the same as doing."

An explosive sound left his throat. "It used to be. You'd think of something one second, and it was out there the next. I'm surprised Sol never lost all his hair because of you."

Isa did splash him then. Droplets of water darkened his faded denims, and he laughed. It was the first time he'd done so since before The Kiss. Their eyes met long enough to resurrect the antics of the night before, and Isa was the first to look away. During the long, silent day's travel, Isa had had plenty of time to examine what the kiss had meant. They hadn't spoken of it, and Junior's mood was too foul to bring it up. She'd eventually concluded that it hadn't meant anything and was all in good fun.

"I never plan on marrying," she heard herself say, carefully avoiding his eyes. "I had considered David, but I only see him as a very good friend."

"The way he went off to lick his wounds with some other female means you made the right choice." When she said nothing, he asked, "What'll you do when you get back home?"

What would she do when she returned home? "I'd like to spend the holidays with family, primarily. Possibly help Minnie at the hotel or Mrs. Hobb at the general store, just to stay busy. And train Mirage when I get her back. What are your plans? Will you stay a while, or will you be off on Ranger business again?"

He was quiet for almost an entire minute. "I don't know." It was so softly said that she hardly heard him.

"You could—" she began, then stopped, pretending an interest in the cypress, pine, and hawthorn trees around them. Orange and yellow leaves littered either side of the creek, and she reached out and grabbed a handful of yellowing leaves from a chinaberry tree, reaching dangerously far over the water. Above them, the sky was a tapering rectangle of blue framed by treetops. Wisps of pink-tinged clouds moved sluggishly in the sky. It was getting close to sunset.

"I could what?" Junior's voice was a rich, low vibration between them.

Isa shrugged as though it didn't matter. "You could stay home for the holidays. Like I am." She didn't look at him. "It's just an idea. I may be...gone for a while."

Junior's interest sharpened into a knife point. "What's that supposed to mean? You're going back to Austin?"

"Perhaps one day. Eventually."

"Hey." Junior crooked a forefinger around her chin, turning her face toward him. "What the hell are you talking about? Are you going somewhere?"

Isa said slowly, "I don't know if I want to tell you."

Smoothing his features into innocence, he released her chin and gestured to himself. "You can trust me."

Isa stared at him, deadpan.

Junior cracked first, his innocent expression twisting back into its normal arrogant one. "I'm not gonna say anything, Izzy. What happens on the trail stays on the trail."

She thrust a pinky out. "Promise me."

His face curdled as though he'd stepped in dog scat. "C'mon, we don't have to—"

"Do it, or I'm not telling you a thing."

Reluctantly, he hooked his rough pinky through hers. "You gonna spit on it, too?"

"Of course not. I'm a lady."

Junior's head went back in laughter. Isa let herself enjoy it, her eyes following the jut of his Adam's apple beneath the old scar that said more about him than his confessions ever could.

She braced herself. "I'm going to travel abroad after the new year."

He stopped laughing to stare. "Travel abroad?"

"Across the Atlantic. I'd like to see London and Paris, Rome and Greece. I'd love to walk the vineyards of Italy—I've read Italy has the most beautiful cathedrals known to man."

"But you're not religious." His voice was as curiously blank as his eyes.

"What if they're so exceptional that I find my religion?"

He waved off her teasing and shifted on his sandy seat. "Who are you traveling with?"

And there it was, the question she dreaded.

"Myself," she said offhandedly, brushing invisible lint from her wrinkled sage blouse. She was beginning to smell ripe. Now that she thought about it, so was he.

The single word seemed to ignite him. "By yourself?" Junior asked carefully, as if making sure he understood. In the filtered sunset, his irises were a paler blue than normal, richly contrasting with the warm colors of fall around them. She didn't like their alertness.

"Yes, *by myself*. And you must keep it a secret." Isa hid the prick of fear that confiding in him was a mistake. The last thing she wanted was for him to blabber to her family before she was ready.

Junior's lips flattened below the golden stubble of a growing mustache. "You could get hurt." He clamped his lips shut. Then, as though he couldn't help himself, added, "You can't just travel to a different continent and not tell anyone!"

He acted like he didn't want to keep her secret at all! "I did tell someone. I told Miss Pickney, David, and now you."

"Hot damn, I'm honored," Junior drawled sarcastically. He pulled his feet from the frigid water and stood. "I can't wait to lose all my teeth to Sol's fist when he finds out I kept something like this from him. I suppose it'll be up to me to tell him if your ship goes down? Or if you get robbed and taken advantage of while you're walkin' those streets in London, hm?"

"I have it all planned out. I'll hire a companion as soon as I touch land. They do things differently there—you can't just travel around unchaperoned, or they'll think you're a loose woman."

His frown dug a groove between his straight, tawny brows, and she began to worry. If he told her brother or (*God forbid*) her mother, she wouldn't step foot out of the county alone again, much less the country.

She clambered apprehensively to her feet and repeated, "You can't tell anyone, Junior. You promised. And a man is only as good as his promise." The space between them was heavy with a resentful hush, and a twitch of panic made her desperate. "I'd never tell anyone *your* secrets. Never."

He didn't respond, and their only congenial tête-à-tête of the day altered into something uncharitable. Worried blue eyes turned flinty, as glass did when struck too hard by something heavy and blunt. Wordlessly, he turned his back on her and readied their animals for another bout of tracking. The lack of communication frustrated her, forcing her to follow his lead.

Isa would never understand men. Just when she thought they were simple creatures driven by their baser instincts, they would roll over and show a side of themselves that was distinctly impalpable. But...infuriating man or not, his condemning silence made her think. Would it be such an unforgivable sin to travel abroad without notifying her loved ones? If something unspeakable did happen while she was gone, would it fall to Junior's shoulders to confess that he had known her plans all along? Troubled, she mounted the livery nag and considered the likelihood that she had just made Junior a whipping boy with her confession.

Mouth pursed, Isa kicked the mare forward, flanking Junior on the trail. He barely spared her a passing glance. "I'll tell them." When he didn't react, she repeated it louder. "I said, I'll tell my family my plans! Just don't mention it to anyone before I get a chance to; I want to be the one to do it."

For a moment, he acted deaf and dumb. Was the impossible man going to ignore her the whole way home? But, after an uncomfortable beat, his stiff carriage relaxed a degree in the saddle, and he nodded curtly.

"Remember the Grenert Brothers?" he asked after a moment's companionable silence.

Isa blinked at the subject change. "Yes. What about them?"

"I'm getting a feel for the men we're following, just like I did with the Grenerts."

"And?"

"I have an idea." Junior glanced at her...and winked.

She was forgiven. The hard block in her chest dispersed into soap bubbles, rising into her brain. Only the boots in her stirrups kept her body from floating away.

Chapter Eleven

I t was midmorning the next day, and Junior and Isa stood hidden at a curve in the road, their animals tethered several yards back. It was the perfect spot for an ambush.

They waited quietly for the two riders and four horses to ride by, and Isa found it difficult to keep her mind from pulling back like a lodestone to The Kiss. It had been easier the day and night before to keep the focus on following tracks and planning their next moves. She and Junior currently stood propped against a hundred-year-old live oak without speaking, a pair of blond heads patiently waiting for the sound of hoofbeats.

Isa watched Junior from beneath her brows as he opened and closed the chambers of his two Colts, ensuring his holsters were clear and smooth on the draw. In profile, his red lips pouted in luscious curves. His beauty enraged her. How trite to desire a man so sensual and beautiful. Would that she could feel such attraction to David, who would have welcomed her attentions with open arms. But to want a man whom every woman desired? It was a dangerous, unstable thing. And want him she did. That was what she would lie awake pondering in the dark and cold, wedged deeply within her bedroll. Isa wanted him the way she'd wanted material things as a child, the way she wanted freedom as a woman. If she were a primordial man and Junior a woman, she'd drag him off, screaming, by his ankle to her cave.

"Something funny?" he asked without looking at her.

"I'm thinking of our kiss," Isa admitted.

Junior's hands stopped their restless movements over his guns. "Why are you thinking about it? I thought it wasn't any good." His bandana was loose today, barely hanging on by its knot, and her gaze dragged from the rope-burn scar to the dark gold lashes framing his hooded eyes.

"It wasn't the worst." She reclined against the tree, motionless. When he looked up at her, she stopped breathing. The little smile on her lips fell away, and his eyes followed the movement. The way they went slumberous sucked all the oxygen from her lungs.

"So you're a liar."

"When it suits me." It was a whisper because all the air had vanished. He had taken it.

Junior's fingers flexed around the gun, then carefully slid it into its holster. Propping a forearm above her head, he turned his body and blocked the view of the road behind him. All she saw was him, golden, stubbled, blue-eyed Junior. She swallowed dryly.

Lids low, he drew his fingertips up the line of her traitorous throat. "What if I just—" He broke off, gritting straight, white teeth. His hand encased her throat, gently squeezing.

Eyes narrowed, breath coming fast, she said, "I'd laugh."

"What if you couldn't laugh?"

"I could. I would laugh, then I'd shoot you."

"Hm." The noise was deep in his throat. He lowered his arm, its sleeve dragging along rough tree bark by her ear until his other hand joined its brother. Warm, rough calluses enveloped her throat, thumbs pushing beneath her chin, elongating her neck. "As much as I want to throttle you sometimes, I don't think I could do it."

"Why not?" Hypnotized by his actions, she dug her fingers into the tree behind her so she didn't touch him and break the spell. "Are you afraid you'd feel bad?"

"Don't know if I'd go that far." Junior's belt buckle pressed against her navel, sandwiching her body between him and the tree. "I'd miss you a helluva lot, though."

All the clever witticisms stowed away in her mind for ready use evaporated. She couldn't have been more surprised if he'd recited the Lord's Prayer in Latin.

Hoofbeats in the far distance brought both their heads up.

"They're coming." He separated from her and handed her the shotgun leaning against the tree. "Get ready."

Their plan was simple: Isa would walk further up the road with the shotgun, and when the men got close, she would aim and shoot the dirt in front of the lead horse, spooking it. Junior would then come out of the woods at the bend, his Colts drawn. Isa's heart raced excitedly when two men appeared up the road. One man rode Champion with Mirage in tow, and the second, who looked suspiciously like Jonesie, was on a travel-worn nag. Their pace was hurried, as if they'd sensed someone on their tail. The black mare was acting up, tugging on her lead rope and attempting to take a bite out of the second man—it *was* Jonesie!—any time his horse got too close.

Isa saw the two men's mouths moving but was too far away to hear. The taller man on Champion yanked the cantankerous Arabian's lead rope in warning, and Jonesie pulled his pistol out. The scarred man aimed the six-shooter at the white blaze on Mirage's forehead, pretending to shoot. His nose was swollen, and both his eyes were black.

Lips thinned in concentration, Isa aimed and shot the dirt a yard away from Champion's feet. Clumps of earth exploded over the men and animals, and the report of the double-barrel shotgun made Mirage scream, eyes rolling and nostrils flaring wide. Jonesie's horse reared. He toppled onto the dirt at his horse's feet, reins still firmly in his fist. Head pulled awkwardly down and to the side, his horse followed and stepped on Jonesie's leg; the man screamed and released the reins.

Junior stepped out of the woods at the bend, aiming his Colts at the men's head. "Hands where I can see 'em."

The taller of the two men stopped trying to control Mirage and immediately did as he was told. Jonesie, however, released the leg he was cradling to reach for his empty holster—his gun had fallen out several feet away.

Junior caught the movement and shot the ground between the scarred man's feet. "You're ugly *and* stupid, aren't you?" he called out, calm and unaffected. "Pull that stunt again, and I'll have my partner shoot you directly in the eastern side of your head. We can bring you in dead or alive. What'll it be?"

They kept their hands raised.

"Izzy," Junior hollered, guns still trained on them. "Bring that shotgun over here and let them get a good look at both barrels while I hog-tie them."

Itching to get in on the action, Isa strode out, rope looped around her shoulders, muzzle trained on Jonesie and ready to blast holes into him with buckshot. Mirage, calmer now, nickered when she saw the tall young woman. "It appears you stole my horse," Isa said conversationally to Jonesie. "That's a hanging offense."

Jonesie sneered. "Goddamned horse broke my nose. I shoulda just killed it."

Isa imagined his nose crushing under the force of a violently swung equine head.

Good girl, Mirage.

To him, she said, "Serves you right. Stealing is wrong."

"Don't talk to him," Junior snapped. Training his gun on the first man, Junior drew the pistol from the lanky fellow's holster and pulled the newly unarmed man down to the dirt. Unraveling the rope from Isa's shoulders, Junior holstered his gun and got to work on the first man, who grunted and swore at the pressure of the rope's knot.

"Why not? You did."

"Not another word." Junior finished tying the man and maneuvered him facedown across Champion's saddle. The thief's hat fell off, blood pooling at his balding pate. The dapple-gray gelding turned to nose at Junior's shirt affectionately. When it was Jonesie's turn, Junior's eyes hardened. "Your turn."

Blackened eyes squinty with hatred, Jonesie cursed something awful, blistering their ears with insults and imprecations.

"Izzy, you have a handkerchief?" Junior tugged roughly on the knots binding the smaller man's limbs.

She scoffed incredulously. "What? No."

"Damn. Here, use this. Stuff it in his mouth and tie it off—don't let him bite you. Might be rabid." Junior pulled his dirty brown bandana from his neck and tossed it to her.

She looked at it, fingers squeezing involuntarily. Isa didn't want anything of Junior's near that humgruffin's mouth. It was too good for him.

"Izzy!"

"Don't harangue me," she groused, wrapping the bandana around the spitting man's mouth and yanking it into a knot with unnecessary roughness. "Be quiet, you fool. Don't you know everything you say can be held up in a court of law? This is a Texas Ranger you stole horses from."

Jonesie froze, his brown teeth bared behind lips peeled back tightly from the bandana. The second man seemed to hold his breath from his precarious perch on Champion. "I thought," the latter said haltingly, "you was a bounty hunter."

Junior's habile fingers stuttered around Jonesie's ankles before completing the complicated knot in two hard tugs.

"More fool you," Isa snorted, shotgun muzzle trained once more on the finally silent man at Junior's feet.

"Stop talkin'," he hissed, eyes shooting arrows at her.

Her brows rose. "Alright, don't get your skirts in a twist."

But Junior had turned his back to her. With a mighty grunt, he hefted the smaller man onto Jonesie's skittish horse's back. The outlaw, hands tied behind his back and ankles trussed up similarly, gave a groan that sounded like he was close to bringing up his breakfast.

"Shouldn't have drunk yourself stupid last night," Junior said unsympathetically. To Isa, he ordered, "Go get the horses and gear."

"Yes, sir!" She mock-saluted him, earning a satisfyingly hot glare.

As she jogged away, she heard the taller thief whisper, "She your sister or somethin'?"

"Hell no," Junior barked. "Now shut your yap."

Glancing behind her, Isa caught the moment Mirage adroitly snatched Junior's hat from his head.

ISA SOAKED IN the hotel's hip bath, physically boneless with exhaustion and mentally alert with elation. They had their horses back!

Junior had turned the two horse thieves over to Bryan's police department—a far more impressive establishment than Navasota's sheriff's office—and the helpful deputy had found a wanted poster with Jonesie's name and description. The scar-faced man had racked up enough offenses to be worth two hundred and fifty dollars alive, and it had taken every bit of Isa's control not to jump for joy at the prospect of splitting the reward with Junior.

That anticipation had deflated when the deputy had refused to hand the reward money over without first confirming the transaction with the sheriff...who wasn't available until the next morning. She supposed a night in Bryan wasn't much of an imposition. For the past two nights, she had slept in her own grit. Every time she had licked her lips, she tasted road dirt and salt. The cool front from the storm had frittered away, and it had been uncomfortably warm again by high noon. Sweat had trickled in dark, dusty trails down their temples.

With the money from selling the livery mare, Junior had bought them supper, ordered two rooms at a respectable hotel (under aliases), and spent extra on a bath for her. Even filthier than she, he'd visited a bathhouse because "it's cheaper" and claimed he needed more tobacco and rolling paper.

The bathwater, foggy from the bar of soap she'd scrubbed with, was tepid. Standing, Isa began the long, arduous process of washing her hair, using scented soap to lather a healthy amount of suds into the itchy roots. An eternity later, her matted knots squeaky clean, Isa climbed from the tub and stretched the kinks from her aching back. After donning her night wrapper, she wreathed her hair in a thin towel and padded barefoot to the plainly made bed in the center of the room. It wasn't as lovingly kept as their first hostel room, but it had the appropriate furniture. She plopped dramatically on the bed with a sigh—and hopped right back up again. The scent of something long-decayed perfumed the air around the mattress.

What the devil is that stench?

Isa ripped the bedclothes off with both hands: quilt, sheets, and pillows. In the center of the mattress was a dark-brown stain, yellow at its edges.

"Jumping Jehoshaphat, someone committed a murder on my bed!" she exclaimed. Then, she trotted to her bedroom wall and pounded a fist against it. A crudely constructed cross vibrated on its nail above. "Junior! Get over here if you please!"

Something heavy dropped to the floor on the other side of the wall, followed by running feet. Junior was already trying the knob before she could get the key into the hole.

"What is it?" he asked, his .45 drawn. He must have been readying for bed. His wrinkled—but clean—work shirt was un-buttoned. Isa's eyes couldn't resist a quick perusal of the sliver of his exposed chest. The top button of his denim jeans was undone.

Clearing her throat, she gestured to the bed. "Look. Someone died in my bed, and the hotel had the cheek to cover it up with bedclothes."

Junior wiped strands of hair, damp from the bathhouse, from his eyes, lowered his gun, and tiredly strode to the bed. He poked the dark stain with the muzzle of his pistol. "What in Sam Hill..."

"I don't know. All I know is I'm not sleeping on that. It's like there would be another person sleeping with me." She crossed her arms beneath her breasts and grimaced.

"I don't think that's blood." Lips twitching, he shot a devilish look at her.

"Oh, *foul*."

"Let's tell the landlady to give you another room."

Chapter Twelve

"I'll have a talking to with Martha, miss, don't you worry," vowed the distressed hotel proprietress. She busily gathered the bedclothes in her squat arms before backing out of the room.

Junior scratched his stubble. He'd need to shave in the morning before meeting with the sheriff. Two hundred and fifty dollars—who knew that pissant Jonesie had been worth anything? "Do you have another room?" he asked the woman, half afraid he knew the answer.

"No, sir, and I'm plumb sorry to tell you that." The woman had gray hair and clean, starched clothes. The little half-moon spectacles on her eyes gave her the appearance of Mrs. Claus from the magazines, and he felt like a bastard for asking.

Isa shifted guiltily on her feet. "Is there, perhaps, a replacement mattress?"

The woman's face sagged. "No, miss, there's not. I'll dock the room from your bill and reimburse you first thing in the morning."

Junior held a staying hand up. "She can sleep in my room. Do you have a bundling board?"

Mrs. Claus' eyes watered alarmingly.

Isa stepped forward, consoling the woman. "Oh, it's fine. He's my brother. I'll make him sleep on the floor." She patted the woman's round shoulder.

As soon as the landlady disappeared down the hotel stairs, heartened by their assurances, Junior turned on Isa. "I'm not sleepin' on the floor, Izzy."

She was already gathering her gunnysack and saddlebags in her arms. Cursing, Junior snatched the saddlebags away and unlocked his door.

"Play you a hand of poker for the bed," she offered on her way in.

"Hell no. You cheat."

Her white smile flashed, and, predictably, his eyes caught on the tempting gap in the center. He hadn't felt the gap during their kiss. It made him wonder what it would feel like on his fingertips. To run his tongue over it.

Damn it, stop thinking of Sol's sister like that.

But it was impossible not to. He'd struggled to keep Isa sister-like in his mind *before* the kiss. Now...all he could think about was all the ways he'd like to defile her. The things he'd do. The positions he'd try with her. He wondered if her curious nature would track in bed.

"Aren't you going to shut the door?"

Junior blinked. He'd been standing in the doorway, vacuously watching Isa set her bag down. Shielding his embarrassment, he shut and locked the door, then dropped her saddlebags to one side of the bed. Pretending not to notice that she was unwinding the towel from her damp hair, he traversed to his side of the bed and grabbed the item he'd purchased from the mercantile next door to the bathhouse.

"Here." He tossed a tortoiseshell comb at her. When she caught it one-handed, he snorted.

Isa glanced at the delicate curve of the comb, touching the handle that was polished to a reflective shine. "A bit pretty for a cowboy, don't you suppose?"

Junior snorted to hide his burning ears and returned to his bags. "It's not mine."

"Is it your mother's?" she asked innocently.

Mama's boy.

The unspoken taunt narrowed his eyes.

"No, I got it for you when I bought my tobacco," he said evenly, pulling his bedroll out to spread it on the hardwood floor.

"Oh." The silence strung out for an uncomfortable minute. There was rustling near the door, and he fought the urge to look. "Here. This is for you."

Twisting around, he caught something hard against his chest. It was a small, circular tin. Hand cream? He raised a tawny brow. "Where'd you get this?"

"Brenham. Your hands are chapped. You should take better care of yourself." The sharp words belied her blissful expression as she combed tangles from the tips of her hair. Knotted skeins, chestnut when wet, tumbled down her back. "I hadn't realized how much I needed this. I left my brush at Miss Pickney's."

At a loss for words, Junior sat on his bedroll, feet spread and knees up, and began to apply the thick salve over his dry hands. It smelled strongly of beeswax and melted into his skin like butter. He sniffed his palm.

"You should put some on every night." Isa had reached halfway up her hair, combing through the tangles the same way she curried the horses' and mule's tails at the end of every evening.

He covertly watched her comb her hair as he massaged the salve into his fingers. Gradually, his hands became smoother, the calluses no longer cutting, their sharp edges blunting. And slowly, her comb ran through the waves without snagging, wide teeth parting thick locks from root to tip. Clean, full, and warm, Junior felt a peace suffuse him. For the thousandth time, he looked upon her and contemplated her wild prettiness. The sage blouse she'd worn for the last two days had made her eyes appear vibrantly green, the flecks of amber only visible in sunlight. Now, the lamplight bathing her from his bedside table made Isa's eyes glow like gold nuggets in a shallow stream.

Hair adequately brushed, she crouched by her bags, dug around, and reappeared with a familiar book that had grown a little more battered by the day. "Shall we?"

Junior shrugged as though he wasn't thrilled to hear more of Sherlock and Watson's adventures. "If you want." He'd no sooner lain back on his bedroll than she was ordering him up again.

"I go hoarse every night trying to get you to hear me. Come up here. I'm not going to bite you."

"I trust you as far as I can throw you," he grunted, rolling to his knees and bouncing onto the bed. "Anything else, Your Majesty?"

"No, this will do," she replied imperially and fell beside him, jostling his arm. "Now, where were we?"

For an hour, she read to him, and his eyes switched between the book and her animated expressions. Occasionally, she'd catch him, her tiger eyes curious, and he'd face the bare wall with its crack down the plaster. Finally, voice scratchy, she closed the book.

"I think this is one of my favorite books," she sighed.

"Mine, too," he agreed. His lids felt heavy. The cracked plaster blinked in and out of his vision. "I'd best get back on my bedroll."

Isa moved to set the book on the table, but she had to reach over him to do it. Her breasts dragged fully across his face; he blanched and sank into the pillow. Unaware, she turned the light down and blew it out. "Just sleep up here."

"You know what would happen if I did," he growled in the sudden darkness. Why was she playing the fool?

"What would happen?" Her ready defiance never ceased to trap him. Never could he let her challenges go unanswered.

Junior grabbed the shoulders hovering over him and rolled her firmly to her back. "*You know what would happen*," he repeated, stressing every word.

Her forearms sliced up, breaking his hold. "We could wrestle for who gets the bed," she teased, putting him in an awkward stranglehold.

Blood rushed through every body part. He broke out of her hold and loomed above her. The room had no windows. Everything felt weighted. Obscure. "Alright. Whoever stops moving wins?"

"Yes." Her excitement was palpable.

Junior lowered his head, tracking the sibilant sound of her "yes." He found her lips and kissed them as tenderly as he would a freshly bloomed flower. Isa went still beneath him, her breath sucking in. Before the surprise wore off and she found control of her limbs, he pulled away, the lush sound of their lips parting loud in the dense quiet.

"I win." He hoped she couldn't feel the effect their innocent kiss had on him.

Her response was delayed. "That's not playing fair."

"You cheat in poker. Why can't I cheat in wrestling?"

"Do that with all the men you wrestle, do you?"

"No, only the women."

"Oh?" Her voice lost its breathiness. "And what women do you wrestle?"

"Only you." He grinned down at her in the dark and wished he could see her face.

Slender fingers threaded through his hair. Her hands pulled him down. "Shall we have a rematch? Kiss me again."

He fully intended to tell her no until soft, perfect lips settled over his.

I'll tell her no next time.

Right now, she was supple and sweet-smelling beneath him, intoxicating him. Her brother—his best friend—was far away, asleep in his own house, in bed with his own wife. Junior had no wife and hadn't been home longer than a week in years. He also couldn't remember the last time he'd lain with a woman. What would a little playing hurt? Surely, that's all he was doing with Isa. Playing. Teasing. Kissing without a means to an end. No expectations of going past the point of no return. She'd remain whole while they were on the trail because he wasn't an animal.

But he sure as hell wasn't a saint.

Not to mention Isa was kissing the sense out of him, mouth wide, tongue questing. Control snapping, Junior broke the kiss and grabbed her wrists. He held them above her head in one hand, feeling the damp silk of her hair against his arm. He kissed her aggressively until she was the one straining, pushing full breasts against his chest, her stomach flush against his. One of her legs rose to wrap around his hip. Without breaking contact, he maneuvered them, settling her deep into the center of the mattress to align his hips with hers, his body insistent. The urge to move, to rock, to grab and pull her was a rampant thing inside him.

If she knew what she really did to him, this mindlessness, she'd laugh. She'd never let him go, and he'd sit like a tome on her bookshelf or a plaything, gathering dust.

It was best if she didn't know the truth.

Isa didn't need to know how deeply her hooks had sunk into him, so embedded he'd never get them out. He'd never tell her about the letter in his billfold that had saved him. Or about the little room he'd rented in Austin years ago just because he wanted to keep an eye on her. Sol knew and kept it secret under the assumption Junior did it for the family's peace of mind. After all, Miss Pickney was only one old woman, and Isa was sly, always up to mischief. He would watch from afar many mornings as she walked to college, tall, elegant, and stylish in her godawful hats and enormous sleeves.

These secrets were to protect him. Not her.

Kissing her exposed one of his most coveted secrets. It was impossible to feel her writhe beneath him without revealing it. With his lips was an admission of how much he thought of claiming her. His pelvis pressing hard against hers was a declaration of how much he wanted her. Junior had never kissed another woman the way he did Isa. Not a whore, not a widow, not a promiscuous neighbor. With Isa, he wanted to brand her. To *own* her. On her lips he would leave a glowing "JS" so no other man could claim them. Everyone would know who this full, wide mouth belonged to.

Isa's legs flexed, hips twisting, and Junior let her roll him to his back. He released her and looked at the black-against-black outline of her face in the dark. The air was heavy around them, their breathing hard. And then, her fingers were on his jaw, down his scarred neck, to his open shirt. Her palms trailed along the crisp mat of hair on his chest, then lower, to his flexing ribcage.

"If I could paint a picture forever in my mind," she whispered from above, barely audible, "it would be of this moment. I'd close my eyes and see you this way with my hands. With my body."

The tendons tightened in his neck. Junior grabbed her hand, lowering it further. When it reached the undone button of his jeans, she hesitated. Raggedly, he said, "And I'd paint one of this moment. The part right before you turn brave and jump into the deep end of the creek. The part where you're a little scared."

"I'm not scared," she breathed, but he felt the fine tremor in her thighs. Could hear it in her voice. He understood. His own hands trembled. To hide it, he gripped her knees which were bracketing his torso and pushed her down until she was seated on his thighs.

"Prove it," he dared. A voice told him he was wrong. That he was the most loathsome and licentious of scoundrels to goad her into slaking her curiosity like this.

Isa didn't hesitate again. One by one, she undid his buttons, knuckles brushing the triangle of hair, until the opened clasp revealed the root of his erection. Junior sucked in a breath, and she stopped.

"What now?" she asked.

With some effort, he sat up, tugged his shirt off, and threw it in the vicinity of his bedroll. He lay back, placing his hands where her nightgown had rucked above her knees. "Your turn."

You're a no-good son of a bitch, Stone, his conscience hissed.

Isa's ugly wrapper whispered to the floor near his shirt. Although he couldn't see her, the knowledge that she was naked within arm's reach stimulated him. Squeezing his eyes shut didn't help; his heart raced as frantically as before. Of their own volition, his palms slid from her knees to her thighs that went on forever, supple with well-developed muscles from years of riding, running, and swimming. His hands mapped them out until they reached her hips, and he tried to picture her sitting naked atop him like a goddess in a mortal man's fantasy. Isa's hands covered the back of his, sliding them over the flare of her hips, along the valley of her waist, pausing at her ribcage. They stalled, held suspended between one action and the next. Drunk with want, Junior brushed the underside of her round, heavy breasts with his thumbs. Air passed shallowly from her lips—her ribs rapidly expanded and compressed—in and out, in and out. The barest touch of her fingertips guided his knuckles now, so he slid his broad palms over her round breasts, feeling their shape. Their weight. The skin was tight and smooth, jutting at the peaks. Her nipples tightened, and she gasped softly when his hands made a slow, sure pass over them. Isa dropped her hands to grasp his lean hips.

Junior released her breasts and pulled her down so that they were flattened against his chest, his mouth hard upon hers. Her clever tongue blanked his mind, and he drew on it fervently, stroking her jaw with his fingers. It felt as though he would bust in his jeans, and he slid his hands down the strong, slim line of her back to grip her buttocks in each hand, squeezing the way he had the first morning they'd woken up together.

Isa pulled back. "*Junior.*" It was the closest thing to a plea he'd ever heard from her, and he tenderly kissed her eyelids, her nose, her soft, swollen mouth.

"I know," he finally managed, gripping her so hard that she shifted up to escape the punishing touch. Her breasts brushed his chin. "I know." He captured a nipple in his mouth, drawing on it the way he had her tongue, and she moaned. She smelled sweet and was softer than satin, and he paid homage to her breasts, rubbing his stubble over the sensitive curves beneath. He bit the skin at the edge of her nipple, sucked hard, then gently laved the hard peak with the flat of his tongue. Tiny kitten sounds escaped her throat, unexpected and unbearably arousing, and she rubbed against the straining edge of his open fly. He broke away with a low groan. Using the handfuls he had of her bottom, he worked her on him leisurely, and her mouth followed in a kiss that was anything but.

Instinctively, he slid one hand down to the hot, damp place hidden between her legs.

Isa stopped rocking; her lips had gone stock-still against his. To calm her, he licked her bottom lip and kissed it. Nipped it with his teeth. Slid his tongue inside the seam of her mouth, then retreated. Playing. Teasing. All the while, his hand moved further south, drifting past shivering skin, past curls, to bracket his fingers around the soft outer lips protecting her sex until he had a palm full of her warm mons. He liked the sounds she made when his fingers parted her, the staccato rhythm of her breath when he touched swollen, delicate skin. And when he breached her entrance, her muscles squeezed him.

Junior had never been inside of someone and felt owned.

He'd never felt the soul of another while knuckle-deep, their heartbeat fluttering around him.

When he disengaged from her, she followed, and he smiled against her lips. Junior's damp fingers traveled only as far as the pleasure point at the top of her sex, making circles around it, hardly touching, in no hurry. Isa's mouth, tucked against his cheek, moaned against his skin. Gooseflesh rose along his arms, his nape. Her mouth opened to trail hot kisses along the line of his carotid artery and peppered little sucking pecks to his skin. Another wave of gooseflesh spread over him, which firmed his touch in response, and the situation in his denims strained to be released. Unsteadily, Junior shoved his jeans down. Stifling a groan of relief when his cock sprang out, he wrapped his hand around it. It was hard as forged iron, the tip leaking.

Isa didn't ask permission to touch it; her hand reached between them, fingers sliding around his knuckles until they were both holding him in hand. Even though he couldn't see her, he sensed her face hovering above, her damp hair fragrant around him. Carefully, he pulled his hand from beneath hers until it was only her flesh on his. The sensation made him throb, almost agonizing in its intensity. Her lips touched his at the same instant his hand resumed its careful exploration between her legs, her tongue dipping in while she stroked him up and down.

Soon, it was a struggle to breathe, to think. Their hands gripped, and their hips moved restlessly. The air between them was humid. Sweat broke out above lips and brows, the skin slippery where their bodies met. Pressure built swiftly on his end. The slicker his fingers became, the faster her hand worked until holding back was no longer possible. He gritted his teeth, grunting. The levee burst, bathing their stomachs in hot, sticky warmth.

"What—oh."

Through the haze of dizzying pleasure, he felt Isa look down in the dark. Isa released him, her hips restless. Having stuttered to a stop when he climaxed, Junior rolled her to her back. His mind was fuzzy. What he wanted to do was dip low and bury his head between her thighs. He didn't; he sensed her closeness. Maintaining a steady rhythm between her legs, he followed the movements of her hips and felt when her body became impossibly lusher. Her noises altered, growing more frequent and higher in pitch until she suddenly grabbed his wrist, pressing his hand hard against her, her lungs like bellows while she climaxed.

Overwhelmed with possessiveness, he tugged his wrist away. Dumb to the mess between them, Junior dropped to his elbows and kissed her slack mouth until he forgot his own hated name.

Chapter Thirteen

I sa awoke from a deep slumber to the jangle of a gun belt. She was naked beneath the hotel sheets, her back exposed to cold air, her hair a mess on the pillows. A fully dressed Junior stood beside the bed, and he watched her with an expression that was both possessive and admiring. Morning light inched into the room through the bottom of the door, and the bedside lamp illuminated what the crack of light couldn't.

"Where are you going?" she asked huskily, pushing her hair out of her eyes with a forearm.

"To saddle the horses and get the bounty from the sheriff." Junior stepped forward, knees against the bed, and let his knuckles drift from the top of her spine to where the sheet lay halfway down her back. "Want to meet at that place we rode past a couple of blocks over for some breakfast?"

His touch stirred memories of the night before. Junior, wiping her clean with a rough hotel washcloth. The way he'd neglected his bedroll to climb back into bed and pull her to him. Naked, they had talked into the early morning hours, blanketed in the kind of darkness that made truths slip out easily. She'd fallen asleep wondering if he'd suffer amnesia by daybreak.

From the way he looked at her now, he hadn't.

A lock of tawny hair falling over studious eyes, Junior bent over and smoothed his palm over the dip of her lower back to the curve of her bottom beneath the sheets.

"I'll meet you there for breakfast," Isa whispered, thoroughly bewitched.

Using her buttock to brace himself, he leaned down for a kiss.

She twisted away, burying her face in the pillow. "Not until I clean my teeth." The words were muffled.

"Get over here," he growled in her ear. Tugging and rolling her with persistent hands, he claimed the lips she'd clamped shut. He pulled away, smiling. "There. That wasn't so bad."

She swept her hair from her eyes again, glaring. Junior's gaze traveled down to her breasts, exposed from their activities. It was the first time he'd seen them in full light.

Impossibly blue eyes met hers, his smile gone. The pad of his thumb journeyed from Isa's cheekbone to the line of her jaw. "You're so damned beautiful."

This time, when he kissed her, she didn't fight him. She wrapped her arms sinuously around his neck, moaning when his warm palms covered the breasts he'd found "so damned beautiful." Minutes—or hours—later, he departed with the utmost reluctance.

For a long time, Isa lay in stunned silence.

TOO RESTLESS TO wait for him at the restaurant as promised, Isa hitched Mirage and Red beside the large gray gelding in front of Bryan's police department. She entered the brick building in clean travel clothes, her skin glowing and hair combed into an elegant updo.

The deputy from yesterday was only too happy to point the way to the sheriff's office. "They just went back," the man eagerly supplied.

"Thank you."

Isa walked confidently down the corridor to an office whose door was partially open. An engraved plate read "Sheriff" in bold letters, and her hand was poised to knock when she heard the elevated nature of the voices inside. A man was conversing loudly, his tone cold and decidedly hostile. Isa lowered her fist. She made to turn away, thinking the deputy had been mistaken about Junior's presence there, when a smattering of words halted her feet.

"...talking big for a Ranger with a dishonorable discharge under his belt—"

Isa's heart skipped a beat.

"The conditions of my release are paid and have been since summer." Junior's voice was stiff. Isa imagined him standing, tall and unbending, in the face of judgment. "I don't work for a fraction anymore, and I'd like to be compensated in full like every other bounty hunter."

The sheriff said something scathing, and Isa strained to hear it.

Junior's words were hot on the heels of that. "Bounty hunters make a lawman's job easier, so I reckon you should thank 'em, not cuss 'em. The poster for Jonesie is on your desk; give me what's owed, and I'll be on my way."

"We're in a depression, son," the sheriff sneered, wholly disgusted. "There ain't any money."

"That so?" Anger sharpened the edge of Junior's tone, and for the first time, Isa wished self-control upon a person other than herself.

"Yep."

"Then our business here is done."

She didn't wait to hear more. Her feet flew down the hallway as though they had sprouted wings. She didn't bother telling the surprised deputy goodbye. Only when the white oak door with its etched glass window had closed behind her did she stop to catch her breath.

Dishonorably discharged? Conditions of his release?

The door she'd just exited swung violently open behind her, so she ducked, pretending to check Mirage's fetlock.

"What the hell are you doing here?" Junior snapped.

Schooling her face, Isa straightened, then shot a surprised glance over her shoulder. "I thought I'd meet you here instead of the restaurant."

"Well, we came to Bryan for nothin'. The sheriff won't pay a dime because of the depression." His stride was long and angry, and when he brusquely untied Champion, the gelding's ears twitched nervously. Junior mounted his horse and wheeled him around.

Isa unhitched the remaining animals and followed behind on Mirage, glancing from Junior's rock-like fists around Champion's reins to his granite jaw. Thinking back, he had never specifically claimed to still be a Texas Ranger, but it was still a lie by omission. Her suspicions that he was being followed felt more sinister now. Without the protection of any sort of military or police force, Junior was a far easier target. And those brothers he'd tracked down and caught? It hadn't been a Texas Ranger operation recovering fugitives; he had bounty-hunted them.

Unable to think on an empty stomach, Isa reached into her bag for a sliver of beef jerky.

Junior's raptor gaze turned on her. "What are you doing?"

Jerky halfway to her mouth, she said, "I assumed we weren't stopping anywhere to eat—"

"Since when have you ever forgone food in town for trail grub?"

Since five minutes ago. "There is no point wasting our remaining money—"

"I'm not hurting for money," Junior fumed. "We'll use some of what we sold the livery nag for. We're stopping at the diner. Might as well get a hot one before we leave."

Isa shrugged and tucked her jerky away. She observed the rigid line of his back and chewed the inside of her cheek. How long ago had he been dishonorably discharged? Why hadn't he said anything to her in all the times she'd mentioned it?

And what had he done?

JUNIOR KEPT HIS feelings to himself during the day-long journey to the farther side of Huntsville. By the time they set up camp, he was sweating bullets.

He was a fraud. His years of bounty hunting for the state had come to a close, and the quagmire of ill-kept secrets was surfacing. One after the other, they rose from scummy depths like bloated corpses in a mill pond.

Isa had confided in him her secrets, and the guilt that he couldn't do the same ate him up. The last time he'd spoken the mortifying truth was when he'd testified in court. Captain Havelard had sat on a courtroom chair, his face pained. Disappointed. It was Havelard's good word that had saved Junior's neck from stretching at the end of a noose, and a sympathetic judge had kept him out of prison. A miner with a vein of pure gold on his plot didn't have Junior's luck.

Still, he had wanted to die.

The weight of wanting to end it all had been crushing, his mind immured beneath a never-ending landslide of faults, one that replenished itself no matter how many times he freed a portion of himself. The fear that his family would discover the truth kept him from home, and his stays were short and sporadic when he did visit. His nephews grew like weeds and forgot him. Ben looked more worried with every visit. Father was livid by his constant absence, lighting into his son at every opportunity Junior deigned to drop by. The old man had to know by now; he was too nosey. Too self-important. One letter to Havelard, and the company would answer every question. The incident was withheld from the papers, but every Ranger knew. Sheriffs at every police department knew the stipulations of his release. Two years of bounty hunting for the state and only receiving twenty-five percent of the profit had been his punishment for being a murdering traitor. A traitor whose oaths were as worthless as stones thrown down a dry well.

"Penny for your thoughts?"

Snapping out of his musing, Junior looked up from scraping dirt and rocks from Champion's hooves. Isa had made silent trips back and forth with their packs to the fire, a reversal of their normal duties. Beneath her brown hat—grimy now from sweat and filth accumulated on the trail—Isa's dirty-blonde hair had unraveled from its elegant updo. Her eyes were gilded jade today.

"What's got you so quiet?" she pressed.

He needed to tell someone. It felt like he was drowning, his thrashing face held down inches from the surface by his own hand.

Tell her.

Speaking as though from a long, narrow tunnel, he said, "Nothing."

The words, the admission, remained lodged in his throat, rooting him to the spot. Isa pursed her lips introspectively, nodded, and walked away. Her heavy hair sagged from its pins, swaying against her back like a pendulum. Tick-tock.

He curried the animals, stalling. More time. He needed more time. The warmth from the mule's and horses' hides soothed him. The flex of big lungs blowing sweet breath into his face steadied his hands. Finished with the animals, he hobbled them and let them graze on leads. Near the fire, his bedroll was already laid out, his saddle propped at one end. An opened can of beans sat on a bed of coals next to a camp-sized dutch oven emitting hints of crispy cornpone. Gratitude assuaged his frayed nerves. Junior hadn't traveled with anyone on the trail since his discharge, and while the solitude had healed parts of him, it had taken with it the ease of companionship. He remembered standing in Miss Pickney's little apartment, dreading the prospect of being on the trail with Isa. He'd just known she'd be difficult. Complaining. A chatterbox with too much in her head that needed to come out.

Junior had forgotten what a good student she'd been. How quickly she'd taken to hunting, training horses, and herding cattle. All the things that took skill, concentration, and long stretches of quiet. Most of their journey was held in companionable silence. It surprised him when he found himself thinking of things to say or do to make her talk. To hear an opinion or fact that made his mouth drop open or his belly hurt from laughing.

"Supper is ready." Isa's voice was husky from fatigue, and he watched her guiltily, hungrily, as she ran the tortoiseshell comb through her loose hair. The ends reached the curve of her waist, pale and shining in the firelight.

They ate in silence, one that lacked the companionship he'd grown accustomed to. He sensed that she wanted to speak, that her words itched to come out, but her fine brows were set in a stern position over her eyes, her fingertips running over her lips the way she did when pondering something.

"I'll clean up," he said to break the void of silence. He took the plates and pan and scraped them out. Rinsed them. Fighting the urge to crumple the tin camp plates into tiny metal pieces, he strode back to the fire. Isa was already lying down, her back to the fire...and to his bedroll. "What are you doing?" It came out like a condemnation.

Isa didn't deign to look at him. "Going to sleep."

Last night, they had slept wrapped in each other's arms. Each time that he'd woken up at the small movements she'd made in slumber, he'd gripped her tighter. There had been no bad dreams, no waking up dreading another day. If he could fall asleep with her in his arms every night, he could face the light of any day. Such sissified reflections used to make him retch. Panic set in now because it rang true.

"Get up," he heard himself say, hands shaking.

"What?" Isa sent a baleful look at him from the corner of her eye.

He didn't repeat himself. Junior closed the distance between them, bent over, and lifted her—bedroll and all—from the ground. Ignoring the outraged squawks from her blankets, he carried her around the fire and plunked her beside his bedroll. While she sputtered and struggled within the confines of her bedding, Junior shoved his boots off and wrapped his legs and arms around her squirming figure.

She wriggled. "What in God's name are you doing?"

"Holding you." It was muttered into her mussed hair.

"Oh." Incrementally, Isa stopped struggling. Her body relaxed in his hold. He loosened the vise of his legs around her but kept his arms tight, pulling her as closely as he could, face buried in the crook of her neck. "Why?"

Why was he holding her? Because he couldn't damned well breathe without her, that's why.

"Because I want to, I reckon," he said.

"You always do what you want?"

"If I did what I wanted, we'd have to stand in front of a preacher come Saturday, your brother's rifle shoving a dent into my backbone." Breathing her in, he let himself imagine it, just for a moment. Isa standing in a confection of ivory, glaring daggers at him through a veil. Sweat would drip from every gland. Their glacier-cold feet would be itching to run.

Isa squirmed again, but closer. "That would be horrid."

"I know."

"Imagine your mother's reaction." She giggled, then suggested slyly, "We could do what we want and *not* get married. No one has to know."

His body responded predictably, and he swatted the lumpy area of blankets where her rear end dwelled. "*I* would know."

"Just once?" Warm lips touched his hand, his wrist. Instead of rousing him further, the soft kisses stabbed directly into his heart.

"I can't. It can't be more than this. You're my best friend's sister. I couldn't live with myself."

"And I couldn't live with myself if we don't."

The edge of teasing in her voice made his lips curve up despite himself. "Guess you'll just have to die."

The fire flared brighter with her laughter. Above them, the night sky was a smooth backdrop of velvet with billions of stars like sparkling diamonds scattered within it. It was warm enough that their breath didn't steam from their lips like chimney smoke, but it was cold enough that the tip of his chilled nose against her neck made her jump.

"It can be a secret," she said, no longer laughing.

He stiffened. "I don't want to keep any more secrets."

Isa's mind was working again; he could feel it against his forehead like a piston. "I didn't know you had secrets. You must be good at keeping them."

"How about I tell you one." He pressed his lips against the fragrant skin beneath her nape, afraid his heart would burst, it was pounding so hard. "I was dishonorably discharged from the Texas Rangers."

The fire popped and crackled in the wake of this sudden announcement, and he sensed her churning thoughts through the centimeter of space separating his head from hers.

"What happened?" she finally asked, carefully subdued.

Another fire flared behind his closed lids. One from the past. For hours, thick, black, and acrid smoke had boiled from it. The smell had lingered on his clothes for days in a jail cell until he was allowed to bathe and change. "I did something very bad."

Delicately callused fingers ran along the length of his forearm, drifting gently through the pale dusting of hair. "Surely it couldn't be so bad. Get two toes out of line, and they drop people like a hot potato."

Junior pressed his forehead tighter against the crown of her skull, eyes shut tight.

Isa pretended he wasn't bowing her neck uncomfortably forward. "Want to know what I've done?" He didn't answer. Couldn't answer. "One time, Mr. Corner made me so angry that I allowed him to believe he'd lost half his personal investments. I let him sweat for a week—"

"I killed six other Rangers in cold blood," Junior interrupted. His tone was emotionless, his palms clammy, his heartbeat swift.

Against him, Isa felt like an ice sculpture. When the thread of silence between them threatened to snap, she whispered, "Why?"

Grimacing into the safety of her hair, he shook his head. "It doesn't matter why. All that matters is that I killed them. And one of them...he was my friend Randal's little brother."

Chapter Fourteen

I sa blew on her steaming cup of coffee the next morning, her hair uncombed and eyes gritty from several hours of heavy sleep. Junior pulled a tin of papers and a tobacco sack from his saddlebag. He had perpetually glanced her way since he'd risen from his bedroll that morning, and it grated on her nerves.

"What are you looking at?" she muttered after another glance, then grimaced at that first astringent sip of coffee. Why he had to brew it to such a tarry consistency was lost on her. She dropped half a handful of sugar in to make it palatable.

"Not sure," Junior replied, carefully pulling a rolling paper from its sheaf. "Haven't figured it out yet."

Isa grunted, finding his joke unworthy of a verbal response.

They sat side by side on their bedrolls, which had lumped together sometime in the middle of the night. Isa squinted against the sun's rays on the eastern horizon. An urgently full bladder had awoken her the hour before, and she'd had to untangle herself from the vise of his limbs so she could answer nature's call. She'd returned and was caught unaware at the sight of him sleeping on his back, neck exposed, an arm thrown over his head in childlike repose. She'd stood, frozen, her chest surging with warm emotion. Helpless against its tide, every wall, every boundary she'd constructed over the years, was ruined by the familiar feelings. Feelings she'd been certain she'd grown out of now returned with disturbing ease. Their resurgence was unwelcome and unsurprising.

It was precisely why she'd so adamantly denied the need to travel with him. Revering someone without being on the reciprocating end of admiration was an experience she never wished to suffer again. Unrequited love was devastating, and Isa was wholly averse to undergoing such illogical anguish ever again.

She refused to. They would be friends. Nothing more.

And she could think of no one in greater need of friendship than Junior. He was slowly opening up, secrets unfurling from every small revelation. She still didn't know why he'd killed those Rangers or who was following him. Questions bubbled up in her, straining to be freed. Isa adored puzzles. Pulling answers like splinters from an enigma was her forte. But something told her to be patient with Junior. He needed someone to listen at a pace he set. Every time she pushed, he pulled. The best course of action was to do nothing at all. To simply exist in companionship.

With new determination, she set her tin coffee cup down. "Teach me how to do that."

Junior glanced up from dexterously tucking and rolling his cigarette. "You'll waste papers."

"I will not," she exclaimed, scooting closer. "I bet I could ascertain how to do it on the first try. Let me watch you roll one. Slowly."

"Alright." He pulled his leather drawstring sack of White Burley tobacco, roughly shredded and fragrant, between them.

Isa watched him thumb out another rolling paper, close the tin, and assemble the cigarette on its metal lid. When he placed a generous pinch of tobacco atop the paper, it looked like far too much; several rough grains spilled from the miniature mountain. After brushing the excess back into the sack, Junior's large, square fingertips folded the paper over the hill of tobacco, then, pinching both ends with thumbs and forefingers, he rubbed the paper back and forth until the action evenly distributed the leaves. Once the contents were secure, Junior tucked and pressed the lower piece of rolling paper down, bringing the top to his mouth. He licked its top edge, then rolled and tucked some more, securing the cigarette. He proffered it for her examination, but she brushed it aside to grab his tin and bag instead.

"I have it," she murmured, reaching beneath the lid for a paper.

Lip quirking, Junior watched Isa pinch and roll the ends of her paper. Several leaves tumbled into her lap. Brow knitted in concentration, she pressed down on the bottom and licked the top edge of the paper. Once finished, she held the cigarette up for his inspection. It was a little loose, a lot wet, and thicker in the center than the ends.

Junior said nothing. He plucked it up with two fingers, put one end in his mouth, and grabbed a stick from the fire. Lighting the tip, he dragged in deeply and winked at her.

JUNIOR TOOK YET another shortcut, and Isa followed along without complaint. She was nauseatingly aware that it was their last day traveling alone together. There would be no more scenic trails of gold and crimson foliage, no more dipping feet into ice-cold creek water. No more stolen kisses. No more secrets.

"I'm starved." They had traveled the same road for miles with only an occasional wagon passing by to break the monotony.

Red clay squished beneath equine hooves from a recent rain. Songbirds flitted to puddles to bathe, feathers ruffled.

"We're just outside Dogwood," Junior appeased. It brought her suspiciously alert. He was never kind if he didn't have to be. "I'm surprised you haven't recognized it by now."

Isa ran an appraising eye over the red clay road, the branching driveways that led to farmhouses in the distance, the thickness of the wood line. "How far are we from town?"

"A few miles west. We should be at the hotel by dinnertime."

"God does answer prayers."

"This is it. Right after this curve." He nodded ahead.

Once the road's curve straightened into a long, narrow path of ocher with a strip of green in its center, Isa spotted the drooping shell of a dilapidated old house. It had once been grand, with a picket fence encasing a tiny yard. The roof had caved in, and all the windows were knocked out by the elements and thrown stones. The forest had nigh taken over it, but Isa felt a flash of recognition. Six years before, she'd ridden on this very road searching for her missing sister-in-law.

"It's where those men took Poppy," she breathed.

"And where you went after them with a sack of sunflower seeds," Junior added dryly. "Look."

He wasn't pointing at the old house. Isa glimpsed yellow blooms on tall green stalks at the tree line, and her mouth opened.

"Are those—"

"Yep. They've been growing wild for years now. There's a trail of 'em going about ten miles in." He nudged his horse forward, and Isa followed behind. A cluster of heliotropes basked in the midday sun. Dead stalks littered the ground. Most had gone to seed, evidence that they had been plentiful in the months before. But, despite it being late October, some flowers still bloomed, their faces turned toward the sun. In the woods behind them, a few tall stalks popped up sporadically, spindlier in the shade than their brothers in full sun.

A trail of sunflowers, she thought wondrously. She'd left a trail of seeds behind her in the summer of '88, praying a posse would discover it. A girl of sixteen in overalls and braids, it hadn't been long before she'd been caught by Poppy's abductors. It had been worth being chained with the other girls. She could still picture the dirty, frightened faces of the hungry girls in the wagon beds, tethered together by their necks. At her first opportunity, she'd lit a wagon on fire, alerting their position to Junior and the other men trailing them.

Yes, it had been worth it.

"Did I ever thank you?" she asked Junior abstractly, reaching over in the saddle to brush her knuckles against the yellow petals of a particularly large sunflower.

Junior studied her profile. "Thank me for what?"

"For saving my life."

"Oh. It wasn't nothing," he grunted.

She didn't bother correcting the double negative. "Don't pretend it wasn't, Junior. It was."

"Reckon you did half the work yourself," he said after a pause. "Led us to them. Lit the wagon on fire. Pushed that bastard's gun up and moved so I could get a clear shot."

As if through some unspoken agreement, the two of them had never talked about it. Isa pulled a petal from the head of the gargantuan flower and scrutinized the yellow spear, softer than a baby's cheek. "We have always made a decent team."

"Still do." He leaned over in his saddle, propped his forearm against the horn, and plucked the sunflower. He handed it to her, eyes intent upon her face. "Can't see sunflowers anymore without thinkin' of you."

Warmth climbed her neck and cheeks as she took it from him. Brushing the petals against her lips, a laugh slipped out. "I was so infatuated with you when I was a child. I'm surprised you allowed me around at all."

The expression wiped from Junior's face like a rag across a blackboard. "What?"

"Oh, yes. I was drowning in puppy love." She'd sworn she would take her secret to her grave, but he had been acting wholly irregular since their journey began. It was only sensible he'd skewed her thoughts to the point she would act in kind.

"I didn't know—"

"For heaven's sake," Isa burst out, flicking her petal at him. It drifted harmlessly onto Champion's coarse mane. "I followed you everywhere. No matter how you teased me, you could do no wrong. Not to mention, you look the way you do."

"I look—"

"And I was a child," Isa finished with gusto. It was liberating, telling him. A release. It lanced wounds that had swollen tight and painful. Now that it was out there in the world, her biggest secret seemed so small. So insignificant. It had lost its power in the course of a few sentences, and now she was free. "Of course I was besotted with you. And now that I'm an adult, I know exactly what to expect when it comes to love."

The way Junior sat on his horse gave her the impression she had aimed a double-barrel shotgun between his eyes without warning. It was as diverting as it was vexing. He seemed to gather himself up, straightening from his slouch. "What do you mean, 'You know what to expect'?" His question was cautious, as though he was unsure he wanted to know.

"I have a theory," Isa said, running her flower over the apple of her cheek. "Well, an analogy, really. Being in love is like being shipwrecked on an island. The object of your affection is the island, and how they reciprocate your love is the level of hospitability your surroundings are. Some islands are beautiful but barren of all sustenance."

"Is this barren island supposed to be me?" Tawny brows settled dangerously low over his eyes.

She laughed. "Hush and listen. Some islands are heaven on earth, but you break your back digging irrigation. You die of thirst catching water, starve for lack of nourishment, and only bushels of money from shipments could keep you alive. And some islands don't look promising at first, but there are trees loaded with fruit, hidden waterfalls of fresh water, and treasures at every turn."

"I'd rather put the work into the barren island. You can plant fruit trees there. Dig a well."

Her mouth curved in a secret smile, and she hid it behind her sunflower. "People make islands habitable all the time."

"Yeah. It doesn't have to stay empty. It just needs a good farmer."

Isa's smile faded. "I learned not to allow myself to be ship-wrecked on a barren island. If I fall in love with someone, they need to sustain me. Not kill me. They need to love me first."

He cleared his throat. "You said you don't want to marry."

"I don't."

"But you're talkin' about love."

A carriage turned the corner in a bustle of rattling wheels and giggles. A courting couple waved merrily as they passed. Isa and Junior nodded back. Isa grabbed Mirage's reins and nudged the mare toward the road. Junior reluctantly followed behind.

"I'm not saying I'll never marry, just that I'd prefer not to. Better women than me have eaten their words over stronger convictions. I'm saying that *if* I marry, it will be to a man deeply in love with me." She considered this for a moment. "More in love with me than I am with him would be preferable. I'd like someone to have powerful feelings for *me*, for once."

Junior said nothing, but she paid little attention to his typical capricious brooding. She was busily basking in the relief born of confession.

Glancing back at him, she called, "Race you to the hotel!"

Mirage's heels threw enormous clods of red clay at the golden-haired man.

Junior didn't move an inch.

Chapter Fifteen

D ogwood Hotel was an immense two-story building that stood familiar and proud on Main Street. The hotel had been the first in the town. It withstood The War, a fire in '79, and near-bankruptcy. It was one of the many focal points in downtown Dogwood, with white clapboard siding, black shutters, and flower boxes. The front porch invited strangers to sit a while on one of the many wooden rocking chairs. The hotel diner's expansive window advertised home-cooked meals in painted calligraphy.

Mouthwatering aromas floated from the building to the street, and Isa's stomach growled loud enough to make Mirage's ears twitch backward. Isa and Junior hitched their horses and mule at the water trough directly below the porch's white railings and hungrily strode up the worn stairs. Several people, mostly old-timers in rockers sipping cups of coffee, bid "afternoon" to the pair as they passed.

Junior held the screen door open for Isa, but she was simply too hungry to comment on this unusual behavior. Telling him of her teenage puppy love had been undoubtedly a mistake, but she could fret about it later. For now, she wanted something hot and fried, a cool drink that wasn't stale canteen water, and familiar faces that weren't Junior's. The familiar scent of lemon wood polish and Minnie's cooking lightened Isa's heart. She hadn't been home since January, as her job and gambling with David had taken up much of her time; she'd had a trip to fund, after all. She hadn't accounted for how much she'd miss the little town.

Behind the concierge desk's glossy countertop, a tall, middle-aged man looked up. The owner, Mr. Ricci, was missing his left arm below the elbow, and his suit was elegantly tailored to fit. He blinked twice at her through spectacles, then his face became animated. Delighted.

"Miss Isa!" Mr. Ricci was around the desk, enfolding her in a familial embrace, before she could respond. Over his shoulder, Isa took in the crown moldings, paintings, and a grand guest staircase before he pulled away.

"It's wonderful to see you, Mr. Ricci."

Junior had halted so close behind her that the hem of her split skirt brushed his boots.

"And young Mr. Stone is with you!" Mr. Ricci cried, abandoning Isa to pump Junior's hand in a pleased handshake.

They made small talk about their journey and how long they'd be home until Mr. Ricci noticed his guest's repetitive glances at the diner. "You must be famished. Go! Get some food in you. Minnie will be tickled you're here."

Relieved, Isa thanked him and turned to do exactly that, then promptly bumped into Junior. Why was he hovering so closely? She had to edge around him to get to the diner.

In the dining room, the space was unchanged except the gingham tablecloths were burnt orange and white instead of blue and white, and the little vases were adorned with dried flowers and fluffy cattails as opposed to spring daisies. The lunch rush had cleared, and Junior chose a table by the open front window while a waitress bussed half a dozen others. Peering through the window screen, Isa smiled at the way her sunflower stuck out of the top of Mirage's halter, giving the horse a winsome appearance. Several bystanders had stopped strolling to look at the Arabian. Junior pulled Isa's chair out for her, and she peered at him as if he'd misplaced his sanity. Once seated across the little square table from her, Junior pulled his buckskin Stetson from his matted yellow crown. He tousled his hair with rough fingers, and the ropey blue veins mapping the back of his hands distracted her. Isa tried to affect boredom, but it was hard when a polite changeling had possessed her normally boorish friend. She doffed her own hat and hung it on the back of her chair.

The waitress momentarily overlooked the dirty dishes on the tables to take their orders. When she disappeared through the swinging door, Isa could hear the busy activity in the kitchen. Through the noise of clattering dishes, frying meat, and scraping pans, the cook's loud, sure orders to the other kitchen workers made Isa smile.

Minnie.

Reading her expression, Junior remarked, "Minnie is gonna tan our hide if we don't tell her we're here."

"If we tell her now, she'll come out and visit, and I don't want anyone else cooking our food," Isa reasoned. Minnie was the best cook in the whole town. Even the mayor ate supper here every Saturday night with his family.

Junior raised his hands as if to say, "Don't say I didn't warn you."

A woman boomed a greeting to Mr. Ricci at the front desk, clomping loudly through the foyer toward the kitchen's side entrance. They could hear her chatting with the kitchen women through the walls. Junior and Isa shared a grin. When the boisterous, statuesque woman made to walk through the foyer and exit the hotel moments later, Junior twisted in his chair and propped an elbow on its backrest.

"You gonna just walk out without saying hello, Mrs. Hobb?" he called.

The woman, taller even than Isa, stopped in her tracks. The linen napkin over her covered plate fluttered. Slack-jawed, Mrs. Hobb looked at them through the doorway, then stomped into the diner.

"Well, I'll be dipped," she barked, setting her plate down to pull them to their feet in back-cracking hugs. "When did you two tumbleweeds roll in?"

"Just now," Junior grunted through the surprising force of Mrs. Hobb's embrace.

"And you came right in here without tellin' anyone?" she huffed, settling on a chair at their table.

"We're not fit company until we eat," Isa explained.

"I 'spect not." Mrs. Hobb's belly moved up and down with her laughter. She was a Viking-sized, jolly woman who owned the general store next door with her husband. Her laugh was as renowned as the skin tags and moles on her face, though no one dared mention those; it didn't do to get on Mrs. Hobb's bad side. Many a recalcitrant man had been thrown out on their backsides for not paying credit owed.

They made small talk and caught up, and when the waitress returned with Isa and Junior's cups of chilled lemonade, Mrs. Hobb patted the slim woman with enough force to rattle her teeth. "Doris, tell Minnie she's got surprise guests. And get me some coffee while you're at it. You know what, bring some of that buttermilk pie, too."

Once the disgruntled Doris disappeared through the swinging door again, Mrs. Hobb pulled her napkin from her plate and updated them on the slowing business of her general store. "Dadblamed depression," she muttered through a mouthful of corned beef.

Minnie glided through the kitchen door with two full plates of food, her smile broad and white against an ageless face. Her curly gray hair was in a tight knot at her nape, her forehead and collarbones shining with perspiration from the cookstove.

"Look at what we have here," she whooped, flourishing the plates in front of Isa and Junior. For the third time, they exchanged greetings. Minnie squeezed into the fourth chair while Junior and Isa dug into their meal, and she and Mrs. Hobb filled the silence with news of Poppy's new baby.

"Poppy had her baby?" Isa asked, covering her mouth with a hand. "I missed it?"

"Happened just a couple days ago, didn't it?" Minnie asked Mrs. Hobb, who was noisily scraping her plate. "Ain't never seen Mr. Sol so proud. Came in to tell us how Ms. Poppy did—she's right as rain, don't you worry none."

Mrs. Hobb wiped the faint mustache above her mouth, chuckling. "He calls her Carrot Top. I plumb forgot her real name. Never seen a man so over the moon to have three girls in a row."

"That's because Sol is the only man to realize that females are the superior of the two sexes," Isa said casually, then huffed in affront when Junior reached over to stab the yeast roll off her plate.

"Sol was dropped on his head as a baby," Junior said through his purloined bite of roll.

"You're foul," Isa sniped, brandishing the dull-tipped knife beside her plate. "Touch my food again, and I'll cut a piece of you off."

Minnie and Mrs. Hobb shared an amused look.

"Long as it's not my favorite piece," Junior shot, then ducked, laughing, as three different things were thrown at him.

"Mr. Stone!" Minnie gasped, wide, coffee-brown eyes showing yellowish sclera all around.

"I oughta let you have a bite of soap, you little chucklehead," boomed Mrs. Hobb.

In between cleaning their plates, Junior and Isa told the story of Mirage and the horse thieves. Minnie gasped several satisfying times; she considered thievery a most mortal sin. Isa noted how carefully he evaded any mention of the Texas Rangers.

"You two goin' to the Fall Dance this weekend?" Mrs. Hobb asked, mouth full of the warm buttermilk pie Doris had begrudgingly retrieved. Dogwood's Fall Dance was an annual event held during the last weekend of October. God-fearing people were mindful not to label it a "Halloween Dance," but families brought their children to bob for apples, play the test of the three bowls, and compete in apple-paring and storytelling contests hoping to win prizes.

"I forgot about the dance," Isa said, pushing her plate away. "I didn't have room in my bags for a dress."

"Pshaw, Franny can fix one up for you," Mrs. Hobb said.

"I can take you if you need a dance partner," Junior offered.

"You think I can't find someone?" Isa narrowed her eyes at him. What did he think she was, a charity case? Of all the nerve!

Mrs. Hobb opened her mouth, but Minnie stepped on her foot under the table and shook her head. She was scrutinizing Junior's face.

"No one that knows you."

Isa didn't like the little smirk on his mouth and dearly wanted to smack it off. "I don't think I'll have you, thank you very much. I'll attend the dance by myself."

"Fine." The smile was gone from Junior's sensual lips. "We can just ride together and go our separate ways when we get there."

"I've ridden with you enough for my taste." Isa sniffed.

"Who said you had a choice?"

She balled her fists and held them up. "These say so."

Junior's smile returned, his teeth strong and white against his trail tan. "Big words from such a little person."

"I am *not* little."

Minnie and Mrs. Hobb shared another look, and Isa grew self-conscious. Junior's mouth opened to say something else, but her expression stopped him.

"Minnie, do you think I can get a bath before I go see Sol?" Isa asked. "I feel like I'm wearing half of Texas on my clothes."

"'Course!" Minnie hopped out of her chair.

Frowning pensively, Mrs. Hobb stood as well, her chair screaming on the hardwood. "Well, I'd best get back. Franny's been pesterin' me to put her new dress in the window."

"Mrs. Hobb," Isa said quickly. "Would you need any help at the store? I'll be home for the holidays."

Mrs. Hobb's eyebrows rose in pleasure. "Well, sure enough, honey, you come on by and do inventory any time. I hate that business more'n anything. Won't be able to pay much—the Panic, you understand."

Isa waved that away. "I'll just be happy to have something to keep me busy." One day, the Panic of 1893 would be a distant dream.

Mrs. Hobb clapped Junior's back, said her goodbyes, and tramped her way outside. Seconds later, she waved at them through the window, headed in the direction of her store. Isa followed behind Minnie. As she passed Junior, she caught his eyes on the curve of her breasts. Isa kicked his boot for his impudence and pretended his low chuckle didn't reach somewhere deep inside, just below her belly.

MINNIE RETURNED TO the kitchen half an hour later, worrying her apron knot. She'd left Isa to her own devices but couldn't shake off a deep unease. At the dinner table, Mrs. Hobb had shared a look with Minnie as though she'd also sensed the underlying sexual tension between the young man and woman. Minnie hadn't liked that tension one bit, no siree. Those two were good as family. Junior and Isa used to run through Dogwood Hotel no better than a couple of misbehaved children, always picking at each other to see who could rile the other up the most. Minnie looked at them now as adults and saw pure trouble. She had seen it coming; two attractive young folks with hot heads and passions right at the surface.

The kitchen women must have seen the disapproval written on the head cook's face and scurried to their duties, but it wasn't their work Minnie objected to. It was that young fool in the dining room who couldn't keep his eyes off Sol William's little sister.

It was plain as the nose on Junior's face that he was keeping some events of his last visit home a secret from Isa, and when that girl found out, it was going to spell trouble. Minnie was watching two sticks of dynamite, each fuse racing to see which could blow the fastest. She feared there wouldn't be enough pieces left to clean up when they exploded.

Chapter Sixteen

They were on another dirt road with a grassy center stripe when Isa stopped Mirage. Sol's house was just out of view. To their right, an immense grassy pasture of Hereford cattle ran parallel to her brother's property. Junior reined in beside her, evening sunlight gleaming off his clean-shaven jaw. He'd paid a visit to the barber shop in Dogwood while she used the hotel's only bath, and the urge to kiss him had persisted since he'd returned to the hotel to collect her. She had posted a letter to Miss Pickney, and they'd made their way to her brother's house.

Several hugely pregnant cows lifted curious heads to watch them on the other side of the fence.

Junior and Isa's journey together was over.

"Come here. I want to do something," she said, nudging her horse closer to Champion. Mirage's black ears slung temperamentally back.

"Why?"

"Just do it." Impatiently, Isa leaned closer, her saddle creaking.

His mouth turned sweetly up as he did her bidding, and he leaned to meet her between their two uncomfortably close horses. "What happens on the trail, stays on the trail?" he asked, his voice deep. Compelling.

Isa pulled her hat off and grabbed him by the jaw. In response, he cupped the back of her neck. Their lips met in a kiss that was at once hot and deep, as if he'd been waiting all day for the opportunity. His tongue thrust, a slow penetration, an even slower withdrawal. Dizzily, Isa wondered how she could begin a kiss just for him to effortlessly steal control away.

She pulled away, but Junior's hand on her neck prevented her from going far. His fingers flexed, massaging the delicate skin of her nape. The confident, languid touch spread all the way to her toes. The deep blue of his eyes burned. They asked: *why?*

"In the event we don't get another chance," she explained, lips damp, eyes glazed.

"In that case..." He brought her in for another toe-curling kiss.

SOL CAUGHT SIGHT of their horses riding in five minutes later, and he hollered so loudly that every horse, mule, and bovine came to attention. An old hound dog on the front porch clambered to his feet, baying at the intruders.

"Legs, is that you?" Sol shouted, abandoning the wagon wheel he'd been repairing. Isa's oldest brother was tall and whipcord lean with the broadest, most genuine smile in the whole world.

Her heart lifted, and she called, "Did you miss me?"

"Is water wet?" Sol started her way, paused, and peeked beneath the wagon bed. "Come out and say hello to your auntie."

Three heads poked out from beneath the buckboard: a dark-haired boy and two towheaded girls. The older children scurried out and ran toward Isa on long, skinny legs, a trait typical of Williams descent. The youngest, an ash-blonde toddler in a pinafore, lifted her hands and whined plaintively. Sol lifted her up high and settled her on his shoulders. Fatherhood suited Sol. He loved children with a fierceness they could sense. They flocked around him, begging for attention and the candy in his pockets.

"I'll take your satanic steed." Junior held a hand out for Mirage's reins.

"Thank you." Hoping her lips weren't as swollen as they felt, Isa handed them over and dismounted. She met her niece and nephew halfway across the yard. Sol jogged, the little one on his shoulders bouncing comically. The hound dog, Hog, trotted behind, his long, thin tail wagging.

"Timothy, Ally, how you two have grown!" Isa gasped, gathering the children in for a hug. "How old are you now?"

"Sixth!" Timothy lisped while Ally chirped, "Five!" Her blue eyes were the same shade as her mother's.

"Why, I hardly recognize you." Isa widened her eyes dramatically. "You were only knee-high to a grasshopper the last time I saw you. And now you're both a whole foot taller."

Sol pulled Isa up from her crouch and dragged her in for a hug. In her ear, he rasped, "Lord, where have you been? I got on my horse a few different times to see if you and dunderhead had gotten lost. Poppy had to stop me."

"Dunderhead?" Junior parroted. He led their horses and Red to the trough beside the well pump.

Isa squirmed out of Sol's crushing hug, discomfited by climbing guilt. "Our horses were stolen—"

"What?" Sol gaped at her.

"—and we had to waste a day getting them back because Navasota's law enforcement is as useless as tits on a boar."

"What are tit-th?" Timothy asked curiously from hip level.

Sol groaned. "You haven't been home two minutes, and already I'll be in trouble with the missus."

Isa grimaced and tugged on her niece's dirty bare foot, which had migrated over Sol's chest toward her face. "Hello, Autumn. You were just a baby when I last saw you." Perched like a canary on her daddy's shoulder, Autumn pulled her foot away shyly. Isa glanced toward the house. "How is Poppy? And the new baby? I'd like to meet her."

Washed in a paternal glow, Sol clapped Junior on the back with a beatific expression on his face and led them up front porch steps lined with carved pumpkins. They walked into the little Folk Victorian home with its cozy parlor and whimsical details while Sol rhapsodized how Poppy had delivered the newest edition without any trouble.

"The midwife got here in the nick of time," he said, pulling Autumn from his shoulders so she didn't bump her head on a doorway.

Poppy, small in stature with cinnamon hair and kind blue eyes, was in her back sewing room. A baby slept in a basket at her feet.

Sol poked his head in and said in a low, excited voice, "Look what the cat dragged in."

Fuller of face and figure from recent pregnancy, Poppy looked up from her mending. Shock drained her cheeks of color as she stood. "Isa, you're home! Sol, I told you she'd be here any day now. He's been pacing the yard since receiving Miss Pickney's wire."

Enduring another tight embrace, Isa winced over Poppy's shoulder. "I'm sorry for worrying you. Truly."

Behind them, Junior gave an account of the events of the past week, and Poppy mirrored Minnie's earlier gasps and little murmurs of disbelief. Meanwhile, Isa crouched over the basket. Something fuzzy and warm grew around her heart at the picture the newborn made in her cushion of blankets. Tiny rosebud lips made sucking motions. Silky hair glowed orange in the light from the little window.

Another perfect niece to love.

"She's beautiful, Poppy," Isa whispered, running the pad of her thumb from the bridge of her niece's upturned nose to the thatch of downy hair. The soft spot on the baby's head was like velvet; the tiny skull bones wouldn't fuse together until well after childbirth. Isa marveled at the phenomenon of the human body. She had never smelled anything better than a baby, not even Junior when he was freshly shaved.

"We named her Agatha," Poppy said.

"Agatha, how distinguished." As though summoned awake, Agatha scrunched her face and stirred, swiping her fist back and forth across a rooting mouth. Isa chuckled. "Looks like it's suppertime."

"It's always suppertime for this one," Poppy said wryly, crossing the room to bend and pick Agatha up. "She has her daddy's appetite."

"Her auntie's, too," Junior drawled, grinning at the way the babe's back arched in an enormous stretch. "Izzy was chewing on something the whole way here."

"And you smoked like a chimney." Isa childishly stuck her tongue out from behind Poppy's back. Autumn, perched on her daddy's hip, giggled.

ISA'S EYELIDS DROOPED after a supper that Sol had rustled up while Poppy fed the baby. She wondered if Junior was as dog-tired as she was. A glance at the pallet in the parlor revealed his stockinged feet sticking out of one end of the privacy screen he lay behind. Isa smiled the whole way upstairs. She had her own room, one that Poppy insisted they keep empty for Isa despite their growing family. Sol had built it with his sister in mind when she was sixteen, and its built-in bookshelves and lead casement window never failed to make her sigh with pleasure. Her sister-in-law's thoughtfulness was why Isa was closer to her than any of her blood sisters.

Poppy and her baby were curled on Isa's blue patterned Crazy Quilt when Isa opened her door, but upon seeing the younger woman's jaw-cracking yawn, the new mother made to slide off the bed. "I'll go so you can get some sleep."

"No, no." Isa rushed to the bed and curved a protective arm around Agatha's little body. "Stay a while. I haven't seen you in almost a year."

"If you insist." Poppy smiled. Faint blue crescents bruised her eyes, offset by the small lines creasing the corner of her eyes and mouth; being married to a man like Sol meant lots and lots of laughter.

"She is going to despise the nickname Sol gave her," Isa mused, stroking her niece's fiery fuzz. "Carrot Top. School children will tease her mercilessly."

"Perhaps. Did you dislike being called Legs?"

Isa sighed. "I've grown accustomed to it. I remember thinking it was a horse's name and would strike anyone who called me thus, but Sol was inexorable."

"That's an excellent word for him."

"It's how he got you to marry him."

Poppy laughed, and the baby jolted. "Your brother can be very stubborn and persuasive."

"When did you finally give in?" Isa asked seriously. Poppy had come to Dogwood for a summer visit, and Sol had pursued the young, widowed seamstress with dogged tenacity.

Kissing Agatha's crown, Poppy frowned thoughtfully. "I suppose I stopped resisting once I realized what a good person he is. Sol never lied or played me false; he was always who he claimed to be. He acted kind because he *was* kind. And he said he loved me because he *did* love me. The way he treats people... he's like an angel in disguise. It still shocks me that he's real." A film of tears magnified Poppy's eyes, and she wiped them away with her cuff, chuckling. "This happens every time I have a baby. I spring leaks."

Isa shuddered at the notion of being out of control of one's emotions. "He's always been that way. Cared for other's happiness. Even when I was little, he made time for me and made me feel special."

"Did you know that he rides to Lufkin every year?"

Isa stiffened. "To see Kat?"

"Yes." Poppy winced guiltily. "I'm not supposed to say anything. He gives your sister a gift and well wishes from the family. I think it's wonderful."

"I wasn't aware she was still alive." Isa pensively rubbed the tiny foot in her hand. "Does she ask after her children?"

Poppy hesitated. "She didn't used to. But, about three years ago, Sol said she started acting curious about Timothy."

"Not the others?" Isa and Sol's parents were currently raising Katherine's three other children.

"I cannot be sure."

"Ah." Isa sensed her friend's cautious diplomacy. Poppy's inherent mansuetude wouldn't permit cruelty, which meant Katherine never asked about the others. How disappointing.

"She asks about you, as well," Poppy added, still with that hesitation.

"Oh?" No one as Machiavellian as Katherine would ask about an estranged family member without reason.

"Sol tells her of all your accomplishments. How you went to college, that you're adept in mathematics…that you're beautiful."

Isa snorted and waved the latter away. *Beautiful.* What a lark!

Surprising Isa further, Poppy nudged her shoulder. "Of course you're beautiful. He even told Kat that you were more beautiful than she!"

Isa gawked. "What a thing to say to a woman whose beauty is the centerpiece of her existence!" *Oh, Sol.*

"She had asked." Poppy shrugged. "Kat had asked him not about your studies but if you had ended up pretty. So, he set her straight. You haven't grown up pretty—you have grown up beautiful."

Although secretly touched, Isa nonetheless scoffed, "Looks never last. It's your brain that makes you interesting."

The baby chose that moment to break wind, which made the two women break into furious giggles. Then, almost as if she were afraid to, Poppy asked, "Were you afraid when those men stole your horses that night?"

Isa settled to her back, thinking. "I didn't know what was happening at first. It was so dark, and they were quiet. Junior woke up before me and pulled his pistol. He told me to stay down, but I don't recall feeling worried." She stopped talking for fear that Poppy would hear how besotted she was.

"Hm."

"He's different," Isa blurted. "Have you noticed?"

"Yes, he's far happier. Almost the way he used to be." Poppy sounded genuinely glad at the fact.

"What?" Brows snapping together, Isa rolled on her side to see if Poppy was exaggerating. "He's moody as a wounded bear half the time. He certainly isn't half as fun as he used to be." She knew why, but did anyone else?

"On the contrary, today is the most I've seen him laugh since he joined the Texas Rangers."

Isa pondered this. She wished to confide in Poppy what she'd discovered about Junior, but it wasn't her secret to tell. Instead, she said quietly, "He was so different when he came to collect me at Miss Pickney's. Colder. I've badgered his old self out of him on occasion since then, but even so, I wonder what changed in him. I thought it was me."

A gentle hand settled on Isa's shoulder. "It wasn't you. He's come home while you were at college, and Sol and I noticed a change even then. Ben is especially worried. Sometimes, he and Sol will go out on the range and talk for hours, fretting."

Isa tried to suppress the relief she felt. "Did Junior ever tell Ben what could be wrong?"

"I don't believe so. Sol supposes it's just the rigors of upholding the law."

Ben would have plenty to say about the healed bullet wound in Junior's side and the hemialgia he occasionally experienced. Everyone knew Ben worried as if he were Junior's father instead of his brother. Isa squirmed in discomfort, knowing about Junior's dishonorable discharge. Why had Junior told her and not Ben?

"I think the difference in him now"—Poppy gathered up a fussing Agatha and rose from the bed—"is that you're home. I think that makes him happy."

They bid goodnight, and Isa was left alone in her room, wide awake and more confused than before.

"ISADORA, WHY HAVEN'T you married yet?"

Mrs. Williams and Isa wiped down jars of canned pears from their water bath. No one who looked at the two women would suspect that they were related. One was short, squat, and coarse-faced, and the other was tall, lean, and had long, fair hair—a stark contrast to the other's graying updo.

"And why would I ever wish to marry?" Isa asked evenly, polishing a lid with unnecessary force. The comfort of being in her small, run-down childhood home soured into something cagier. Wariness grew unbidden. She dearly wished Sol had joined her at their parent's sharecropper farm. Even Junior's irritating presence was preferable to being alone with her mother. Isa pondered how strange it was being away from Junior after several days of uninterrupted togetherness. He'd left Sol's house first thing that morning to visit his brother, and it felt...odd.

A noise Isa recognized better than her own name snorted from her mother's hooked nose. "I knew you was stubborn, but to tell your suitors 'no' a dozen separate times? I don't know what goes on in that head o' yours, child. It's best to accept one of those offers afore that bloom of youth is gone."

"Why does everyone keep expanding upon the number of men who have asked my hand in marriage?" Isa mused aloud.

Mrs. Williams wasn't listening. "Bein' an old maid is fine and good if you're an ugly woman, but you're not. You got lots to offer a man."

"Because of my *face*?" The object in question scrunched as though it had sucked on a lemon. Isa popped her mother's broad backside with her polishing towel. The older woman yelped and made a threatening lunge for the broom, but Isa was already dancing away. "What does any man have to offer *me*?"

"I knew it would come to that," Mrs. Williams moaned. "Can't say as I'm surprised you'd need some man to invent the wheel before you'd consider him."

Amused, Isa tucked several jars between arm and bosom and strode to the dry larder, her mother clucking for her to be careful. "Maybe I'll choose a man the way men choose women. A suitor with no brains, just a pretty face. If I'm lucky, he'll be rich as well."

From across the kitchen's worn, sagging floor, Mrs. Williams muttered, "Money ain't everything." Then, "If I didn't know better, I'd say you just described that young rascal, John Junior."

Isa almost dropped a jar. Luckily, the dark room hid her fumbling. "Him? Ha! He'd make a terrible husband."

Mrs. Williams cackled. "And you think you're such a fine catch? Half the time, you can't decide if you're a man or a woman. Goin' to college, ridin' astride, scrappin' in the dirt with your cousins and brothers. 'Sides. That one's already taken. You'd better pray the Stones have another brother holed up somewhere."

"What do you mean, 'That one's already taken'?"

The woman was truly disturbed to mistake the eldest Stone brother for the youngest. Isa's mother acted more and more like Granny every year, Lord rest her soul. But Mrs. Williams had turned a deaf ear. Her skirt hem swayed as she bent to dig into the cluttered cupboard, grousing and banging pots and pans.

"Ma!" Isa shouted from the larder's doorway. "Junior isn't 'taken.' You know better than to spread untruths." Gossip was the better word for it, but her mother pretended she never partook in such an unchristian pastime.

"Sure is!" Mrs. William's voice echoed in the cabinet, and her grunt was loud when she straightened. "Since his visit this summer, accordin' to Poppy. His ma's been crowin' to everyone about Miss Kristy something-or-other. Hear she's a pretty little thing, too. Don't think our Poppy approves of her."

Isa's mother continued in this vein until all the jars were in neat rows in the dry larder and cupboards. Meanwhile, Isa worked soundlessly. It felt like she'd been knocked upside the head with a frying pan, dumb to everything but the sound of her mother's droning voice. By the time her pa and cousins came in from planting greens and root vegetables in the field, Isa knew everything about Junior's fiancée, from the many bows she wore on her dresses, to the frequency of her church outings with Mrs. Loretta Stone. Junior's mother had taken one look at the girl's southern belle pedigree and was smitten, pulling her beneath the wing of the Stone name. As per the grapevine, Junior was never home long enough to properly court his fiancée, so the wedding had no set date.

And Poppy knew.

Why had her sister-in-law not said anything? They had talked about Junior at length last night. It would have been a perfect opening for this type of juicy information. And Lucy, with all her letters. Why hadn't her friend written of this news in all their weeks of correspondence?

Outwardly, Isa was cool as a cucumber. She teased her cousins playfully when they entered the kitchen, laughed at her father's favorite jokes, and caught up with the family until the sun began to sink lower in the sky. When it was time to leave, she hugged her tall, skinny pa's neck and pecked her mother's cheek. A smile was carved as deeply into Isa's face as one of the jack-o'-lanterns on Sol's porch.

The broad smile slid off like butter in a hot pan during the ride back to her brother's house.

Junior had made no mention of a fiancée during their week-long journey home. He had kissed her. Touched her. Held her. Even told her his deepest secret whilst acting every part the available bachelor.

Yes, but he'll never be available for you, will he?

Mirage's ears twitched back as if sensing her rider's tumultuous mood.

God.

Why was history repeating itself? Hadn't Isa sworn to never feel so downtrodden and lovesick again? There were rocks in her belly, so she reined in and dismounted. She strode to the expansive pasture of Hereford cattle, clenching her stomach with her hands the whole way. It was close to the site of that last forbidden kiss. Sickened by the reminder, Isa hitched the black Arabian's reins to a fencepost and tried to control her breathing. Fingers digging hard into her stays, Isa paced the fence line.

"Pull yourself together, Williams," she said through spasms from belly to chest. "You have endured it before. You can do so again."

She would speak sense into existence.

After a minute, Isa's heart began to calm. After five, her breathing evened. Deepened. *There we are,* she told herself, relieved that she wouldn't have an apoplexy right there on the road. Her science professor—the one who had so admired her brain—had recently written to her about the newfound concept of muscle memory, a theory of how the brain retrieves and stores information. With repetition and continued practice, a muscular movement will become more efficient. Much like aiming and shooting at a target. Or riding a horse. Could falling out of love with Junior become easier the second time around? An evoked muscle memory? At sixteen, it had been nearly impossible.

One simple truth had forced the agonizing feelings into submission.

"Loving him means wanting the best for him," she whispered aloud. "Even when he's a damned, cowardly *liar.*"

Isa stood beside the field for endless minutes, thinking. Beneath her manufactured strength was a simmering rage. She tamped it cruelly down.

Had he promised himself to her?

No.

Had he told a lie?

A lie by omission is still a lie.

And Poppy had known. That hurt nearly as much as Junior's deceit. Isa's brain whirred, straining to make sense of these unnervingly strong emotions. If she wasn't in love with him, she wouldn't feel so betrayed. But she wasn't in love with him. Was she?

There was no reprieve from these looping, miring thoughts. There were no answers. Not even when the birdsong stopped and the crickets began.

Chapter Seventeen

A far calmer Isa trotted up Sol's driveway just as the hot-pink sun set over the Hereford pasture, washing everything in a romantic glow. Sol and Poppy's whimsical white house was cast in a rose hue, and Isa's stomach dropped at seeing another wagon parked beside Sol's in the yard.

Junior had returned with his brother's family in tow.

Two dining tables stood end to end between the tree and the cozy front porch. The children played on the rope swing while the men hung lanterns on hooks along porch eaves. A dark-haired woman busily set the table. Ben, Junior's older brother, surreptitiously patted the brunette woman's bottom as she walked by. She glanced back at him playfully, mouthing something. *Lucy.* Junior's sister-in-law was lovely, inside and out.

She was also observant. Isa's teeth clenched together. If something was wrong, Lucy would be the first to notice and drag Isa into a room to spill her secrets.

Hog loped to her, jowls flapping, tail wagging. Poppy saw this and waved from her rocking chair in a porch corner, baby Agatha at her breast.

Isa considered rebuffing the greeting. Instead, she raised a hand, her features smooth and posture relaxed. The decision not to confront her brother's wife was sound. Poppy had just given birth and was gracious and caring, and any withholding of information was most assuredly made with good intentions.

Ben and Lucy's three boys, aged seven to eleven, walked cautiously toward Mirage with their mouths agape. Living on a ranch where their father bred quarter horses, they knew a quality horse when they saw one. Seeing the awe in their eyes made an honest smile spread across her face.

"You may want to stay back," she warned them, dismounting. "I'm not entirely certain how she feels about children."

"I can get a sugar cube from Aunt Poppy's kitchen," offered the middle boy, Samuel. He had riotous brown curls and mischievous hazel eyes.

"Here. Try these." Isa reached into her saddlebag and brought out a handful of sweetened grain compacted into little biscuits. "You know how to hold your hand?"

Samuel rolled his eyes and took the biscuit without deigning to comment.

The oldest boy, Matthew, said solemnly, "Yes, ma'am." He was his father's mirror image with heavily lashed blue eyes and hair black as a raven's wing.

"And you?" Isa asked the youngest boy sternly.

"Yes'm." Lucy's last child had a shock of nearly white hair and vivid cerulean eyes. He was always smiling, even when he got into trouble. Which was often. Isa wondered if Junior had been like little Jack as a boy.

"Wonderful." She dropped a biscuit into Jack's hand, which remained properly flat and still.

Mirage took the treats with gentle, nibbling lips, her ears perked forward and her stance friendly. When she licked each hand for crumbs, the boys laughed. At the swing, Timothy and Ally shouted and began running in their direction.

"Don't run at horses, you'll scare 'em that way," Samuel shot over his shoulder.

"I'll get 'em," Matthew said calmly. He rounded up the two excited children and held their hands. Then he showed them how to hold the treats so they didn't get their fingers bitten. Ally looked scared at that and decided not to feed the horse after all. Isa chuckled and picked her up. The child was light as a feather.

"Here, you can sit on her." Glancing at the other children, Isa asked, "Would you like to accompany me and put Mirage up for the night? I'll show you the best places to scratch her."

Together, the five of them walked beside the horse, chattering and telling stories, with little Ally perched proudly up top. Isa was grateful for this disruption from her twisting, calamitous thoughts. She took her time showing the children the steps to get Mirage bedded down for the night. By the time the spoiled horse was curried, fed, and watered, the little lean-to stable was filled with eerie, opaque shadows. Timothy and Ally clung to Isa's riding skirts while Samuel told spooky stories.

"Samuel, if you keep on this way, the younger children will never go to sleep," Isa chastised, dismayed that, as the only adult around, she had to take on the uncomfortable responsibility of reprimanding another person's child. Typically, it was she who got into trouble for instigating mischief with the cousins.

"I ain't scared," Timothy said. That bravado was immediately snuffed when a shadow moved in the corner of an empty stable.

Narrowing her eyes, Isa pushed the children behind her and walked forward. It could just be a barn cat stalking one of the rats that was after horse grain.

A hulking figure with a burlap sack for a head exploded out of the dark corner, and all the children screamed. Isa's throat closed up; she reflexively balled her fist and slugged one of the cutout eyeholes. Ally began to cry.

"Ow, shit!" cried a masculine voice, muffled by the burlap sack. "Why'd you do that?"

Junior!

"Because you deserved it!" Isa shouted, pushing his shoulders for good measure. He stumbled backward, holding his face and laughing. "Come, children. Let's tell your mothers what mean old Uncle Junior did to you." She plucked a sniffling Ally up and marched out of the stable.

"Aw, come on. I was just playin'!" Junior called after them, pulling the sack from his head to touch his left eye.

The other adults peered up at the hullabaloo in the well-lit front yard. Isa stopped the children halfway to their parents. With Ally still on her hip, Isa crouched to their level and whispered, "What do you say you and I get back at Uncle Junior?"

Five pairs of eyes gleamed, especially Samuel's and Jack's, and they all gathered in to listen to her plan.

SOL WAS SOON privy to the prank Isa and the children were cooking up, and he'd supplied a length of rope, and red and yellow paint. Sol was keeping Junior busy while Isa and the young ones huddled around the rope in the weak light of the kitchen window. Lucy and Poppy checked on them occasionally, smiling benignly at their secretiveness. Finally, the huddle broke, and the children skipped, giggling, to their positions.

Isa, gingerly holding the painted rope in her hands, scampered behind the outhouse. It was absent of any light, and her breath streamed from her mouth in white gusts from the dropping temperature. In the recesses of her mind, inflamed emotions threatened to rupture. Every cousin of anger and betrayal was a finger's breadth away from escaping. Part of her wished to give the emotions free rein. She'd drop the sticky rope, stomp over to Junior, call him a liar and a dozen other names, and disappear from Dogwood without another word.

A greater, more rational part of her knew such antics were melodramatic and beneath her. She'd be apart from her family for months—possibly a year—while she toured Europe. Why should one no-good, lying snake take time with family away from her?

"Yeah, I must've left it in the outhouse," came Sol's faint voice from the front of the house.

Isa straightened in readiness, holding her steaming breath in.

"Don't know why the hell you'd do that," Junior muttered from a yard away. Lantern light undulated across the grass, and his footsteps paused. "What are you youngsters up to?"

Ally giggled nervously. Isa bit her lip. Then Samuel saved the day. "We're playin' hide and seek."

"Well, you're not doin' a very good job standing out in the open like that," Junior snorted.

"It's Jack's turn. He runs slow as a turtle in mud." The lies slid so easily from Samuel's lips that Isa felt a stab of sympathy for his mother.

Junior's footsteps continued. Light illuminated the outhouse. Isa tucked her body even tighter along its back, the tacky rope dangling in her hands. As soon as the door shut behind Junior, Isa burst into action. Just off the path, she furtively laid the rope along the grass, manipulating it until it looked coiled and ready to strike. After shushing the children, who held their sides in silent laughter, Isa scurried back into position. Muttering could be heard in the outhouse—whatever fool's errand Sol had sent Junior on had proved to be fruitless.

When the outhouse door swung open, Isa jumped out and screamed, "Snake!"

Junior, who hadn't taken more than one step, saw the painted red and yellow rope and cursed. The lantern dropped, and everything was doused in darkness. The children screamed with laughter. It was common knowledge that both Stone men were deathly afraid of snakes, and a trickle of satisfaction soothed some hurting part in Isa.

"Let that be a lesson to you," she said in the darkness.

She turned on her heel toward the well pump, intending to wash her hands before her fingers were stained forevermore with paint. Two strong, vise-like arms wrapped around her.

"You're gonna pay for that," a voice growled in her ear, the humid warmth sending gooseflesh down her arms and spine.

"Get off," she grunted, attempting to flip Junior from her person. It only managed to bring him flush against her back. In the protection of darkness, he nuzzled her neck. Then he bit it gently and forced her to her knees. Her physical response to this was instantaneous and wholly unwelcome, and she gasped inaudibly with want and hate. In a last effort to keep her dignity, Isa screeched, "Children...get him!"

One child—likely Samuel—made a war cry and pounced onto Junior's back like he would a bucking bronco. Isa was soon lost in the bottom of the dogpile while Junior screamed with contrived shrillness, trying to protect his head and face. A fresh lantern brought visibility back, and Sol, Lucy, and the others guffawed nearby. Isa had just managed to wriggle her way from the bottom of the pile, breathing hard with the effort, when a broad hand grabbed her ankle. *Oh, no.* She twisted her head to find Junior's gleaming blue eyes and face screwed up with the effort of holding her between breaks in the writhing bodies around him.

"Get. Back. Here." With inexorable strength, he slowly dragged her to him.

Weakened from the absurdness of it, Isa gave in...and laughed.

LUCY FILLED AN enormous platter with fried deer meat while Isa vigorously mashed potatoes with red-stained hands. No amount of washing could get the blasted paint off. She stoically accepted the good-natured ribbing of being caught "red-handed."

"Careful, you'll make glue," Lucy teased from the wood stove.

Isa paused thoughtfully. "Does Poppy *have* glue?"

From the hallway, Sol called, "Do not give her glue, shug."

"I hid it away when she and Junior arrived," Poppy replied from the worktable. She cut thick squares of cornbread and placed them in a gingham-lined basket.

"That's a shame," Isa sighed, smacking the wooden masher on the side of the bowl. Wiping her hands on a borrowed apron, she leaned into the hallway to speak to Sol. To her consternation, her brother had disappeared, and Junior was walking in. Hiding her dismay at being face-to-face with him, she asked, "Why don't you make yourself useful and bring all this food to the table?"

Mussed and grass-stained from his romp outside, Junior looked up from wiping his boots on the rug. "What makes you think I'd do anything for you?"

"Do it for Lucy."

"What makes you think I'd do it for her?"

His eyes sparkled at her.

She wanted to poke them out.

"Hey," Lucy said from the stove.

"Then do it for Poppy," Isa said through her teeth.

"Well, why didn't you just say so?" Junior edged past her into the kitchen, tugging her braid as he went. She knocked his hand away, and he laughed from deep in his chest. Poppy and Lucy smiled secretly at each other, and Isa peeled her attention from his broad back, seething. Hating.

On a return trip for more food, he whispered in her ear, "Have you told your family your New Year's plans?"

She didn't act coy. "No. I haven't."

"Why not?"

"It's hard." Her words were clipped.

"You'll have to tell them at some point. Secrets aren't good in a family."

"You're one to talk," Isa snapped. When he turned wary eyes on her, reminiscent of a wounded puppy, she grabbed a pitcher of water and escaped through the hall.

Supper was a fun outdoor affair despite the chill; the children were bundled up at one end of the table, the adults in flannels at the other. Lucy, Sol, and Junior shouted to hear one another over the din of childish laughter. Even the laconic Ben cracked wide smiles, his gold tooth glinting. Isa had a hard time finding her appetite and pushed her corn cob around in its coagulating pool of butter, forcing her rigid facial muscles into smiles at the appropriate times. Across from her, Poppy glanced at Isa often but was thankfully distracted into cutting Autumn's meat into small bites.

Isa strictly ignored Junior, whose laughter tapered off the more he looked in her direction.

Stop looking at me! she wanted to shout but stifled the impulse. College had taught her that women who threw tantrums were viewed as hysterical. Something to be laughed at. A woman ruled by her emotions was not a human capable of sophisticated beliefs and opinions of her own.

She took a sip of her warm apple cider and fed Hog from beneath the table.

During a lull in the conversation, Lucy asked from Isa's immediate right, "Isa, are you attending the Fall Dance this Saturday?"

Isa caught Junior straightening in his seat from her periphery. "I suppose."

Undeterred by this lackluster answer, Lucy pushed forward. "Would you like to ride with us? We can escort you since Sol is staying home with Poppy and the new baby."

Junior set his cutlery down. "I'm taking her."

Isa's mouth moved before she could stop it. "And have me on one arm and your fiancée on the other? I think not."

Sol and Ben were in the middle of a conversation and didn't seem to have noticed the hush that fell over the table. Poppy and Lucy looked at each other again, driving Isa to distraction. They both *knew*. They had known, and not once had they notified Isa in any of the letters they'd sent. Feelings of betrayal grew and tripled in size, whetting the razor edge of Isa's tongue.

Junior's jaw had turned granite-hard. "What are you talking about?"

"I believe she's speaking of Kristy Anne," Lucy piped in, cutting into her fried deer steak.

"Or have you forgotten her?" Isa asked, stabbing a piece of meat and shoving it into her mouth. She rudely spoke around it. "You're probably not around enough to recall. I suppose she escaped your mind."

"Who?" Sol had finally noticed the dissension among the others.

Poppy, normally the peacemaker, said quietly, accusingly, "Kristy Anne. Junior's intended."

Ben shifted in his seat on the other side of Lucy. Isa set her chin on her hand, indicating an innocent interest in this turn of conversation.

"Hell, you're still walkin' out with that one? I thought she was just some skirt—er, *lady*—your ma shoved under your nose this summer." Sol winced apologetically at his wife.

"She is," Junior gritted out, staring holes into Isa's face.

Isa suppressed a derisive snort.

"And," he continued, "I haven't seen or talked to her since. She didn't take the hint to drop whatever intention she had with me. I don't plan on marrying."

"That's not what she and your mama are telling everyone who will listen," Lucy argued.

"I haven't been home to stop them, have I?" His tone grew steadily angrier.

Recklessly, Isa leaned back in her chair to peer around Lucy's trim back. "What about you, Ben? How do you like Miss Kristy Anne?"

Out of all of them, Ben was the most soft-spoken. But he was always honest. And it was honesty Isa wanted most of all. Scratching the back of his neck, Ben sighed. "I don't rightly know her. I've never even seen Junior spark her. Pa's wife gets matchmakin' notions in her head and can be a force to reckon with if she doesn't get her way."

"Kristy Anne sparks my mother and father more than she ever has me," Junior snapped, his hands fisted on the table.

Sol laughed at this.

"What's she like?" Isa asked, fluttering her lashes. "Ma says she's from good stock. Pretty. Social connections. Has supper with your parents every weekend."

"I wouldn't know." Junior's eyes warned her not to continue, which she blatantly overlooked.

"I highly doubt your mother and father would accept her if she wasn't at least obscenely rich," Isa said, laughing as if he were being very silly. Only the children were talking; all the adults were silent. All except Sol, who groaned.

"Isa, that ain't a nice thing to say—"

"No, let her say it. It's true," Junior interrupted. He gulped his water without meeting anyone's eye.

Ben looked uncomfortable.

Poppy cleared her throat. "Isa, have you a dress for the dance?"

Isa shrugged. "Mrs. Hobb said Franny will fix one up for me."

Lucy, who had glared at Junior for the last five minutes, pointedly turned in her chair to face Isa. "I have a red one that may fit you. The hemline is far too long on me."

"Red is for hussies," Junior said, scowling at Lucy's profile.

"A subject of which you're an authority," Isa shot back. "I'd love to wear your red dress, Lucy. It could make a statement. I wonder if Gareth Glen will attend."

"Gareth—that fellow we caught you kissin' a few years back?" Sol asked. "He's the deputy in Dogwood. What do you want him for?"

"A dance partner." Isa's smile was all teeth. "Is he married? Or *engaged*?" She refused to look at Junior.

"Neither, but you don't need to be messin' around with him, Isadora." Sol wagged a finger at her. "Now that you're home, we don't need any scandals."

"Since when is dancing with a man in a public place a scandal?" Isa laughed scornfully.

Junior stood stiffly from his seat and dropped his napkin on his empty plate. "Supper was good Lucy. Poppy. I think I'm gonna go get Champ ready to head home."

"Oh, but you can stay the night," Poppy fretted.

"I won't put you out. It's been a while since I've been to the house. I need to check on some things." Junior kissed Poppy's cheek, shook Sol's hand, and clapped Ben's back. He didn't spare Lucy or Isa another glance.

Good. Go home and sulk.

"Look at him leaving without even offering to help clean up," Lucy muttered.

"Luce," Ben said lowly, frowning at Junior's departing figure. Lucy wrinkled her nose but quietened.

The rest of supper was subdued, and Isa returned her attention to her cold cob of corn. Agatha fussed in her basket, so Sol picked her up, kissing the crown of her head. "Come here, Carrot Top."

When the children began to rub their eyes, the men tended to their yawning offspring while the women quietly brought plates and platters into the kitchen. Lucy and Isa scraped plates over a slop bucket, the silence between them suffocating. Lucy opened her mouth several times, then stopped herself. Her dark, winged brows were set in a worried line over her eyes.

Finally, Lucy began, "Isa, I'm sorry we didn't—"

"It's fine," Isa interrupted evenly.

Lucy shook her head. "It isn't. He comes home sparking you while the rest of the town thinks he's engaged to be married to that—that woman. Junior's mother even put it in the paper!"

Isa's nostrils flared, but she held her tongue.

"But that's just like his mother. She's a termagant. I've not so much as heard him speak Kristy Anne's name—"

"And if I have to hear it again, I shall scream." It came out sharper than Isa intended. Lucy's lips parted in shock, and her dark eyes were wide upon Isa, who had never used anything but a level tone with her before. Dropping the jocundity, Isa whirled and whispered, "Why didn't you or Poppy ever say anything?

We wrote dozens of letters to each other. Surely, you'd have found some opportunity to mention it."

From the dry sink, Poppy looked close to tears.

Lucy licked her lips, considering her words carefully. "Did something happen between you and Junior on the way home?"

"No." It came out hotly. Angrily. Isa could tell that neither woman believed her. "I'm just upset that you and Poppy handle me with kid gloves and treat me as though I cannot take...*news*. I hate being played the fool. I had a schoolgirl affection for him years ago, but I've moved on. What I don't understand is why the two of you can't."

"Oh, Isa. We're dreadfully sorry," Poppy whispered, her mouth turned down, her blue eyes swimming with compassion.

Feeling inexplicably hunted—and worse, embarrassed—Isa rubbed her eyes, worsening their irritated state. "I'm sorry, too. I just—I hate not knowing things. Being withheld information is a trial for me. And it shouldn't matter, anyway. It *doesn't* matter." But she couldn't speak further. Humiliation sealed her larynx with a horrible squeak, and rather than have her two best friends witness her loss of control, Isa squeezed past Lucy to speedily exit the kitchen. Nodding blindly at Ben and Sol, who were surrounded by the children in the parlor, Isa ascended the stairs toward the sanctity of her room.

"LEGS? YOU AWAKE?"

Sol's voice through the door was both welcome and infuriating. Isa watched her reflection in the tiny vanity's mirror. In her hands she twisted a tortoiseshell comb, glinting amber and gold.

"Yes, come in." Isa ran the comb through her hair, relishing every snag and snarl.

Sol slid in and shut the door gently behind him so as not to wake up the little ones. His tall presence was odd in her narrow childhood bedroom. He perched his narrow rear on the edge of her bed, watching her with a bemused expression. "I've seen you comb horse tails with a gentler hand than that."

"That is because they get fractious if you're rough."

"You're lookin' a mite fractious yourself, if you don't mind my saying."

"I do mind."

They made eye contact through the mirror, and his face sobered.

"You and Junior havin' a tiff?"

Isa returned her attention to her reflection. "We're always fighting. It's nothing new."

"He hasn't..."

The pause was so unnerved that Isa whirled on her backless stool. "Hasn't what?"

Sol shifted on her bed. "Hell, I don't know. He hasn't bothered you more than normal, has he? I know y'all spent an awful lot of time together during the trip here."

Never having enjoyed lying to Sol, Isa struggled to appear unaffected. "Of course not. He's like a brother to me. A particularly irksome one."

"Alright, don't fuss. I was just making sure no one was messing with my baby sister."

Isa wrinkled her nose, set her comb down, and reluctantly approached Sol for a one-armed hug. His long, lean arms wrapped tight around her. He ruined the moment the next instant by rubbing his knuckles against the part in her hair.

"Sol!" Hating that form of sibling torture more than anything, she pinched the skin over his ribs until he released her.

"Uncle!" he gasped dramatically, falling away. His broad, white grin drooped a little as he stood to leave. "You can always talk to me, you know."

"I know." The guilt of lying ate her alive. She swallowed past the discomfort.

"And if Junior—or any other man—tries to bother you, all you gotta do is tell me."

She lifted a brow. "What will you do? Committing a murder is a hangable offense. Not to mention, Ben will never speak to you again."

"I wouldn't kill anyone," Sol said blithely from the doorway. A promise lingered in his teasing hazel eyes. "But they'd damned sure wish they were dead."

Chapter Eighteen

Junior left his empty house and rode Champion back to Sol's the next day. He was no better than an old cur dog that had been run off but slunk back, tail tucked and hopeful. An excuse for returning to the Williams' home was ready on his lips, one he'd thought up last night when sleep was impossible. Between the faintly damp, musty sheets of his bed, he'd sweated and worried. *Kristy Anne.* He'd forgotten all about that nuisance. He'd never kissed the woman. Never even held her hand. That summer, when Mrs. Stone announced what a perfect wife Kristy Anne would be for Junior, he had sarcastically agreed, seeing as the young woman was a miniature of his mother. Wouldn't that be just perfect? Two women of similar caliber to dictate his every move whenever he had the gumption to be home.

How was he supposed to know his mother would take the caustic acquiescence and run with it?

He'd laughed about it with Ben, Sol, and Lucy before he'd left, brushing off their warnings as silly concerns. Now he was in hot water, and he'd rather face a firing squad than verbally spar with Isa over this calamity.

It was overcast and gray, and the treetops swayed and rustled overhead as he rode along Sol's property line. To his great relief,

Isa was in the yard alone. No children were afoot, and the buckboard was gone. She had settled on the rope swing with her long hair down and floating around her body, snagging on the taut ropes bracketing her.

The moment she saw him, her chin lifted, and she gripped the ropes hard on either side of her face. Junior halted Champion with a low "whoa" and stared at her from his position in the road. When she didn't move, he dismounted and warily approached her.

"Izzy." From six feet away, he could see her ribs expand with a deep breath.

"I do not wish to speak to you," Isa said calmly.

Mouth compressing, he tied his horse to a bush and closed the distance between them. She wore a simple white blouse and a navy skirt that was too short for her, revealing long, slim feet bare in the dirt beneath the swing. With her skeins of rippling hair, clear skin, and baleful gaze, she looked like an angry, beautiful witch.

It was the challenging look that made him speak without thinking

"You've got no right to be mad at me. Didn't you hear a word I said at the table last night? My mother is behind all this. She's got some fool notion of tying me down no matter how many times I tell her I'm not interested. I am not marrying that woman."

"It sounds like a whole lot of excuses to me."

"They're not excuses, damn you. They're the truth." He strained to keep his voice low, mindful of the dark windows facing them from several yards away.

"No, damn *you*. You do not get to kiss me and...other things while being promised to another woman!"

Her growing anger ignited his. "That's rich coming from someone who traipses around with a married man!"

"I'm only friends with David." Isa rubbed her temples. "And even before he married, he asked for my hand."

"Yeah, that's right, you've got men lined up to be with you. How could I forget?"

"You don't get to be angry."

"I'm not!"

"I was trying to say that David never used me!" She checked behind her after this outburst, inspecting the yard for eavesdroppers.

Ears burning, he walked forward until their knees brushed. Isa had to crane her neck to look up at him. "I thought we were friends, too. You think I used you?" he asked, breathing rapidly.

"We are not friends." She was dodging his question.

"Then what are we?" The question dangled in the silence, broken only by dry leaves rustling on the ground. *What are we?* They damned sure weren't friends. Not anymore. It was hard to look at her face, to see the greenish gold eyes burning into his like live coals.

"I don't know! I just know friends don't kiss, Junior. I don't like that you kiss and touch me one day, and the next, I discover you're to marry another woman—from my ma, of all people."

A tendril of her hair floated against him, and he caught it, rubbing the silky strands between his rough fingers. "I am not marryin' anyone, Izzy! I never kept anything from you because I never intended to be with Kristy Anne."

Her lips thinned. "And yet I still feel lied to." She stood from the swing, toe to toe with him. "Did it not occur to you in all the times we kissed that I'd find out about her? That I'd feel hurt?"

As though Junior was watching someone else do it, he grabbed her arm and pulled her behind the live oak, shrouding them from the house's view. "I don't remember making any promises to you," he said, his eyes burning into hers. She shrugged his hand off. "Whatever secrets I kept had nothing to do with you."

Isa's jaw firmed. "I am aware of that."

"Then why are you punishing me?"

They were within arm's reach of each other, the air between them heavy. Full of hurt. It infuriated him. Reaching with his right arm, he cupped the back of her neck to bring her in for a hard kiss.

She angrily shoved him away.

"You don't get to do this now!" Her eyes flashed sparks. "I used to worship the ground you walked on, but I've grown up. I will not be a last resort, a consolation prize!"

Junior raked his fingers through his hair, mussing up the macassar oil he'd applied in the hopes he would see her. "What in God's name are you talkin' about?"

"I'm talking about the women you've gone through over the years, Junior." Isa's face was twisted with emotion, even wilder and prettier in her rage. "Your whores and your widows. The way you discard them once you've finished with them. Even this Kristy Anne. I'll bet half the gold in England that you let her entertain the idea of marriage with you, then you disappeared again before it was set in stone. And she was so desperate for you that she never gave up the hope of being with you one day. And now...now you want to parade me around at the Fall Dance and kiss me without even having spoken to her directly. Tell me if I am incorrect in my assumption."

His teeth clacked shut. He couldn't tell Isa anything because she was right. Kristy Anne was his mother's first choice of a wife for him. His mother was closer to the woman than he was himself, and the young southern belle was present at holidays, weekend suppers, and church socials. Junior had abided by Kristy Anne's unwelcome appearances because it made his mother happy.

Hearing Isa's perspective made him distinctly uncomfortable. Censure from this twenty-two-year-old woman with little worldly experience made something stick in his craw. And he couldn't admit to being wrong. He was always wrong. For once, just once, he'd like to be right.

Her face softened with a different emotion. He didn't like it.

"Don't you see?" she whispered. "It's not right to touch me the way you do while another is out there, pining for you, expecting your loyalty. It doesn't feel good. In fact, it's the worst feeling in the world."

Junior's teeth slackened from their unbreakable clench. "Is that how you used to feel?"

"Yes." Isa's throat worked above her crisp white collar. "I felt that way about you often, too young to have a name for it. You would have laughed in my face if I had ever told you. But seeing you spark other women—it was insuperable, like seeing someone I loved die. I may loathe this Kristy Anne on principle, but I relate to her. No woman should be left wondering."

His numb lips moved of their own accord. "I'll tell her, Izzy. I'll call everything off."

Isa's pale hazel eyes were dark and limpid beneath the shadowy tree boughs. "You'll speak to her?"

Champion snorted nearby, his tail swishing lazily.

In an echo to his Texas Ranger's oath years before, Junior raised his hand and murmured solemnly, "I swear it. You have my word. First thing tonight during my supper at the big house."

"And then what?"

"Then you stop bein' mad at me. And you dance with me at the Fall Dance."

Not taking her eyes off his, she took a step toward him. And another. His belt buckle brushed her stomach, and the softness of her made him hard. Another lock of her hair blew in the wind, draping across his wrist like a lover begging him not to go. He caught it, made a glossy loop, and pulled his knife from its sheath on his gun belt. They watched breathlessly as he gently sawed the blade through the dark-blonde strand. The hair attached to the root drifted against her breast, quickly lost amidst the forest of its brethren. He tied the tress in his hand into a loop knot and tucked it into his vest pocket.

He wondered if she would reject him again if he bent to kiss her, but the rattle of a buckboard in the distance swept the notion away. A child screamed happily out of sight, and Junior and Isa dispersed. She loped across the yard and into the house while he untied Champion and mounted him. By the time Sol and the children rolled into the empty yard, the only movement was the rope swing swaying in the breeze.

THE RIDE TO his childhood home gave Junior plenty of opportunity to ruminate on all the ways he'd betrayed Sol in the last couple of weeks. The shift in his loyalties concerned him. When had he become more dedicated to Isa than his oldest and best friend?

It was nearing twilight when Champion rode through the gates of the Big Stone Ranch. The farmhouse stood in the center of everything, immense, white, and cold. Despite the constant flow of activity around the outbuildings, many corrals, and barn, the ranch had never felt friendly. Never felt like home. Several ranch hands noticed him and waved their hat or called greetings. He made his way over to a group of them and dismounted to shake hands and shoot the breeze. For half an hour, he stalled, catching up with cowboy gossip. He knew his mother was wringing her hands somewhere inside the house, hoping he would show up.

According to the men, Loretta had let five cowhands go since that spring. It shocked and stymied him that his mother was making important decisions, not his father.

"My pa didn't mind?" he asked Chuck, a veteran cowhand.

Chuck scratched the back of his neck. None of the men looked Junior in the eye. "Ms. Loretta told us to keep it to ourselves. The big man has enough to worry about."

A young, eager cowboy let slip that John Stone spent more and more time out of town on business. Then he delicately implied that the depression had provoked the old man into almost constant antagonism.

"Father home now?" Junior asked idly, flicking ash from his cigarette.

"He, er, takes to spending weekends in town." Chuck's hangdog eyes shifted away.

Junior shook his head and stubbed out his cigarette. "To think he used to chew my hide for whoring and worrying my ma. Now look at him."

The men laughed warily, glancing at the house for listening ears of the female variety.

"Guess I better go in." Junior stifled a sigh and took his horse's reins.

"Need me to stable him?" Chuck held his hands out for the reins.

"I reckon I'm not so far up on my high horse I can't put my own mount up."

The laughter was more genuine this time. They ribbed him as he walked into the barn, and Junior took his time feeding and watering Champion. He kept the gelding saddled; he didn't plan on staying longer than it took to eat and tell Kristy Anne to look elsewhere for a husband. He pictured Isa's shrewd eyes watching him, waiting for him to put his money where his mouth was. The words he'd told her by the rope swing remained true. One day she'd learn that he'd always call her bluff.

"JUNIOR, DEAR," LORETTA Stone cried after the housemaid alerted her of his presence. "You can't imagine my happiness when Chuck told me you would come for supper."

Junior stoically accepted his mother's ecstatic greeting, hugging her with a single arm and pulling away first. "Mother. You doing well?"

"My, yes, we're just fine." Loretta Stone laughed, dabbing at the corner of her eyes with a handkerchief. The last few years had aged her a decade. Her blonde hair was a full cap of white, fashioned in one of those fussy hairstyles with a fringe of a bunch of frizzy curls. "Adele, tell Cook we'll be ready for supper in ten minutes."

The housemaid gave a little bob and exited the foyer.

"Hello, Mr. Stone," said a voice from the parlor doorway.

Bracing himself, Junior turned on a heel to face Kristy Anne. "Ma'am."

The woman his mother had chosen for him was expensively dressed and soft-featured except for a long, sharp nose. Her eyes were watchful, and her thin lips were turned down as though he'd denied her the pleasure of a dance. In the stilted silence following his underwhelming greeting, Loretta fluttered around him to draw the young woman further into the foyer.

"Don't be shy, dear. It's only Junior. There's no need to call him 'Mr. Stone.'"

Molars grinding, Junior skirted both women to hang his Stetson on the hat rack. His jacket followed, and he heard a disapproving little noise behind him when Loretta saw the six-shooters in his gun belt. For years, she'd striven to get him to leave his guns with the coats. Such a notion was laughable.

"How is your Ranger work?" his mother asked, a slight emphasis on the word "Ranger." Another thing she disapproved of.

"Good," he lied. "How's Father?"

A small pause. "He's well. Business keeps him restricted to town often."

I'll just bet it does. "That's too bad."

"Kristy Anne's mother was elected chairwoman of the Women's Council in Huntsville, have you heard?"

"Nope."

Loretta went into an animated account of Kristy Anne's accomplishments, from volunteering at the local orphanage, to her sewing skills in the quilting circle, to speaking her testimony at church a few months before. He imagined Kristy Anne with a bit in her mouth, his mother holding the reins, showing a disinterested buyer the lines of her flanks and the length of her teeth. If Isa was there, her dismay would be palpable. Junior smiled at the thought.

Emboldened by Junior's seemingly indulgent mood, Loretta added, "She has also stood in a few times for the teacher when she was out with putrid throat."

It was hard to imagine this quiet young woman taking over a schoolhouse full of children. When he was a young boy, he would have run circles around any teacher as soft and quiet as she. "Did you like teaching?" he asked to be polite.

Before his mother could speak for her, Kristy Anne vehemently shook her head. "No, I daresay. The children were loud, unkempt creatures. Terrible grammar and manners, and hardly any of them wore shoes."

Junior's half-smile disappeared. "Not all families can afford them."

"I don't see why not. If you can bear the child, you should be able to decently clothe it." Her voice was harsh, and distaste twisted her features. He thought of a young Isa, easily the most brilliant student in her schoolhouse, with secondhand bib overalls and dirty bare feet. The sharecropper family she was born to, with their many children, always had welcome, laughing faces. They were a more loving family to him and Ben than the one inhabiting this ranch.

"Many of them are poor in the flesh but rich in love," he said, striving for patience. "Money isn't everything."

It was as though he'd said a particularly nasty word; his mother and Kristy Anne blanched and shared a disquieted look. Patience waning, Junior was grateful when the housemaid chose that moment to announce that supper was served, and asked if they would they like to quit to the dining room?

Halfway through the meal, the two women chattered as happily as a couple of magpies about Kristy Anne's family and acquaintances. Junior didn't know of any of the names they lobbed around like little snares, waiting for one tempting enough to snag him. Truthfully, he'd never been so bored in his life. He found the conversation dull and yawned several times behind a fist; each time, his mother's eyes would flash. As Kristy Anne became more comfortable talking about herself, her opinions revealed a scathing, mean-spirited streak. Blinking tired, itchy eyes, Junior wished Isa was there to properly set the girl down a peg or two.

Without a thought of the consequences, he asked, "You hear Izzy's back home?"

Silver clinked onto fine china. Movement ceased. "Who?" his mother asked.

Junior leaned back and hooked an arm around the straight-backed dining chair's top rail. "What do you mean, 'who?' Sol's little sister."

Kristy Anne sat straighter.

"Ah. No, I did not know she was home. In truth, I was not aware she had left." Loretta's words were tipped with frost.

Smiling incredulously, he asked, "You weren't aware she was in Austin getting her mathematics degree? I thought the whole county knew."

"I make it a point to not associate with the same rabble as your brother," she replied stiffly.

The little smile playing around Junior's lips tightened. His mother wouldn't look at him, so he slid his eyes to an uncomfortable Kristy Anne. He pulled a cigarette from his vest pocket.

"We do not smoke—" Loretta began but broke off at the flare of Junior's match.

"Yep, Izzy grew up pretty sophisticated despite being *rabble*." Junior's voice was light. Conversational. "But she's still got a backbone under all that. Our horses were stolen on the way home, did I tell you? No? Well, she wouldn't stay behind and tracked the thieves down with me."

He was deaf to his mother's squeak.

"That's what took so long, you see. We were on the trail for about a week," he added for a white-faced Kristy Anne's benefit. "Izzy didn't complain once. She was better company than several of the privates I've had in my company. Maybe I can bring her by next Sunday for dinner, Mother. Probably the most well-informed, interesting person you've ever had at the table."

The barb struck his mother harder than it did the young woman.

"Junior," she breathed. "If this young woman has anything to do with the atrocious manners you are displaying, then I have no shadow of a doubt that she will be unwelcome at this table. And to speak of another woman before your betrothed…I'm speechless. Apologize to her this instant."

Smoke billowed from his nostrils as he observed the bloodless features of his betrothed. "Did you put our engagement in the papers, Kristy Anne?"

Not a pin drop was heard in the ensuing quiet. The longer the silence stretched, the more sinister it felt.

Loretta dabbed her mouth with her napkin and set it carefully on the table. "I posted that announcement some months back."

"I don't recall ever asking for anyone's hand in marriage," he said, flicking ashes into his full wine glass. No matter how many times he told his mother he wasn't a drinking man, she still insisted that wine at supper was different. Tasteful.

"If it were up to you, son, you would grow old alone just to spite me." Loretta's voice shook. "I would have no grandchildren to bounce on my knee."

"You do have grandchildren." There was an edge to his tone.

"Your brother's offspring do not *signify*. I have no grandchildren."

"If you think I'm going to marry this woman you've handpicked and start giving those grandbabies to you, then you've lost your damned marbles." Junior pointed the two fingers holding his half-smoked cigarette at Kristy Anne; she looked close to tears. "I haven't said more than two sentences to this woman at a time, and frankly, I don't appreciate coming home to a passel of people asking about upcoming nuptials that are never going to happen."

"But her whole family expects you to marry," Loretta whispered.

"And I don't remember proposing," he repeated.

The wobble in his mother's lower lip belied the venom in her words. "Ever since your father's oldest son came home all those years ago, you have been a man changed. It's as though I hardly know you anymore, Junior. You used to be so much kinder to me—"

"Mother, before Ben came back, I was pissing all of Father's money away at the local whorehouses and drinking down what little sense I had left," Junior countered cruelly. "If I was kind to you, it was because I was hungover and couldn't hold a thought in my head. Or the old man was standing over me, threatening to beat me within an inch of my life if I upset you. The best thing that ever happened to me was when Ben came home."

A tear fell from one of her sagging eyes. "How can you possibly say that when he was the one who killed your cousin Leonard?"

"Please," Junior growled, stubbing the cigarette out on his plate. "That fool rode into floodwaters so drunk he could barely sit a horse."

"If your brother had not been such an incompetent trail boss, it would never have—"

Junior sat forward from his comfortable recline against his chair and said softly, "I won't have you talk about my big brother like that. Not in front of me. We've discussed this."

Another tear leaked. That she did not dab it away with her handkerchief, but let them fall silently, dramatically, down her cheeks, set Junior's teeth on edge. "Considering he almost had you killed alongside your cousin—"

"My cousin was a drunkard with a penchant for whoring and had me down that same path. He went into the river first. Ben's twice the man your nephew ever could have been. Good riddance, I say."

"Junior!" She began to cry in earnest now, but he was hardened to it.

"And if you won't be civil about my family, I'll see myself out." He stood.

"No!" Loretta sniffed and finally, blessedly, wiped her face. She rose and made her way to his side of the table. "No, dear. Stay. I hardly see you."

I wonder why, he thought, exasperated. "I don't think there's anything left to say. Kristy Anne, it was nice to see you again. I'm sure you'll tell your family that our engagement was just one big misunderstanding?"

Small in her seat, her eyes enormous, Kristy Anne nodded.

"Thank you kindly." He gave her one nod, rounded his mother, and made his way to the front door where his coat and hat waited.

Junior frowned during the journey home. While moonlight lit his way, he pondered his mother's frantic reaction to him breaking off all ties with Kristy Anne and how it just didn't fit.

Chapter Nineteen

He shouldered through colorfully dressed women and soberly dressed men, hard blue eyes searching for a tall blonde in red. Junior's heart pounded as forcefully as the music jumping from the corner stage of the dance hall, his tanned skin covered in a fine sheen of sweat. The crush was sweltering, suffocating, and he clenched hands into fists until engorged veins wound along the tendons and knuckles. He couldn't stop thinking about Isa and what he'd say to her. What he'd do.

Her hair lay coiled in his vest pocket, a dark gold noose against his heart.

Junior had arrived late to the Fall Dance. Champion had thrown a shoe a mile out from the house, and by the time the gelding, and his newly restored horseshoe, was settled in the Dogwood Hotel's stable, Isa had already departed.

Cursing his rotten luck, Junior shouldered his way to one of the open double doors. He considered lighting a cigarette. Lanterns were lit, and through the double doors, he saw children run hither and thither, jumping over the fire, roasting nuts, bobbing for apples, and participating in three-legged races.

Finally, he saw the broad back of a man with curling black hair, arm in arm with a woman in blue. Ben and Lucy. Junior strode back into the sea of skirts, feathered hats, and felt bowler hats. Lucy, whose side was to him as she spoke to another woman, noticed him.

"There you are." Lucy reeled him into the group of people. The woman she'd been talking to stared at Junior. He avoided her ogling and searched once again for a red dress.

Lucy was talking but he didn't hear her. Impatience crawled along his spine, tightening his muscles. "Where's Izzy?"

"Dancing, I think," Lucy said. "She's been on the dance floor since Gareth brought her."

"I thought you brought her," he snapped.

"Gareth rode by the hotel to look at her filly, so they rode here together." Lucy spoke lightly, unbothered by his terseness. "The children weren't ready yet, in any case."

He was already straining to see over the heads of the men around him at the dance floor. There! A flash of dark crimson satin and black lace snagged his attention. Isa wore her gleaming hair in an evening coiffure with two black wings at the crown. She and her dance partner towered above the other dancers. Junior's lip curled.

Jealousy stabbed deep into his gut and twisted.

Lucy had continued her conversation with the woman, and Ben's deep voice could be heard discussing mundane things with a couple of men. Meanwhile, a woman in a blush pink gown sidled over from a neighboring group. From the corner of Junior's eye, he saw a lot of teeth and smelled a heavy application of gardenia toilette water. Something in her bearing reminded him strongly of Kristy Anne. Sinuses burning, he struggled not to lose sight of Isa's tapered waist, the flare of her red pleated skirts.

"Why, Mr. Stone. I've not seen you in these parts for some time," simpered the young woman to his right.

He grunted something. There was a roaring in his ears as Isa's head went back, her white teeth flashing with laughter. His fists clenched. A tinkling giggle escaped lips too close to his ear; he wanted to scrub the sound out with a finger.

"I see you are without a dance partner," the woman hinted.

Irritation flared.

"I'm dancing with her next dance." He nodded in Isa's direction.

The many teeth disappeared. After several moments' pause—was she waiting for an apology?—the female flounced off, cheeks the color of Ms. Ruth's spiked punch. Junior didn't care. Once upon a time, he would have twirled her around the floor and lavished her with praise for whatever dancing skill she may or may not have possessed on the off chance that Isa would see and be jealous. Such games didn't appeal to him tonight. That sharp twisting in his gut hadn't abated. He was too pent up to pretend with anyone. Too angry.

Finally, the string bass played its last jolly note of "The Yellow Rose of Texas." The dancers laughed, curtsied or bowed at each other, and dispersed from the dance floor.

"Oh, here she comes." Lucy waved Isa over. "Junior, have you met Gareth Glen?"

Unsmiling, Junior met the eyes of the man he'd walloped for kissing Isa six years before. He shook the young man's hand with enough strength to make the tendons in their hands pop. Beside Lucy, Ben straightened, a sleepy guardian dog coming to attention.

"Sure, I've met him." Junior's lips barely moved.

"How could I forget?" Gareth replied, his eyes dark shards above a pleasant smile.

Isa dabbed at her collarbones with a handkerchief, frowning at Junior and Gareth's endless handshake. "Are you two going to hold hands all night, or can I persuade one of you to get me a cider?"

Reflexively, Junior said, "Your legs work."

Gareth's answer was far smoother. "I'd be honored."

The handshake ended, and circulation returned, maroon fingers gradually returning to their normal shade. Gareth kissed Isa's gloved hand before he melted into the crowd, and Junior watched her surreptitiously wipe it against her skirts.

Lucy cocked a hip and looked at her husband. "I've missed something."

"That's the fellow who stole a kiss from Isa right before she and Poppy went missing," Ben reminded her. "We weren't at that dance."

Mouth rounding into a little *o*, Lucy opened her fan and vigorously fluttered it.

"What makes you think I wasn't the one doing the stealing?" Isa nicked Lucy's fan and began to wave it in front of her shining pink face. "I'm sweating like a pig in this dress. It'll be a miracle if Gareth comes back."

Isa didn't look like a pig. She looked dewy and sensual. He wanted to lick every inch of her exposed skin. It was damned hard to keep his eyes from the square neckline of her bodice and the swells of cleavage it revealed. It boggled the mind that Lucy let her show up without one of those little hankies tucked over her bosom. A black choker necklace with dangling obsidian beads drew the eye, and the dress's sleeves were slips of intricate lace. Elbow-length black gloves contrasted starkly against deep red skirts, and Junior itched to peel them off, one by one.

And then he wanted to choke her with them.

"Stop glaring at me," Isa hissed for his ears alone, waggling her fan in front of his face.

He folded his arms and stared. "I wasn't even looking at you."

"Yes, you were."

"A man can't stretch his eyes without a woman accusing him of something?"

Across the dance floor, the woman-scorned in pink chatted to a group of young women, pointing his way.

"Stretching your eyes?" Her lips flattened.

"Yep."

"You're unbelievable."

"Here you are, madam," said a voice to Junior's left. Gareth's center part looked foolish to Junior, especially paired with his wispy mustache. How old was the boy now? Twenty-two? Twenty-three? "Would you like to dance?"

Isa threw back the cider and shoved the empty cup and fan into Junior's unwilling hands. "I'd love to."

The handsome couple disappeared onto the dance floor, the hardwood vibrating with the stomping feet of an upcoming square dance. Lucy murmured something to Ben, then asked louder, "Junior, will you take me for a spin while Ben checks on the children?"

Releasing the tight clench of his jaw, Junior nodded and passed the cup and fan to a disgruntled Ben.

Lucy, the little devil, placed them right beside Isa and Gareth. For torturous minutes, he was forced to hook Isa's arm with his and twirl them around before returning to his position. She scowled when paired with him and beamed when paired with Gareth. It was enough to make him howl. To tear at his hair and run from the dance hall screaming. He wanted to go to the nearest saloon and drink his way through a bottle of whiskey. Then he'd fight the biggest man at the bar.

But to do that, he'd have to leave Isa in the company of this young, lean deputy, whose dark eyes marked the way her heels kicked up her skirts and the way her breasts bounced with each step. Junior, a fair-fighting man, wanted to gouge those eyes out. If the young man thought about pawing Isa again in some darkened alley the way he had six years prior, Junior would finish what he'd started. This time, he wouldn't stop. It was all he could do to dance this ridiculous dance and glare impotently from afar, hating.

A woman's high-pitched scream, followed by a ruckus from the sidelines, brought the music to a wrenching halt. People turned as one toward the end of the hall nearest the first set of double doors. Without hesitation, Junior and Gareth broke free from their partners and waded through the curious onlookers to the scene of the scuffle. Two men were in a scrap by the cider table. A faint woman was held up by two others a short distance away.

"Break it up," Gareth barked, hauling the younger of the men away.

Junior hooked his arms beneath the damp armpits of the older, burlier man and brought him back a few steps. "Might want to cool that temper before you spend the night in the hoosegow."

"That sonuvabitch owes me money," the man growled, straining against Junior's hold. "He had the nerve to show his face here, braggin' about the ring he bought his strumpet."

Several women nearby gasped.

"This is a family event," Junior said softly. Menacingly. "Keep your yap shut while you're around women and children or I'll shut it for you."

"Get your goddamned hands off me." The belligerent man began to struggle in earnest.

Junior strengthened his hold.

From his suit pocket, Gareth pulled free a pair of handcuffs and neatly shackled Junior's captive. "I'll take it from here," the deputy said, meeting Junior's eye. "Can't have him starting this up again around a bunch of families."

"Need a hand?"

"I got it. The other gentleman involved said it was unprovoked, backed up by eyewitnesses."

Before walking off, Gareth nodded grudgingly at Junior, then frog-marched his prisoner through the double doors into the night. Junior watched them go, irritated at the sneaking respect he felt for someone he hated on principle.

"What happened?" Isa asked from behind him, so close he felt her breath on his neck. It hadn't taken long for her to come sticking her nose right into the fray.

He considered leaving. It would be strictly an act of self-preservation. Instead, he reluctantly gave her a quick breakdown of events. Ben and Lucy were nowhere to be seen—probably gathering their children up during the melee. Surrounded by strangers, he and Isa were alone. Through the hum of gossip around them, the band started up a sweet, slow song. He turned to face her, and they observed each other warily.

Without a word, he drew her into the dance.

She let him.

It felt dreamlike, whirling her around with the other couples. No family was looking on, and no jealous suitors were nearby. It was just the two of them, like when they were on the trail.

"You ever miss being on the trail?" he asked, then cursed himself for asking.

She answered candidly. "Yes. I miss it all the time. It was peaceful."

"Yep. Quiet."

She nodded, and her eyes, pale as gilded whiskey, drifted from the top of his styled hair, to the black kerchief at his neck, to the tailored fit of his dove gray vest. His own gaze trailed from the onyx bird wings in her hair to the delicate strength of her shoulders under the revealing dress's sleeves, then stopped. He'd be damned if she caught him ogling her breasts, no matter how tempted he was.

"You look pretty," he said softly so no other dance partners could hear him.

Her eyes shuttered. "Where is your fiancée?"

Not this again. "I told you. I don't have a fiancée."

"That's not what everyone else believes." She shrugged a nonchalant shoulder, but her temple flickered.

"I called it off like I said I would." It was hard to keep his anger in check. She made him feel violent. Desperate. "Which shouldn't have been necessary as I've never asked anyone to marry me before, Izzy. You want me to go up on stage, grab the megaphone, and announce it to the whole town?"

"Be my guest."

"Alright." He released her and strode purposefully toward the band, weaving between twirling couples, ignoring dirty looks. A hand gripped his arm at the elbow. He hid his smirk before Isa turned him around. They continued their dance, her color heightened. More seriously, he said, "I'll always call your bluff."

She looked intently at him beneath lowered brows. "I know."

They danced in silence, breathing each other in, gazes tangled together.

JUNIOR RODE IN the back of Ben's wagon around midnight. Two of his nephews listed to one side of the wagon bed. Jack had already nodded off on the bench seat; his little head rested on Lucy's lap, drooling onto her skirts.

"I'll put the wagon up," Junior murmured to Ben once they had parked in the hotel stable.

Arms full of his two oldest sons, Ben grunted his thanks and followed Lucy and Jack through the back door. In the stable breezeway, the sounds of Isa putting away Mirage's tack made the quiet night less lonely. Once he inhaled long and slow, Junior freed Ben's horse from the yoke and took him to an empty stable beside Isa. He and Isa worked in silence, the stable wall between them. There were so many things he wanted to say that pride wouldn't give voice to.

The silence was choking him.

Then, "How was your supper with your mother?" Isa's tone was deceptively offhand.

His hands paused beneath the horse's halter. "Quick."

"Quick?"

He needed to see her face. Junior abandoned the horse and entered the stable adjacent to him. A disinterested Mirage's jaw worked around a mouthful of hay, loud in the stillness. Even in the watery street light, her coat glistened. Meanwhile, Isa paid him no mind, warning him that whatever truce they had come to during their last dance was still quite shaky.

"Mm." His jaw worked while he watched the jut of her bustle beneath her slim back. "I reckon my pa is looking everywhere to hand me an ass whippin' I won't forget for the way I spoke to Mother and Miss Kristy Anne."

"That bad?" Her back was to him, but she'd ceased moving.

Junior closed the stable door behind him and treaded closer, boot heels muffled by straw and dirt. "I reckon it was for them. My ma wants to manage me. Tell me how to live, who to talk to, who to marry. I can't wrap my head around why it has to be this woman; I've barely spoken to her."

"I heard she has a bloodline the queen herself would nod to," Isa said. Her neck was long and vulnerable beneath her twisted updo. Fine hairs drifted to her nape, soft as feather down.

"Like I give a damn about that in a woman."

Her hands stopped moving. "How *do* you like them?"

Junior had never seen her so motionless. Licking his dry lips, he stepped closer, his hip brushing her bustled skirt. "I like 'em feisty." Giving into the temptation, he ran his thumb from the downy hairs at her nape to the line of her spine. Her skin broke out in gooseflesh. She shivered. "I miss your braid."

"What are you doing to me?" Isa whispered, head bowed.

The question rang alarm bells, and he whirled her around to face him, chucking two fingers under her chin. But it wasn't despair clouding her eyes. It was desire. Lids heavy with want, she gripped his shoulders, neck, biceps—anywhere her gloved hands could reach. What was he doing to her? What was *she* doing to *him*?

"The same thing you're doing to me, Izzy. I'm going crazy here."

"What happens now?" she breathed, her dilated pupils focused on his lips. When his hands spanned her waist, her back arched into him until they were flush, their faces separated by inches.

"Anything you want," Junior said truthfully. He'd do anything for her, something he'd only just discovered. His irredeemable soul felt less heavy with her. Isa's presence was like rain washing muck and filth from his spirit.

"Anything?"

"If you don't want to marry, we won't marry. None of that matters to me anyway. I just want you." And if he couldn't have her, he'd throw her over his shoulder and convince her. He didn't care what it took.

Isa lowered her hands to his chest...and shoved him. Once, twice, thrice, until the stable door was at his back and he was forced to grip her delicate wrists and hold her still.

"Damn you," she choked out. Her attention was on Junior's eyes, lips, neck, and eyes again. "I was through with you."

"No," he grated, throat compressing like some invisible fist gripped it.

"I was." She grimaced and tried to pull free from his hold. "Release me."

"No," he repeated. Her upper lip looked slightly rouged, begging to be licked. He'd been dying to kiss her all night.

This time, she pulled harder and lost her balance, and they tumbled onto the hay at Mirage's feet. The horse scarcely gave them a second glance; her mouth steadily worked to put hay in her belly. Isa's mouth opened at the impact, and Junior took full advantage, kissing her. Her soft lips made him dizzy. Her scent, the way she groaned, vibrating his mouth. Her taste. His whole body went hard: arms, thighs, cock, the grip he had on her. It made him lightheaded, and he closed his eyes, tongue twining with hers. Straddling her voluminous skirts, he trapped her with his knees and attempted to overwhelm her presence the way she did his.

A deep voice called out in the darkness, bringing them both up, wide-eyed.

"Junior, you need help with the wagon?" Ben called from the hotel's back porch.

"Shit," Junior hissed, adjusting himself.

From her newly upright position, Isa rested her forehead on his stomach, breath uneven and hot through his shirt. He froze. When she kissed him directly over his navel, his heart stopped. Hands shaking, he cupped her cheeks and lifted her face to his. She was the most beautiful, sensual thing he'd ever seen.

"Meet me in the attic when everyone is asleep," Isa ordered softly.

A gun to his head couldn't make his voice work. He nodded, helped her up, and watched her walk unsteadily out of the stable. While she spoke conversationally to Ben across the yard, Junior squeezed his eyes shut, grabbed himself with a rough, staying hand, and cursed the day he was born.

"WHAT THE HELL are you doin'?" growled a voice from a rocking chair.

Junior's hand was halfway to his holster before he realized it was his brother, shrouded in darkness.

"What do you mean?" Junior asked cautiously, pulling a cigarette from his vest pocket and lighting it with a match.

"Something is goin' on between you and Sol's little sister."

The accusation was quietly said, but it affected the accused as though it had been screamed directly into his ear; he jumped.

"Why the hell would you say that?" Junior's tone was defensive.

"Don't give me that, boy." Ben leaned forward. Moonlight revealed a shirt stretched across a brawny chest and the lower half of his face. The lower half looked furious. "Me and Lucy see it clear as day. You were raised better than that."

Guilt took the sharp retort from Junior's lips. He inhaled a drag from his cigarette, its dizzying sensation reminding him of Isa's kiss. He rubbed his eyes with a thumb and forefinger.

"Just"—Ben sighed, stood from the chair, strode to Junior, and clapped him on the back—"don't do anything stupid. Don't compromise her. Because Sol will kick your ass. And I'll let him."

Ben left Junior to his thoughts. His demons. The ex-Texas Ranger stood in the quiet of the back veranda, both exhausted and buzzing with energy.

Meet me in the attic when everyone is asleep.

The hotel's attic room was where Isa stayed in the Dogwood Hotel. Lucy and her family bunked in the family rooms on the second floor. Shame and guilt wrestled with need. With obsession. If he was a decent man, he would heed his brother's advice. He would treat Isa like a sister, not like a woman who made him laugh, made him hard, made him crazy. He finished smoking, at war with himself. Then he stubbed his cigarette out against his boot heel and gave in.

Junior had made peace with himself a long time ago about a fundamental truth.

He was not a decent man.

Chapter Twenty

His feet wouldn't budge beyond the foot of the attic stairs. They were rooted to the glossy wood planks. A few doors down, occasional thumps announced that his brother's family was settling down to sleep.

Ben's warning thrummed like an insistent headache, and Junior massaged his forehead with a callused palm.

A creak from the staircase above alerted him, and he hastily dropped his hand.

"What are you doing?" Isa whispered. Her fine lawn nightgown was just visible in the dark stairway, white and billowing around her bare feet. It was a far cry from the old maid wrapper she'd slept in while traveling.

"Ben and Lucy suspect something," he answered softly, glancing down the family hallway at the other doors. He half expected Ben to be standing in an open doorway, staring in accusation. But every door was closed. Everything was quiet.

"But they aren't certain?" she asked, closing the distance between them. She stopped on the last step, just tall enough to meet him eye to eye.

"No. But they're suspicious."

"Without evidence, there is no argument." Isa's hands lifted to Junior's hair and smoothed it back, nails raking his scalp.

It made his eyes close, and his body shudder. Her soft body pressed against him. Long, sinuous arms wrapped around his neck. "Take me upstairs."

She smelled powdery and feminine with a hint of wildness. Her hair was down, cloaking her back, and the ends tickled his forearms when he gripped her bottom to pick her up. The time for indecision was gone. Her legs wrapped tight around his lean hips, and he began the careful journey upstairs, swathed by her body. Enveloped in her scent.

Isa trailed her lips from his ear to his jawline. His ability to think vanished.

The attic space was long and narrow, with a single, circular window at one end. A strip of dim streetlamp light stretched across the floor to the stair railing, and his feet followed it. Junior dipped his head to capture lips like pliant satin. His knees hit the narrow little bed against the wall, and he stood her on its firm mattress. Bent to avoid the attic's sharply vaulted ceiling, Isa watched his hands slide from her hips to the hem of her nightgown, disappearing beneath.

Neither spoke.

She reached up and untied the ribbon at her neckline; the nightgown opened, drooping down her shoulders. Junior stifled a groan and pulled the garment over her head. Her yards of gilded hair fell over her shoulders, scarcely disguising how gloriously naked she was before him. Although he knew Isa was an equestrian and sportswoman, her physical strength caught him unawares. Junior couldn't stop touching her. His hands mapped out the areas between her full breasts and the flare of her hips. Burying his face in the silky seam above her navel, he brought her close, breathing her in.

Slowly, she unknotted his kerchief until it drifted to the bed below.

He allowed her to touch him, to unbutton his vest. His shirt. Suspenders were unclasped and dangled to his knees. He shrugged everything off and went still as her cool hands familiarized themselves with his body. Breathing hard, he watched her get to her knees to press a kiss to his healed bullet wound. Biting his lip, he ran his fingers through her hair, noting its wavy thickness, wild and untamed as a mustang's mane. When her fingers busily worked at his belt and fly, he fisted the hair in his hands and pulled her head back. Her neck arched delicately.

"What are you doing?" His question was almost inaudible.

"Kissing you," Isa breathed, placing her hand directly over the bulge straining behind his fly. "Here."

It didn't shock him that she knew of such things. She was the nosiest busybody he'd ever met. As a child, she'd ask the most inappropriate questions after hours of eavesdropping on her brothers, the cowhands, and teenage boys at church. If any innocent knew about kissing a man below the belt, it was her. Junior wanted to ask if she'd ever done such a thing before. Another part of him never wanted to know. If he asked uncomfortable questions, she would ask them in return. The notion was enough to make him sweat. Hell, he was sweating now. His heart thumped like a herd of buffalo against his sternum. Sudden possessiveness made it hard to release her, to allow her clever fingers to complete their task. He couldn't stop touching Isa's hair. Her neck. Her delicate jaw.

Once Junior's pants were pulled down, his cock sprang out, thick and heavy with arousal. It pointed right at her. For a breathless moment, he experienced an adolescent fear that she would laugh at him. She didn't. Her wide-set eyes were enormous, and she touched him lightly, running a fingertip along the sensitive head to the thin skin behind its flared crown. Then, eyes closing, she leaned forward and kissed it. He couldn't look away. The image of her—knees slightly spread on the quilt, back arched, his tanned hands holding her dark-blonde hair from her face—would be burned like a brand behind his eyes. The kiss deepened; her lips spread. Wet warmth enveloped him, long lashes fluttering against her cheekbones. He tilted his head back, eyes closed, his throat swallowing something hard that had lodged in it.

Isa began to move, her mouth gliding slowly upon him, then away. Unable to resist, he looked down again. Their eyes met. Fingers trembling, he carefully guided her mouth from him. A hint of a frown shadowed her brow before her lips were crushed beneath his. He kissed her ravenously, pausing only to step out of his boots and rip off his remaining clothes.

They were naked together, hot skin pressing against heavy breasts, his chest hair tickling. He tumbled her onto the thickly padded bed.

Their mouths learned each other: soft kisses and hard, gentle plucks and deep pulls. Junior had never felt so eager to merely kiss. If it was all they did tonight, he'd be content. But his body felt the response in hers, the way her movements shifted from languid to urgent. Demanding.

Hard as iron against her, he broke away from her lips, gasping for air against her neck. Tension strummed his muscles like bass strings. His limbs trembled.

"Touch me," she demanded, moving insistently against him.

Junior wedged his body between her thighs, then slid down to breathe in the satiny area between her slightly flattened breasts. With his hands, he pressed her breasts together, kissing each on its peak, tracing each nipple with his tongue until they were hard and wet. Isa's fingers were rough in his hair, and he grinned around her breast. Taking the hint, he laved a nipple with the flat of his tongue and sucked it in deep. Her exhalation was fast and shaky, her grip on his hair fierce. Junior showed both breasts equal treatment, then moved down, down. Her breath stuttered. His pulse pounded so fiercely in his ears that it was a wonder he heard her at all. Gripping her beneath her slightly damp knees, he pushed her legs up and apart.

Isa squeaked, and her hands left his hair to grasp at the quilt.

"Sh." He planted a soothing kiss on the area above her pubic hair.

The room was bright enough that he could see her outlined against the coverlet. She was beautiful, the most beautiful thing he had ever seen. Lying flat on the mattress, he allowed his eyes to drift closed and did what he'd been dreaming of since their first kiss; he kissed the incredible softness between her thighs. Junior had only done it once before, a disappointing experience. As an adolescent who spent most of his weekend nights at cathouses, he'd tumbled a good amount of women who loved to tease him for never burying his face between their legs. But he knew of the vinegar douches the more responsible whores availed themselves to, could smell the chemical tang in the air during a romp. It made him skittish.

Isa did not smell of chemicals. Her scent was clean. Sweet. It made him want to burrow, to fill her with himself until she was no longer one, but two. Him and her. His lips pressed harder, lower, against the supple crease between her thigh and sex.

From the sound of the soft moan escaping Isa's lips, she knew exactly what he was planning. Her eyes gleamed at him from the headboard, her lower lip pulled between her endearingly gapped teeth. She was waiting, breath held, curiosity and excitement alive in her expression. At any other time, he would have grinned. But not now. He was aflame. Shaking, weak, dying inside to do depraved things to her that he'd never done to another woman. Closing his eyes again, he lowered his mouth and traced the seam of her with his tongue. She jumped.

"Tickle?" Junior whispered.

"Like you took a feather down there with you," Isa whispered back.

Chuckling softly, he asked, "What if I did this instead?" And he bit her on top of her fuzzy mound. It was just like biting into a ripe peach.

Her hand swatted his head. He ducked in self-preservation, but her thighs were quicker, closing in on his ears with a muffled clap.

"Am I going to have to train you like my horse?" Amusement and affront strained the words.

"Have mercy!" He shook with mirth, ears ringing, overcome with soundless hilarity.

Isa had had enough. She rose to her knees and tried to shove him into the blankets.

Junior was ready for her. Smiling broadly, he got to his knees and, in a flash, wrestled her back down. Limbs wrapped around each other, muscles straining and defiant. He clapped a hand over her mouth and began tickling her. Her writhing was in earnest now. Breath erratic, eyes tearing up, Isa twisted and turned to get away from his tormenting fingers. Her ribcage and hip bones were the areas he targeted most, and soon, they were both sweating, gasping for air, giggling silently while trying to gain the upper hand.

Finally, he had her pinned and shoved tightly against both the wall and mattress. The play had stimulated him further; his erection had swelled to an unbearable degree.

"Give in," he breathed against her lips, nibbling on the lower one.

"You." She wrapped her fingers around his cock.

Smile dropping off, Junior watched from beneath lowered lids as her face settled into a sort of glazed triumph while she worked him with her hand. He bent and kissed her forehead. Her cheek. Her chin. Everything that made her so dear to him.

He slipped his tongue between her lips, tracing the gap in her teeth.

Close to exploding, he grabbed her wrist with a steely grip. Isa didn't release him. The silence was louder than before. Their earlier amusement evaporated as he cupped her between her slightly spread legs. He heard her swallow. Heard his own heartbeat in his ears.

Isa's hand moved. It guided him down. Down. To the place he was testing with careful fingers. She was slick; he searched, found, and dipped two fingers inside her to the first knuckle. The hips beneath his flinched at the invasion, inner muscles protesting. And still, her hand guided. Junior released her wrist, removed his other hand from her body, and allowed her to line them up. Sliding a palm up her thigh to her back, he shifted her away from the wall to the center of the bed. The head of his erection notched against her. The heat radiating from her was intense, and he couldn't resist flexing his hips.

There was significant resistance despite how ready she was.

For a long, tense moment, he looked at her. They said nothing. All those years of college as a modern woman, all the beaus, her gentleman friend—she still remained untried. It stalled him. Isa was born to experience, to unveil every secret, to discover things people try their damnedest to conceal. He'd always thought she'd treat sex as just another challenge to overcome. Yet, somehow, some way, she lay beneath him, frozen and braced as though...

"Izzy?" he asked softly.

Her lips compressed stubbornly. She brought him closer until his sensitive crown pushed in an inch. Junior groaned softly.

Dropping his forehead to hers, he shook his head. "We can't." *It's wrong.*

"Yes. We can." *Don't stop.*

He pulled out, jaw clenched at the sensation. She wrapped her legs tight around his hips until he was once again notched against her. *A saint couldn't resist this woman*, he thought, panicking. "We shouldn't."

"Just a little bit," she urged. Almost a plea. "Just one more time."

Yes. Just a little bit. Just one more time.

He pushed forward again, and this time, with less resistance. He went in deeper. They both gasped.

Isa's hand touched his cheek, and he looked into her eyes from an inch away. "It was always meant to be you."

Gooseflesh rippled over his back, vulnerable in its nakedness. It was as though she'd spoken an oath, one as familiar as prayer. Something invoked so often it became truth. Beneath him, she undulated, her hips rising like a sea swell. Her long, long legs tightened around his hips, and her lips rose to meet his. Tempting. Persuading.

I am not a good man.

Junior kissed her deeply, lost in her, and carefully thrust to the hilt.

ISA FELT INEXORABLE pressure, insistent and unavoidable. She had always wanted to examine, to gauge, the exact force of pressure it took to penetrate one's hymen. Inconceivably, now that she was experiencing it, her focus was too clouded with arousal to contemplate the drier details of the sexual act.

What her brain centered on was the lithe, strong weight pinning her. Junior was built like a mountain lion, with bulging arms and muscular shoulders tapering to the lean hips her thighs cradled. He was kissing the sense out of her, and the discomfort below warred with mounting excitement. The pain of losing her virginity couldn't compete with her mind's intoxication, made drunk by his lips, tongue, and the clever fingers bracketing where their bodies met to stroke the top of her sex. There was a word for such a body part. A scientific one she had memorized. It escaped her now.

When he was fully seated, skin to skin, she gasped, all coherent thought muted.

Incredible fullness, heat, the instinct to move.

Junior began to rock slowly, carefully, and she couldn't catch her breath at all. He penetrated her body the way he did her mind. She had never been more present in her flesh, aware of every brush of skin. The movement of damp, sleek muscles bracketing his spine, the way his hand found her hair and tightened into a fist. Their bodies grew slick, their pace quickened, and limbs became vises as lissome movement roughened. Isa was climbing, reaching, straining for the moment that would explode her into a thousand blistering fragments.

He groaned, cursed, and suddenly, his heavy weight was gone. Withdrawing quickly from her body, he sat back on his heels. Between them, one fist held his glistening erection, and his other hand protectively cupped its head. Something warm and viscous dropped to her thigh. Isa touched it, testing its lubricity between her forefinger and thumb. She was throbbing, exposed to the air, a few touches away from climax.

"Junior," she whispered, brows knitted, the soles of her feet moving restlessly on the mussed quilt.

Eyes still glazed, Junior snagged her nightgown from the floor, roughly wiped his hand upon it, and lowered to a prostrate position between her legs. "I'll help you, darlin'," he said against her inner thigh, brushing his mouth down to the swollen, aching center of her. "I'll take care of you."

The touch of his soft tongue was like the first surge of electricity she'd experienced in her science class, a small shock followed by increasingly stronger currents. Her lips parted, a silent scream that she cruelly quashed. Biting her lips hard, she grabbed his head, needing him closer, closer. God, she couldn't think. She couldn't *breathe*. The sensitive tissues he worked with his surprisingly wily, indomitable tongue made her race to her peak faster, faster, until she was crashing headlong like a wave against a surf, or a coal popping in a fire, showering the sky with sparks.

When awareness returned—which it did with slumberous leisure—it was to discover his hand on her mouth, his breath gusting into her ear. Blindly she tugged his hand from her face, and it rested with proprietary ease on her breast. He was doing something strange against her shoulder; his chin bumped her collarbone repeatedly.

"What are you doing?" She was hardly conscious. Barely curious. Her brain was lethargic, like a cat that had awakened from its nap with every intention of stretching and falling back to sleep.

Junior lifted his head, eyes glittering. His face was a damp mess. "Seeing if my jaw still worked." He opened his mouth, stretching his jaw from side to side as though he'd been hit with a hard fist.

For a moment, she could only gape at him, and then she began to shake. His own shoulders moved, his dimples deep in his cheeks, the cleft in his chin more defined. She planted a kiss on the latter, and he stopped laughing.

"I'm relieved it still works," she announced, raising her arms and extending her legs, stretching her entire body in naked bliss.

"Yeah?" He didn't move off her, and his hand lovingly caressed her breast. She did not protest.

"Yes."

"That's downright generous of you."

"It's for selfish reasons, I assure you." Her mouth widened in a smile.

"Why's that?" He touched a gentle fingertip to her front teeth.

With her lips moving around the digit, she said, "Because I'd like for you to do that again."

JUNIOR HELD HER tightly against him as they settled down to sleep, and when she woke up the next morning, groggy, sore, and disoriented, his arms and legs were still heavy upon her. Like at the campsite, she rolled over to discover him sleeping with that same childlike abandon. Relaxed, his face was angelic.

Then eyes the deep blue of an arctic glacier opened in panic.

Morning sunlight streamed across the attic floorboards, and voices echoed in the hall below the stairs.

They both scurried from beneath the covers, completely naked.

Isa threw his clothes at him while he struggled to get his trousers right side out.

"Isa? Are you awake? Come join us for breakfast." Lucy called from the foot of the stairs.

Frozen in terror, Isa noticed several things at once. Junior would not get dressed in time; he was hopping on one foot to get his leg into his dark trousers. The motion did interesting things to his genitals. On the floor was her nightgown, but Isa couldn't don it; she merely held it out in horror. It had stiffened into a wrinkled ball from Junior's seed. Traces of blood stained it.

She and Junior goggled at each other, their eyes giant blue and gold saucers, respectively, in their faces.

"Isa?" Lucy sounded curious. Any minute now, and she'd be walking up the attic stairs.

Silently, Isa motioned for Junior to hide behind the changing divider, then threw the stiff nightgown at his departing buttocks. She had just enough time to kick his boots beneath her bed when the stairs creaked.

"Don't come up," Isa yelped, diving beneath the covers.

"Why not?" Lucy sounded flummoxed. The top of her head was just visible through the stair railings.

"Because I'm in my birthday suit," Isa blurted, incapable of thinking of another reason why Lucy couldn't come into the attic.

"Oh." The silence stretched.

"There are many benefits to sleeping in the nude if you must know," Isa babbled defensively from beneath the covers.

"Are there?"

She couldn't tell if Lucy sounded suspicious or intrigued.

"Oh, yes. The air flow is much better for your skin. I sleep so hot, you know. Additionally, you won't need to wash as many nightgowns. I hate the blasted things, always choking me in my sleep."

Junior, tucked deeply into the corner behind the divider, covered his face with a hand. She could spy gooseflesh on his chest and arms from the bed. His nipples had tightened into little points from the morning chill in the air.

"Well, in that case, shall I just meet you in the diner?" There was a trace of amusement in her voice but, thankfully, no suspicion.

"I'll be quick!" Isa chirped.

As soon as the stairs creaked from Lucy's receding footsteps, Isa flew out of bed and rummaged through her wardrobe. As quiet as a couple of church mice, she and Junior dressed, bumping into each other and grinning. He kissed her once on the lips, stopped, and came back for a second. After she checked that the coast was clear in the hall, Junior slunk into his room like a guilty polecat. Isa smiled all the way downstairs.

Chapter Twenty-One

Isa felt detached from her body at the breakfast table. Like a specter with an aerial view from above, she appraised herself. She looked normal; she had donned a day dress the shade of claret that made her dark-blonde hair appear brighter. It had buttons in the front and didn't need a bustle or crinoline, and she felt half naked sitting there at the end of the table from the Stone family. Her cheeks bloomed with every memory of the night before, all encouraged by the ache low in her gut and between her legs. Matching her cheeks, Isa's hands were red-stained and conspicuous. Isa was a woman changed. Evolved. Some hybridized flower created in a hothouse. To the naked eye, her material was the same, but upon closer inspection, minute deviations appeared. She was somehow different. Altered.

Junior had transformed her.

As if she had summoned him, Junior walked into the dining room, adjusting a faded red kerchief over his neck. His great height and handsomeness truly were absurd. Deep-blue eyes met her gaze, and his fingers stopped fidgeting. Isa straightened fractionally, shoulders back, trying to halt the slow flush of heat rising from her chest to her collarbones.

"Jack, let Uncle Junior have that seat," Lucy ordered absently, stirring sugar into her coffee.

"Naw, it's alright." Junior playfully shoved a standing Jack back down into his chair. "Scoot down, Izzy."

The normal Isa would have asked Junior why he thought she'd want to sit by him.

Instead, she moved down a seat so Junior could take the chair beside her at one end. On her other side was Matthew, oblivious to everything but his breakfast. Wedged between the table and wall, Junior eased in beside her. The dining room's coffee and smoked meat scents disappeared until all she could smell was Ivory soap, tobacco, and the musk of his skin. It sparked an olfactory memory of his weight upon her, the smoothness of his broad shoulders between her knees.

Beneath the table, Isa noticed the way his faded denims stretched tight around his hard, muscular thighs. Hours earlier, she had dragged her nails along the fine blond hair that dusted them.

How was she supposed to sit beside him and eat with such lewd images bedeviling her? She'd never felt less hungry in her life. When the waitress arrived to take Junior's order, Isa took a bracing sip of her coffee...then almost spit it out.

Junior possessively placed his broad hand on her thigh beneath the table.

His palm was so hot, she could feel its warmth through her skirt and petticoats. So he was not unaffected. Peering at him from the corner of her eye, she took advantage of his attention on the waitress to study him. A lock of golden hair fell over his brow. She had pulled on that hair hours before. Had run her fingers through it. Mussed it.

The waitress left, and everyone made polite conversation around her.

"Mama, it ain't fair that I got third place in the sack race," Samuel complained to Lucy, who hid a yawn behind her hand.

"When I save up enough money, I'm gonna get a horse like Uncle Junior's," Matthew was saying to Ben, whose lip quirked up at this announcement.

Jack was teasing Samuel, pointing at him with a syrupy fork. "I got first place."

"Nobody asked you," Samuel said. "'Sides, you won runnin' with the little kids." Jack stuck his tongue out, and Lucy was forced to intervene.

Meanwhile, Junior's hand slid higher and squeezed. From the corner of his mouth, he murmured, "You feelin' poorly?" He didn't look directly at her, but his brows were furrowed.

Isa covered his hand with hers. They sat so close together that their arms appeared innocuously side by side above the table. "I'm a little sore."

Blue eyes flicked to her face. "Where?"

Checking that no one was paying undue attention to them, she slid his hand higher until he was cupping her gently between her legs. "Here."

In her periphery, the tips of his ears reddened. He swallowed. "How bad?"

"Not bad. It's like when you get saddle sore." She couldn't hide a wicked grin.

"You know what I want to do when you smile like that?" he asked. Junior had leaned so close that his breath tickled her ear.

She was considering how to reply when Ben spoke up from the other end of the table. "I got an invitation to a couple of Stock-Raisers' Association meetings up in Graham. You want to ride with me?"

Beneath the weight of everyone's stare, Junior withdrew his hand from under the table and tugged at his kerchief. "How long will it take?"

"A couple of weeks, I reckon. I promised Lucy I'd bring her home a turkey for Thanksgiving."

"Yeah, I'll go."

While they planned back and forth, Isa forced herself to eat. Junior's food was brought out, and when he tucked in, Isa's mischievous nature lured her hand up Junior's firm thigh. He stopped chewing. Normally, Isa would have smiled at his startled reaction, but she found herself incapable of it now. Her heart was in her throat, her blood thick and hot in her veins. She couldn't drag enough air into her lungs. Of its own volition, her left hand slid dangerously close to the bulge a few inches north. When it seemed as though he had turned to stone by her soft touch, she cleared her throat and bumped his boot with her foot.

Junior responded with a warning glance, and he hooked her foot with his. His mouth resumed its chewing, so Isa completed her mission by laying a caressing hand on the hardening bulge behind his straining fly.

"Did you get enough sleep?" she asked softly, her brain muzzy.

"Nope." He was cutting his ham steak into a dozen pieces, his eyes unfocused. "I reckon I need to sleep again soon. Wish I could sleep right now."

If that wasn't a double entendre, Isa didn't know what was. Licking her lips, she moved her biscuit around in its pepper gravy. "I could nap, too. Maybe I'll find the time after Lucy and your brother go home."

Air hissed out of Junior's parted lips, and he shifted in his seat, spreading his thighs wider. Beneath her curious hand, he was long, thick, and hard. "God, yes."

"What are you two talking about?" Lucy asked curiously.

Isa's left hand froze. She took a bite of her cold, soggy biscuit. "We were just saying how late we came in. That we didn't get enough sleep."

"Aunt Isa wants to take a nap," Jack said through a mouthful of hotcakes.

"Jackie, don't speak with your mouth full," Lucy said. Her brown eyes were sharp on Isa. "Junior, whatever happened with the fight at the dance?"

Isa nervously eased her hand back into her own lap while Junior summarized the scuffle beside the dance floor. She was losing her sanity. If she didn't get hold of herself, she was going to get them both into big trouble.

"ISA, MAY I speak with you in my room?" Lucy asked brightly in the hotel's foyer.

Damnation.

"Of course," Isa said in the same bright tone.

The boys disappeared through the hotel's back door to play in the yard, and Isa resolutely followed Lucy up the family staircase as if she were ascending the gallows. Junior and Ben had already made their way to the feed store to stock up on supplies for their journey north to the Stock Raisers' Association meetings. Isa's mind raced the whole way to Lucy's favorite room—one decorated in blue with an enormous bed overlooking the backyard—and she scrambled to hone her wits when Lucy questioned her. Because Lucy had most assuredly noticed something strange between Isa and Junior.

Sure enough, Lucy snapped the door shut behind them and asked, "Do you know what you're doing?"

"Pardon?" Isa made a show of blinking in confusion.

"Don't give me that." Lucy's lips twisted. "You didn't insult Junior once at breakfast. And Junior—he couldn't keep his eyes off you."

At her friend's strained features, Isa opened her mouth to deny knowing anything. Closed it. Opened it again. "Lucy, I—"

"Don't bother lying to me. I can smell one a mile away. Ask Samuel." Lucy folded her arms beneath her breasts.

Flustered from this direct interrogation, Isa lifted her hands helplessly. "I don't know what you want me to say."

"The truth, if you please," Lucy said crisply. "What is going on between you and my husband's brother?"

None of your business, Isa wanted to snap. She wouldn't, of course—Lucy was one of her best friends. But Isa wasn't ready to talk about it. Not yet. She didn't have words for what was happening between Junior and her. Whatever *it* was, it was a newly hatched fledgling, weak and precarious on a nest's edge. One wrong word, one wrong move, and it would plummet to its death. She needed time. Needed privacy to mull things over.

Lucy's eyes widened expectantly.

Isa took a deep breath. "Junior and I formed a truce last night after the dance."

"A truce."

"Yes. I've been..." Isa chewed a lip, considering how to express herself.

"Angry with him?" Lucy's tightly crossed arms loosened.

"Well, yes." It wasn't a falsehood. Isa had been very angry with him. And the closer to the truth she was, the more Lucy would believe her. "I heard about the engagement, and he'd not once told me of it—"

"You two *did* get close during your travels," Lucy broke in softly, lips parted in wonder. "I knew it. Even Ben sees it, and he's always half-blind where Junior is concerned."

"Junior and I have done nothing wrong." There was an edge to Isa's words.

Lucy dropped her arms and softened fully. "I didn't say you were doing anything wrong. I just want you to be careful. Don't let him hurt you."

"He would never hurt me. If he did, I'd hurt him back, and worse."

"Which is why you went with Gareth to the dance?"

"I didn't *go* with Gareth. He just happened to ride with me and asked me to dance," Isa muttered.

"Junior had smoke coming out of his ears."

"Such a thing is impossible."

"Isa."

Isa rounded the wrought iron bed frame to look out the window at the boys playing in the backyard. One brown head, one black, and one fair.

She sighed. "Very well. Junior and I got close on the trail. But we didn't do anything," she said quickly before Lucy could interject. The lie tumbled free, and it sounded believable even to Isa's ears. Lucy was an honest person; if she knew the full extent of their relationship, she would either cajole Isa into telling Sol or would put a stop to it. And Isa would do neither. It was no one's business but their own if she and Junior enjoyed a little harmless fun. Who was it hurting?

"Did you two do anything last night?" Lucy sounded as though she were afraid to ask.

Isa took her time answering. "We talked. We kissed in the stable." They weren't lies, but the Spanish Inquisition wouldn't get more out of her.

Lucy's footsteps approached, and her hand rested carefully on Isa's shoulder blade. "That's wonderful."

Eyes widening incredulously, Isa turned around. "It is?"

Lucy's face was full of understanding. "Oh, yes. You make him happy, it's obvious to everyone. Even Sol. You may want to consider that. Your brother won't always have blinders on when it comes to Junior. What I saw today at the breakfast table..."

"What did you see?"

"I saw Junior acting very flustered around a woman." Lucy chuckled. "I've never seen such a thing in my life. And last night? Last night, he was so jealous he could spit."

Isa had the sudden urge to jump on the bed and kick her feet in the air. Alarmed by this revolting impulse, she nervously edged away from Lucy. "I don't think he was all those things. You're being fanciful."

"I'm not!" Lucy followed, prowling behind her like a zealous merchant with wares to sell. "I see it. Ben sees it. Poppy saw it years ago."

"Lucy—"

Lucy leaned in. "You even smell like him."

"I do not!" But she did. The musk of Junior was all over her. Serious brown eyes bore into hazel. "Junior loves you."

Isa whispered, "What?"

"And I think you love him, too."

"You're mad."

"I know what I see."

They were staring at each other, Isa horrified, Lucy sympathetic, when several pairs of boots stomped up the family staircase. The door burst open.

"Mama! Mama, tell Jack this is a toad and not a frog!" Samuel bellowed from the top of his lungs. Lucy saw the toad in question and jumped back.

Isa took advantage of her friend's distraction and fled.

SHE FOUND REFUGE in Hobb's General Store's storage room. Tightly packed with parcels and wooden crates, the store room muffled all sound from the front. Woody scents of pallets and burlap allayed her racing thoughts. Dust motes swirled lazily in the stream of light from the single window near the roof.

After Isa begged for work, Mrs. Hobb gave her a clipboard with instructions to take inventory from Saturday morning's supply load.Half an hour ago, Isa had spied Junior's buckskin Stetson across the street behind a group of men through the front window. Now she was counting pine boxes of nails and writing crisp numbers in the margins when a shift in the air made her pause. A pair of strong arms wrapped around her waist and hoisted her effortlessly into the air. The clipboard and pencil clattered at her captor's feet as Isa struggled in earnest. She struck back with an elbow, connecting with the man's head, and the owner of the offending arms released a masculine grunt.

She would recognize that grunt anywhere.

From the doorway came bellowing laughter. Isa caught sight of Mrs. Hobb leaning against the storage room's doorframe, her stomach jumping beneath pendulous breasts that hadn't felt the restriction of stays in a score of years.

"I'd think twice before taking that one on again, Junior," Mrs. Hobb said.

"I can handle her," Junior growled close to Isa's ear. She cocked an elbow, and he set her down like a hot potato.

Color high, hair mussed, Isa bent down for her clipboard and pencil. "You're hardheaded. I'm sure you didn't feel a thing."

Junior touched a tender spot above his ear, wincing for dramatic effect.

A bell tinkled above the store's door in the front room.

"While you two hash it out, I'm gonna make a post office run. Mr. Hobb's in the front if you need anything." Mrs. Hobb winked at Junior and departed, leaving the door cracked behind her.

Now that they were alone, the air grew charged between them, crackling with static electricity. Isa dusted off her papers and side-eyed Junior, taking in the golden stubble, full lips, and indigo eyes that didn't waver from her face. He took a step toward her. Then another. He stalked her like the mountain lion he so resembled.

"If you pounce on me again, I'll be forced to use this," Isa warned, holding up the clipboard.

"Think I'm scared of you?" he asked, his eyes intense upon her.

"You should be."

His hand was a blur as it snatched the clipboard from her fingers and set it on a shelf beside them. Crowding her, Junior maneuvered them behind the lip of the shelf and into a dark little alcove, out of sight. Her back pressed tight against the wall, his hips flush against hers. Helpless not to, she ran her fingertip beneath his metal belt buckle, brushing the firm stomach behind his shirtfront.

"Did you get everything you needed for your trip?" she asked, dipping her fingers a little deeper.

Running his knuckles beneath her jaw, Junior watched her intently. "Yep."

"When are you leaving?"

"Tomorrow." He gripped her hips, pulling her until her feet were on either side of his, their pelvises even more snug together.

"Will you miss me?"

Junior took his hat off and nuzzled his soft lips against her neck. "I already miss you, darlin'."

"Mm." Isa couldn't think when he did that. She ran her fingers lightly through his hair, loving its coarse-silk texture.

"I think this is Ben's way of getting me away from you." He pulled away and pressed his lips against the top of her head, breathing her in. "He'll probably try and talk sense into me."

"Perhaps he just wants to spend time with you," Isa reasoned. "I don't believe you and I are being very convincing in our *friendship*. Lucy cornered me after you and Ben left."

He cursed and cupped her shoulders, meeting her eye. "What did she say?"

Junior loves you. And I think you love him, too.

"She knows there is…more between us. I may have told her we kissed."

Brows rising, Junior licked his lips and smiled. "You did?"

"Why do you look so happy?" she groaned.

"Because you're my girl. And people knowin' isn't necessarily a bad thing. Is it?" His eyes went slumberous, his lips in a boyish curve.

"Pff." The small noise was swallowed by his mouth moving hotly upon hers. It drove every sentient thought from her brain, and she returned the kiss with equal enthusiasm. Happiness was a bright note in the maelstrom of intense need. Always, his kisses tasted dark and exotic, but today, it was flavored with joy.

"I don't want that deputy sniffing around while I'm gone," he mumbled between kisses, plucking her lips with his.

"Who?" Sense returned sluggishly. "Oh. Am I supposed to control who visits the store or eats at the hotel, Junior?"

His fingers delved into the base of her updo, displacing pins. "No. But that's alright. Just so long as you know."

"Know what?"

"That you're mine."

This next kiss was so deep that it made Isa's jaw ache. Her pulse was erratic. Her skin throbbed. Every place he touched begged to be handled harder, wanting more, more until he was as deep inside her as she could get him. Isa moaned and clung to him, her body relaying a need her voice could not.

"Sh," he said against her lips, but he was gasping as loudly, as breathlessly as she. "I wish I could take you right now, right here, in this corner."

Intoxicated by his scent, by the strength of his sensuality, Isa lightly bit his cleft chin. Kissed it. "I would let you."

Grabbing two handfuls of her bottom, he tucked his head between her shoulder and neck, groaning. "Lord Almighty, I need to calm down. Talk to me about something. Anything."

"Yes. Excellent idea." Isa sifted through the muck of her brain. "Tell me about the Stock-Raisers' Association meetings. Tell me about the trail."

They spoke of normal, comfortable things, her hips still wedged securely against his. Junior's tawny head lowered repeatedly to steal a kiss, to murmur something shocking in her ear, the space between them filled with the scent of leather and laundered skirts. Isa never wanted him to leave. And when he finally did, it was with a goodbye kiss that made her toes curl in her boots, their lips damp and swollen when they broke apart. He had to exit through the back entrance door, adjusting himself through tented jeans, and his backward glance and tipped hat touched something deeper within her than the soul-stealing kisses.

Chapter Twenty-Two

"I've been keeping something from you," Junior said in the silence across the campfire.

He and Ben had camped a day's ride northwest of home. The weather was clear, they had made good time, and life had returned to normalcy since being in his brother's quiet presence. If only that blasted secret wasn't hanging over his head like a rain cloud threatening to pop. The more time he'd spent around Ben, the larger it loomed.

Ben paused in the middle of pouring his coffee, forehead wrinkling above straight, black brows. His shrewd eyes were the same hue as Junior's. "Does it have anything to do with Sol's little sister?"

Junior froze. "What makes you say that?"

"You two aren't real good about hidin' your feelings."

To hide his burgeoning panic, Junior laughed. "I don't know what you're talkin' about."

"Horse shit."

"You know how me and Izzy are."

"I know how you two used to be, Junior. But it's gone a mite past that." Ben's broad chest swelled with a breath as though he was struggling for patience. "And I think unless you're plannin' on marrying her, you need to leave her alone. Cut ties."

Sudden, helpless fury choked Junior. His words came tumbling out, heated. Impassioned. "I *did* cut ties. I stayed as far away as I could, Ben. And then I still found myself in Austin, watchin' over her like God had sent me to be some guardian angel. More fool Him. The things she's been up to…"

Silence followed this explosion, and they watched each other, a mountain lion and a panther meeting in unknown territory.

Warily, Ben gestured with his tin cup. "I reckon she feels the same about you, considerin' how she acted when she found out about Kristy Anne."

"Christ, not that woman again. That name pops up like a bad penny." Junior scrubbed his face with both hands until his vision blurred. "Whatever fool notion Kristy Anne had about us, I settled it. I broke it off and told Mother to stop yammering about nuptials that were never gonna happen."

"You tell Isa this?"

"Who the hell do you think I did it for?" Junior looked at his brother, defenseless. "What am I going to do, huh? I don't think I can keep away from her. She's under my skin."

Pensively, Ben scratched the dense black stubble hiding the cleft Stone chin. "Have you considered askin' Sol and their pa's permission to court her?"

"She's not interested in marriage. The life Isa wants"—Junior struggled to put it into words—"it's not traditional. She wants to go places. See things. Experience life. Imagine having her brain but being raised in a family that multiplies like rabbits and never makes it past primary school. Izzy's had a taste of the family life. A dozen siblings and double the nieces and nephews—she doesn't want that. She wants something different."

Ben's expression was indecipherable. "You know her pretty well, don't you?"

Uncomfortable, Junior pulled a cigarette out from his vest pocket and busily worked on lighting it. "I reckon I do." Desperate to change the subject, he veered the conversation away from Isa. "I've been meaning to ask, have any drifters shown up in town and asked about me?"

Eyes narrowing, Ben said, "No. Should I be worried?"

"I have to tell you something, and it's not an easy thing to say."

"I'm listenin'."

The cigarette trembled slightly between Junior's two fingers. "I'm not a Texas Ranger. Not anymore."

Ben set his cup down and clasped his hands together between his knees. "What happened?"

"Got discharged." Though it was easier talking to Ben than their father, it was difficult imparting news proving how much of a disappointment he was. "Dishonorably."

The word rang out like a cymbal crash. Ben pulled the coffee pot from its bed of coals and refilled his cup, a deep crease between his two black brows. "When was this?"

"Two years ago."

Ben set the coffee pot back in its place, picked up his mug full of black, shimmering liquid, and cradled it between his palms. "Why didn't you tell me?"

"Christ, Ben." Junior shook his head at the little fire. "It was a *dishonorable discharge*. I've done enough fool things over the years that I was in no hurry to tell you I'd dug myself into a hole again."

Mouth pursed, Ben took a tense sip of his coffee. Then he surprised Junior. "You said two years ago? I knew something was wrong. Couldn't put my finger on it, but I knew. You'd stopped sending letters, didn't talk much when you came home...if you came home. You looked like—" He broke off.

Clenching his trembling hands together, Junior demanded, "I looked like what?"

"Like you were thinkin' life wasn't worth livin'." Ben's jaw flexed. "Lucy and I were both scared."

Junior held silent.

"But I didn't push it," Ben added cautiously. "'Cause you made me a promise that you wouldn't do a fool thing like you did in the hayloft again without talkin' to me first."

Junior released the tight clench of his jaw and admitted softly, "I did think about it. But I won't break my promise. I just didn't want to talk to anyone about it. About what I've done."

"You wanna talk about it now?"

"I don't know." Junior's voice was barely audible. "I don't think I'm ready to tell you yet. It's bad. Real bad."

"Not bad enough to hang."

"Almost did. Captain Havelard had some words with the judge."

"Jesus. Neither Pa nor I were notified you went to court."

"At my request. But the case—it was sensitive. Not open to civilians."

They sat in the tense quiet for several minutes. Then Ben said gently, "I'm glad you told me. Must have been damned hard."

Junior could only nod, throat painfully tight. He felt the cloud above him break apart piece by piece. The pain was there, but it was less. And soon, he'd tell Ben everything, and the past would be vapor over the horizon.

TWO WEEKS LATER, Junior's spirits were high as they rode across Ben's pasture. A turkey squawked and gobbled on Ben's pack mule in a flimsy cage. They hadn't had another uncomfortable conversation since that first night, and Junior was light as a feather. The only thing that would make a perfect end to their journey would be if Isa coincidentally visited the ranch.

A tall, shirtless Sol caught Junior's eye along the distant fence line.

Face splitting into wide, toothy grins, the two men rode closer to the foreman. Junior called out, "Don't you know it's almost winter? Put your damned shirt on."

Sol stopped digging the post hole and turned, shading his eyes with a filthy, callused hand. "When Hell freezes over!"

Ben chuckled, but he didn't slow his mount down. "I'll meet with you later, Sol. I'm gonna give the missus a turkey and a kiss."

"Give her a kiss for me," Junior called after him, laughing at the rude hand gesture Ben sent over his broad shoulder.

"Better not let his boys catch him doin' that." Sol chuckled, wiping his face with a forearm.

"Pretty sure Samuel invented that one," Junior said wryly, tossing his full canteen at Sol.

"How was the trip?" Sol asked before taking a swig.

They talked about the weather during the trail; it had rained on them the night before, and Junior was certain he was coming down with something. He told Sol about the meeting with the Stock-Raisers' Association and the changes in prices for the upcoming year.

"Damned depression," Sol growled. He tossed the canteen back.

"We'll make do," Junior sighed, hanging the empty container on his saddle horn. "Ben's got a good head for business. It'd be even better if we got Izzy in his corner."

"Ain't that the truth."

"Is she around?" Junior kept his tone innocent.

Sol scratched a fine dusting of dirt off the back of his neck. On a fence post, his shirt fluttered in the wind. "At the ranch? Nope."

"Oh. She still in Dogwood, then?" Junior's question was carefully offhanded.

Laughing, Sol sent a questioning glance in Junior's direction. "Why do you want to know so bad? You courtin' her or something?"

Sweat broke out on Junior's lip. "What? Hell no!" Good thing he hadn't dismounted. He had never beaten Sol in a footrace, and Champion would have a far better chance of outrunning the lanky cowboy.

Sol barked out a laugh and turned back to his work. "Good. You ain't good enough for her anyway."

Junior's stomach sank, and he had to smooth his expression when Sol glanced back at him, still with a curious frown wrinkling his brow. Junior cleared his throat. "You can't just say something like that and not expect a man to jump a little."

"Hell, Junior, I know you wouldn't do me like that. I trust you more than anyone not to start sniffin' around my baby sister."

"Yeah."

"Oh, I almost forgot. Your pa rode by last week. He wants you to come by the big house as soon as you're settled."

"Appreciate it."

Junior rode along the edge of Ben's property toward home. He had no plans to ride to his father's house. If anyone could bring his mood down into the dirt, it was John Stone, Sr.

The black cloud was back. Worse, it was akin to an anvil, crushing Junior with the heavy weight of guilt. He was the sorriest son of a bitch alive. What sort of friend vowed to protect a beloved little sister just to carry on with her behind the brother's back? Was he supposed to resist Isa?

He certainly couldn't anymore.

He was well and truly tied.

If he was a righteous man, he would stay away from her. Too bad he wasn't.

Already, he was planning on getting a night's shut-eye, then riding into Dogwood first thing in the morning.

Junior patted his pocket. Something small and hard dug comfortingly into his thigh. He'd seen the trinket in a glass case during a supply run in Dallas, and it had glittered, stylish but different. It made him think of Isa. The price had lightened his wallet, and he'd left the store with a secret smile. Even now, the thought of gifting it to his girl and stealing a kiss replaced any residual self-reproach.

Two hours later, he sank into his bed, cleansed of trail dirt and exhausted. Thoughts of Isa's response sent him into blissful sleep.

HOOFBEATS BROUGHT JUNIOR awake the next morning.

Automatically, he slid stealthily out of bed, grabbed his .45 Colt off the bedside table, and crept down the hall. His throat was on fire, and he had to stifle an explosive sneeze at the front window. An unfamiliar horse was tethered to the front porch post. Several harsh knocks pounded on the door. Junior cocked his gun, teeth clenched together, glassy eyes fixed.

"Come on, boy, I know you're in there!" a voice barked through the solid door. The man tried the doorknob; it was locked.

Nostrils flaring, Junior lowered his gun.

Father.

Junior unlocked the front door, opened it, and stepped back, squinting at the invasion of midmorning light. John Stone's great silhouette spread a dark shadow, stretching halfway across Junior and beyond. His father stomped in and slammed the door shut.

"Do you know how long I've been lookin' for you, damn it?"

"Mornin', how are you? Good? Hell, I'm grand, thanks for asking." Junior's sarcastic retort was trailed by a tickling cough.

"Morning? It's noon on a Sunday. Couldn't pull yourself outta bed for church? Didn't those Rangers teach you any discipline?"

Too busy coughing to answer, Junior turned his back on his sire and shouldered his way through the kitchen door. Without asking John if he wanted any, Junior readied a pot of coffee to brew and stoked the banked fire in the stove. His father followed, casting disparagements against the red union suit Junior wore in broad daylight, carping on about how he'd had to ride all over creation to find him.

"I was with Ben at the Stock-Raisers' meetings," Junior said without heat. Lord, he felt like hell. "Now I'm dying of the bubonic plague, and you couldn't give a damn."

John snorted, narrowing a jaundiced eye on his son. "Your mama told me you jilted Miss Kristy Anne."

"I didn't jilt anyone, considering I didn't ask the female to marry me in the first place." Junior looked hard at John.

"Don't you look at me like that, boy."

"I won't when you and Mother keep your noses out of business that doesn't concern you."

John took a threatening step forward. "Big words comin' from a pissant I used to whoop till he was twenty."

You just try it, you old sonuvabitch, Junior thought. The thought of overpowering his father made him revolt deep inside, but he was too sick and tired to keep the peace, literally and figuratively. Swallowing his words and being the bigger man was hard when he felt cold and shivery, and his throat had turned into a red-hot brand.

As if realizing he was getting nowhere fast, John pulled the dining chair out and took a seat. The wood creaked under his weight. "If you don't want Kristy Anne, who do you want?"

Scoffing, Junior turned back to the blue enamel coffee kettle. "What makes you think I want anyone?"

"Your mama said something about that Williams girl." Said with the same tone reserved for diseased cattle, full of disgust and indignation.

"If you know everything, why ask?" Everything was a test with this man.

"I just wanted to check that you weren't tellin' your mama any balooey."

Nostrils pinching, Junior pulled a mug from the cabinet and scraped petrified sugar out of the enamel dish with a spoon. The spoon bent. "Just 'cause I talked about Isa Williams doesn't mean I'm courting her. I was just trying to get Mother off my back. That woman's still playing tug-o-war with the apron strings."

John chuckled reluctantly. "Make me a cup while you're at it."

Both men sat at the table for a while, speaking civilly as they sipped their coffee. Then John impatiently set his elbows on the table.

"I need you to go with me to Lufkin Wednesday."

"It's Thanksgiving this week, and I just got back from—"

"Stop that whinin' and listen," John said sharply.

Junior's teeth clacked shut, turning his jaw to granite.

"You look just like your brother," John groused, pulling his mug to him. "I need you to hold the Circle S book here until we can go. A lawyer named Carl Rafferty in Lufkin is gonna take a look at it."

Sitting stiffly in his straight-backed chair, Junior gritted out, "I told you I don't want any part of the business. I don't want the ranch."

John waved that off. "Want in one hand and spit in the other. You need to be more involved. When I die, you're the one who's gettin' everything. The ranch needs a strong hand and someone who knows how to run it. Your mama does the books, but you—you'll do everything else."

"Take Ben with you." Junior didn't give a damn about the ranch, or the book, and especially about riding to Lufkin. Nonchalantly, he picked his mug up to sip his coffee. It was a good thing he did because John slammed his fist on the table so hard that the remaining mug jumped and overturned.

"Enough! I've built a legacy, and by God, you're going to take the reins when I'm gone."

Junior wasn't daunted by the purple vein bulging in his father's forehead. He watched a trickle of coffee pool to the table's edge. "And I don't want your legacy. I'll make my own way."

John sat back in his chair. "You're plumb stupid, you know that?"

In John's eyes, everyone was stupid.

Exhausted physically and mentally, Junior took their mugs to the sink while his father lectured about his lack of ambition. But when John mentioned Loretta being embarrassed by her only son, Junior couldn't resist a little jab. "Is she embarrassed of me? Or is she embarrassed that you galivant in town with whores every weekend?"

There was an ominous, telling silence.

Recalling Isa's words at the campfire, Junior added, "You could get something catching."

The purple vein in the elder Stone's head pulsated. John stood, stormed outside, and came back with a ledger the size of Maryland. Slamming it down on the dry corner of the breakfast table, John growled, "Keep the book here, son. Let no one else see. I can't trust it at the house, and the banker in town is crooked as a barrel of snakes. We'll ride out Tuesday."

He left before Junior could get a word in edgewise.

Without sparing a second look at the Circle S ledger, Junior tossed a ragged mustard-colored dishtowel on the table spill, stumbled to his room, and crawled back into bed.

Chapter Twenty-Three

He'd been a slugabed all Sunday evening and night, and Junior still felt like something scraped out of the bottom of a trash barrel the next morning. He sat at the breakfast table with a shaving mirror propped against his coffee mug, hoping his shaking hand wouldn't slice his throat. His ears were stopped up from constantly blowing his nose, and he was stricken by recurring coughing fits. Therefore, he didn't notice the rider passing the kitchen window. He had just leaned over to run the trembling blade from throat to chin when the kitchen door slung open, and Isa Williams waltzed in without knocking.

The blade had no sooner clattered to the floor than his hand was on the .45 on the table. When he saw flashing gold-green eyes and a thick, waist-length braid, he released the gun's grip like it was a red-hot coal.

"Isa?" Junior gawked.

Shrewd hazel eyes took in his raw, red nose. "You *are* sick. Here I was thinking you were avoiding me." The forced humor in her voice belied her stiff posture.

Worry suddenly ate at him. Isa was angry. *Damn it.* "What're you doin' here?"

Smiling tightly, she set two jars down with twin clunks atop the little round breakfast table. "Lucy sent these."

He didn't look at the jars; his eyes didn't waver from hers. A dollop of thick, white soap dropped from his chin onto his lap. The silence stretched like saltwater taffy between them. He hadn't realized how much he'd missed her until she was standing right in front of him, fresh and lovely in a navy riding skirt and white blouse. The curls by her ears were lighter in color than the rest of her hair, bright against her tan skin and pale eyes. Junior's hands spasmed.

God, you're in love with her, aren't you?

It yanked the rug right out from under him.

"You look like a caricature of Santa Claus," she said, and her wide lips curled up reluctantly.

Junior stopped staring to peer at the little mirror on the table. Ivory foam coated him from jugular to cheekbones, his red lips vivid against it. While he and his reflection shared a flabbergasted look, Isa whirled to his cupboards. He knew how bare they were—not even a crumb graced their shelves. Shaking her head in disgust at the sink of dirty dishes, Isa reached for a clean pot from a hook over the oven and set it on the greasy stovetop.

"Didn't your mama ever teach you how to clean up after yourself? Mine would have switched me."

Junior was too busy reeling to answer. Out of all the women he could have fallen in love with, it was this one. This sharp-tongued, fiery-tempered female. Just looking at her busying herself at the stove made his throat seize up. What if she was his? What if, one day, he'd get to sit at this table and watch her with the knowledge that she belonged to him and he belonged to her?

"I'll heat these up for you," she said, returning to the jars on the table.

"You don't have to—"

"Don't be ridiculous."

Unwilling to sit there and ogle her like a scoundrel, Junior picked up his razor and resumed shaving his neck. His fingers trembled worse than ever. He loved her. God, but he loved her so much he could howl. Blissfully unaware of his turmoil, Isa kindled the stove's fire higher, fed its hungry blaze two logs, then closed one damper and opened another. She poured the contents of both jars into the pot and wiped her hands on a semi-clean dishcloth on a peg.

"It's a right state in here."

"So you've said." Junior sneezed and blew his nose with the damp kerchief in his pocket, wiping off half his soap in the process.

"You're going to cut your own throat." Isa propped her hands on her hips. Wouldn't it irk her to know how much she looked like her ma at that moment? "Here. Give me that." She strode over in a waft of fragrant skirts and took the straight razor from his hand.

Too exhausted to argue, Junior groaned and rubbed his eyes, praying the pressure his sneeze had caused would ease. He heard her drag the soap bowl and the shaving brush closer, and he made only the weakest attempt to dodge the horsehair brush when she began reapplying soap to his face. All struggles ceased when she grabbed a handful of his golden hair and held him still.

"Were you going somewhere today?" Isa asked over the sound of the blade scraping stubble.

Lips hardly moving, Junior said, "I'm supposed to take the books to Lufkin with Father Tuesday and Wednesday. I wanted to ride by Dogwood today and let you know before I left."

The grip on his hair loosened considerably. "Books? You read?"

"Ha ha," he deadpanned, eyes closed. The pressure in his head was slowly improving. "The Circle S books. The old man wants to take it to some banker he knows. Said he didn't trust his old one anymore. Hell, he won't even keep it at the big house."

Fingertips brushed his hair from his brow, smoothing over his forehead comfortingly. "Why didn't he just go himself? You're obviously in no state to travel."

"It's his way of getting me involved in the business. He still wants me to take over the ranch."

"And you don't want that."

Junior waited for her to finish shaving around his lips and under his sore nose before replying. "Never have. Ben would be better at it, but…"

"But your folks treat him like a stain that just won't wash out," Isa mused.

He opened his eyes to see her peering thoughtfully down at him. "Yeah."

"Instead of taking over your father's business, you want to…" Isa trailed off and resumed her shaving, waiting.

It took several rasps of the razor for him to formulate a response. "I don't know anymore. I haven't thought about the future since—well, in a while."

Pensive, she finished shaving him, cleaned the blade, and set the straight razor beside the basin of cooling water. Holding the little hand mirror up while he wiped his face clean with an ugly mustard dishtowel, she said, "Maybe it's time for you to start thinking of one."

AFTER JUNIOR CONSUMED the soup straight from the pot, he shuffled to his bedroom to begin packing, coughing all the way. Isa watched him disappear down the hall, worrying her lip with her teeth. If he traveled to Lufkin in this condition, his cough could turn into a serious respiratory illness.

Sol had told her at church that Junior and Ben were back, and she'd felt a cautious fear rise in her that he'd decided to turn taciturn toward her again. A quick visit with Lucy this morning had proved that he hadn't turned cold—he *had* a cold. Now she was worried all over again; the damned fool was going to ride himself into an early grave.

Feeling an uncomfortable dose of hopelessness, Isa found his galvanized steel tub and filled it with chilly well water while pots of water heated on the stovetop to a boil. When Junior returned to the kitchen with a bag of clothes and supplies, it was to a sweaty Isa smacking the side of a steaming tub.

"Get in."

"I don't need a b-bath." He was sneezing before he'd completed the sentence.

Face twisting doubtfully, Isa argued, "I beg to differ. Here." She handed him a washcloth and a bar of Ivory soap. His cheeks were chapped into twin spots of color, and his eyes were dull. Isa touched his forehead with the back of her hand. "You're feverish. You're in no condition to travel. Take your bath before the water gets cold, and I'll see to your bedding."

"I'll take your bath only because you went to the trouble." Junior dropped the rag and soap into the hot water and sluggishly began to peel himself out of his rumpled clothing. He paused. "What's wrong with my bedding?"

"Ben said you caught a cold on the trail. If I know men the way I do, you haven't changed your bedding since before you left, and your sheets are atrocious. There's nothing better than sliding between clean sheets after a bath."

He chuckled weakly. "Since when were you ever domestic?"

Glaring without heat, Isa said, "Just because I don't go about making a house a home doesn't mean I don't know how to make a cozy life. Or how to take care of a family."

As though the teasing had drained him, Junior ceased arguing and stepped, naked and unselfconscious, into the bath. He was so beautiful that her breath caught. Gooseflesh stood from his shoulders to his kneecaps, and she felt a pang of protectiveness. Sweat popped out on his forehead and upper lip, and his nose began to run.

"You're staying home," Isa said firmly, handing him her soft cotton handkerchief.

Junior blew his nose and shook his head weakly. "I can't, Izzy. I have to ride with my pa to get his books looked at, or he'll make my life hell. It isn't worth the fight."

Steam rising all around, she bent until she was at eye level. "It's always worth the fight. Just get the books looked at without riding to Lufkin."

His brow pinched. She didn't like his fever-bright eyes. "I told you, he doesn't trust—"

"No. I meant *I* can look at the books. Between the two of us, we can discover where the ranch is losing money."

While Junior considered this, she left him to his bath and stripped the sheets from his bed. The clean bedding from the linen closet smelled of cedar, and she aired them out as best she could. Isa took the clean clothing out of his packed bag and set the pile on the kitchen table, tutting at the way he dripped water onto the floor. Junior was a horrible patient and wanted to do everything himself. She wouldn't hear of it.

Within the next hour, he was tucked into bed wearing a fresh set of red underwear, and she was setting a glass of water and a stack of clean kerchiefs on the bedside table. Feeling the dry, chapped heat radiating off him, she ran back to the kitchen for a basin of water and a rag. Once the wet cloth was draped over his forehead, she turned to leave...and was stopped by a hard hand wrapped around her wrist.

"Wait." He didn't open his eyes, and she felt a pang at seeing the length of his lashes against his flushed cheekbones. "The ledger is on the parlor table. Help yourself to it. I trust you."

"Thank you," she said softly, stroking his damp hair back from the cloth.

He fell asleep within minutes.

Forehead creasing, Isa wondered how much trouble she'd be in if she stayed the night.

No, Lucy was understanding, but not to that extent. It was better to come back in the morning before John arrived. Frustrated that she didn't have the right to stay overnight with him while he lay on the bed, handsome and vulnerable, Isa grudgingly stepped into the hall, quietly shutting the door behind her.

Then she entered the parlor and settled herself on the settee in front of an enormous ledger with the Circle S brand on its leather cover. Isa opened its gilded pages and got to work.

JUNIOR'S FEVER BROKE the next morning, and he grumpily ate the breakfast Isa brought with her from Lucy and Ben's house.

"I don't need you babyin' me," he groused when she cleaned up his empty plate.

"Don't get used to it. I'm only doing this because Lucy asked me to. She didn't want to come herself and possibly bring something catching back to the children. There's too much work to be done for Thanksgiving."

"So you're the sacrificial lamb?"

"Precisely."

A smile cracked his face. "Did you figure anything out from looking at the books?"

Excitement rose in her chest, and Isa abandoned the dishes in the sink to sit next to Junior. "Yes. I found loads of errors. Whoever your bookkeeper is should be tarred and feathered."

"That would be my mother," he said wryly.

Isa winced. "I apologize."

He laughed. "You ain't sorry for shit."

"You're right." Isa pulled a sheet of notes out of her hidden skirt pocket. "She's truly horrid at arithmetic. I would suggest that your father hire someone else immediately. I do, however, have a few questions. Let's go over the facts.

"Your father sells beef for up to seventy-five dollars a head in San Francisco, and, as he's a sound businessman, he doesn't sell them for a penny less. After paying the hands and the remaining men on the ranch, your father makes a profit of about sixty-nine thousand a year. Divide that by twelve months, and he has a comfortable six thousand monthly. But it's expensive running a ranch, so he only pockets a fraction of that."

Junior whistled. "Did you stay up all night reading that?"

She wrinkled her nose. "If only. I had to reach Lucy's house by sunset, or they'd send someone over." Turning the page over, she showed Junior her notes. "Typically, Circle S expenditures lower after trail drives. This year, there has been no change in expenses, which I find odd, even with the depression. If you compare it to last year's bank deposits, there has been a thousand-dollar monthly discrepancy since May. It's balanced, but I bet half my savings that the answer is in that ledger. I simply don't know enough about the particulars to get a clear picture."

Sobering, Junior pulled the paper to him. A thousand dollars missing a month was a helluva loss in this economy. "What do you need to know?"

"Even with the books, it can be difficult to narrow it down. I've worked at a bank long enough to identify certain patterns. Businesses are always bringing their books in, suffering from the same things the Circle S Ranch is—mysteriously disappearing money. Often, they're making a series of unsound investments. But it could be any number of things, embezzlement being the most common. Payroll fraud is always worth looking at—the bookkeeper will keep employees' names on the payroll despite having fired them and will just pocket the money. I'm sure it's not that, considering your mother does the books."

Junior stiffened visibly at the latter, but instead of lashing out at her as she'd expected, he quickly stood from his chair and stomped toward the parlor. Half-afraid, half-curious, Isa followed. In the parlor, Junior sat in the space she'd occupied the day before and rifled through the ledger's gilded pages.

"Where the hell is spring of this year?" he muttered.

"Here." Isa sat beside him, their thighs snug, shoulders brushing. Reaching past his large, clumsy hands, she found the place she had bookmarked with a scrap of paper. "I noticed nothing wrong with the balance at first, as everything was the same since January: payroll, feed, everything. But according to this"—she pointed at the bank deposits—"your father is pocketing less profit between May and October of this year."

Junior licked a thumb and flipped the pages until he reached April's payroll. He combed through them, lips moving as he read, then repeated the process with May, June, July, and so on. Patiently, sensing he knew something she didn't, Isa said nothing and waited.

Finally, he cursed and sat up. "When I visited the ranch a few weeks back, I was told five ranch hands had been let go. But on here—"

"Everyone is all accounted for." Isa bent over the book to furiously flip back and forth. "According to this, no one was let go since the cattle drive's cook was fired."

Junior slowly shook his head. "I figured it was because Father was visiting the whorehouse every weekend."

Isa glanced back at him. "He's not."

"What? How do you know?"

Why did she have to open her big mouth? Isa slid her eyes back to the ledger. "Lucy may have mentioned it."

"Who the hell is he spending weekends with?" When she didn't say right away, Junior wrapped his fingers around the tail of her braid and tweaked it. "Tell me, Izzy."

Her mouth twisted at this unpleasant turn of events. Slowly, Isa said, "He's keeping a mistress in town. Lucy said the woman is my age."

Junior made an explosive noise of disgust. "I wonder if Mama knows."

"Do you suspect that's why she's embezzling a thousand dollars a month out from under your father's nose?"

"I reckon that's as good a reason as any. But—if I'm bein' honest, it doesn't feel right. She wouldn't leave the ranch, her friends. She'd pretend everything is fine and expect everyone else to do the same." Junior absently stroked her braid.

Isa tried to not let the glide of his hand over her hair hypnotize her, but she was a snake in a basket, and he waved the pungi, charming her against her will. Junior's introspection shifted incrementally. He was watching her expression, his eyes dark, the lids sleepy. His fist ran down her braid from root to tip, this time pulling the tie off at the end.

"Junior—"

"I can't kiss you, but I can touch you," he said and proceeded to unravel her thick plait into endless skeins of honey-colored waves. "You don't know how bad I've wanted to do this again."

Isa pretended stoicism, but her face and body felt hot. Docilely, she let him run his fingers through her long, loose tresses. Junior's eyes glittered as he untangled every knot until her hair flowed through his fingers like water. The sensation was so pleasant and arousing that she closed her eyes and clenched her thighs together. She was tempted to kiss him even though he was sick, damn the consequences.

She had just slid her hand from his large, square knee to his groin when they heard it.

The rattle of a buggy just outside.

Chapter Twenty-Four

T hey shared a wide-eyed look, and then both were moving. Isa frantically braided her loose hair, searching for the tie on the settee while Junior strode to the picture window. He cursed.

"It's my pa and...why the hell did he bring *her*?" Junior said it with so much disbelief Isa didn't bother asking who "her" referred to. "Stay here." He left the parlor without waiting for a reply.

John Stone parked a flashy buggy pulled by a couple of glossy bays with powerful haunches and feathered feet. Through the window, Isa watched Junior step onto the porch. His whole demeanor had hardened into square angles and rigid lines. A brawny, aging man helped an elegantly dressed woman from the buggy. Her sleeves were enormous, and her hat was a veritable cornucopia of decorative fruit.

Kristy Anne?

Isa looked down at her own ensemble. There would be no standing ovation for her rust-colored riding skirt and sensible shirtwaist. Her hastily plaited braid was messy and thick, bristling over her right shoulder like a frayed rope. Unwilling to sneak out the back door, and disinclined to meet the visitors in the yard, Isa snagged Junior's tobacco sack off the central table and made herself comfortable on one of the parlor chairs.

When Junior reluctantly led his father and ex-fiancée inside, Isa was reclined in his favorite chair, legs outstretched and ankles crossed. She leisurely rolled tobacco into cigarettes, as unconcerned with their entrance as a cat in the middle of its hourly bath. The woman who was smiling hopefully up at Junior in the foyer froze when she spotted Isa through the open parlor door. A curious maelstrom of emotions threatened to discompose Isa, and by willpower alone could she appear relaxed. Continuing her ministrations, she licked the paper and sealed the cigarette.

"Oh. I wasn't aware you had company." The woman's voice was breathy, and her features were a tad too sharp. She was nonetheless attractive, stylish, and of appropriate height for a woman; the top of her head just reached Junior's shoulder.

"Company is far too formal a word for my presence," Isa responded, pulling out another paper. It helped to concentrate on this rather than the three people staring at her. "Consider me a part of the furniture and think of me no more."

"Easy enough," John Stone said, taking up the rear. His blue gaze was that of a raptor, absorbing her relaxed position in his son's chair.

Cupping a hand around her mouth, Isa shouted, "Hello, Mr. Stone! How are you? How is your rheumatism faring?"

Junior quickly averted his face and succumbed to a coughing fit. Isa caught a glimpse of his profile behind his fist; his dimples cut deeply into his cheeks.

John's eyes narrowed in speculation. "I ain't deaf, girl."

"It's *Miss Isa Williams,*" Isa corrected patiently, still using what Lucy called her "outside voice."

As though cobwebs had been brushed from whatever store of manners he had left, Junior tucked his handkerchief in his pocket and nodded in Isa's direction. "Pardon me. Iz—Isa, you remember my pa, John Stone? And this is Kristy Anne Guthrie."

"Your predecessor, yes. Of course I recall." Isa set aside the papers and tobacco. When she rose to her feet and approached the little group uncomfortably clustered by the door, she saw Kristy Anne's eyes widen to the size of dessert plates as the brown eyes looked up...and up. "It's a pleasure to meet you, Kristy Anne."

"Likewise." Kristy Anne neither offered a hand to shake nor gave a dip of a curtsy.

Isa felt a surge of dislike but remained placid. "Junior, do you have coffee or tea that I can heat up for our guests?"

Kristy Anne stiffened at the word "our."

"Uh, yeah. I've got some coffee in the cupboard."

"I do not partake of coffee," Kristy Anne said stiffly. The babyish quality of her soft voice sounded particularly insufferable now that a hint of haughtiness had leaked into it.

"Of course not," Isa tutted understandably. "Not every woman has the constitution for it. I'll get the men and myself coffee and bring you some warm milk."

Cheeks reddening, Kristy Anne sputtered, "Oh, no, I do not—"

"No? Cold milk it is." Isa glanced at the elder Stone and raised her voice a decibel. "And do you like your coffee black?" *Like your soul?*

John muttered something, but Isa was already walking away, winking conspiratorially at Junior as she passed. It took some time to make coffee; the pre-ground canister was empty, so she spent ages grinding the blasted coffee beans. Voices floated to the kitchen, and Isa discovered that John had brought Kristy Anne to be escorted back to her family in Huntsville before the men journeyed to Lufkin. By the time Isa brought a tray out, Junior was stiffly sitting in the chair she'd vacated. John scowled ferociously at the thick, gold-embossed ledger, and Isa wondered if he spied the several sheets of notes she had left within its pages. Kristy Anne sat perched at the end of the settee like a sparrow tempted to take flight.

As if nothing was amiss, Isa set the tray on the table between them. "Unfortunately, Miss Guthrie, any milk in residence is more solid than liquid, and I wouldn't serve such a concoction to my worst enemy. Junior, when was the last time you shopped?"

"I've been sicker than a dog," Junior retorted.

"Miss Guthrie, I've brought an extra cup in case you change your mind about coffee."

Miss Pickney would be so proud that her lessons in etiquette had finally found purchase in her young charge. Isa poured fragrant black coffee into four white mugs and settled herself on the fringed ottoman beside Junior's chair. If she didn't know any better, she'd speculate that John Stone was angry and annoyed by her presence. Looking at Isa beneath thick, imposing eyebrows, the elderly man snapped the ledger shut and set it on the coffee table beside the tray. An uncomfortable silence ensued. Kristy Anne held her cup in her tiny gloved hands but didn't drink it. Junior sat straight in his chair, jaw working. All the while, John looked at Isa as though trying to peer into her very being.

Isa looked back, unperturbed. She knew a bully when she saw one. Nothing would please her more than to be a splinter in his side.

"I recall you," John said finally. "Doesn't your sister work at The Hound Dog Saloon?"

Junior, who had just taken a sip of coffee, went impossibly still.

Isa smiled. "Yes, she works with your mother."

An explosion of coughing erupted to Isa's right. Junior choked on his coffee, his eyes bulging and cheeks the color of bricks. Across the table, Kristy Anne's mouth had dropped open to reveal crowded bottom teeth.

"What's that, girl?" The shelf housing John's bristling eyebrows dipped so low that the folds of his eyelids almost encompassed his eyes. "Speak up."

Raising her voice to a shout, Isa replied, "I said you have mistaken her for another!"

"Let's get back to the matter at hand," Junior said, clearing his throat. His watery eyes refused to look anywhere near Isa.

"Are you well, Mr. Stone?" Kristy Anne asked, the picture of concern.

Isa's eye twitched. "If a bullet couldn't kill him, I doubt a bit of coffee can."

The other woman gaped. "You were shot?"

"When was this?" John snapped.

Shooting a betrayed look in Isa's direction, Junior gave a watered-down version of the confrontation with the Grenert Brothers. Isa picked at the fringe dangling from the ottoman's cushion, eyes glazing over as the conversation moved from Junior's healed gunshot wound to his mother.

"She wants to know what time you'll come by for Thanksgiving. Miss Guthrie's family will attend, and no expense will be spared." John leaned back comfortably on the settee, sipping his cooling coffee.

"Do you think that's wise, considering you're losin' money?" Junior's question was sharp.

John stopped sipping. "What maggot's diggin' around in your head, boy? You better keep men's business out of female's ears."

"Izzy has a degree in mathematics. I reckon she can catch on just fine."

"What's come of this country when women are allowed to gallivant around, claiming young men's educations, taking over their jobs?"

Junior stood so fast that his chair almost overturned. Both women looked up at him; Kristy Anne seemed tense and ready to move out of the way; Isa's muscles warmed in readiness to come to his aide. Fists clenched at his hips, Junior ground out, "Father? A word outside?"

Surprising everyone, John Stone stood from his recline without argument, and both men exited the parlor, leaving the two women alone.

"Well," Isa said after the front door had snapped shut, and she glanced beyond Kristy Anne through the picture window. Junior and his father gesticulated in the yard. "Your family is going to spend the holiday with the Stones. They must be very close. How long have you known each other?"

Kristy Anne set her full mug on the table, and her timid expression firmed into something less pleasant. For an instant, she looked just like Junior's mother with her nose in the air. "For a while now." She spoke with the thread of reluctance, a queen forced to speak of the weather with her scullery maid.

"Since this past spring, at the very least," Isa said conversationally, thinking of the summer engagement.

Kristy Anne's eyes darted to the ledger. "Why do you say that?" Her voice was tight. Nervous.

Isa straightened from her laggard slouch on the ottoman at this curious reaction. "Isn't it quite obvious?" Testing a theory, Isa slid her eyes meaningfully to the ledger.

Eyes flitting between Isa and the heavy book on the table, Kristy Anne stammered, "I won't pretend to know what you're prattling about—"

Prattling?

"—but I'm very certain that I do not have to explain my family's relationship with the Stones to *you*. I have been told all about you."

Resting her fingertips over her heart, Isa asked, "You've been told about me?"

"You're money hungry," Kristy Anne spat, glancing behind her at the window to ensure the men were still occupied. "Mrs. Stone told me all about your...sharecropper family." The latter was said in an impugning whisper.

"Oh, I see." Isa was whispering, too. She leaned forward as though to share a secret. "And everyone knows just how desperately poor we are."

"Yes."

"Marriage to a man like Junior would set my family up for life. We could put our feet up and swill rotgut until we die. We'd never have to work the fields again."

Kristy Anne nodded, her entire face puckered with contempt. It made the hairs on Isa's neck stand up. She didn't give the woman across from her the satisfaction of a reaction. For years, she'd been heckled by male college students and angry protesters outside the college grounds for being a woman attending their alma mater. She'd been mugged twice in the last five years—only once successfully—and had dealt with plenty of hateful comments and ill-treatment at the bank when Mr. Corner's back was turned. Even before that, as a young girl, she'd suffered the discrimination of her father's trade and its financial lack. Not to mention the many jokes at her expense about her height, her gapped teeth, and how she failed in every way at being a perfect example of femininity. This angry, bitter woman across from her was no different than those many naysayers. And no more special. Kristy Anne was just another consciousness in the twenty percent of living bodies who despised Isa on principle.

But something else became clear.

Junior would never have married a woman like this. Never. She was his mother made over, a little shadow of Loretta Stone, only separated by years and sharper features.

Disappointed and bored, Isa moved from the ottoman to Junior's favorite chair and made herself comfortable. While she gathered the tobacco and papers back into her lap, she made conversation. "Do you want to know what I've learned about money during my terms at university, Miss Guthrie?"

Kristy Anne stared resentfully and made no response.

"I've learned that there is more than just one way to make it. And for a woman, it's considerably harder. Heavens, the obstacles females must overcome to earn coin hand over fist are bountiful. I'm sure you grasp our plight." Isa ran her tongue over her paper. Seeing that her cigarettes were neater and tighter than Junior's pleased her, another skill mastered. "But if you are willing to bend the rules, learn the tricks of the trade, and even manipulate situations in your favor, an income is possible. Some women are born into riches. Some marry into it, as you're desiring to do."

The young woman finally found her voice. "I do not—"

"And some ingratiate themselves into a family of means." Isa ignored the offended squeak across the coffee table. "Loretta Stone is a woman of means. She's also a shameless social climber. And your family, Miss Guthrie, is at the top rung of the social ladder in Huntsville, is it not? It would be nothing to weave a tale of financial woe to a woman with stars in her eyes. But I'm curious—were you ever truly interested in a marriage with Junior? He can't have been home long enough for you to have fallen madly in love with him."

"What you are insinuating—it is all lies! You are deplorable!" Kristy Anne cried. "I-I will—" She broke off, rhythmically clenching her skirts in her small gloved fists.

Brows climbing her forehead, Isa asked slowly, "You'll what?"

Cheeks blanched of color, the young woman abruptly stood and vacated the parlor, tripping over the leg of the coffee table on her way out. The wild fear on Kristy Anne's face had revealed her hand. Isa's suspicions of where John Stone's money was disappearing to had just run out the door as though her skirts were afire.

"What the hell did you say to her?" John Stone barked five minutes later from the parlor door.

"Don't talk to her like that," Junior shouted, hot on his heels. "Izzy, what happened to Kristy Anne?"

Isa set the tobacco and papers on the side table and picked up the Circle S ledger. "I told her I knew Loretta Stone is giving money to her family."

"The hell you did," John growled. He stomped across the parlor and wrenched the book from Isa's hands. "I knew you were trouble as soon as I saw you."

"Don't talk to her like that," Junior said softly. He was inches away from his father and looked seconds away from swinging. "Izzy, come here." He held a hand to her, beckoning her to come around the other side of the coffee table to him.

Isa ignored it and stood toe to toe with John Senior, feeling her brain crack its knuckles for a round of verbal sparring. "There's no need to be angry, Mr. Stone. I'm sure you would have made the connection eventually."

A vein bulged in John's forehead. His brown teeth were slightly bared. "You're just like my first son's wife. Got that same mouth and spit-in-your-eye look. I can't for the life of me understand why my boys attract such rabble."

"Perhaps it's because good men find us irresistible."

Junior had apparently had enough; he hauled his father back with a hard hand and shouted, "Get the hell out of my house!"

He placed himself between Isa and his father, who didn't budge from the parlor.

"I said, get the hell off my property," Junior said, low and serious.

Isa's muscles tensed.

It was the moment after cannon fire when both sides were deaf and dumb, waiting for someone to make the first move. The moment dangled, a weighted object on a string threatening to snap. Then...John whirled on his heel and strode from the room without another word.

JUNIOR WAS STONILY quiet after his father left. He mumbled something and disappeared out the back door. Through the kitchen window, Isa saw him enter the barn. Hopelessness flooded her usually logical train of thought.

During the weeks he'd traveled with his brother, she had kept herself busy training Mirage and working at the hotel and general store. She'd visited her parent's farm for an exhausting weekend. The children of her many siblings were perpetually underfoot and always up to mischief, so her mother never sat down for more than ten minutes as a result. Isa had found herself missing the quiet of her job at the bank, the scratch of a pencil to paper at her university classes, and even the incessant chatter of David Corner after a successful night of gambling.

But most of all, she had missed Junior.

He occupied her thoughts as much, if not more, than travel. An old dream and a new one at war with one another, battling for space within her future. Taking a deep breath, Isa followed him. Once in the insulated quiet of the barn, however, she veered into Mirage's stall instead of following the sound of Junior pitching hay from the loft to the breezeway. The ebony mare, in the last few days of her season and irascible, tried to nip at Isa's skirts when she attempted to dig through the saddlebags.

"Don't bite me, you cow," Isa hissed, flicking the mare's sensitive ear.

Back in the dusty breezeway, Isa held a stack of books and pamphlets, watching Junior climb down the ladder. Wiping his forehead with a kerchief, he took in the pile straining in her arms.

"What'd you do, rob a library?"

"No, they're for you. Come look." Together, they walked across the yard and into the kitchen. She dropped the stack on the empty kitchen table and showed him each book, all on carpentry and architecture. "I know you're fond of building and thought you would enjoy these."

Junior sat, bewildered, and grabbed a book titled *The Carpenter's New Guide* to thumb through its eighty-four plates. He stopped at two pages titled "Hand Railing" and "Staircasing," studying them.

Pointing, he said, "Look at this. I always wondered how they get these handrails to bend this way and that. See how sharp the wood has to turn to fit the curve of the staircase?"

Isa listened closely, his excitement contagious. She pulled a travel pamphlet out of the pile. "Look at the architecture section in this." Black and white printed photographs of spectacular buildings and bridges occupied its pages, some of the architecture too intricate to be believed.

Eyes devouring the photos, Junior stroked his fingertips down the Gothic Revival architecture of one building in particular. "It looks like a queen lives here."

"This is the Midland Grand Hotel in London."

"That's a *hotel*?"

"Yes, and one I plan to visit," Isa said excitedly, her eyes sparkling up at him. "Just for one night, as I imagine it is exorbitantly expensive."

He looked back at the picture, more subdued. Something cinched her throat into uncomfortable tightness. "You could come with me and see it, if you'd like."

It was said half-jokingly, but Junior looked up at her with a telling swiftness. "Yeah?"

"Certainly. I wouldn't have to get a chaperone if you accompanied me. Think of all the money I'd save."

The shy smile that spread across his face was one she hadn't seen before. She wasn't accustomed to boyish, enthusiastic Junior. "I'm not exactly hurtin' for money, either, you know."

Dryly, Isa said, "I know."

His lips straightened into a firm line. "And that doesn't have a damned thing to do with my pa. I haven't taken a cent from him since I was eighteen."

Isa widened her eyes dramatically and held her hands up. "I would never presume otherwise. I'm sure being a Ranger paid a fortune."

"No, it didn't," Junior said, turning his attention back to the travel pamphlet. "Not even when I was a lieutenant. Bounty hunting, though...that paid decent, even at a percentage. Especially when I brought in the real nasty ones."

Intrigued, Isa leaned forward. "Tell me more."

They talked until the sun sank dangerously low in the distance, and Isa was forced to cut their visit short. They parted reluctantly.

"I'm glad you're feeling better," Isa said, gathering her pamphlet—then thought better of it and dropped it. "You can keep that. I have it memorized."

"I'm sorry my pa was a bastard to you," Junior said seriously. His nose was still chafed, but he hadn't sneezed or blown it since that morning. His eyes were clear, no longer red-rimmed.

"You need never apologize for him."

"Well, I am." His jaw was angled obstinately, and Isa stifled a smile.

"Think nothing of it."

"Is what you said true? Is Mother giving Kristy Anne's family that money?"

Isa chewed the inside of her cheek. "It's a possibility. I may have bluffed a little just to see what she'd do. Kristy Anne's reaction to my accusations was certainly suspect, but I'm sorry if I made it worse between you and your parents."

"I'm not sorry. It's been bad with them since I can remember. Has nothing to do with you." Watching her closely, Junior held the pamphlet up and changed the subject. "We can take this with us when we travel."

We. The word did funny things to her insides.

She touched the tip of his nose. "Don't forget to put petroleum jelly under that nose, or you'll be teased mercilessly at Thanksgiving."

Junior's hand was quick, snagging hers in midair. He kissed her fingertip. "Thank you for takin' care of me."

Chest aching from heart to ribcage at the terrifying strength of her feelings for him, Isa cleared her throat. "It was nothing."

"It was."

"Being ill makes you maudlin," she teased, but her heart was twice its normal size, rising in her chest, surpassing her reason.

She thought, *I will do anything for this man.*

Chapter Twenty-Five

Thanksgiving at the Stone Ranch was a noisy, happy event.

The breeze was blessedly chilly, trailing through open windows, cooling the hot flurry of activity in the kitchen. Isa and Poppy helped Lucy prepare dinner while the menfolk minded the children. Sol had brought his dining table over in the back of the buckboard, and he and Junior lined it up with the Stones'. Junior's hair beneath his brown Stetson caught Isa's eye from the dining room window, gleaming like a golden coin, distracting her from setting the table. He was playing football—a growing favorite amongst the general population—and allowed himself to be tackled by five exuberant children. Samuel was the victor of the dog pile, holding the oblong pig bladder full of air aloft with a triumphant yell. His father ran past and neatly snatched the pigskin up. The children's outraged screams were audible through the window screens.

Later, the family said grace at the two tables. The children's end was adorned with bright decorations and games, and the boys wore turkey tail feathers in their hat bands and shirt pockets. Ally used her feather to tickle her little sister. Everyone gorged themselves with turkey, stuffing, and pickled vegetables. The air was redolent with savory stewed onions and roasted sweet potatoes. A cured ham was picked clean. Pumpkin pie was passed around despite the groans of full bellies and claims of being unable to eat another bite. Isa entertained everyone with a discussion about automobiles, dams, and electricity.

When the older children went outside to play within view of the yard. Poppy fed Agatha beneath a blanket while Sol spooned bites of pie to a sleepy Autumn. Everyone sagged contentedly in their chairs, and Isa felt the urge to speak up. What better time to spill the beans than while everyone was present...and too sluggish to catch her if she had to flee?

"I have an announcement to make," Isa declared, purposefully avoiding Sol's eye.

To her left, Junior set his coffee down. His nose was no longer raw, and his voice had lost the thick sound of congestion. He looked braced for the worst.

Isa lifted her chin fractionally and said, "I'm not returning to Austin after the new year."

Before she could take her next breath, Sol was happily slapping the table. "You're stayin' home! Hellfire—"

"No, I'm not." Isa held up a staying hand. "I quit my job at the bank and have plenty saved up for what I truly want to do."

Everyone's eyes were on hers. Blue, hazel, brown—all curious. Why was it so hard to say?

Poppy, the most considerate of everyone, asked gently, "What do you wish to do?"

"I wish to travel abroad," Isa said. "I'll take a transatlantic ship to England, and once I arrive, I can procure a companion to travel with me." She was very conscious of Junior beside her. Of their conversation.

You could come with me and see it, if you'd like.

Yeah?

After a beat of shocked silence, everyone began talking at once.

"Oh, how exciting!" Lucy cried, clapping her hands a little. Her husband lifted alarmed brows at her.

"That's quite a journey," Poppy said, mouth smiling, eyes worried.

"Like hell you are." Sol's voice was the loudest of all. The spoon he held in front of Autumn's face wavered, and her open mouth followed. "Wasn't there a bunch of women gettin' killed overseas?"

"There were a series of murders a few years ago in London, but they stopped." Isa pointed her fork at him. "We had something similar happen in Austin in '85, if you'll recall? The Servant Girl Annihilator?"

Sol's mouth clacked shut. Then he seemed to notice that Junior was the only person who hadn't acted surprised at this news. "Did you know about this?"

Junior held his hands up. "Since when have I ever been able to control her?"

Again, Poppy tried to smooth the conversation. "Tell us where you're planning to go when you get there. I've never traveled outside the country."

Sol shot his wife a look of betrayal.

Isa refused to let Sol smother her excitement at the prospect of travel. "It will be a Grand Tour. I'd like to begin in England for a month, then cross the English Channel to Calais, France. I only know passable French, so I'd prefer for my companion to be French-speaking. Then we'll sojourn to Geneva before crossing the Alps. Once across, I shall stop in Italy and spend much time visiting Florence, Pisa, and Venice."

Lucy's eyes lit up. "My papa hails from Italy."

Sol looked unhappily on, mouth opening and closing as though he'd like to interrupt but didn't quite dare.

"Italian men are very passionate," Lucy explained. When Ben cast a jaundiced eye her way, she hid a smile. "Or so Papa says. He's told tales of village boys following behind beautiful women in the street, sweet-talking and whistling."

Lucy, Isa, and Poppy laughed. The men looked horrified.

"She's definitely not goin' now." Sol set Autumn down from his lap and leaned across the table to catch Isa's eye. "How can you afford somethin' like this? You been plannin' it for a while?"

Isa sobered. "Yes. I wrote the itinerary during my first year of college. That's all the college boys would talk about. Their *Grand Tour*."

Sol ran a hand over his straight chestnut hair. "I don't know. I don't like the thought of you bein' an ocean away and me not knowing how to get to you. I wouldn't even know if you were in trouble."

Reaching her hand across the table to hold his, Isa made her face as serious as possible. "I promise I will not veer off the well-known paths. No risk-taking, no looking for trouble. Apparently, the only trouble I might have is with amorous locals."

The weak attempt at a joke fell flat with the men, but Poppy's lip quirked and Lucy teased, "My money is on a handsome stranger sweeping her off her feet. Isa will be back this time next year with a besotted new husband."

"I have no interest in that." Isa laughed awkwardly. Beside her, Junior was as rigid as a stone pillar.

Lucy waggled her eyebrows. "When it comes to tall, beautiful American women, you won't have to show interest; they'll court you anyway."

"If any man gets within three feet of her, they can court the business end of my pistol." The words came out hot and angry to Isa's left. Blond locks of hair trailed over Junior's forehead, and beneath them, his eyes seared into Lucy.

Bewildered, Sol asked Junior, "What, are you goin', too?"

Shoulders relaxing as though the effort cost him, Junior took a bite of dried apple pie. "Why shouldn't I go and chaperone her? Who else is gonna keep her out of trouble?"

Hiding her hands in her lap beneath the table, Isa asked, "Are you quite serious?"

"Why not?" There was a stubborn tightness to his chewing jaw that disallowed any argument. "I don't speak French, but I can keep Lucy's lusty countrymen from sniffing around your skirts."

"Then it's settled!" Lucy said quickly. She stood and widened her eyes at Isa. "Isa, will you help me clear the table?"

Isa grabbed her plate and followed Lucy into the kitchen before Sol could get a word in edgewise.

"I'm goin' for a smoke," Junior grunted behind them.

"I'll come with," said Ben.

Poppy and Sol were left alone to gape at each other at the table.

IF SOL HADN'T been suspicious of Junior's intentions with Isa before, he was now. Junior knew his friend wanted to have a word with him, but Poppy had insisted Sol help her put their youngest daughters down for a nap. Lucy and Ben made themselves scarce and took plates to Tia and Frank, the old couple who lived a short distance away, their arms bumping each other as they strolled along the path.

The screen door to the kitchen slapped shut, and Junior turned his head from watching the children play on the corral fence. It was Isa.

Leaning on the railing beside him, she asked, "Did you mean it?"

Her eyes looked as green as the dress she wore. It had been damned difficult not to look at her for too long. Her skin glowed. Her pink lips snagged his attention so often that it made him senseless.

"Did I mean what?" Focusing on her words was difficult when all Junior could smell was the perfume of her skin, the clean, powdery scent of her upswept hair. He would lie awake at night thinking of the way it had felt through his fingers in his parlor, how it had looked splayed on the pillow while he took her from above in the attic, and he'd fist himself beneath the sheets. Even when he was feverish and sick at home, his nose dripping like a cracked faucet, he'd wanted to crush her to him.

"Did you mean it when you told them you'd chaperone me during my Grand Tour?" Her question was carefully neutral, and he'd come to learn that meant she was anything but. But which answer did she want? Did she want him to stay here and not tag along like a nanny? Or did she want the opposite?

Junior decided the truth was the best course of action.

"'Course I'm going with you. We talked about this at the house." He nudged her with his shoulder, and she caught herself against a post.

"I suspected you were only joking." Eyes twinkling, Isa bumped him with her hip; he smacked his elbow on a wooden post before he could right himself.

"Ouch, you little wildcat."

They were busily tussling for the upper hand when hoof-beats in the yard brought them up short.

Junior released Isa's wrists, muttering, "What the hell is he doin' here?" as he hopped down the porch steps. He hadn't seen or heard from his father since their argument two days before, and yet, here he was, tying up his thoroughbred at the water trough by the well house.

John Stone ignored his youngest son and strode to the middle of the yard where Ben and Lucy's boys were running to meet him with cries of "Grandpa!" He ruffled the three boys' hair and gave Jack a silver dollar.

John said, "Walk with me." He didn't look at Junior or even appear to notice Matthew and Samuel's crestfallen faces.

Cursing the old man under his breath, Junior dug into his pocket for loose change. A slim hand settled on his wrist. Isa had sidled up to him.

"Children," she said, her face lit with impish delight. "How about we get the rest of you silver dollars, and you can help me saddle up Mirage for a ride. Would you like that?"

Matthew and Samuel whooped and raced each other to the barn. Isa wrinkled her nose in dislike at the old man's back.

"I'll pay you back," Junior muttered, wishing he had the right to swat her bottom.

"Yes, you will." Cheekily, she smiled and followed the children to the barn, gathering up young Ally and Timothy on the way.

Longing to trail behind her like a lost duckling, Junior sighed and joined his father on the porch. John sat on the swing, his widespread arms and legs sending an unmistakable message. Junior folded his arms and leaned against the kitchen windowsill.

"You know," John said, pulling a cigar and a matchbook from his fine jacket pocket. A gold chain swayed against the red silk lining. "I talked to Loretta about the books. Had a look at them when we got home. Chuck told me about the men your mama let go, so she fessed up to everything."

Biceps tense over his fists, Junior asked, "And her reasoning?"

"Damned fool woman has been giving money to the Guthries." John sounded deceptively nonchalant.

"No wonder she wanted me to marry that woman so bad," Junior said, discomfited. "Izzy was right."

John ignored the latter. "Your mama figured they were as good as family."

Junior snorted softly. "But to give them a thousand a month? You don't even treat your own family that well."

"Watch your mouth." John wrenched his cigar from his mouth, his craggy face going from weathered brown to brick red. "I'm not too old to knock your front teeth out."

Expressionlessly, Junior eyed the man on the swing whose shoulders were not as broad as they used to be, the hair not as thick around the pate. He didn't feel anger or even hate towards his father. He felt nothing at all. "Anything else?"

A resentful silence expanded between them until the color in John's cheeks returned to normal. "I got a mite more to say to you. Might as well be now. I don't expect you know anything about a cripple runnin' around asking for your whereabouts?"

The only change in Junior's expression was the intensity of his eyes. They glittered like chips of sapphire.

Unabashed, John brought his cigar up, damp at the base, for another puff. "He was spouting all kinds of tomfoolery about you getting dishonorably discharged. Wanted to talk to you in a bad way, he did. 'Course, I had to run him off with my shotgun before your mama heard that kind of talk. How long has it been since the Texas Rangers kicked you out on your tail?"

Junior didn't speak. He couldn't. A tic in his jaw flickered, and it felt as though his tongue had become glued to the roof of his mouth.

John, however, looked satisfied. "Usually, it's your brother tucking tail and runnin'. Quite a change of pace, eh?"

Giggles interrupted the tension. Both men turned their heads as Isa walked Mirage past, Ally and Timothy on the mare's back. The sight of Isa—tall, elegant, beautiful—grounded Junior.

Everything in his life was falling apart. Everything except her. He was an open wound. Infected. Drawing flies and vermin. And Isa...she was the cure in a brown medicinal bottle. Not bothering to acknowledge the bear trap his father had sprung on him, Junior turned his back on the swing and walked alongside Isa on the porch. He caught her eye and beckoned her over to the steps with a crook of two fingers. Face scrunching to show just how impudent she thought his behavior was, Isa reluctantly led Mirage closer. On the top step, Junior crouched so that he was eye level with her. He took his hat off and set it on her head.

Ally giggled when it fell over Isa's eyes.

While Isa pushed the brim up, Junior said in a carrying voice, "My pa apologizes for his poor behavior the other day. He knows better than to talk that way to a lady."

At the other end of the porch, John blew cigar smoke past his nostrils and down-turned lips, much the same way his youngest son did.

"Did he?" Isa asked.

"Yep. He also said you were right about where the money was goin'."

Instead of gloating, she only appeared mildly interested. "I'm happy the mystery is solved." Without sparing a glance at the elder Mr. Stone, Isa settled Junior's Stetson more firmly on her head and walked away. Junior winked at the children.

His father heaved himself up from the swing and made his way down the porch steps. He paused, his speculative gaze on the Stetson on Isa's head. "You know what you're gettin' into with that one?"

"Reckon so."

"Well, don't expect any wedding gifts from us." Junior didn't comment, so John dropped the cigar in the dead grass beside the porch and said over his shoulder, "Don't forget to ride by the house. You know how your mama misses you."

Junior descended the porch steps and ground out the small flame the cigar had ignited in the grass. In the distance, his father was but a speck.

IT WAS MIDNIGHT in the bunkhouse, and the men who had returned early from holiday celebrations were groaning and complaining as Isa won yet another round of faro. Junior had followed to keep an eye on her and leaned in a shadowy corner, watching.

Raking in coins and bills, Isa called out, "I can't believe you won't play with me, John Junior."

He shook his head, arms firmly crossed.

"I've never seen such a chicken," she cried, shuffling cards with frightening adeptness. A bold young man, eyeing the way Isa's hair fell from its pins, made soft clucking noises.

Junior stared until the young man looked down.

"Just play one game," Isa cajoled, laying cards out into a horseshoe shape. "You already owe me two dollars."

"Hell no. You cheat."

"Prove it."

"You know I can't."

"There's no argument without evidence," she said, eyes gleaming from across the room.

That smart mouth had said similar words on those attic stairs just before he'd picked her up and had his way with her. Junior gripped his biceps hard with his right hand, wishing it was her throat he was strangling. She was driving him crazy on purpose. Every look, every taunt.

He let her finish one last game before he grabbed her by the arm and pulled her from the bunkhouse, much to the disappointment of the cowhands.

"I wasn't finished taking all their money," Isa complained. She tugged at the grip he had on her arm.

"Oh, yes, you are. I know you're cheating, and it isn't right."

"I don't have an ace up my sleeve, nor am I drawing from the bottom of the deck. Counting cards is not cheating."

"What the hell is counting cards?"

Isa went on about high cards, low cards, and neutral cards. She waxed poetic about percentages and strategy, shuffle tracking and hot decks. All he heard was balderdash, especially when she said words like "variable change." He tightened his grip on her arm and turned them to the barn.

"Why are we going to the barn?" she asked when he shut the enormous double doors behind them.

"Because you're driving me to distraction," he growled, cupping the back of her neck and bringing her in for a hot, open-mouthed kiss. She released a moan that turned his semi-hardness to iron, and he backed her into the feed stall. Her hands were everywhere, delving into his hair, spanning his shoulders, dragging nails down his back, tugging his belt. But when one clever hand unbuttoned his fly and made its way down the front of his trousers, it was his turn to groan.

Junior's hands found their way up her skirts, one on her buttocks, the other cupping her mons. Then lower, testing her readiness. The kiss that had started out rough grew rougher, their breath choppy, their moans stifled. Hands shaking, muscles straining, they tumbled into a pile of hay.

Needing her more than he'd needed anything in his entire life, Junior rolled her over and lifted her to her knees. After a slight hesitation, Isa reached beneath her skirts to fumble at the buttons hiding the opening of her combinations. Having taken what felt like hours unbuttoning his own clothing, he yanked the material of his trousers down and shoved her skirts high, exposing the open slit of her underwear. Filling his palms with her bottom, he pressed close, brushing against warm silk. Her back arched, and she pushed demandingly backward.

"Hurry," she whispered unevenly.

A monk couldn't have told her no.

After giving her a pathetically cursory caress, Junior lined himself up and slowly, carefully, eased his way in. His eyes closed, and his lips parted. He'd never felt anything as good as she did at that moment. And when she started rocking to and fro, carefully taking more of him in, one inch at a time, his fingers bit into her hips. He wanted to be gentle. But he couldn't.

He thrust in to the hilt.

Isa flinched and inhaled a shocked breath.

"You're doin' good, darlin'," he crooned. "Be still for me. You make me too crazy."

For once, she listened and held still. He could feel her inner thighs tremble minutely. Junior kept his thrusts slow and long, tip to root, gauging for the moment when her rigidity slackened into loose-limbed ardor. It happened in increments. Her thighs ceased trembling. Her movements returned, and her breath came in excited pants. The base of his shaft all the way to the tops of his thighs was drenched, and he instinctively roughened his thrusts, feeling the euphoric sensation of an oncoming climax centering at the sensitive place beneath the head of his cock and spreading all the way to his toes.

"Izzy, I'm getting close."

"So am I," she gasped.

Christ, that didn't help him a bit. Desperate, Junior concentrated on not climaxing and ordered, "Touch yourself. Catch up to me."

"Are you"—she contorted her body to comply—"challenging me to a race?"

"I'll beat you in this particular race every time," he gritted out, still holding back, still trying his damnedest not to finish first.

"Want to bet?" she moaned, her movements erratic. He felt the change in her internal muscles as they squeezed him, milked him, clenched harder almost than he could stand.

The minx *had* beat him. And that made him wild. Hissing a hard exhale through his teeth, he yanked out of her, swiftly grabbed himself in hand, and pointed down while he stroked himself through his end. The beat of his heart throbbed against his palm, and he missed what she said.

"What?" he croaked, sitting back on his heels, his heartbeat pounding hard and slow through every vein in his body.

"I said I beat you." In the darkness, he could just make out the exposed portion of her rear as she lay on her side in the hay.

"I let you win." Winded, Junior slapped her right buttock with the flat of his hand before falling to his side with her, cock still out. When the fog cleared from his mind, he kissed the back of her neck and said, "Come to my house tomorrow night."

Isa snuggled closer. "If you insist."

Chapter Twenty-Six

J unior had built his home with his own two hands after Ben and Lucy had married. Located not far from his brother's land, his white house sat beneath the sprawling branches of a black walnut tree, its wide-open porch braced by thick, tapered columns. Exposed beams, brackets, and rafters gave character to an otherwise square frame, its low-pitched roof and over-hanging eaves prettying up what Isa considered fairly masculine architecture. Her favorite aspect of the home was its welcoming front porch and the picture windows facing the expansive land surrounding it.

The yard was empty, and no Junior came outside to greet her, so she walked Mirage to the little barn off to the side. Champion's head stuck out of his stall at the sound of their approach, nostrils flared in a whinny of welcome. Mirage's ears perked forward, and her pace quickened.

"Happy to see him again?" Isa grinned, dismounted, and hitched Mirage outside the gelding's stall so the two horses could greet and scent each other to their hearts' content.

As was her habit, she walked into Junior's house without knocking but stopped in her tracks at the smell of frying food—or what was supposed to be frying food. Despite her mental exhaustion, a smile spread across her face when she opened the kitchen door and found Junior frantically scraping charred lumps off the bottom of cast iron skillets. A plume of smoke hovered menacingly beneath the ceiling.

"What in heaven's name are you doing?" she asked, smothering her grin.

He jumped at the sound of her voice. Grease splattered on his arm, and he cursed. Shirtless and barefoot with his messy hair uncombed, Junior looked good enough to eat. The contents of the skillets, however...

"I am *not* eating that." She walked past him to open the back door. "You're in luck. Ma always sends me on my way with more than I can eat. Are you in the mood for fried rabbit?"

"Lord, yes," he coughed. Eyes watering, he toted the smoking pans outside to smolder beneath the well pump.

Once the stove top was cleaned and the windows were opened, they ate the rabbit from Isa's pack with buttered slices of bread.

"Ma almost didn't let me leave," Isa said around a piece of crust. Remembering her manners, she wiped fingers greasy from butter onto Junior's ugly mustard dishtowel. After a second thought, she cautiously brought it to her nose for a tentative sniff, then drew back in surprise. "You washed this?"

"I'm not helpless. I can do my own wash." He looked and sounded so offended that she laughed.

"You could have fooled me." She threw the clean towel at his face; he caught it one-handed.

"Why didn't your ma want you to leave? Did you tell her you were coming here?" Junior lit a lamp in the center of the little round table, and the dim kitchen glowed saffron.

"Why would I do a fool thing like that? So she and Pa could follow me here with a preacher and a shotgun? No, I told her my plans to travel." Isa hesitated, wondering if she should admit everything. "Ma and Pa acted like I would be molested the moment my feet touched foreign ground, so I panicked and told them you were accompanying me."

His broad, square shoulders stiffened. "And you don't think that'll have them hearing wedding bells? What did they say?"

"They were still unhappy that I'm leaving American soil—frankly, they seem doubtful of my intelligence—but eventually allowed that it would be much safer if I had a Texas Ranger at my side." Isa realized too late what she'd said and could have slapped herself. But Junior didn't bridle the way he usually did. He merely appeared weary.

"It'll probably get out before too long that I'm not a Texas Ranger anymore, Izzy." Strong, callused hands loosely intertwined with hers on the table.

She brushed her thumb over his knuckles. "Why do you say that?"

"Father told me at Thanksgiving that Randal—"

"The Ranger friend whose leg was amputated?" *The friend whose brother he'd killed.* Those words lay unspoken between them.

"Yeah, him. Randal showed up at the Big Stone Ranch and told my pa all about my discharge."

Defensiveness straightened Isa's spine. "That's none of that wily old goat's business."

"Everything is his business." Junior's white teeth gleamed in a mirthless smile. "And if Randal found my pa, it's only a matter of time before he's pointed in this direction."

Isa squeezed his fingers and bent so he would meet her eye. "You don't think he'll come here and try to start trouble, do you?"

"I don't know. I wouldn't blame him for wanting his revenge."

"I would!" The very notion made Isa's insides go cold. "I would blame him very much. And then I'd have revenge against *him*. It would be a dreadful cycle of violence, and it should cease immediately before any harm is done.”

“Before any *more* harm is done,” Junior stressed, his forced smile fading. “He has a worthy motive to find me. It’s what he’s gonna do when he has me that I’m not so sure about. I haven’t seen him in over two years. If Havelard told him about the court hearing, Randal was too injured to make it, and he doesn’t have any other living relatives. All Randal had in this whole wide world was his brother.”

And Junior had killed him.

Isa found she had no ready comment, no witty rejoinder. Instead, she covered his hands with hers and squeezed.

“YOU’RE TELLIN’ ME this was built in the year eighty?”

Junior held up the picture of the Colosseum in Rome, Italy for a closer look. They had migrated to the parlor and sat side by side on the same settee his father and ex-fiancée had reposed upon a few days prior. Spread out on the coffee table were Isa’s itinerary, travel pamphlets, and sheaves of notes and clippings.

“Yes, the Romans had extreme ingenuity. The professor at UT could talk for hours about Roman roads. It was a civilization who loved their blood sport as much as they loved their conquering.” Isa pointed at the illustrated diagram of the interior of the Colosseum. “People would gather and watch from these seats as gladiatorial events took place. Have you heard of gladiators?”

He sent her a narrow look. “I know what gladiators are.”

Hiding her amusement at his struck nerve, she continued, “They would hold huge events of fighting gladiators and mythological reenactments, and they would bring in all manners of beasts from other countries—the more deadly of which would be placed into the arena with naked men condemned to execution.”

"Makes hanging seem like a kindness," Junior said softly, unconsciously scratching the scar on his neck. He was beyond distracting with his messy blond hair, bare back, and feet peeking out from behind faded Levi Strauss jeans.

"Oh, yes. The civilization was as bloodthirsty in their sport as they were in war; they had the best fighting army in history."

"Maybe you were a Roman in a past life."

"Or a Viking leader."

"So humble," he said dryly, setting the picture down on the coffee table. "What time next year will we be in Rome?"

Isa smothered her surge of enthusiasm at the word "we." Too much anticipation made her nervous and on guard. She was used to dousing her hopes and could hardly believe they were planning such an intimate trip, one where they'd be together every day for half a year's time. It was too new. Too ineffable. A small, distrustful part of her wondered if he would change his mind at the last possible minute. "I hope to be in Italy in late spring or early summer. I have more than enough funds to get us through June before we come home."

Junior reached over, captured a lock of her hair, and tweaked it. "You're crazy as a bed bug if you think I'll let you pay my way the whole trip."

"It was my idea, so I'm spending my money. Call me crazy if you wish." She swatted his hand away. Not only did he catch her hand, but he pulled her up from across the settee until she was chest-to-chest with him. His skin was hot, the fine mat of hair across his pectorals glittering like gold dust in the kerosene light.

Isa had known the purpose of her visit when she rode up the narrow driveway. Her brother thought she was at her ma's, and her ma thought she was at her brother's. A fresh change of clothes lay neatly folded in her gunnysack, and in the morning, she'd ride into Dogwood for a day's work with no one the wiser.

What she'd forgotten was the size of him in a well-lit room. Every meeting of their bodies before now had been in darkness, every noise stifled. Now, they were alone in an empty house several miles away from another living person. They could look at each other as long as they wished and be as loud in their passions as they pleased, and Isa wanted him more than she wanted her Grand Tour. To want another person more than one wanted their dream? What a terrifying prospect. Such a concept was fraught with potential heartbreak. She'd had a taste of heartbreak and was not fond of it.

Junior's eyelashes were pale at the tips and so low that they concealed the blue fire of his irises. He looked at her lips when he spoke. "We agreed to share the financial burden. This is one area where you won't win."

"Is that so?" His mouth was inches from hers. It wasn't fair for a man to have lips women had to rouge to get.

His answer was a kiss. They had learned each other, and their mouths met with perfect synchrony, their tongues matching rhythms like a rehearsed dance. Kissing him halted the rapid pace of her brain. Her thoughts changed from coherent words to colors and sensations. She was swimming in honey, slow and languid, her breath slow, her heartbeat fast. It weakened her. Junior's fingers, warm as the rest of his body, cupped her face, her neck, her heavy breasts. They were so sensitive when he touched them that she broke away from his kiss, moaning freely in the open air of his parlor.

Grip roughening, he pulled her to straddle him on the settee. He plucked the buttons of her blouse open and pressed his face between her breasts, massaging them with gentle force. His lovemaking was different this time. More intentional. She kissed the satiny skin of his shoulder, and he pulled her loose bodice down to expose her breasts to the hazy lamplight.

"These are the prettiest things I've ever seen in my life." His voice was deep. Worshipful.

"I used to bind them," Isa admitted breathlessly, brushing his hair out of his eyes. "They popped up around thirteen or fourteen when I was still wrestling in the dirt with you and wearing overalls. I stopped binding them when I was sixteen."

"When Poppy came to Dogwood?" He kissed the tender skin above each pink nipple, then held each breast up like a vendor weighing a couple of melons. She was both exasperated and entertained.

"Yes. The first week I met Poppy, she fitted me with a new dress. You should have seen her face when she saw I had bosoms." Isa pantomimed a shocked expression, eyes wide, mouth open.

Junior chuckled. "That's about my reaction when you showed up in a dress with your chest stuck out to here when the day before it was flat as a washboard. I thought you'd stuffed your underthings."

"Shows how much you know," she murmured, leaning in to kiss his lips.

They kissed forever. There was no hurry.

Isa wasn't sure when it changed. Their movements became more deliberate, and clothes soon littered the parlor floor until they were both naked and entirely visible to one another. She'd only seen him fully nude the morning they woke up in the attic, but he hadn't been aroused. Her eyes settled at the apex of his thighs, where his sex stood proud and flushed. Neither had a shy bone in their body, and they looked their fill until looking wasn't enough. Hands joined in, touching, caressing, spreading, and gripping until they were both gasping and coming together in a frenzy.

For the first time, there was no discomfort when he entered her, and Isa liked the control she had straddling him on the settee. It was like riding a horse, yet not. She loved the tight glide of him inside of her, which was evident by the embarrassing sounds coming from her mouth. She loved the way he looked up at her from below, like he was seeing something both painful and lovely. And when his hands gripped her hips and forced her to go at a more vigorous pace, she was racing again, determined to reach her end before him. To win. By the grimace of his face, he wanted her to win. The slick friction of their skin, the beads of sweat on Junior's forehead and chest, the way his blue eyes couldn't decide whether to look at her face, her breasts, or where their bodies met—it was too much.

She grabbed one of the hands gripping her hips and brought it to where their bodies met; he understood immediately. Three passes of his warm, slick fingertips over her sensitive sex, and she was shuddering upon him, her climax sharp and deep. Throaty cries escaped her, the kind she'd never made before, and he was cursing, displacing her from his person. Dazed, empty, Isa caught herself on his knees and sat back while spurts of white exited the tip of his cock, painting a sensual picture on her breasts and stomach.

"That's not very gentlemanly," she blurted, still trembling from the aftershocks of her orgasm.

"Well, you weren't actin' very ladylike," Junior panted, squeezing the last of the viscous fluid from the slit at the tip. His seed was a translucent white, and some had leaked down the knuckles of his fist.

Curious, she swiped her first finger through it and brought it to her nose. The aroma was hard to decipher, and she touched the tip of her tongue to it. He made a choked sound. The taste was earthy and salty, but the texture was not to her liking; she wrinkled her nose.

"It's not very good," she said, looking at her finger in disappointment.

"It's not a sweet you get at a general store, Izzy." He sounded as though someone was strangling him.

"I know. I don't imagine anything naturally secreted from the human body tastes very good, but I was curious."

"Curiosity killed the cat." His dimples deepened in his cheeks.

"This won't kill me, will it?" Isa asked coyly. To his horror, she brought her finger closer to his face. "Like poison? Here. Try it. We can be Romeo and Juliet."

"Hell no!" he shouted, and she was on her back on the settee in a flash, laughing like a madwoman while he held himself a safe distance away. Like a naked primordial man guarding himself from a threat, Junior's roving eyes spotted her crumpled combinations on the floor, and he swiped it up in his fist. Only then did he approach her, scrubbing at the drying fluid on her breasts and abdomen with the balled-up cloth. It was becoming a habit, his use of her undergarments to clean up. Once she was dry, he wiped his hands on the damp underthings and lay atop her. Isa wheezed her breath out dramatically at his weight. Junior kissed her chin and looked into her eyes. "If you ever got in the family way, I would do right by you."

The statement derailed her train of thought. Sobering, she wrapped her legs around his hips and squeezed him to her. "I know you would."

"You do?"

"Of course I do. You're a good man, Junior. Despite what you think."

He absorbed this for a moment, then wrapped his arms around her back and lifted her from the settee. She kept her legs tightly secured around him while he carried her to his back bedroom. In the little fireplace, coals radiated a pleasant warmth that was lacking in the parlor. Junior pulled the bedcovers and sheets back and tumbled them into bed, Isa clinging like an orphaned opossum. Then he swore and rolled out of bed because he'd left the lamp in the other room.

Later, when the lamp was on its lowest setting and another log fed the fire, Isa ran a palm over the divot of his healed gunshot wound. "What does getting shot feel like?"

Junior looked half-asleep, but he propped his elbow on his pillow to face her. "It's like...getting hit with a hammer. Then, nothing for a few minutes. It's just wet and cold from the blood comin' out of you. But once the shock wears off, it feels like someone ripped a hot wire through you, and it burns like hell. That was the worst part at first, that burn. Like your blood's boiling out instead of just leaking, and there's not a damned thing you can do about it but stanch the flow. I'd packed it the best I could with bandanas until I got a doctor in town to sew me up. Later, I was sore in every part of my body. Movin' hurt, so I walked around like an old granny when her bones would ache. Felt like I had a fever for days, always breaking out in cold sweats. When I came to get you, I'd had three weeks to recover. I was godawful sore, though."

"Is it sore now?" Isa asked.

Thoughtfully, Junior settled his hand over hers and pushed down, forcing her to press harder until he winced. "Not too bad."

"Stop that." She tugged her hand away and bent to kiss his scar. Even now, there was faint, greenish-yellow bruising around his side. "It's a miracle the bullet didn't pierce your intestines."

"I thought it had for a while. Even though the sawbones told me it hadn't." He chuckled.

"Why? Were you very sick?" Sepsis was no laughing matter. Concern knitted her brow.

Remarkably, Junior's ears reddened. "No, but it's not fit for a lady's ears."

"We've established that I am not a lady."

"Yes, the hell you are," he scoffed, running his fingers through her hair from root to tip. He'd done so countless times, seemingly entranced by its length, its texture. "Fine. After I'd been shot, I didn't have to visit the outhouse for a week. I thought maybe it was all trapped inside of me, festering. Figured I'd die soon."

Isa's features cleared. "Ah. Perhaps it was the trauma of being shot?"

Junior twisted her hair into his fist and released it slowly, watching honey locks fall to the blanket, then repeated the process. "I didn't know you went to doctor school." The sarcasm was at odds with his engrossed attentiveness.

"I didn't. But David did."

"Hmph. *David*." No name had ever been said so petulantly.

"He spoke so often of things he learned from textbooks and cadavers, I feel as though I could go into practice myself." Isa leaned over to kiss a freckle on his collarbone. "But I don't need a medical degree to know you weren't dying. Just full of shit."

The fist holding her hair yanked, and she exploded into helpless giggles.

They grappled naked on the bed until they were drenched in sweat and weak-limbed. Once she was properly subdued beneath him, he hovered above her, the fringe of his hair brushing her shining forehead.

"I win."

Junior's smile was wide and impish, and Isa felt an answering throb between her spread legs. "Claim your reward, then."

Having conquered her, he sunk into her with his eyes closed. His mouth whispered words she couldn't hear but could feel with every swell of him reaching the deepest parts of her. He stroked into her body in a way that was more than a means of release; it was reverence. It was making love. The old fear crept in. It made her squeeze her eyes shut just before she shuddered through her second climax of the night.

Isa was deeply in love with Junior. Again.

Chapter Twenty-Seven

Deputy Gareth Glen loved his job.

Though it shamed him to admit it, he felt fulfilled as a sheriff's deputy in ways he hadn't as a poor miner's son. His daddy, a hardworking man with permanently blackened hands and ragged clothing, had died in a cave-in in '88. He'd refused to let his only son go into the trade and pushed him to finish schooling. To find an occupation that didn't fill his lungs with sediment or keep him from sunlight six days out of the week. Lord, but Gareth missed that man. Maybe the old miner was looking down at him, proud and smiling.

A significant drawback of policing a small town was knowing everyone's business.

Rumors circulated through the people inhabiting Dogwood, and they all found their way into the sheriff's office. Gareth had intimate knowledge of people's households, their deepest secrets, domestic troubles, and whether they owed money. Lawyers came and went in the jailhouse as often as the prisoners, and Gareth knew them all by their Christian names.

So, when a severe man in a suit with a well-groomed mustache walked into the sheriff's office, Sheriff Ellis and Gareth came to attention. They had never seen this man before. The stranger had a severe limp; his left leg was straight and unbending. The cane gripped firmly in his left hand stabilized him, and his gait was confident despite its rolling nature.

"Help you, sir?" Sheriff Ellis asked, eyes shrewd above his smile.

"Be a miracle if you could," the man said. Gareth stood and offered his seat, but it was declined with a curt head shake. "No one 'round these parts seems real willin' to give up information. I'm looking for a man named John Stone."

Sheriff Ellis reclined further in his old chair, its squeak ominous. "And what does this pertain to, Mr.—?"

"Talbot. Randal Talbot. Former Texas Ranger." Mr. Talbot tapped his stiff leg with his cane; it made a muffled knocking sound. The leg was wooden. "Honorable discharge."

"I'm Sheriff Ellis, and this is Deputy Glen. Now. Tell me about old John Stone. What sort of business do you have with him?"

"Not old John Stone," the man corrected. Something ugly flickered across his face. "The son. John Stone, Jr. I got business with that murdering bastard."

The sheriff asked him to elaborate, and Mr. Talbot complied with folded papers from his jacket pocket and a tale that widened the lawmen's eyes.

Gareth listened carefully from the sidelines as the story unfolded, and if it had been about any other man, he was sure that Sheriff Ellis would have written everything down word for word. But the moment Mr. Talbot called Junior a "murdering bastard," Gareth knew Ellis wouldn't give this man's words a passing thought. Ever since the Stone brothers had helped catch a caravan of stolen girls, the sheriff had held them in high esteem. After an hour of Randal Talbot making some grave allegations, unfolding wrinkled, faded paperwork and a copy of a court-martial dated two years before, Sheriff Ellis told the man he'd consider everything and would inform Mr. Talbot if he learned of John Stone, Jr.'s whereabouts.

When Sheriff Ellis didn't ask where Mr. Talbot was staying or where he could be reached, the stranger's face tightened in displeasure. He gathered his paperwork and stalked out, almost—but not quite—slamming the door behind him.

Gareth frowned and watched from the barred window as the one-legged man limped to his horse. At Randal Talbot's hip gleamed a military-grade Colt revolver.

ISA SPENT EVERY night with Junior that week, and if the laws of physics weren't in question, she'd be floating amongst the clouds. Minnie, Mrs. Hobb, and even Mr. Ricci commented on the changes in her demeanor, the ready smiles, the flush in her cheeks.

"It's because I have my family's blessing to travel abroad," she told them serenely.

Minnie and Mrs. Hobb's eyebrows rose when they discovered Junior would be traveling with her, but Isa pretended not to notice. The imminent travel made lying easier; no one questioned her claims to spend every night at her parent's farm after a full day's work. After all, she wouldn't see them for months.

It didn't matter that it took nearly three hours to reach Junior's house. His house became an insular meeting place, a world where they could be together with impunity. The first night, he was waiting on the porch for her to ride up the driveway. He'd pulled her off Mirage before she had a chance to dismount. But every night since, he waited for her just outside of town, his .45 at the ready in case of danger.

Isa was so in love with him that it terrified her. Something large and out of control loomed overhead, some presence moments away from stealing this happiness from her like taking candy from a baby. Because surely her trysts with Junior were candy. Delicious, irresistible, and perilous when consumed in high quantities. And consume him she did. It was that or be consumed first; he met her hunger with a ferocity of his own. A gripping, clinging hunger with an edge of desperation amongst all the lust. The way he loved had to be more addictive than the substances in the opiate dens in low town.

Was it love? It felt like more. It was an obsession close to madness. A driving need. There wasn't a word in the English language for it. She wanted evidence. Hard data. Neither of them had made statements of love despite the eloquent conversations of their bodies.

"I saw Sol yesterday," Isa said when they returned from their moonlit ride one night. "He saw what you left on my neck and started asking questions."

"What?" Junior leaned over Champion and shoved her hair to the side.

"You won't see it in the dark, numbskull. Besides, it's on this side." She shook her loose hair back into place. It pleased him to release it from its pins and watch it come tumbling down. "Don't be vexed. I told him it was a burn from my curling iron. It does look remarkably similar. I don't think Poppy believed me, but she won't say anything."

"Izzy." In that one word was a wealth of meaning.

Her jaw clamped shut. There it was. That looming presence, that giant God's hand that wanted to take her candy away. But now that the threat was nearer, it didn't feel like candy anymore.

It felt like a piece of *her*, and one of her favorite ones at that.

Junior was lecturing, and she resentfully listened.

"—think we need to be more careful. If Sol found out, if any of them found out...maybe we need to slow down." He was more than concerned; he sounded truly afraid that what they were doing would come to light.

It hit Isa all at once. His need for secrecy, his fear of discovery—the blow should have struck her mind, but it swung and hit directly into her heart. It hurt. His description of what it felt like to be shot came to mind. The hammer strike, the subsequent numbness.

He was *ashamed* of what they were doing. What she considered beautiful was, to him, something to be hidden. Concealed.

And hadn't she wanted to keep it a secret? Hadn't she insisted she wasn't too tired after working to ride to his house? Wasn't she lying to her family, over and over again, to be with him? It hadn't hit her until just now that she didn't like keeping secrets. Not about this. Not about him. It made her feel dirty. Unwanted.

They pulled their saddles and tack from their horses and hung them neatly up. Junior was still talking to her, but his deep voice in the dark held no substance. Isa's expression remained blank, her eyes downcast. She combed Mirage's thickening winter coat with a currycomb without once meeting his eye. He stopped talking, and his footsteps were muffled near the barn entrance. A match flared; an old kerosene lamp was lit. She turned her back to its light, mouth pinched.

"Izzy."

For the first time, Isa was sick of hearing that name. She could feel his eyes on her back, watching.

"What's wrong?" He stepped into her horse's stall.

"Nothing." It was all she could get out of her bloodless lips. She felt cornered, a wild hare avoiding a child's soothing, petting hands.

"Did I make you mad?" The little flare of disbelief, the undertone of humor, enraged her.

"I'm not mad, Junior. I think you're right about slowing down. We should stop this." It was impossible to keep her tone light. The raw, exposed nerve was too close to the surface.

"What?" All vestiges of humor disintegrated.

Fed up, Isa whirled to face him, her hair fanning out behind her. She wore his jeans and a soft, faded cambric shirt. She'd never felt so childish. So foolish. "I would hate for people to find out and for you to feel embarrassed. I should never have expected you to ever be proud to be with me the way I am with you. I'm not certain why I'm endeavoring to have some semblance of a relationship with you when you clearly don't want one with me."

"How the hell can you say that?" Junior's voice rose, and the lantern swung dangerously in his gesticulating hands. He set it on the floor outside the stall, and the shadows shifted ominously. "You're the one who doesn't want to get married! What the hell do you think will happen if people find out?"

He made a succinct point, and it enraged her further. "You act as though my brother finding out about us would be the worst thing that happened to you. Pardon the hell out of me for feeling insulted."

"It *would* be one of the worst things that ever happened to me, Isa!"

Isa disliked the range of emotions surpassing her levelheaded logic: the insecurity, the doubt. Disgusted in herself, she stormed past him. She needed air. Space. The stall was too small and close with him in it.

Junior blocked her passage. "Sol is my friend. My *best* friend. I don't like two-timing him. And being with you is like stabbing him in the back."

Something ugly inside of her broke free of its tether, and she laughed humorlessly in his beautiful, earnest face. "You had no compunction betraying him, *John*. You're only afraid he'll find out, like a child who's not sorry for what he does until he's caught."

His handsome face paled. "Don't call me that."

Isa took advantage of his shock and hurt and slid around him to escape down the barn's narrow breezeway. "Don't be a goddamned coward, and I won't."

"Don't call me that, either!" Behind her, Mirage's stall door slammed shut. Isa was quickening her pace when his hand wrapped around her elbow.

"Let go!"

"Stop running away and talk to me!" he shouted. "Who's bein' the coward now?"

Chin high, Isa tried to free her elbow but couldn't, so she stood rooted to the spot. "Fine. I'll talk. I don't like being dishonest with my family. I don't keep secrets from them no matter how hard it is. What we're doing feels wrong."

"You call dressing like a man and gambling in secret bein' honest?" His shout of laughter was cruel.

"I mean the important stuff!" she snapped. "I knew how disappointed Ma would be when I told her I wanted to move away and get an education. I knew how angry and afraid Sol would be when I told him I wanted to go abroad. *I told them anyway*. I can't be like you, holding onto my secrets like a lead bullet in a gunshot wound, letting it rot me from the inside out. You're so worried you'll betray Sol like you did with Randal that you're killing what you have with me!" She struck her chest with an open palm.

Junior released her arm, white-faced. "I never should've told you anything."

That hurt. Isa pretended it didn't.

"Well, I'm glad you did. That way, at least one person can be honest with you. You're just mad that person is me." Isa's words tumbled out faster than her racing thoughts, and she wondered if she looked as wild as she felt. "And do you know what else? I'll make this easier for you. I'm ending this...this attachment and I'll never speak of it again. This way, you'll have no more guilt with my brother, and you won't have this *shameful* secret—"

Junior's incoherent shout stopped her words. He stalked off in the other direction, his knuckles white spikes in his clenched fists. At the dark end of the barn, an explosive sound made her and the horses jump; he'd struck an empty stall.

"I won't do this with you," Isa croaked, striding to Mirage's stall. She would leave. This was too painful.

His footsteps were loud behind her. "You did this," he accused, and his voice was no better than hers, full of grit and hurt. "If anyone is to blame here, it's you."

Isa scrubbed her irritated eyes hard with the cuff of her borrowed shirt. He wouldn't let her open the stall door. "You're raving."

He moved around her until he was between her and the stall, his face twisted up, unrecognizable. "I mean it. Ever since Austin, you've been a splinter in my side. Everywhere I turn around, there you are, bothering me and wrestling with me, irritating the hell—get back here, I'm not done! And now that I need you, can't sleep without you on my mind, can't wake up without thinking of you, can't go to the outhouse because there you are! Now that I can't live without you, you want to stop this—whatever the hell this is. Well, I won't have it!"

"And I've told you. I will be someone's first choice, not their last. You can't even decide what you want more: to be my brother's best friend or to be with me."

Red-rimmed eyes as dark as the northern sea, Junior spread his arms wide and vowed, "I'll tell him tomorrow. Hell, I'll tell him tonight if you want. You're betting I won't, aren't you? I'll show up on his doorstep and shout it up at his window right now. I'll go to your ma and pa's house and tell them. And if they take us straight to the preacher tomorrow, then that's the bed you get to lie in. A lifetime with me. If that's what you really want, Izzy, I'll give it to you. All of me, every day, until we're so old, we can't even fight anymore."

He'd do it. Junior was calling her bluff and daring her to do the same. He'd do everything he just threatened, no matter how she begged and pleaded for him to stop.

While her mouth was ajar at his pledge, his promise, he closed the distance between them and wrenched her to him for a hungry kiss. She wasn't aware of him carrying her to the house or of being stripped naked on the bed. They made love with all the anger and hurt burning inside of them. It was rough, and their need put bruises on each other's skin. Their cries and groans echoed in the empty house.

Later, when the sweat dried on them and their racing hearts slowed to normal, Junior pulled her as close to him as she could go and said softly, "I want to tell you the truth about what happened."

Chapter Twenty-Eight

He loved her. God, he loved her so much it scared him.

And he thought, though it was wishful, maybe she loved him, too.

I can't be like you, holding onto my secrets like a lead bullet in a gunshot wound, letting it rot me from the inside out.

Isa was right. Junior hated it when she was right. If he was going to tell her, he may as well do it now before he fell in deeper with her. He was already so deep that he didn't think he could claw his way out. His biggest shame was a weighted chain dragging him down. Holding him back.

"Randal Talbot and I were privates together under Captain Havelard. When we got ambushed and peppered with bullets, Randal was shot in the leg and Havelard was seriously wounded. Randal was able to cover me while I snuck around and got two of the bastards; the rest of them got on their horses and rode off. After that, I was promoted to lieutenant. One day, I was visiting them in the hospital when Havelard waved me over. He got a letter sayin' that a company of Texas Rangers had gone rogue near the border."

The memory was patchy.

Captain Havelard, old before his years, lying in a hospital cot. The letter explaining in convoluted military jargon that half a dozen Rangers were terrorizing civilians along the border, and local law enforcement wasn't doing enough about it for the citizen's liking.

"Need you to investigate this for me, Stone," Captain Havelard had said, his eyes closed above his sunken cheeks. The bullet to his chest had just about killed him. "And Stone. One more thing."

"Sir?" Junior had been busily scanning the wrinkled missive.

"One of them is Talbot's little brother."

"Shit."

"It gets worse. He's impersonating a captain and leading the other Rangers—"

"*Shit.*"

"—and there have been Mexican-American fatalities. They're all poor farming families."

A noise hissed between Isa's teeth as he told her this, and he rubbed the soft skin of her arm.

"Did your friend know?" she asked, looking up from the crook of his shoulder.

"Captain Havelard ordered me not to tell him anything." Junior had resented the orders mightily. "I'd told Randal I was going to the border but didn't explain why. By the time I was released, a superior officer told him, and I was too chicken to meet him face-to-face."

Junior had ridden to the dusty little town south of El Paso, where the activity was most prevalent. His orders were clear: gather enough evidence to incriminate the men, discover their location, and send for reinforcement. The local sheriff was old and short on help. According to him, the group of young men was showing off their homemade Texas Ranger badges, abusing their power, and their leader claimed to be Captain Bill Talbot.

"There *was* no Captain Bill Talbot. The sheriff gave me his blessing to investigate, so I visited some nearby farms and asked about the men's whereabouts. Most of the families wanted to be left alone. I reckon they thought their involvement would incriminate them in case things turned ugly. But a few of them—the ones brave enough to contact the U.S. Marshal—were angry. They gave statements on the men's movements, the usual spots they'd hole up at, and the pattern of places they ran off to after a night of mischief. According to them, these men stole, bullied, and even had their way with some of the farmers' daughters."

Isa made a noise in her throat, and Junior realized he'd stopped stroking her forearm and was instead gripping it. He peeled his hand from her, dismayed to see a white impression on her skin.

"I'm sorry, darlin'." He kissed the top of her head, breathing in her sweet scent, and chafed her arm.

She waved this off and scooted up until she was propped on her elbow. "Did you end up finding them?"

"Yeah, I did. First, I reported back to Captain Havelard on my initial findings, then scouted for a couple days around the places the rogue Rangers were known to frequent. I met a farmer named Paulson. He thought I was one of them at first and pulled a gun on me till he came closer." Junior chuckled. "He was a tough son of a bitch. He was a white man married to a Mexican senorita and knew fluent Spanish. Only ever saw him smile for his woman and two little girls. They were just about the sweetest things you've ever seen, Izzy. The oldest one—she was about Ally's age—had these great big eyes and was always smilin'. I remember her name. Leticia. Paulson called her Leti."

He stopped talking. This chapter of his story was ugly. Tainted. One he relived when he couldn't sleep, wishing over and over again that he'd done more to prevent it. A hand slid into his, fingers linking, sharing strength. He squeezed tight.

"With Paulson's help, I finally found where Bill Talbot and his men were hidin' out."

Junior and Paulson had spent an afternoon tracking the six men's movements when they found them. The men were holed up in an abandoned shanty on the outskirts of town, and Paulson had wanted to confront them immediately. Junior explained how that would have been a mistake.

"Even with a militia at our backs, it could have turned into a shootout," Junior explained. "I had orders not to let things escalate. Havelard wanted federal troops to put the fear of God into these men so no one else would get similar ideas. Meanwhile, Paulson's in my ear talkin' about forming a posse to bring them in by force." He ground his teeth together at the memory and stared across the foot of the bed. In the little fireplace, the coals glowed red beneath a crust of white ash.

Gently, Isa asked, "Did Paulson listen?"

"Not a damned bit."

Junior had no sooner ridden to El Paso to send a wire to Havelard than Paulson was forming a posse of angry neighboring farmers to surround the shack housing the group of rogue Rangers.

"Paulson underestimated what men will do when ruled by fear," Junior said. "One of his neighbors betrayed him and notified Bill Talbot."

Isa groaned softly. "Why would anyone do such a thing?"

"Could be the neighbor was scared it wouldn't be a successful mission, and his family would pay the price." By the time Junior returned to the dusty little town, the sheriff had informed him the men had cleared out from their hiding spot, alerted before the posse could arrive at the scene. "I visited Paulson's ranch that evening. Lord, I was ready to tear into him. He didn't come out to greet me, which was strange. His dog didn't, either, and that should've warned me. I remember dismounting and being pistol-whipped from behind."

The six Rangers had surrounded the ranch with plans to execute Paulson before fleeing. Junior's arrival alerted one of their posted men, and it had been all too easy to sneak up behind the tall, blond Ranger. It was not quite as easy to disarm him, however.

"I'd managed to pin their lookout down when four more of them were on me, punching, kicking, stirring up sand. One of them shot me, but it only grazed me." He pointed to a withered scar on the roundest part of his left shoulder. "I remember Bill ordering them not to shoot. They all carried military-grade Colts. If I'd been killed by one of those, it'd fall back to them. The best course of action would be to beat me unconscious and disappear over the border. That's how I got this." He brushed a thumb over the scar beneath his eyebrow.

It wasn't until later that night that Junior regained consciousness. He'd woken to a pitch-black sky lit by the blazing farm beside him.

Beside him, Isa listened rigidly. Afraid of hurting her again, Junior pulled his hand free of hers and gripped the blanket, discreetly wringing it between his fingers.

"The fire was raging. Had been goin' on for a while. It was the heat that woke me." He had wanted to scream a warning to Paulson and his family but couldn't get his jaw to open. "The barn was a shell, and the house was engulfed. It was loud; I never knew fire could be so loud, not even when you lit those wagons on fire back then, remember?"

Isa nodded, but he wasn't paying attention, not truly. He was lost in the memories. Bottled up since his testimony in court, the words came flooding out. "I found Paulson inside the front gate. He'd been shot, execution style, and had probably been dead before I'd even ridden up. I wanted to look for the rest of them, but it was hard to see; one of my eyes was swollen shut. But I could hear them. Laughing. Shouting. They were excited. They had taken the .45 Havelard gave me, the engraved one, but I still had my military Colt. I pulled it out and walked around the house. Everything was lit up like it was daytime, and the heat comin' off the house had sweat pouring into my good eye. I kept having to wipe it on my shoulder. I found them in the backyard. Five of the men were grouped around Paulson's wife. She was naked on the ground. I didn't think twice about it, Izzy. I shot them all.

"I emptied five rounds into them, and they all dropped like flies. That's when I saw movement by the outhouses. It was Bill Talbot. He was running, shooting at me. He was a piss-poor shot—used up all his ammo before I'd even thought about chasing him. I was in no fit state to catch him. Thank God they'd tied Champ up nearby. I got on him and lassoed Talbot before he could get on his horse. It was when I was draggin' him to me that I saw what the bastard had been doing by the outhouses. He'd been with Paulson's little girl, Leti."

Junior covered and scrubbed his eyes, willing the image to wipe away.

"Junior..." Isa's voice was as broken as his.

He touched her, and she quietened. He had to finish it.

"I'd like to say my mind walked away from me after that. In court, Havelard's lawyer argued that I was concussed. But I wasn't, Izzy. I was crystal clear. I dismounted, disarmed Bill Talbot, and tied him up with a spare bit of rope I had. Then I put the lasso around his neck."

Bill Talbot had talked, shouted, and begged for his life. Junior had ignored him. He'd led his friend's little brother by his neck to the nearest tree and threw the rope over it. Then he'd secured the rope around his saddle horn, mounted Champion, and slowly pulled Talbot up. The man had ceased to be human to Junior. In his mind, Talbot had become nothing more than a vessel that inflicted pain and suffering. A monster. Junior had watched the body swing and kick until it stopped moving. Until piss ran down its legs, dripping off weathered boots into the dust. Until it was dead.

"I made sure he was," Junior said numbly.

He'd tied the end of the rope to some scrub brush, limped over to Paulson, his wife, and Leti, and covered them as best he could with spare blankets and clothes in his saddlebags. When a search for the smallest child had proved fruitless, Junior had dragged the men's bodies away and contemplated ending his own life.

Isa wiped at her nose.

The silence was too loud. Junior talked to fill it. "I cried when I shot those men. Isn't that pitiful? I was so mad it turned into tears. I did that as a kid and hated it. My pa always called me a 'sissy female.' But I didn't shed a tear for Talbot. I hanged him and felt glad." He cleared his throat. "I turned myself in when the sun rose. They called me a traitor. A murderer. But I'd do it again. I reckon that's why I can live with myself."

To give her privacy while she subtly blew her nose into one of his bandanas, Junior reached for his wallet in his bedside table drawer and gently withdrew a frayed, folded letter.

"I read this. To give me strength."

Isa's shaking fingers held the sheaf of paper she had written on several years before, and her next words, so sincerely spoken, were what finally crumbled his reserves.

"I love you, Junior."

He allowed her to pull him close, like a mother would a child. For a long time, she stroked his bare back and made no mention of the dampness against her shoulder.

Chapter Twenty-Nine

"I reckon Isa is sneaking off with some fellow."

Poppy looked up from sponge-bathing Agatha, and Sol glimpsed a flicker of panic in her soft blue eyes before she could hide it. "What do you mean?"

"I saw Ma this mornin' on her way home from church and asked how it felt to have Isa underfoot all the time again. Damned if she knew what I was yammering on about. Then she went and tried to get nosey, so I had to lie to her. I said Isa must've decided to hole up at the hotel. Shug, I haven't lied to my ma since the last time she came after me with the rug beater." Despite his teasing words, there was a hard set to his face, an expression normally reserved for cattle rustlers and wife beaters.

"Surely there is some other explanation than her being with a man."

It would be easier to believe Poppy if she would meet his eye.

"Maybe not, but I can smell when Isa is up to mischief, and she's up to something." He grabbed his sheepskin coat off the peg beside the bedroom door. There was a nip in the air, and it was too busy at the ranch to afford catching a fever. "I think I'll go pay the deputy a visit."

"Oh, I don't think notifying the authorities—"

"I'm not notifying anyone of anything. I'm gonna see if Isa is shacking up with that boy she went to the dance with."

"Gareth?" She couldn't have sounded more stupefied if he'd announced he was taking a trip to the moon. "You think she's disappearing at Gareth's house?"

"Who else would she be canoodling with?"

"Who says she's canoodling at all, Sol!"

Mulishness firmed the line of his jaw. "I know what I saw on her neck, and it wasn't no curling iron burn."

Poppy's eyes brimmed with worry as he gave her and Agatha a smacking goodbye kiss before walking out the door.

DEPUTY GLEN LIVED in a little second-story apartment a few blocks from the sheriff's office. It was a Sunday afternoon, and Isa was supposed to be at their ma's.

She wasn't.

According to a concerned Minnie, Isa wasn't at the hotel or general store, either. Sol had the unsettling impression he'd been through this before. Isa had gotten it into her fool head to follow Poppy's abductors six years before, and he'd been beside himself.

Now, he was beside himself for a different reason.

He took the outside stairs three at a time, and his fist was hard against the apartment door. In the ally below him, a couple of town kids looked up from whatever bug they were poking. The door opened, revealing Gareth in his Sunday best. His shirt was creased, and the back of his hair had a cowlick. Seeing it was Sol, he opened the door without hesitation.

"Afternoon." Gareth was Isa's age with dark hair and eyes, and he yawned and scratched the back of his head like he'd just woken up from a nap. "Everything all right?"

Sol didn't get much further from the front door and studied the younger man's face for any hint of reticence. "Isa been by here?"

"What?" Gareth's shock seemed genuine.

"My sister. You haven't had her over any, have you?"

"Hell no!" The offense was real. Gareth eyes snapped angrily. "Why would I ever have Isa up here? I don't bring any women up here; it's a stipulation of the lease."

The two men stared hard at each other, one bewildered, one searching for deceit. Finally, Sol's tense posture sagged. "I reckon I got it wrong. I shouldn't have barged in here accusin' you of anything."

"I'll say." Concern replaced the other man's cautious hostility. "Everything well with your sister?"

"Yeah, she's just—it don't matter. I'll see myself out."

"Wait." Gareth put a hand on Sol's shoulder, and the gravity in his eyes made Sol straighten. "I've been meaning to talk to you. There's some fellow by the name of Randal Talbot looking for Junior. I know he's your friend, and the sheriff and I reckon we smell trouble. I was plannin' on visiting him myself come Monday."

Sol's eyes flared. "Appreciate that. I'll ride over today and let him know. Did that fellow say why he's lookin' for Junior?"

Gareth winced. "I don't think you're gonna like it."

Five minutes later, Sol shook Gareth's hand and sped down the stairs to his aging roan gelding. The mystery of where Isa was disappearing to would have to wait—he had to find Junior and warn him. Blanched of color beneath his tan, Sol kicked his roan north, racing to his friend's house.

Trouble was coming.

Chapter Thirty

It was hard to saddle a horse with a man's hard body pressed against her. The ticklish sensations of lips against her ear made Isa duck her head, laughing.

"Junior, if I don't show up at the hotel this evening, Sol will start asking questions. He thinks I'm with Ma right now."

Two tanned hands gripped her hips and pulled her back against a pair of hard thighs. "Let him ask. How about I go with you? We can tell him what we've been up to together."

Isa shuddered at the thought. "We should break it to him slowly. Perhaps you should make your intentions known and start courting me. They don't need to know about...this." She rubbed the curve of her bottom against the line of his lengthening erection.

Face against her neck, Junior cupped one hand on her breast and the other between her legs. "Stay a little longer."

Isa wasn't a woman who believed in giggling, yet here she was, giggling uncontrollably while Junior herded her into the clean, empty stall, its dirt floor insulated with hay. They played a little, laughing and teasing, and didn't hear the horse riding up in the yard. He'd pinned her down but allowed her to roll them until she was on top, her honey-blonde hair a pincushion of hay. She bent to kiss him, and neither noticed the shadow that fell over the stall opening.

The kiss had deepened, sobering all playfulness—when Isa was unceremoniously ripped off Junior by two powerful hands.

"I came here to warn you, you goddamned bastard!" her brother's voice bellowed.

From her sudden position on her back, Isa caught sight of Sol's long arms pumping as he pummeled every inch of the prone man on the ground. Junior protected his face with his arms and hands but didn't fight back.

The utter grief in Sol's voice broke through Isa's shock. She crawled to her knees and tried to pull her brother off by his gun belt. "Sol!"

"Fight back," he was gasping, oblivious to his sister. His hat lay on the ground beside him from the scuffle. When it was obvious Junior would not reciprocate the blows, Sol shakily got to his feet and dragged the younger man up.

"Get away from him," Isa cried, attempting to shove her body between the two men.

"You shut up!"

Junior's stricken face twitched. "Don't talk to her like that. It's my fault, not hers."

"You're damned right, it's your fault—Isa, get off!" Sol shoved Isa from his person and gestured disgustedly at Junior. "He charms every pretty girl in the county into his bed, and you make yourself one of them?"

It felt like a doubled fist to the solar plexus, solidifying her.

To Junior, Sol said, "I always told myself the one girl you wouldn't mess with was my little sister. You're my friend, and friends don't do that to each other!" His voice rose with every word until he was shouting again.

"It isn't like that," Junior defended, his face dark red from either blows or heightened emotion. His eyes were glossy. Isa knew he considered crying a sign of weakness, and her heart went out to him. Her own tears choked her as she stood helplessly off to the side.

"The hell it isn't. You probably only wanted her because you knew you couldn't have her!" Sol sneered unfeelingly. His normally attractive face was a twisted, ugly mask. He looked like a stranger, and his words repeated in her head like an echo in a cavern.

You probably only wanted her because you knew you couldn't have her!

"I love her!" Junior shouted, spittle flying, his face finally animated.

Sol roared, lunged, and struck Junior on his cleft chin with a hard fist. "You're not good enough to lick her boots!"

Junior stumbled backward.

Isa cried out and ran toward him, but Sol's hand whipped around her biceps and pulled her roughly back. "Let me go!"

"Did you know he was discharged, Isa?" Sol shook her a little. "Did you know he murdered men in his own company?"

Junior looked up at them, the blood drained from his cheeks. He listened, blue eyes glittering in his white face.

"I don't know you anymore," Sol continued. "The Junior I knew wasn't a murderer and a liar. Didn't kill men, get court-martialed, and keep it a secret from everyone for *years*. And he didn't roll my sister in the hay with no intention of marriage."

"I was the one who didn't want marriage," Isa broke in angrily. "And roll me in the hay? That's rich, Sol, considering Poppy was already with child when you married her!"

"That's beside the point!"

"That's the whole point. Junior isn't stupid enough to get me in the family way, and he wasn't alone in the seducing. We are equally at fault, though it's no business of yours what we do."

Sol's laugh was unpleasant. "Is that so? You're such a hifalutin modern woman, with your college education and plans to travel to foreign countries. You think getting' your skirts flipped up by a womanizing murderer doesn't affect you? I never thought I'd say this, but you're just like Kat."

It was Isa's turn to pale.

"That's enough." Junior's attention was no longer on Sol's face but on Isa's. "You're hurting her when you should be hurting me."

Jaw ticking, Sol refused to look at Junior. "Isa, you're too good to get shackled to someone like this. Get your ass on your horse before I kill him."

"I'm not leaving." Her words sounded watery and weak, and it made her hate Sol even more.

"Izzy." Junior's voice was soft. He looked bloodless, like he'd been shot again, the life slowly draining into a puddle at their feet. "Go with him."

"No—"

"Please."

She wouldn't make him beg. And she didn't dare approach him for comfort with Sol watching. Junior had been hit enough. Hurt enough. She nodded, refusing to blink so as not to overflow the tears. She would leave because he had asked. It was the hardest thing she'd ever had to do. Before she exited the stall, she stopped and said quietly, "Just...stay, Junior. Don't leave."

She was afraid to return to his house and find him gone, this time forever.

He nodded once in understanding.

Only then did she walk away.

Chapter Thirty-One

Junior stood in the empty stall long after Sol had chased after a galloping Isa in wordless disgust. When the sun threatened to sink below the horizon, he got on Champion bareback—no saddle, no bit—and led the gelding with only a bridle and lead rope to his brother's house. He didn't bother locking up his house; he never wanted to step foot inside that house ever again unless Isa was with him. It was no home without her. It was void of warmth. Empty.

The sky had darkened. The north star winked beside the sliver of moon above. Junior didn't notice. He stared blindly ahead and revisited Sol's words repeatedly in his mind.

"You were my friend," and "womanizing murderer," and "get on your horse before I kill him."

If Junior could scrub his ears out and never hear them again, he would.

Did you know he murdered men in his own company?

At the time, he'd been too stricken with grief to defend himself. Now that he was sound of mind, he wanted to know just who the hell had told Sol. Junior doubted it had been his father. Guilt and shame wrangled with self-preservation. He needed to talk to someone with a clearer head than him, and the person he knew with the soundest mind was his brother.

Lucy opened the kitchen door when Junior knocked, and her eyes sharpened.

"Junior. What happened?"

"Is Ben home?" He hated how childish it sounded.

Opening the door wide to the warm, fragrant kitchen, Lucy said, "Of course, come in. Get yourself a cup of coffee while I get him."

Junior followed orders mechanically while Lucy scurried off to the barn for Ben, who was probably doing the evening milking. He poured rich, black coffee into a mug, splashed sugar and cream into the swirling liquid, and sat at the rough work table. The mug was still full when Ben stomped his boots off at the door and stepped inside. His older brother may be shorter by a few inches than he, but Ben made up for the disadvantage with an enormous presence and shoulders as broad as a barge. His blue Stone eyes homed in on the bruises darkening Junior's chin and cheekbone.

Something in the younger man's expression stymied any questions, so Ben eased the kitchen door shut behind him and made use of the coffee kettle on the stove. Lucy and the boys were conspicuously absent. By the time Ben sat in his usual place at one end of the table, Junior had organized his thoughts into some semblance of order.

When Ben took a sip of his black coffee, Junior found the strength to speak. "I messed up."

The black-haired man set the mug down and steepled his fingers on the table. "Can it be fixed?"

"I don't know." Junior felt his breath leave his lungs in a trembling exhalation and pressed his thumb and forefinger against his closed lids. "God, I don't think so. Everything's been going to hell for so long."

"I wish you'd tell me about it. All of it, instead of just skirting around what's goin' on." There was no accusation in Ben's voice, but the words nonetheless made Junior's heart race.

"It's not just one thing; it's endless things. Problem after problem after problem." Junior laughed hollowly and dropped his hand to the table. The coffee trembled in his mug, reminding him to take a sip. It settled like ashes in his mouth, and he set it back down, sick to his stomach.

Ben, however, had no issue with his own coffee. He'd already finished his first cup and stood to get a refill. "How 'bout we start with the problem that put those bruises on your face?"

It was easier to talk now that Ben's eagle eyes weren't staring into his forehead. Junior braced himself and said, "Isa and I—you were right. We got close after the trip from Austin."

From the corner of his eye, Junior saw Ben's shoulders go very still.

"How close?"

"Close enough that when Sol came by the house earlier, he tried his damnedest to see what my brains felt like with his fist."

"Guessin' by those bruises, you didn't hit back."

"Naw, I deserved the licks." Junior scrubbed his tender cheekbone and groaned into his hands. "I was gonna tell him. Izzy and I had planned to do it together."

"But he caught you first." For the first time, there was censure in Ben's voice. His back remained facing the room, and the sounds of liquid pouring and clinking metal against ceramic filled the room. "You shouldn't have gone behind his back like that. Sol's good as family. Better than family, in fact. He'd die for you."

"I know, Ben, you don't have to tell me. *I know*."

"What're you gonna do to fix it?" Ben turned around, mug tiny in his hand. Under the firm stare was a wealth of understanding. "We've all been tempted by the women we love. Even

Sol. Hell, even me. And for all your faults, you never chased after innocents. Never accepted any offers from 'em, either."

"Just widows and whores," Junior murmured, looking at the rag rug on the floor. "Older women who didn't want ties to a man. None that wanted marriage."

"It's looking like marriage now, brother."

Junior had often thought that Ben had filled the role of father better than brother, and this was proving correct now. Firm and direct is what he gave Junior. No shouting, no berating. Just honesty. It settled something frantic in Junior's chest, something that had been clanging like an off-key note. Soothed it.

"I told her last night it looked like marriage. She never wanted it, you know. And I was more than happy to oblige her."

"I'll bet." Ben hid the smile, quirking his full lips behind his mug.

"But it changed. The sneaking around. I wanted her more and more. And she'd come without a single complaint, even though she was riding three hours each way to and from Dogwood. I worried about her so much, I'd ride to Dogwood and back with her. Haven't gotten a lick of work done all week. When she'd get to the house, it would feel like home. I don't want to let her go." Junior laughed awkwardly. "Listen to me. I sound like one of those sissy poems the teachers made us read at school."

Ben wasn't smiling anymore. His straight brows lowered. "You sound like you love her."

"I love her so much I'm about to throw away a twenty-year friendship over it." Junior turned his mug a full rotation, then another. "Sol said he won't let me marry her. Said I'm not good enough for her. He's right."

"Sol's right about a lot of things, but not about this." Ben straightened from his lean against the counter.

"Yes. He is. And I'll tell you why." Junior looked miserably up at his brother. "You might want to sit down."

Without hesitation, Ben sat. It was black as tar outside, reflecting the two brothers, as Junior told Ben everything. They faced one another, one man stiff with worry, the other beaten. Junior spoke of Captain Havelard's letter, the investigation of the terrorized Mexican-Americans, and Bill Talbot swinging from a tree at dawn. Even the court-martial, which had been kept relatively quiet, was a distasteful case no politician wanted to rouse the public with.

"That's why my next of kin wasn't notified. And...because I asked Captain Havelard not to send letters to you or Father. He was good to me. Disappointed, hurt, angry, but good to me. Wouldn't even take back the .45 he gave me." Throat dry, Junior took a sip of cold coffee. An hour had gone by, and he glanced at the back door. "Where are Lucy and the boys?"

"I asked them to go to Tia and Frank's." There was something in Ben's eyes, but Junior couldn't decipher it. It was different from the discontent that had etched premature lines in Havelard's face.

Fear of condemnation made the sick feeling return in Junior's stomach. "I'm sorry, Ben. Everything I do, I mess up. Even love. I finally fall, and I'm the wrong man for her." The words didn't feel right in his mouth, and he wanted to take them back as soon as he said it. Ben beat him to it.

"That ain't true. I've never met two people more suited to each other. It's just the way you went about it."

Junior swallowed some obstruction in his throat. "I reckon you're right." His nostrils flared. "I've got to tell you something else. The man who's after me? I think he finally caught up. That's why Sol came by. He said he was warning me."

"I thought you were acquitted?" An edge of fear sharpened his brother's voice.

"I was. This is Bill Talbot's brother. Randal was my friend, one I'd saved. Guess that don't matter much if you hang his brother right after."

"He gonna try to kill you?"

"I don't know."

They sat in charged silence for a time until Ben leaned forward, arms on the table between them. "I've got a plan."

JUNIOR RODE HOME the next day with clear instructions to grab enough belongings for a lengthy stay at Ben's. Christmas was two weeks away, and Ben said seeing his little brother's face for the holidays would be good. Junior suspected it was because Ben thought he'd flee.

But he was tired of running. Tired of hiding out, tired of the lies. The cat was out of the bag; Randal was hot on his trail, telling anyone who'd listen about Junior's inexpiable crime. The whole state probably knew what happened in '91.

A flock of red and brown cardinals took flight when Junior rode across his front yard, and he narrowed his eyes on the empty house. The weather vane squeaked, lazily pointing south. Neck hairs prickling, Junior brought Champion around to the back of the house and hitched him away from any windows. He pulled his gun, heartbeat swift, and sidled along the siding to the back door. It was unlocked.

Had he locked it last night?

No, he'd left as soon as Isa and Sol had ridden off.

Cocking the hammer back on his revolver, Junior carefully turned the knob and pushed the door open wide. There were no shouts. No gunfire. Still, he couldn't shake that uneasy feeling, the same sensation that clung to him just before he'd been ambushed. Or the time he was hunting and caught sight of a mountain lion in a tree above him.

"You can come in. I'm not gonna shoot you, Stone."

The voice sent chills through Junior's bones; he hadn't heard it in years. It came from the direction of the kitchen.

Randal Talbot had found him at last.

Chapter Thirty-Two

"How do I know you're not gonna shoot me?" Junior called out, stalling for time. If only his sluggish brain would *think*. He stared blindly at the door trim, wondering what the hell to do. This was different from capturing a known criminal, a stranger. Inside was a man he'd once risked his life for. A friend who now had a vendetta against him.

"I'm not gonna shoot you. Can't get answers from a dead man, can I?" Randal's voice was just as affable now as it had been years ago. "I'll make it easy on you. I swear on my dead brother's grave that I won't shoot you when you come in."

"That doesn't mean a damned thing to me." It was out before Junior could stop it. Like in a dream, he saw a small figure on the dirt, illuminated by hot, yellow firelight. *Leti*.

I'd do it all again, Junior thought wildly, that old hate rising like bile. *Would that I could go back and do it sooner to spare them.*

Randal must have sensed the animosity exuding from Junior from the doorway; he didn't speak for a long spell. Then, "Alright. I won't swear on him. You saved my life once. How about you come in, talk to me, and I leave? Then we'll call it even."

Junior pictured Isa shaking her head at him, eyes shooting citrine sparks of warning. He thought of Ben and his unflinching bravery, his steady calm.

He uncocked the hammer.

"I'll come in." He said it so quietly it may not have reached the kitchen.

But Randal heard. "I'm sitting at the table, both hands in plain view."

Junior peeked around the doorframe as if he were on the wrong side of a bounty-hunting exchange. It was as Randal had said; the man sat at the breakfast table, lit by the window over the dry sink. He looked frail. Old. His hands lay flat on the tabletop, so Junior holstered his pistol and strode in. Seeing Randal in his house was like encountering a missing pet, one who had disappeared for several days and returned with evidence of rabies. Was Randal the same man he'd been two years ago? Or was he all twisted up inside, inclined to bite?

Hands mindfully on the tabletop, Junior sat at the table. Seeing Randal in a suit instead of cowboy attire was off-putting. The suit was blue. Oil shone in his styled brown hair, and his mustache was combed, curling at the ends.

"It's not real safe to keep your door unlocked," Randal said conversationally, analyzing Junior with similar intensity and lingering on the bruises.

"I left in a hurry yesterday."

"It's been a trial to find you," Randal continued. "I've been all over Texas. Couldn't remember where you said you was from—you never talked much about your family, you know that? You come from good stock. Not like me and Bill. We came from a boy's orphanage in Dallas."

"I remember that." Junior's teeth clenched at this second mention of Bill Talbot.

"I always figured you were raised in the same squalor as us. Don't know why. Maybe it was the way you worked, the way you talked." Randal rolled his shoulders in a shrug. "Imagine my surprise when, after asking around for you in Huntsville, someone pointed me in the direction of a ranch the size of Rhode Island."

Junior said nothing.

"Then I talked to your pa and understood. He's a mean sumbitch, ain't he?" A hint of the old Randal appeared, familiar as a set of old woolen socks. "Thought he'd blow a hole right through me when I asked questions about you. I s'pose you never told him what happened?"

Mouth dry, Junior shook his head.

"Not an easy thing to tell your family."

More silence.

"Almost as hard as hearing it from the other side. In a hospital bed. Not able to walk. Not able to do a damned thing for months until you learn to use a pair of crutches and walk and ride again." Old Randal was gone. New Randal pinned hard brown eyes into the man opposite him. "I didn't find out what happened until Captain Havelard came back. He wanted to tell me in person. I'd been fightin' gangrene for weeks. Felt like my stump would never heal."

"I'm sorry you had to hear that way," Junior forced out. Guilt and righteous anger sparred with one another.

"You're sorry." Randal chuckled. "What I don't understand is why you never just told me yourself."

Incredulously, Junior met the other man's gaze. How could he ask that? "You'd have shot me on the spot before I'd had a chance to speak my piece."

"I wasn't as hotheaded as all that," Randal scoffed. But there was a fire in his eyes, a burning. Not a vengeful flame—a righteous one. "I deserve answers, Stone. Havelard's story didn't add up. There were holes the size of Texas in it, and once I was discharged, the bastard moved east. When I approached his superiors, I was shut out as surely as a beggar on the street. *No one would tell me anything.*"

The hurt in his old friend's voice was harder to stomach than the indignation. If Junior had been in Randal's shoes, if something had happened to Ben, he would've stopped at nothing to learn the truth. Nothing. He straightened in the chair and nodded once, his lips compressed and pale. "I'll tell you everything."

And he did.

Not a single detail was spared.

At first, Randal peppered questions at him like birdshot. What did Junior mean, Bill was leading the rogue Rangers? How was anyone confident Bill was impersonating a captain? Captain Havelard had only mentioned Mexican-American casualties, not fatalities. That didn't sound like Bill. No, that sure didn't sound like him at all.

But the more Junior recited everything calmly and with absolute certainty, the more Randal's questions tapered off until he sat in his chair, unmoving. Unspeaking. When Junior expressed his own anger at himself for trusting Paulson not to get involved after leaving for El Paso, Randal looked at his hands. And when the reopened wound of Leti's demise made an appearance in the tale, Randal's hands covered his face. Junior tried to keep his account of what he did to Bill Talbot clinical, but Randal still held a hand up. *Stop.*

It was too late for that. Junior completed his account, ending it with his court-martial, his dishonorable discharge, and bounty hunting for the state. He didn't think mentioning the years of secrecy and avoiding his family were necessary.

Several minutes of quiet passed before Randal revealed a countenance that had aged a decade. He opened his mouth to speak, but couldn't. Instead, he nodded once, grabbed his cane, and walked out of Junior's kitchen.

Junior suspected he wouldn't see Randal Talbot again, so he walked to the window and watched the man awkwardly mount a horse behind the barn and ride away. A noise startled him, and Junior reflexively whipped his .45 out. Ben was walking through the kitchen doorway, holstering his pistol.

He'd been in the hallway, gun drawn, the entire time.

Chapter Thirty-Three

Junior approached his brother's round pen the next day. A tall, shirtless man was putting a horse through its paces, but when he saw the approaching figure, he threw the quirt down and climbed the rungs of the round pen.

"Sol," Junior called, jogging to keep up. "Sol!"

Sol refused to talk. His long legs ate up the distance between the round pen and the barn. Junior chased him, cursing, then noticed a lariat looped on a fence post. He snagged it up, swung his loop, and the circle of rope settled over Sol's head.

Furious, Sol ripped the rope off before it could cinch. He backtracked toward Junior, his eyes promising violence.

"Now that I have your attention," Junior said calmly, throwing the rope down. All that calm scattered when the angry cowboy closed in on him; Junior skipped backward. "Damn it, Sol, I'm trying to apologize to you!"

"I don't want your sorries. They ain't worth spit." The venom in Sol's words was potent, but he stopped stalking Junior to stand by the round pen, fists like rocks.

"Well, you're gonna get it!" Junior held his palms out guardedly. "And I'm going to start by telling you I've loved Isa like a sister since she was knee-high, and those feelings didn't change until she went off to college."

A sneer curled Sol's lips, and he took a threatening step toward Junior.

"I swear on my life, Sol," Junior said. "But the feelings did change, and I couldn't stop it. If you want me out of your life, I'm gone. But I won't stay out of hers. I'm gonna ask her to marry me. She might not even have me. Lord knows she's never wanted to be shackled down."

Sol finally spoke. "What makes you think I'll let you have her?"

Isa would throw a wall-eyed fit if she heard the two of us talking about her like this, Junior thought distractedly.

Aloud, he said, "I figured you'd think that way. Which is why I called on your parents this morning and got their blessing. If I can't have yours, I reckon I'll take her pa's."

Red climbed Sol's neck at an alarming rate. "You sneaky polecat. You've got stones bigger than that pea brain of yours."

"I have to. Have you met your sister? She'd run all over anyone else, and you know it."

Sol ripped his gloves off and slapped them against his thigh, looking off in the distance. His jaw worked. "What happened with that feller lookin' for you? Is what he told Deputy Glen true?"

It rankled more than anything that Gareth knew Junior's business. He swallowed his pride and told Sol, "Yes."

Junior divulged the whole rotten tale, but by the end of it, Sol was begrudgingly meeting his eye.

"God almighty," Sol whispered.

"I should've told you, but I was so goddamned ashamed. Some of those men...I shot them in the back. You don't do that. Not if you're a real man."

Sol shook his head and settled his hat further back on his head, squinting to see Junior clearly. "Remember those men who stole Poppy, Isa, and those other girls away? I'd have shot the lot of them in their beds and not lost a lick of sleep over it. Sounds like those Rangers were of similar ilk and had it comin'. So, yeah, you should've said something to me. That way, I knew to tell you how stupid it was to feel ashamed of something that had to be done."

Incapable of speech, Junior nodded curtly.

"People in power should never abuse it," Sol continued, his deep voice carrying across the space between them, cracking the glacier of Junior's pride. "They were hurtin' innocents. How many more would have been hurt if it hadn't been for you? How could you have let it keep happening?"

It was Junior's turn to look out at the pasture, watching cowboys make their rounds amongst the herd.

"You still goin' to Europe with Isa?"

The question brought him back. "Hope so." It sounded rough, and he cleared his throat.

"Good. Legs needs some lookin' after. I reckon I wouldn't trust anyone else with the job."

Swallowing became difficult. "I—"

Sol shifted his feet and raised his hands. "What are you waitin' for? She's at the hotel where I threatened her with Ma and Pa if she didn't stay. Go get her."

"But you—"

"Don't be a jackass." When the younger man didn't move, Sol threw his gloves at Junior. A big, white smile spread across his face, cutting creases into brown cheeks. "That was my blessing, stupid butt. Now, git."

Junior didn't say a word. He strode to the taller man and yanked him in for a back-clapping hug before jogging to Champion. He rode the horse with a smile on his face because Sol, his best friend, had reciprocated the hug with ferocious slaps of his own. The sun had never felt sunnier.

Chapter Thirty-Four

One thing kept Isa from racing to Junior's house (Sol's threat be damned), and it was the unexpected visitor who had arrived at Dogwood Hotel with a wrapped gift in tow. Mr. Ricci gave Isa and her guest leave to use his office for their visit so long as the door remained cracked.

"You're telling me," Isa said slowly from Mr. Ricci's plush leather desk chair, "that you fell in love with your wife during our time apart?"

"Quite like a fairy tale, isn't it?" David Corner quipped around one of Mr. Ricci's fine cigars.

"The one where the maliferous witch is sent to a faraway land so the prince and princess can live happily ever after?" Isa could almost laugh if she wasn't so torn up by the circumstances of her own love life.

David, whose world was finally set to rights, did laugh. "Just so. I imagine I needed some time apart from you to see what had been in front of me all along."

Isa's brows rose. "Spoken like a true philosopher."

"I've become wise in your weeks away. Also, Father refuses to retire and begs for your return." He blew a plume of smoke at the ceiling, smiling benevolently.

"Give him my apologies, but I am not returning to Austin." She dropped her head against the chair's backrest and looked out the bay window. The street teemed with people busily living as they did daily. How did they do it? How did they exist in the same place, day after day, and not want to flee?

"Something is wrong," David said from his seat across the enormous desk. "I've never once seen you melancholy. Perhaps it's good that I showed up when I did."

A small huff of mirthless laughter escaped Isa's pinched nostrils. "I am not melancholy. Just—not in control."

"Oh?" David leaned forward, his boyishly handsome face wreathed with intrigue. "What's out of your control? I've never seen you with a feather out of place, not even when you were soaked with beer and stumbling out of the gaming hall."

Isa never lied to David. In fact, the more shocked he was, the more it amused her. But, curiously, she was not in the mood for sharing. "I'm telling you nothing while you're as euphorically happy as you are. Misery loves company, or haven't you heard?"

"Ah. You must be having trouble with a man. Mr. Suffix, I presume?"

Her eyes narrowed on him. "Why do you say that?"

"Because I know what unrequited love looks like, Dora, and I'd say you have quite the case of it. As the only man you've ever loved is your childhood sweetheart, I'd wager from your brooding that he does not share these affections."

"You'd bet wrong," said a deep, menacing voice from the doorway.

Isa and David jumped from their seats in unison. David's cigar fell to the hardwood and rolled several feet away. The door opened wider, and the owner of the deep voice stepped through and crushed the burning ember with his boot heel. Isa's heart did somersaults in her ribcage, an anatomical impossibility, yet there it was, twisting and flipping like a banked fish.

"Junior," she croaked, panicking. For him to come here, now, while she was entertaining another man...

"I'm in love with my wife," David blurted, his hands up as though at gunpoint. "I arrived with a Christmas gift for Dora, but it's from my wife, I swear to you."

Junior, dressed in a dark-blue shirt, faded jeans, and no bandana, ignored the other man. His indigo eyes were on Isa and Isa alone. No kerchief hid his scar from view, and no hat covered his wavy golden hair. Thanks to a fresh shave, dimples and a cleft chin were visible. His footsteps were slow and measured as he passed David and rounded the desk.

"Isadora Williams, I love you. I'll always love you, no matter how many men pant after you."

"Well." David cleared his throat but quietened when Isa shot him a nasty look.

As if he and Isa were the only two people in the room, Junior continued, "You told me once that if you were to ever marry, it would be to a man who was more in love with you than you were with him. Well, here I am. I want to fight with you for the rest of my life. I want you to make lists of all the places we'll go and all the things we'll see because I'll be right there beside you until we've been everywhere. Until the only thing left to see is the wrinkles poppin' up on our faces."

Something hard was choking her. A ray of sun must be blinding her. She couldn't speak and could hardly see. Even drawing breath was difficult.

Junior wiped a callused thumb beneath her eye and gently lifted her bloodless hands to his mouth. "I spoke to your pa, your ma, and even your brother. Sol would rather have horsewhipped me than listened. We both knew I wasn't worthy of you, but I'm a selfish bastard. It took a lot of convincing, but I got your family's blessing. All I need now is yours."

From the corner of her eye, she saw David smile and surreptitiously leave the room. Isa hardly noticed. "My blessing for what?" she asked, her lips trembling into their first smile since she'd left him in that barn.

"You gonna make me spell it out for you?"

"If you're going to propose, you may as well do it right," she said, sniffling.

"Alright." Junior grinned, released one of her hands to pull something out of his pocket, and bent to one knee. "Izzy, will you do me the honor of becoming my wife?"

He held between his fingers a delicately wrought gold ring set with a large, square-cut citrine, which glittered in the afternoon sun.

"I'd love to be your wife," she said through a haze of irritating tears, laughing when he whooped, stood, and swung her around.

Junior slid the ring on her finger with shaking hands. "I got it because the gemstone looks a lot like your eyes."

Isa kissed him.

JUNIOR RETURNED THE kiss enthusiastically, then immediately dragged her from the office. After checking the hall and down the stairs, he led Isa up into the attic. In broad daylight, they disrobed, neither caring a damn if they were caught; they were engaged now, weren't they?

"Remember the first time we did this?" he asked her between kisses. Her skin was incredibly soft against his.

"Hm, perhaps you should remind me," Isa murmured, nibbling his full lower lip.

Junior growled playfully, and she laughed when he picked her up as if she were light as feather down and threw her on the bed.

"Wait, I remember something!" Isa climbed to her knees and positioned herself at the edge of the bed where he stood. In this position, Junior's eyes snagged on the sensual crease between her hips and legs.

His smile wavered, and he licked his lips; Isa was kissing the warm, taut skin of his stomach. Instead of going lower, her moist pink lips rose and skated over his pectorals. The narrow gap in her white teeth flashed when she bit the fleshy muscle of his chest. It made him instinctively grip a handful of her thick hair in warning, but she only grinned. Then the little minx wrapped her lips around his nipple and drew on it.

"What are you doin'?" he asked, laughing.

"Seeing if this feels as good for you as it does for me," she said, kissing his hardened nipple.

He thought about it while he pulled the pins out of her hair, enjoying the way the heavy waves unraveled down her back to her waist. "It feels pretty good."

"When you do it to mine, I feel it all the way down here." Isa pulled his hand between her legs until he was cupping her.

Junior lost the ability to speak. His fingers parted her, spreading her damp heat to the part of her that drove her wild, but she wriggled free to kiss down his flexing stomach. Below her chin, his cock bobbed insistently. He could feel the cool air on its tip; it was already leaking. And when she palmed the heavy sac below, he grunted. Isa licked him from the bottom of his shaft to the slit of his crown. Unsteadily, his fingers pulled her hair back until it lay in a thick rope in his fist. Every time her eyes met his, he felt his control slipping a little more. Finally, *finally*, Isa's lips spread around the flushed crown of his cock, and his groan was pure gravel. She sucked him past the roof of her mouth to that soft place in the back of her throat. Without realizing he was doing so, he used the hair in his fist to guide her up and down. Every time he pulled her back, her cheeks hollowed, the suction increasing as though she were afraid to unlatch. Isa's breasts swayed below, heavy and full, and a remembered fantasy of those breasts resurfaced.

"Sit up," he growled, pulling her off him with a little *pop*. Isa's lips were red and swollen from abuse. "Push your bosom together."

"What?" She looked dazed.

"Like this." Junior stepped so close that his erection grazed her breastbone. He filled his hands with her bountiful breasts and pressed them together until they sandwiched his shaft.

"Oh." Isa watched the broad head of his sex disappear and reappear between her manufactured cleavage. Her cheeks flushed. "You, sir, have a dirty mind."

"I know," he groaned. "You make me that way."

It didn't take long of whispering filthy things to her, of her following the unlikeliest of orders, before he was close to his end. She had stuck her pink tongue out to lick him and had replaced his hands with her own when he gasped, "Izzy, open your mouth."

Abandoning her breasts, he slid back between her welcoming lips, noises grunting out of him that he could feel ashamed of later. The hot pull of her mouth was too good, and he exploded, completely forgetting to pull out. Besides a surprised noise, she didn't protest.

Junior weaved on his feet while she worked him, and with his thumbs, he stroked her silky brows, her flushed cheeks, her lips tight around him. Thighs shaking like jelly, he disengaged from her mouth; the top half of his cock was dark red. Isa had turned it into one big love bruise. Heart hammering, he crouched and kissed her forehead, her nose, her lips. When they opened, the expression in her eyes was one of adoration, obstructing any ready words. She'd never looked at him like that before.

If only she knew how much he loved her. Revered her.

Gradually, he pushed her to her back and got to his knees on the rough attic floor. This was where he always wanted to be. On his knees before her. Pulling her smooth thighs over his shoulders, he buried his face between her legs. She was unbelievably soft, the petals of her sex practically melting beneath the flat of his tongue. With his two longest fingers, he tested her, felt the give of her narrow passage and the flutter of her muscles when he pushed them in deep. Her fingers delved into his hair, mussing it, and he lost track of time as he paid homage to her. The noises she made, the gasps—he would never forget them as long as he lived. When her fingers roughened in his hair, and he was in desperate need of air, he still didn't stop. If this was how he succumbed to his death, so be it.

From far away, Junior heard her sobbing, begging, pleading through a fierce orgasm. Her inner walls sucked his fingers in, and her thighs quivered around his ears. He resurfaced, pulling his wet face and fingers free, breathing hard. Wild for her.

Maintaining her ankles' position on his shoulders, he surged to his feet and guided himself to her slick, swollen entrance. Isa was unbelievably tight in this position with her endlessly long legs together and elevated, and they both gasped when he worked himself in and out of her. He was talking again, voicing how much he loved her, how beautiful she was. He couldn't stop and was too intoxicated to care.

When her noises reached boisterous pitches, he leaned over and covered her mouth hard with his hand, a movement that forced him deeper, to the very end of her. She screamed behind his hand, clenched hard around him, and he saw stars. Teeth gritted so he didn't shout, he yanked out of her and rode out a tremendous climax between her tightly clamped legs.

An eternity later, Junior remembered to release her mouth. Isa lay there, winded, her breasts heaving, her eyes closed. Gingerly, he pulled away from her closed legs and let the boneless limbs fall open. Splayed open in the sunlight, she was damned beautiful. He lovingly stroked and patted her damp, exposed sex, then soundly slapped the round cheek of her rear end. Something about the way her flesh jiggled following the friendly swat filled him with masculine appreciation.

One of Isa's eyes slit open. "How can you even stand?" Her voice was almost hoarse.

"I have no idea, darlin'." It was true. His legs were shaking. Weak. Junior felt he had run two miles and wanted to do nothing more than sleep. Instead, he walked to the washstand and wet a cloth.

After he had tidied them up, he pulled the quilt back and tucked them in. While she stroked his back between the sheets, he lifted his head and admired her. One of her breasts was exposed to the chilly attic air, its pink nipple puckered. Lovingly, he palmed it, warming it. Then he manipulated it this way and that, squeezing, squishing, and plucking.

"Ouch. Those are attached." She sounded half-asleep.

"Imagine if they weren't. I could put 'em in my saddlebags so I don't miss you when I'm away."

"You're vile." But a wicked grin spread across her cheeks.

Junior kissed her softly on the lips. Something beneath her pillow caught his eye, and he tugged it out. It was a black bandana. He suspected it was the one he had worn to the dance. Hiding a delighted smirk, Junior slid it back under her pillow.

"You know," he said after a beat. He had eschewed her breast to play with her hair, another choice diversion. "You're pretty good at...what you did earlier."

Isa's eyes blinked open. "Which part?"

He told her and felt his ears warm.

"Have you ever done it before?" He tried to sound as though it didn't matter.

"Fellatio?" she asked. "Yes."

Hot jealousy welled up in him. "That so?"

"Yes, but I'm not telling you with whom."

"I already know with *whom*," he said dryly, wishing the lock of hair in his hand was David Corner's neck. "Christ, I didn't think I could hate that city boy more than I already do. I was wrong."

Isa didn't correct him, and he had a brief urge to stomp downstairs naked and challenge her "friend" to a showdown on Main Street. But her next words dampened the hot flare of violence. "Tell me about the first time you performed cunnilingus, since we're sharing."

Damn it. He knew asking her would end up piquing her own curiosity. And *cunnilingus*, what a mouthful of a word. "Alright, then." Junior cleared his throat. "I did it one time and one time only before you. She was a whore in Huntsville. I remember she—well, it was like I took a swig of our housemaid's cleaning solution. Vinegar and carbolic. I told myself I'd like it better the next time I tried it and not with a prostitute. The next time was a neighbor girl who got around. I went beneath her skirts and came right back out."

Isa was struggling to keep a straight face. "How unfortunate."

"Unfortunate for her. Judgin' from the noises you make, I reckon I'm pretty good at it."

"Cad." She grabbed one of her smaller pillows and smacked him with it.

They laughed and scuffled beneath the bedclothes before he popped his head out of the sheets like a straw-haired gopher. "I forgot to ask you something."

"What?" Isa was dreamily admiring the ring on her finger.

"Where are we traveling to first?"

The dreamy smile became incandescent.

Epilogue

The same preacher who married Ben and Lucy agreed to marry Junior and Isa after Christmas.

Isa expected Christmastime to allow them to express their love now that everyone knew about their surprise engagement. Instead, their upcoming nuptials gave everyone the incentive to meddle. Sol and Ben tried their utmost to keep Isa and Junior appropriately apart before their wedding. Sol took Isa to Huntsville for a Christmas shopping trip for their family. As soon as they returned, Ben spirited Junior away to shop for the Stones. Poppy was determined to make Isa's wedding gown, so Isa was obligated to assist with the children.

When Isa did see Junior, it was always in the company of several other well-meaning people. Her skin felt tight and hot when he looked at her, and it was obvious to everyone what he was thinking. She couldn't tease or laugh it off; she was too miserable. Now that she'd had his kisses, had felt the weight of his body on hers, had experienced the fullness of him inside of her...it was all she could think about.

She wanted him so much it hurt.

Christmas was to be held at Junior's house—her future home—this year, and already, she had plans to corner him and have her way with him. Plotting how to go about it in her finest dress, a dusky blue velvet that matched the Stone eyes, she mixed savory biscuits at Junior's kitchen table. Lucy and Poppy had just stepped outside for a cool breeze.

"What are you doin'?" asked a deep voice in her ear.

Every one of her hairs stood on end, and Isa suppressed a shiver. "Helping with Christmas dinner. What are you doing? Avoiding work?"

Junior nuzzled her sensitive neck, and her eyes drifted closed. Immediately, her body was heavy and painfully aroused. "No, I'm comin' in here to bother my future wife."

Isa turned her head, and they shared a hot, open-mouthed kiss that went on and on...until a child's shriek broke them apart.

"Uncle Junior is kissin' Aunt Isa!" shouted Samuel. When he caught the look in Junior's eye, he whirled and ran outside to tell anyone who would listen.

"Shit," Junior hissed. But, instead of clearing out, he turned back around, cupped the back of Isa's neck, and kissed her again with that same hungry ferocity.

"That's enough, you two!" Lucy shouted behind them. "I'm going to hear about this from Samuel for months."

Junior broke away with a reluctant groan. "But I have this." He held up a green sprig for Lucy's inspection.

Lucy smacked it to the floor. "That isn't even mistletoe, you scoundrel."

Isa laughed, and he turned on her, his darkblue eyes twinkling. "I figured you'd appreciate a little Christmas kiss."

She would appreciate much more than that, but now that Poppy was walking in, Isa wasn't about to announce her deepest longings before the sisters of her heart. "Well, you've had it. Now, make yourself scarce, or we're putting you to work."

"Aw, come on, Izzy—"

"Stop your whining." Isa laid her sticky, doughy hand against his mouth, effectively silencing him.

It was the wrong thing to do.

Junior grabbed her, snatched a handful of flour off the table-top, and smeared her face with a streak of white. After that, it was pandemonium. By the time Ben and Sol burst inside the crowded kitchen to see what the fuss was about, Isa and Junior had fallen to the floor, coated with a fine dusting of flour and weak with laughter.

"I think they went crazy," Lucy muttered to Ben, her lips twitching.

"I'd be crazy, too, if I didn't get to touch you for weeks," Ben murmured back, dimples creasing his cheeks.

Suddenly, a wide-eyed Matthew appeared at the door of the kitchen. "Pa, some old lady is here sayin' she's Uncle Junior's mama."

The laughter ceased. Junior and Isa scrambled up, sharing a panicked look.

"I'm a fright," she hissed at him. She had never met his mother before, and here she was, looking like she had fallen face-first in a flour sack.

Junior patted her shoulders and wiped her face, helped by Lucy and Poppy. Then he abruptly stopped. "Stop. You're perfect the way you are. Look at us."

His grin made her wonder if he really had gone mad. "I see us. We look like bedlamites."

"No, we look crazy for each other. Come on. Meet my ma."

And so, Junior and Isa met Loretta Stone in the foyer, coated in flour and grinning ear to ear.

A change had come over the elder Mrs. Stone. A softness. Whether she was temporarily inspired by the holidays or moved by fear to make more of a conscious effort to be a part of Junior's life, Isa didn't know. All she knew was the woman looked half scared to death in her enormous hat and expensive dress, holding a large, wrapped parcel like it was a branch and she was swept up in floodwaters.

"Mother," Junior said simply. He held out his hand to take her hat.

"I'm not staying long, dear," Loretta said tremulously, her eyes darting to the open kitchen doorway where Lucy and Ben Stone stood. "I-I brought a present for the children."

Lucy's dark, winged brows shot up, and she stepped forward. "Thank you, Mrs. Stone." She accepted the package from the woman before falling back, shoulder to shoulder with her husband.

Loretta swallowed visibly and nodded her head at Ben. "Hello, Benjamin. Merry Christmas."

"Merry Christmas, Loretta," Ben said gravely. Lucy slid her hand into his.

Finally, the woman's faded-blue eyes met Isa. "And you must be Isadora. How do you do?"

Isa didn't correct her. "Very well, Mrs. Stone. Merry Christmas."

"Please call me Loretta."

"Loretta, then." Isa's eyes skated to Junior, and he jerked out of his frozen gawking.

"Did you get our invitation to our wedding? It'll be in Dogwood this Saturday."

"I did indeed," his mother sniffed, and everyone held their breath, waiting for insult. Instead, a fire lit Loretta's eyes. "Your father shan't attend, but no old general or even an army could keep me from sitting in that first pew. When are you leaving for the Continent?"

"Right after the new year." Junior sounded as surprised as everyone felt.

"I expect a postal card from every country you visit, dear." She pecked his cheek, nodded once to everyone, and left.

"Well, I'll be damned," Junior murmured. "My mother just gave us her blessing."

"Let's hope her blessing doesn't curse us," Isa said thoughtfully, then squeaked when Junior pinched her.

The rest of Christmas was merry indeed. Junior gifted Isa a Colt revolver engraved with a sunflower on each side of the grip. When she opened it, she jumped in his lap, lamenting that she'd only bought him a traveling suit. He whispered in her ear that he loved it, and he expected her to take it off him any time she wanted.

Later, Poppy distracted Sol with the baby long enough for Isa and Junior to escape outside. They made it only to the nearest outbuilding, where Junior took her roughly against the wooden siding. It didn't last long for either of them.

"Merry Christmas," Isa breathlessly murmured against his lips, then opened her mouth for his plundering tongue.

They were married the next week, he in a black suit with an emerald vest and she in an intricate gown of the same green hue, her hair in cascading, ironed curls down her back. Loretta Stone dabbed her eyes on the first row, and Lucy dabbed along with her, accidentally letting it slip later that being in the family way made her leak like a faucet.

Isa couldn't remember ever being so happy.

JUNIOR COULDN'T REMEMBER ever being so happy.

The last seven months felt like a dream.

He hadn't realized the world was so big, so different, especially compared to small-town life in Texas. It made his problems feel small, made *him* feel small. The rigors of traveling in foreign lands had changed them. And yet, time flowed differently in Europe. Everything was slower. Leisurely. He and Isa shared how they felt like entirely different people, yet not. Junior loved the long days of hearing other languages and dialects, seeing unfamiliar animals, and gaping at extraordinary geography. One of the wedding gifts he'd received from Isa was a small, leather-bound sketchbook, and half its pages were filled with intricate drawings of architecture and landscapes. The most beautiful place he'd seen thus far was Switzerland. It was a place from a painting, otherworldly and vivid.

But his favorite place in the world, he discovered, was bedding down with the woman who had come to symbolize comfort and familiarity.

Isa had bloomed.

She smiled so big and often that seeing her gapped teeth was commonplace. At her breast lay a locket he'd gifted her on their wedding day. Inside was a miniature daguerreotype of them in their wedding finery, and even Junior was impressed at the handsome couple they made. It was no wonder they turned heads no matter the country they were in. Isa chalked it up to their uncommon height, but Junior knew it was because he walked arm in arm with the most beautiful woman in the world.

It was late summer, and they were spending steamy evenings in a rented villa in Tuscany.

"This is my favorite place," Junior mumbled around a crust of herb and oil-soaked bread. They lounged half-nude on the bed, the window opened to let in air fragrant from nearby olive groves.

"Shall we stay here forever?" Isa asked, lifting a hand to touch the white, gauzy curtain floating toward her in the breeze. Her golden wedding ring sparkled on her finger.

"Why not? The renters like us alright."

"Like us? We're practically family. You wouldn't invite strangers you 'like' to your daughter's wedding," Isa explained, rubbing her bare foot along his hairy calf. She wore one of the silk chemises Poppy had sewn her as a wedding gift, and her nipples stood out against the cream material.

Feeling himself rousing—an hourly occurrence, married to Isa—Junior reached across the wooden tray for a grape they'd harvested just that morning. "I think they just wanted to show us off to their family members like a couple of circus performers."

"They do quite like when Mirage steals people's hats and gloves." She chuckled, then flinched. "What are you doing?"

Junior had pulled her chemise over her waist and set a grape in the exposed dip of her navel. It balanced there, lush, round, and purple against Isa's pale skin. The rest of her skin was just as pale; the tan on her arms and face had faded after a winter in London and France. While they traveled, Isa dressed piously to avoid cultural upset. Alone in villas and inn rooms, however, she lived in her little silken confections.

"Be still," he ordered softly. "Don't let it roll off."

Curious, Isa followed instructions. She'd tamed somewhat over the months. They hadn't fought since crossing the Alps when Mirage had turned up lame from the rough terrain, and another layer of depth had been lain over the foundation of their shocking marriage. Their passion wasn't just conflagrant—it had grown as deep as a Scottish loch. Junior had studied her body with a woodworker's intensity, running hands over every curve, memorizing every lush dimension. With that study came trust.

Isa held still while he carefully pulled the straps of her chemise down her shoulders, revealing her breasts. He grabbed two more grapes, bit each in half, and tried to balance them on her nipples.

She began to laugh, knocking them off completely. "What in heaven's name are you doing?"

"I'm trying to recreate one of those paintings where fruit and fig leaves hide the woman's private parts. Hold still, now. You're ruining my masterpiece," Junior said sternly.

Still laughing, but quietly, Isa lay motionless to his ministrations and allowed him to bare her completely until she was fully exposed except for an array of oddly placed fruit and bread.

"There. See? *Bellissima*." He kissed his fingertips as he'd seen done on the streets of Siena.

Isa looked down, saw the strange assortment of antipasti on her body, and broke into laughter again. Everything rolled off, and Junior made an exaggerated noise of affront that sounded convincingly Italian.

"You ruined my art, madam," he growled. He replaced everything back on the tray and rolled atop her. He was already randy, but her whooping laughter didn't subside. It wasn't until he trailed kisses down the seam of her ribs, over her navel, and past the dark-blonde curls between her legs that she sobered. Their lovemaking never failed to be intense, often creative, and always shattering. Once she was properly subdued and making a different set of noises completely, Junior rose to his knees, twisted her body this way and that, and entered her in a slow, luxurious stroke.

"Oh," she moaned into the sheets.

Another bonus of this little sequestered villa—they could be as loud as they wanted.

Much later, the sun had sunk beneath the olive groves, and they were tangled up in each other.

Junior asked sleepily, "Where else do you want to go?"

"We could go home," she murmured against his neck.

He kissed the top of her mussed hair. "That's anywhere you are."

"Mm." Her arms tightened around him, and he felt her lips curl into a smile against him. "Rome, perhaps?"

Junior perked up a little. "The Colosseum?"

"It's the last thing on our list."

"The Colosseum it is." Tucking the sheets around them until they were enfolded like a large cocoon, he whispered, "I love you, Izzy Stone."

"I love you." Sighed against his skin the way it was, Junior squeezed his eyes closed and gave fervent thanks for all the beautiful things this woman had brought to his life.

Author's Note

During my research of Texas Ranger history, I discovered a period where their role was questioned during a very violent and scandalous period in the 1910s. Along the Mexican border, their frontier hero status swiftly shifted into something more sinister. As tensions rose between Anglos and ethnic Mexicans along the border, Governor James Ferguson sent hundreds of Texas Rangers to quell uprisings and explosive violence between the two groups. Unfortunately, to restore order, Rangers implemented lynch laws and, without trial or conviction, executed up to 300 "suspected Mexicans." For years this continued until Representative José Tomas Canales of Brownsville requested an investigation in 1919. Found guilty of unwarranted violence, several companies of regular Rangers and almost all appointments of Special Rangers were canceled. New and existing members became subject to stringent qualifications (Bullock Museum).

As I outlined Junior and Isa's story, this information unsettled me. I wondered what Junior would do if he encountered violence, dehumanization, and abuse of power in a company organized to keep people safe. To him, being a Texas Ranger meant to honor and serve the people. I took creative license by suggesting that Ranger/civilian unrest along the Texas-Mexico border could have started years before its culmination in the 1910s. Bill Talbot and his group of Rogue Rangers are fictional, and we can only speculate if similar horrible events could have occurred. I hope, however, that there *were* good Rangers out there who tried to be the voice of reason even at risk to themselves.

Something also to note, I took a few creative liberties with a few things such as, but not excluded to:

Automobiles weren't introduced in Texas until 1899, but it was just too good to pass up as Isa most definitely found them fascinating (and who is to say a few people didn't own them here and there and it was never recorded?)

Card counting is also something I abuse using my Get Out of Jail Free Card (creative license), as that wasn't exactly a "thing" until the mid-twentieth century. However, I thought, wouldn't Isa, with her mathematician's brain, use a similar, albeit more primitive, form of card counting? In this book, I consider her a self-taught card counter before it was cool and I stick to that.

Also by Tanya Fischer

A Texas Bloom Series

Letters to Dogwood
Poppies and Silk
Trail of Sunflowers

Short Stories

Crew and the Goat Lady

Acknowledgements

I'm so grateful for the loyal readers who have been an enormous support during the process of writing this series. I wrote book one for fun without ever thinking of publishing. I didn't even want it to be a series. In the original epilogue of Letters to Dogwood, Sol barely gets mentioned, and Junior marries a faceless, nameless neighbor girl. I didn't even imagine that I would write more than one American Historical Romance; I have more book ideas set in Europe than in any other place. But something changed during my publishing research. Why not write a series? Why not give more meat to Sol and Junior's stories? We can give this fictional little town a life of its own, and if readers enjoy it, great! If not, it'll just be a series for me. Little did I know that I would grow relationships with some of the most supportive, wonderful fellow readers.

Thank you, Susan, for being my very first review from a complete stranger (before you, it was only family members and friends). You shared my book in several Facebook groups, and from there, it was history. I loved your historical romance recommendations so much and felt our reading tastes were so aligned that I couldn't help but become friends with you in real life. The same goes for Dagmar: thank you from the bottom of my heart for all your shout-outs and your matter-of-fact loyalty to the authors you stand behind. You're my sister in our love for grit and rough-around-the-edges heroes, and every book you've recommended, I have loved! Thank you, Rasa, for your *stellar* support in all avenues. You're the best reader with the most incredible recs and a fantastic hype man who really knows how to talk an author up from feeling quite low.

Without these three, I would have far less confidence in my abilities and would not have the attitude about writing that I do today! May every author have readers as wonderful as them.

About the Author

Tanya Fischer lives on a little Texas homestead with her husband, two children, and their pets (of which there are chickens). When she's not reading, she is writing. She has a passion for romance of every genre, though her heart lies in Historical Romance. She left her job in education and has pursued her dream of writing full-time.
She can be found on: Facebook, Twitter, Instagram, and her Website

www.ingramcontent.com/pod-product-compliance
Lightning Source LLC
Chambersburg PA
CBHW031113160726
47991CB00004B/1355

9798986408521